P9-CDM-444

THE ELF QUEEN
OF SHANNARA

THE

LF QUEEN

OF

HANNARA

TERRY BROOKS

A Del Rey Book

BALLANTINE BOOKS • NEW YORK

A Del Rey Book
Published by Ballantine Books
Copyright © 1992 by Terry Brooks

All rights reserved under International and Pan-American Copyright
Conventions. Published in the United States by Ballantine Books, a
division of Random House, Inc., New York, and simultaneously in
Canada by Random House of Canada Limited, Toronto.

Library of Congress Cataloging-in-Publication Data

Brooks, Terry.
The elf queen of Shannara / Terry Brooks.—1st. ed.
p.   cm.
"A Del Rey book."
ISBN 0-345-36299-3
I. Title.
PS3552.R6596E48   1992
813'.54—dc20   91-73257
                                                  CIP

Manufactured in the United States of America
First Edition: March 1992
10 9 8 7 6 5 4 3 2 1

FOR DIANE
WHO IS MISSED

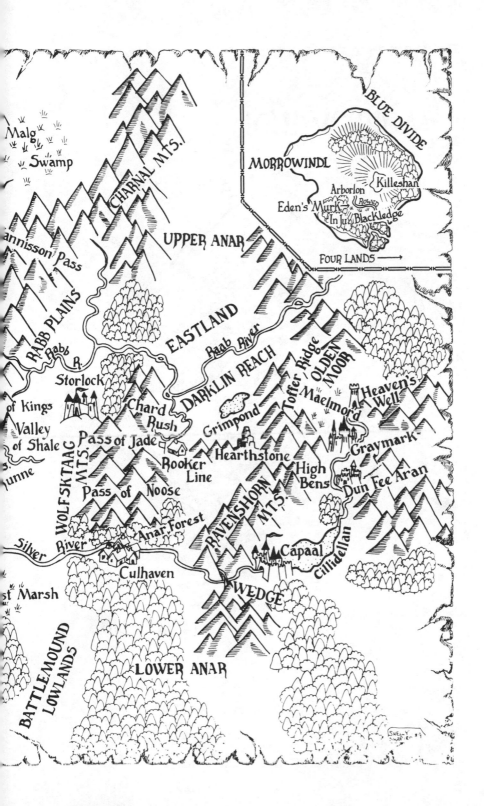

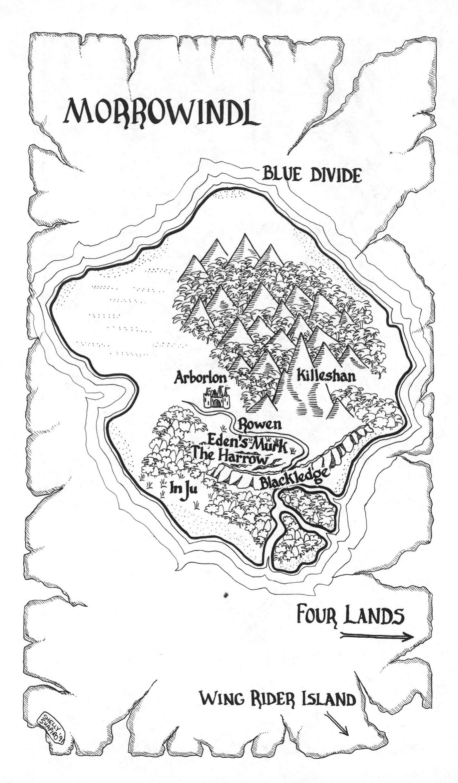

THE ELF QUEEN
OF SHANNARA

1

FIRE.

It sputtered in the oil lamps that hung distant and solitary in the windows and entryways of her people's homes. It spat and hissed as it licked at the pitch-coated torches bracketing road intersections and gates. It glowed through breaks in the leafy branches of the ancient oak and hickory where glassed lanterns lined the treelanes. Bits and pieces of flickering light, the flames were like tiny creatures that the night threatened to search out and consume.

Like ourselves, she thought.

Like the Elves.

Her gaze lifted, traveling beyond the buildings and walls of the city to where Killeshan steamed.

Fire.

It glowed redly out of the volcano's ragged mouth, the glare of its molten core reflected in the clouds of vog—volcanic ash—that hung in sullen banks across the empty sky. Killeshan loomed over them, vast and intractable, a phenomenon of nature that no Elven magic could hope to withstand. For weeks now the rumbling had sounded from deep within the earth, dissatisfied, purposeful, a buildingup of pressure that would eventually demand release.

For now, the lava burrowed and tunneled through cracks and fissures in its walls and ran down into the waters of the ocean in long, twisting ribbons that burned off the jungle and the things that lived within it. One day soon now, she knew, this secondary venting would not be enough, and Killeshan would erupt in a conflagration that would destroy them all.

If any of them remained by then.

She stood at the edge of the Gardens of Life close to where the Ellcrys grew. The ancient tree lifted skyward as if to fight through the vog and breathe the cleaner air that lay sealed above. Silver branches glimmered faintly with the light of lanterns and torches; scarlet leaves reflected the volcano's darker glow. Scatterings of fire danced in strange patterns through breaks in the tree as if trying to form a picture. She watched the images appear and fade, a mirror of her thoughts, and the sadness she felt threatened to overwhelm her.

What am I to do? she thought desperately. *What choices are left me?*

None, she knew. None, but to wait.

She was Ellenroh Elessedil, Queen of the Elves, and all she could do was to wait.

She gripped the Ruhk Staff tightly and glanced skyward with a grimace. There were no stars or moon this night. There had been little of either for weeks, only the vog, thick and impenetrable, a shroud waiting to descend, to cover their bodies, to enfold them all, and to wrap them away forever.

She stood stiffly as a hot breeze blew over her, ruffling the fine linen of her clothing. She was tall, her body angular and long limbed. The bones of her face were prominent, shaping features that were instantly recognizable. Her cheekbones were high, her forehead broad, and her jaw sharp-edged and smooth beneath her wide, thin mouth. Her skin was drawn tight against her face, giving her a sculpted look. Flaxen hair tumbled to her shoulders in thick, unruly curls. Her eyes were a strange, piercing blue and always seemed to be seeing things not immediately apparent to others. She seemed much younger than her fifty-odd years. When she smiled, which was often, she brought smiles to the faces of others almost effortlessly.

She was not smiling now. It was late, well after midnight, and her weariness was like a chain that would not let her go. She could not sleep and had come to walk in the Gardens, to listen to the night, to be alone with her thoughts, and to try to find some small measure of peace. But peace was elusive, her

4

thoughts were small demons that taunted and teased, and the night was a great, hungering black cloud that waited patiently for the moment when it would at last extinguish the frail spark of their lives.

Fire, again. Fire to give life and fire to snuff it out. The image whispered at her insidiously.

She turned abruptly and began walking through the Gardens. Cort trailed behind her, a silent, invisible presence. If she bothered to look for him, he would not be there. She could picture him in her mind, a small, stocky youth with incredible quickness and strength. He was one of the Home Guard, protectors of the Elven rulers, the weapons that defended them, the lives that were given up to preserve their own. Cort was her shadow, and if not Cort, then Dal. One or the other of them was always there, keeping her safe. As she moved along the pathway, her thoughts slipped rapidly, one to the next. She felt the roughness of the ground through the thin lining of her slippers. Arborlon, the city of the Elves, her home, brought out of the Westland more than a hundred years ago—here, to this . . .

She left the thought unfinished. She lacked the words to complete it.

Elven magic, conjured anew out of faerie time, sheltered the city, but the magic was beginning to fail. The mingled fragrances of the Garden's flowers were overshadowed by the acrid smells of Killeshan's gases where they had penetrated the outer barrier of the Keel. Night birds sang gently from the trees and coverings, but even here their songs were undercut by the guttural sounds of the dark things that lurked beyond the city's walls in the jungles and swamps, that pressed up against the Keel, waiting.

The monsters.

The trail she followed ended at the northern most edge of the Gardens on a promontory overlooking her home. The palace windows were dark, the people within asleep, all but her. Beyond lay the city, clusters of homes and shops tucked behind the Keel's protective barrier like frightened animals hunkered down in their dens. Nothing moved, as if fear made movement impossible, as if movement would give them away. She shook her head sadly. Arborlon was an island surrounded by enemies.

Behind, to the east, was Killeshan, rising up over the city, a great, jagged mountain formed by lava rock from eruptions over the centuries, the volcano dormant until only twenty years ago, now alive and anxious. North and south the jungle grew, thick and impenetrable, stretching away in a tangle of green to the shores of the ocean. West, below the slopes on which Arborlon was seated, lay the Rowen, and beyond the wall of Blackledge. None of it belonged to the Elves. Once the entire world had belonged to them, before the coming of Man. Once there had been nowhere they could not go. Even in the time of the Druid Allanon, just three hundred years before, the whole of the Westland had been theirs. Now they were reduced to this small space, besieged on all sides, imprisoned behind the wall of their failing magic. All of them, all that remained, trapped.

She looked out at the darkness beyond the Keel, picturing in her mind what waited there. She thought momentarily of the irony of it—the Elves, made victims of their own magic, of their own clever, misguided plans, and of fears that should never have been heeded. How could they have been so foolish?

Far down from where she stood, near the end of the Keel where it buttressed the hardened lava of some long past runoff, there was a sudden flare of light—a spurt of fire followed by a quick, brilliant explosion and a shriek. There were brief shouts and then silence. Another attempt to breach the walls and another death. It was a nightly occurrence now as the creatures grew bolder and the magic continued to fail.

She glanced behind her to where the topmost branches of the Ellcrys lifted above the Garden trees, a canopy of life. The tree had protected the Elves from so much for so long. It had renewed and restored. It had given peace. But it could not protect them now, not against what threatened this time.

Not against themselves.

She grasped the Rukh Staff in defiance and felt the magic surge within, a warming against her palm and fingers. The Staff was thick and gnarled and polished to a fine sheen. It had been hewn from black walnut and imbued with the magic of her people. Fixed to its tip was the Loden, white brilliance against the darkness of the night. She could see herself reflected in its facets. She could feel herself reach within. The Ruhk Staff had given strength to the rulers of Arborlon for more than a century gone.

But the Staff could not protect the Elves either.

"Cort?" she called softly.

The Home Guard materialized beside her.

"Stand with me a moment," she said.

They stood without speaking and looked out over the city. She felt impossibly alone. Her people were threatened with extinction. She should be doing something. Anything. What if the dreams were wrong? What if the visions of Eowen Cerise were mistaken? That had never happened, of course, but there was so much at stake! Her mouth tightened angrily. She must believe. It was necessary that she believe. The visions would come to pass. The girl would appear to them as promised, blood of her blood. The girl would appear.

But would even she be enough?

She shook the question away. She could not permit it. She could not give way to her despair.

She wheeled about and walked swiftly back through the Gardens to the pathway leading down again. Cort stayed with her for a moment, then faded away into the shadows. She did not see him go. Her mind was on the future, on the foretellings of Eowen, and on the fate of the Elven people. She was determined that her people would survive. She would wait for the girl for as long as she could, for as long as the magic would keep their enemies away. She would pray that Eowen's visions were true.

She was Ellenroh Elessedil, Queen of the Elves, and she would do what she must.

Fire.

It burned within as well.

Sheathed in the armor of her convictions, she went down out of the Gardens of Life in the slow hours of the early morning to sleep.

CHAPTER

2

REN OHMSFORD YAWNED. She sat on a bluff overlooking the Blue Divide, her back to the smooth trunk of an ancient willow. The ocean stretched away before her, a shimmering kaleidoscope of colors at the horizon's edge where the sunset streaked the waters with splashes of red and gold and purple and low-hanging clouds formed strange patterns against the darkening sky. Twilight was settling comfortably in place, a graying of the light, a whisper of an evening breeze off the water, a calm descending. Crickets were beginning to chirp, and fireflies were winking into view.

Wren drew her knees up against her chest, struggling to stay upright when what she really wanted to do was lie down. She hadn't slept for almost two days now, and fatigue was catching up with her. It was shadowed and cool where she sat beneath the willow's canopy, and it would have been easy to let go, slip down, curl up beneath her cloak, and drift away. Her eyes closed involuntarily at the prospect, then snapped open again instantly. She could not sleep until Garth returned, she knew. She must stay alert.

She rose and walked out to the edge of the bluff, feeling the breeze against her face, letting the sea smells fill her senses. Cranes and gulls glided and swooped across the waters, graceful and languid as they flew. Far out, too far to be seen clearly, some great fish cleared the water with an enormous splash and disappeared. She let her gaze wander. The coastline ran unbroken from where she stood for as far as the eye could see, ragged, tree-grown bluffs backed by the stark, whitecapped mountains of the Rock Spur north and the Irrybis south. A series of rocky beaches separated the bluffs from the water, their stretches littered with driftwood and shells and ropes of seaweed.

Beyond the beaches, there was only the empty expanse of the Blue Divide. She had traveled to the end of the known world, she thought wryly, and still her search for the Elves went on.

An owl hooted in the deep woods behind her, causing her to turn. She cast about cautiously for movement, for any sign of disturbance, and found none. There was no hint of Garth. He was still out, tracking . . .

She ambled back to the cooling ashes of the cooking fire and nudged the remains with her boot. Garth had forbidden any sort of real fire until he made certain they were safe. He had been edgy and suspicious all day, troubled by something that neither of them could see, a sense of something not being right. Wren was inclined to attribute his uneasiness to lack of sleep. On the other hand, Garth's hunches were seldom wrong. If he was disturbed, she knew better than to question him.

She wished he would return.

A pool sat just within the trees behind the bluff and she walked to it, knelt, and splashed water on her face. The pond's surface rippled with the touch of her hands and cleared. She could see herself in its reflection, the distortion clearing until her image was almost mirrorlike. She stared down at it—at a girl barely grown, her features decidedly Elven with sharply pointed ears and slanted brows, her face narrow and high cheeked, and her skin nut-brown. She saw hazel eyes that seldom stayed fixed, an off-center smile that suggested she enjoyed some private joke, and ash-blond hair cut short and tightly curled. There was a tautness to her, she thought—a tension that would not be dispelled no matter how valiant the effort employed.

She rocked back on her heels and permitted herself a wry smile, deciding that she liked what she saw well enough to live with it awhile longer.

She folded her hands in her lap and lowered her head. The search for the Elves—how long had it been going on now? How long since the old man—the one who claimed he was Cogline—

had come to her and told her of the dreams? Weeks? But how many? She had lost count. The old man had known of the dreams and challenged her to discover for herself the truth behind them. She had decided to accept his challenge, to go to the Hadeshorn in the Valley of Shale and meet with the shade of Allanon. Why shouldn't she? Perhaps she would learn something of where she had come from, of the parents she had never known, or of her history.

Odd. Until the old man had appeared, she had been disinterested in her lineage. She had persuaded herself that it didn't matter. But something in the way he spoke to her, in the words he used—something—had changed her.

She reached up to finger the leather bag about her neck self-consciously, feeling the hard outline of the painted rocks, the play Elfstones, her only link to the past. Where did they come from? Why had they been given to her?

Elven features, Ohmsford blood, and Rover heart and skills— they all belonged to her. But how had she come by them?

Who was she?

She hadn't found out at the Hadeshorn. Allanon had come as promised, dark and forbidding even in death. But he had told her nothing. Instead, he had given her a charge—had given each of them a charge, the children of Shannara, as he called them, Par and Walker and herself. But hers? Well. She shook her head at the memory. She was to go in search of the Elves, to find them and bring them back into the world of men. The Elves, who hadn't been seen by anyone in over a hundred years, who were believed by most never even to have existed, and who were presumed a child's faerie tale—she was to find them.

She had not planned to look at first, disturbed by what she had heard and how it had made her feel, unwilling to become involved, or to risk herself for something she did not understand or care about. She had left the others and with Garth once again her only companion had gone back into the Westland. She had thought to resume her life as a Rover. The Shadowen were not her concern. The problems of the races were not her own. But the Druid's admonition had stayed with her, and almost without realizing it she had begun her search after all. It had started with a few questions, asked here and there. Had anyone heard if there really were any Elves? Had anyone ever seen one? Did anyone know where they might be found? They were questions that were asked lightly at first, self-consciously, but with growing curiosity as time wore on, then almost an urgency.

What if Allanon were right? What if the Elves were still out there somewhere? What if they alone possessed whatever was necessary to overcome the Shadowen plague?

But the answers to her questions had all been the same. No one knew anything of the Elves. No one cared to know.

And then someone had begun following them—someone or something—their shadow as they came to call it, a thing clever enough to track them despite their precautions and stealthy enough to avoid being caught at it. Twice they had thought to trap it and failed. Any number of times they had tried to backtrack to get around behind it and been unable to do so. They had never seen its face, never even caught a glimpse of it. They had no idea who or what it was.

It had still been with them when they had entered the Wilderun and gone down into Grimpen Ward. There, two nights earlier, they had found the Addershag. A Rover had told them of the old woman, a seer it was said who knew secrets and who might know something of the Elves. They had found her in the basement of a tavern, chained and imprisoned by a group of men who thought to make money from her gift. Wren had tricked the men into letting her speak to the old woman, a creature far more dangerous and cunning than the men holding her had suspected.

The memory of that meeting was still vivid and frightening.

The old woman was a dried husk, and her face had withered into a maze of lines and furrows. Ragged white hair tumbled down about her frail shoulders. Wren approached and knelt before her. The ancient head lifted, revealing blind eyes that were milky and fixed.

"Are you the seer they call the Addershag, old mother?" Wren asked softly.

The staring eyes blinked and a thin voice rasped. "Who wishes to know? Tell me your name."

"My name is Wren Ohmsford."

Aged hands reached out to touch her face, exploring its lines and hollows, scraping along the skin like dried leaves. The hands withdrew.

"You are an Elf."

"I have Elven blood."

"An Elf!" The old woman's voice was rough and insistent, a hiss against the silence of the alehouse cellar. The wrinkled face cocked to one side as if reflecting. "I am the Addershag. What do you wish of me?"

Wren rocked back slightly on the heels of her boots. "I am searching for the Westland Elves. I was told a week ago that you might know where to find them—if they still exist."

The Addershag cackled. "Oh, they exist, all right. They do indeed. But it's not to everyone they show themselves—to none at all in many years. Is it so important to you, Elf-girl, that you see them? Do you search them out because you have need of your own kind?" The milky eyes stared unseeing at Wren's face. "No, not you. Why, then?"

"Because it is a charge I have been given—a charge I have chosen to accept," Wren answered carefully.

"A charge, is it?" The lines and furrows of the old woman's face deepened. "Bend close to me, Elf-girl."

Wren hesitated, then leaned forward tentatively. The Addershag's hands came up again, the fingers exploring. They passed once more across Wren's face, then down her neck to her body. When they touched the front of the girl's blouse, they jerked back as if burned and the old woman gasped. "Magic!" she howled.

Wren started, then seized the other's wrists impulsively. "What magic? What are you saying?"

But the Addershag shook her head violently, her lips clamped shut, and her head sunk into her shrunken breast. Wren held her a moment longer, then let her go.

"Elf-girl," the old woman whispered, "who sends you in search of the Westland Elves?"

Wren took a deep breath against her fears and answered, "The shade of Allanon."

The aged head lifted with a snap. "Allanon!" She breathed the name like a curse. "So! A Druid's charge, is it? Very well. Listen to me, then. Go south through the Wilderun, cross the Irrybis and follow the coast of the Blue Divide. When you have reached the caves of the Rocs, build a fire and keep it burning three days and nights. One will come who can help you. Do you understand?"

"Yes," Wren replied, wondering at the same time if she really did.

"Beware, Elf-girl," the other warned, a stick-thin hand lifting. "I see

12

danger ahead for you, hard times, and treachery and evil beyond imagining. My visions are in my head, truths that haunt me with their madness. Heed me, then. Keep your own counsel, girl. Trust no one!"

Trust no one!

Wren had left the old woman then, admonished to leave even though she had offered to stay and help. She had rejoined Garth, and the men had tried to kill them then, of course, because that had been their plan all along. They had failed in their attempt and paid for their foolishness—perhaps with their lives by now if the Addershag had tired of them.

Slipping clear of Grimpen Ward, Wren and Garth had come south, following the old seer's instructions, still in search of the disappeared Elves. They had traveled for two days without stopping to sleep, anxious to put as much distance between themselves and Grimpen Ward as possible and eager as well to make yet another attempt to shake loose of their shadow. Wren had thought earlier that day they might have done so. Garth was not so certain. His uneasiness would not be dispelled. So when they had stopped for the night, needing at last to sleep and regain their strength, he had backtracked once more. Perhaps he would find something to settle the matter, he told her. Perhaps not. But he wanted to give it a try.

That was Garth. Never leave anything to chance.

Behind her, in the woods, one of the horses pawed restlessly and went still again. Garth had hidden the animals behind the trees before leaving. Wren waited a moment to be certain all was well, then stood and moved over again beneath the willow, losing herself in the deep shadows formed by its canopy, easing herself down once more against the broad trunk. Far to the west, the light had faded to a glimmer of silver where the water met the sky.

Magic, the Addershag had said. How could that be?

If there were still Elves, and if she was able to find them, would they be able to tell her what the old woman had not?

She leaned back and closed her eyes momentarily, feeling herself drifting, letting it happen.

When she jerked awake again, twilight had given way to night, the darkness all around save where moon and stars bathed the open spaces in a silver glow. The campfire had gone cold, and she shivered with the chill that had invaded the coastal air. Rising, she moved over to her pack, withdrew her travel cloak, and wrapped it about her for warmth. After moving back beneath the tree, she settled herself once more.

You fell asleep, she chided herself. *What would Garth say if he were to discover that?*

She remained awake after that until he returned. It was nearing midnight, the world about her gone still save for the lulling rush of the ocean waves as they washed onto the beach below. Garth appeared soundlessly, yet she had sensed he was coming before she saw him and took some small satisfaction from that. He moved out of the trees and came directly to where she hid, motionless in the night, a part of the old willow. He seated himself before her, huge and dark, faceless in the shadows. His big hands lifted, and he began to sign. His fingers moved swiftly.

Their shadow was still back there, following after them.

Wren felt her stomach grow cold and she hugged herself crossly.

"Did you see it?" she asked, signing as she spoke.

No.

"Do you know yet what it is?"

No.

"Nothing? Nothing about it at all?"

He shook his head. She was irritated by the obvious frustration she had allowed to creep into her voice. She wanted to be as calm as he was, as clear thinking as he had taught her to be. She wanted to be a good student for him.

She put a hand on his shoulder and squeezed. "Is it coming for us yet, Garth? Or waiting still?"

Waiting, he signed.

He shrugged, his craggy, bearded face expressionless, carefully composed. His hunter's look. Wren knew that look. It appeared when Garth felt threatened, a mask to hide what was happening inside.

Waiting, she repeated soundlessly to herself. Why? For what?

Garth rose, strode over to his pack, extracted a hunk of cheese and an aleskin, and reseated himself. Wren moved over to join him. He ate and drank without looking at her, staring off at the black expanse of the Blue Divide, seemingly oblivious of everything. Wren studied him thoughtfully. He was a giant of a man, strong as iron, quick as a cat, skilled in hunting and tracking, the best she had ever known at staying alive. He had been her protector and teacher from the time she was a little girl, after she had been brought back into the Westland and given over to the care of the Rovers, after her brief stay with the Ohmsford family. How had that all come about? Her father had been an Ohmsford, her mother a Rover, yet she could not remember either of them. Why had she been given back to the Rovers rather than allowed to stay with the Ohmsfords? Who had made that decision? It had never really been explained. Garth claimed not to know. Garth claimed that he knew only what others had told him, which was little, and that his only instruction, the charge he had accepted, was to look after her. He had done so by giving her the benefit of his knowledge, training her in the skills he had mastered, and making her as good at what he did as he was himself. He had worked hard to see that she learned her lessons. She had. Whatever else Wren Ohmsford might know, she knew first and foremost how to stay alive. Garth had made certain of that. But this was not training that a normal Rover child would receive—especially a girl-child—and Wren had known as much almost from the beginning. It led her to believe Garth knew more than he was telling. After a time, she became convinced of it.

Yet Garth would admit nothing when she pressed the matter. He would simply shake his head and sign that she needed special skills, that she was an orphan and alone, and that she must be stronger and smarter than the others. He said it, but he refused to explain it.

She became aware suddenly that he had finished eating and was watching her. The weathered, bearded face was no longer hidden by shadows. She could see the set of his features clearly and read what she found there. She saw concern etched in his brow. She saw kindness mirrored in his eyes. She sensed determination everywhere. It was odd, she thought, but he had always been able to convey more to her in a single glance than others could with a basketful of words.

"I don't like being hunted like this," she said, signing. "I don't like waiting to find out what is happening."

He nodded, his dark eyes intense.

"It has something to do with the Elves," she followed up impulsively. "I don't know why I feel that is so, but I do. I feel certain of it."

Then we should know something shortly, he replied.

"When we reach the caves of the Rocs," she agreed. "Yes. Because then we'll know if the Addershag spoke the truth, if there really are still Elves."

And what follows us will perhaps want to know, too.

Her smile was tight. They regarded each other wordlessly for a moment, measuring what they saw in each other's eyes, considering the possibility of what lay ahead.

Then Garth rose and indicated the woods. They picked up their gear and moved back beneath the willow. After settling themselves at the base of its trunk, they spread their bedrolls and wrapped themselves in their forest cloaks. Despite her weariness, Wren offered to stand the first watch, and Garth agreed. He rolled himself in his cloak, then lay down beside her and was asleep in seconds.

Wren listened as his breathing slowed, then shifted her attention to the night sounds beyond. It remained quiet atop the bluff, the birds and insects gone still, the wind a whisper, and the ocean a soothing, distant murmur. Whatever was out there hunting them seemed very far away. It was an illusion, she warned herself, and became all the more wary.

She touched the bag with its make-believe Elfstones where it rested against her breast. It was her good-luck charm, she thought, a charm to ward off evil, to protect against danger, and to carry her safely through whatever challenge she undertook. Three painted rocks that were symbols of a magic that had been real once but was now lost, like the Elves, like her past. She wondered if any of it could be recovered.

Or even if it should be.

She leaned back against the willow's trunk and stared out into the night, searching in vain for her answers.

3

AT SUNRISE the following morning, Wren and Garth resumed their journey south in search of the caves of the Rocs. It was a journey of faith, for while both had traveled parts of the coastline neither had come across caves large enough to be what they were looking for or had ever seen a Roc. Both had heard tales of the legendary birds—great winged creatures that had once carried men. But the tales were only that, campfire stories that passed the time and conjured up images of things that might be but probably never were. There were sightings claimed, of course, as with every fairy-tale monster. But none was reliable. Like the Elves, the Rocs were apparently invisible.

Still, there didn't need to be Rocs in order for there to be Elves. The Addershag's admonition to Wren could prove out in any case. They had only to discover the caves, Rocs or no, build the signal fire, and wait three days. Then they would learn the truth. There was every chance that the truth would disappoint them, of course, but since they both recognized and accepted the possibility, there was no reason not to continue on. Their only concession to the unfavorable odds was to pointedly avoid speaking of them.

The day began clear and crisp, the skies unclouded and blue, the sunrise a bright splash across the eastern horizon that silhouetted the mountains in stark, jagged relief. The air filled with the mingled smells of sea and forest, and the songs of starlings and mockingbirds rose out of the trees. Sunshine quickly chased the chill left by the night and warmed the land beneath. The heat rose inland, thick and sweltering where the mountains trapped it, continuing to burn the grasses of the plains and hills a dusty brown as it had all summer, but the coastline remained cool and pleasant as a steady breeze blew in off the water. Wren and Garth kept their horses at a walk, following the narrow, winding coastal trails that navigated the bluffs and beaches fronting the mountains east. They were in no hurry. They had all the time they needed to get to where they were going.

There was time enough to be cautious in their passage through this unfamiliar country—time enough to keep an eye out for their shadow in case it was still following after them.

But they chose not to speak of that either.

Choosing not to speak about it, however, did not keep Wren from thinking about it. She found herself pondering the possibility of what might be back there as she rode, her mind free to wander where it chose as she looked out over the vast expanse of the Blue Divide and let her horse pick its way. Her darker suspicions warned her that what tracked them was something of the sort that had tracked Par and Coll on their journey from Culhaven to Hearthstone when they had gone in search of Walker Boh—a thing like the Gnawl. But could even a Gnawl avoid them as completely as their shadow had succeeded in doing? Could something that was basically an animal find them again and again when they had worked so hard to lose it? It seemed more likely that what tracked them was human—with a human's cunning and intelligence and skill: a Seeker, perhaps—sent by Rimmer Dall, a Tracker of extraordinary abilities, or an assassin, even, though he would have to be more than that to have managed to stay with them.

It was possible, too, she thought, that whoever was back there was not an enemy at all, but something else. "Friend" was hardly the right word, she supposed, but perhaps someone who had a purpose similar to their own, someone with an interest in the Elves, someone who . . .

She stopped herself. Someone who insisted on staying hidden, even knowing Garth and she had discovered they were being followed? Someone who continued playing cat and mouse with them so deliberately?

Her darker suspicions reemerged to push the other possibilities aside.

By midday they had reached the northern fringe of the Irrybis. The mountains split off in two directions, the high range turning east to parallel the northern Rock Spur and enclose the Wilderun, the low running south along the coastline they followed. The coastal Irrybis were thickly forested and less formidable, scattered in clusters along the Blue Divide, sheltering valleys and ridges, and forming passes that connected the inland hill country to the beaches. Nevertheless, travel slowed because the trails were less well defined, often disappearing entirely for long stretches. At times the mountains ran right up against the water, falling away in steep, impassable drops so that Wren and Garth were required to circle back to find another route. Heavy stands of timber blocked their path as well, forcing them to go around. They found themselves moving away from the beaches, higher into the mountain passes where the land was more open and accepting. They worked their way ahead slowly, watching as the sun drifted west to sink into the sea.

Night passed uneventfully, and they were awake again at daybreak and on their way. The morning chill again gave ground to midday heat. The ocean breezes that had cooled the previous day were less noticeable in the passes, and Wren found herself sweating freely. She shoved back her tousled hair, tied a scarf about her head, splashed water on her face, and forced herself to think about other things. She cataloged her memories as a child in Shady Vale, trying to recall once again what her parents had been like. As usual, she found that she couldn't. What she remembered was vague and fragmented—bits and pieces of conversation, small moments out of time, or words or phrases out of context. All of what she recalled could as easily be identified with Par's parents as with her own. Had any of it come from her parents—or had it all come from Jaralan and Mirianna Ohmsford? Had she ever really known her parents? Had they ever been with her in Shady Vale? She had been told so. She had been told they had died. Yet she had no memory of it. Why was that so? Why had nothing about them stayed with her?

She glanced back at Garth, irritation mirrored in her eyes. Then she looked away again, refusing to explain.

They stopped to eat at midday and rode on. Wren questioned Garth briefly about their shadow. Was it still following? Did he sense anything? Garth shrugged and signed that he was no longer certain and that he no longer trusted himself on the matter. Wren frowned doubtfully, but Garth would say nothing further, his dark, bearded face unreadable.

The afternoon was spent crossing a ridgeline over which a raging forest fire had swept a year ago, leveling the land so thoroughly that only the blackened stumps of the old growth and the first green shoots of the new remained. From atop the spine of the ridge Wren could look back across the land for miles, her view unobstructed. There was nowhere that their shadow could hide, no space it could traverse without being seen. Wren looked for it carefully and saw nothing.

Yet she couldn't shake the feeling that it was still back there.

Nightfall brought them back along the rim of a high, narrow bluff that dropped away abruptly into the sea. Below where they rode, the waters of the Blue Divide crashed and boomed against the cliffs, and seabirds wheeled and shrieked above the white foam. They made camp in a grove of alder, close to where a stream trickled down out of the mountain rock and provided them with drinking water. To Wren's surprise, Garth built a fire so they could eat a hot meal. When Wren looked at him askance, the giant Rover cocked his head and signed that if their shadow was still following, it was also still waiting. They had nothing to fear yet. Wren was not so sure, but Garth seemed confident, so she let the matter drop.

She dreamed that night of her mother, the mother she could not remember and was uncertain if she had ever known. In the dream, her mother had no name. She was a small, quick woman with Wren's ash-blond hair and intense hazel eyes, her face warm and open and caring. Her mother said to her, *"Remember me."* Wren could not remember her, of course; she had nothing to remember her by. Yet her mother kept repeating the words over and over. *Remember me. Remember me.*

When Wren woke, a picture of her mother's face and the sound of her words remained. Garth did not seem to notice how distracted she was. They dressed, ate their breakfast, packed, and set out again—and the memory of the dream lingered. Wren began to wonder if the dream might be the resurrection of a truth that she had somehow kept buried over the years. Perhaps it really was her mother she had dreamed about, her mother's face she had remembered after all these years. She was hesitant to believe, but at the same time reluctant not to.

She rode in silence, trying in vain to decide which choice would end up hurting worse.

MIDMORNING CAME AND WENT, and the heat grew oppressive. As the sun lifted from behind the rim of the mountains, the breezes off the ocean died away completely. The air grew still. Wren and Garth walked their horses to rest them, following the bluff until it disappeared completely and they were on a rocky trail leading upward toward a huge cliff mass. Sweat beaded and dried on their skin as they walked, and their feet became tired and sore. The seabirds disappeared, gone to roost, waiting for the cool of the evening to venture forth again to fish. The land and its hidden life grew silent. The only sound was the sluggish lapping of the waters of the Blue Divide against the rocky shores, a slow, weary cadence. Far out on the horizon, clouds began to build, dark and threatening. Wren glanced at Garth. There would be a storm before nightfall.

The trail they followed continued to snake upward toward the summit of the cliffs. Trees disappeared, spruce and fir and cedar first, then even the small, resilient strands of alder. The rock lay bare and exposed beneath the sun, radiating heat in thick, dull waves. Wren's vision began to swim, and she paused to wet her cloth headband. Garth turned to wait for her, impassive. When she nodded, they pressed on again, anxious to put this exhausting climb behind them.

It was nearing midday when they finally succeeded in doing so. The sun was directly overhead, white-hot and burning. The clouds that had begun massing earlier were advancing inland rapidly, and there was a hush in the air that was palpable. Pausing at the head of the trail, Wren and Garth glanced around speculatively. They stood at the edge of a mountain plain that was choked with heavy grasses and dotted with strands of gnarled, wind-bent trees that looked to be some variety of fir.

The plain ran south between the high peaks and the ocean for as far as the eye could see, a broad, uneven collection of flats across which the sultry air hung thick and unmoving.

Wren and Garth glanced wearily at each other and started across. Overhead, the storm clouds inched closer to the sun. Finally they enveloped it completely, and a low breeze sprang up. The heat faded, and shadows began to blanket the land.

Wren slipped the headband into her pocket and waited for her body to cool.

They discovered the valley a short time after that, a deep cleft in the plain that was hidden until one was almost on top of it. The valley was broad, nearly half a mile across, sheltered against the weather by a line of knobby hills that lay east and a rise in the cliffs west and by broad stands of trees that filled it wall to wall. Streams ran through the valley; Wren could hear the gurgle even from atop the rim, rippling along rocks and down gullies. With Garth trailing, she descended into the valley, intrigued by the prospect of what she might find there. Within a short time they came upon a clearing. The clearing was thick with weeds and small trees, but devoid of any old growth. A quick inspection revealed the rubble of stone foundations buried beneath the undergrowth. The old growth had been cut away to make room for houses. People had lived here once—a large number of them.

Wren looked about thoughtfully. Was this what they were looking for? She shook her head. There were no caves—at least not here, but . . .

She left the thought unfinished, beckoned hurriedly to Garth, mounted her horse, and started for the cliffs west.

They rode out of the valley and onto the rocks that separated them from the ocean. The rocks were virtually treeless, but scrub and grasses grew out of every crack and crevice. Wren maneuvered to reach the highest point, a sort of shelf that overhung the cliffs and the ocean. When she was atop it, she dismounted. Leaving her horse, she walked forward. The rock was bare here, a broad depression on which nothing seemed able to grow. She studied it momentarily. It reminded her of a fire pit, scoured and cleansed by the flames. She avoided looking at Garth and walked to the edge. The wind was blowing steadily now and whipped against her face in sudden gusts as she peered down. Garth joined her silently. The cliffs fell away in a sheer drop. Pockets of scrub grew out of the rock in a series of thick clusters. Tiny blue and yellow flowers bloomed, curiously out of place. Far below, the ocean rolled onto a narrow, empty shoreline, the waves beginning to build again as the storm neared, turning to white foam as they broke apart on the rocks.

Wren studied the drop for a long time. The growing darkness made it difficult to see clearly. Shadows overlay everything, and the movement of the clouds caused the light to shift across the face of the rock.

The Rover girl frowned. There was something wrong with what she was looking at; something was out of place. She could not decide what it was. She sat back on her heels and waited for the answer to come.

Finally she had it. There were no seabirds anywhere—not a one.

She considered what that meant for a moment, then turned to Garth and signed for him to wait. She rose and trotted to her horse, pulled a rope free from her pack, and returned. Garth studied her curiously. She signed quickly, anxiously. She wanted him to lower her over the side. She wanted to have a look at what was down there.

Working silently, they knotted one end of the rope in sling fashion beneath Wren's arms and the other end about a projection close to the cliff edge. Wren tested the knots and nodded. Bracing himself, Garth began lowering the girl slowly over the edge. Wren descended cautiously, choosing hand and footholds as she went. She soon lost sight of Garth and began a prearranged series of tugs on the rope to tell him what she wanted.

The wind rushed at her, growing stronger now, pushing at her angrily. She hugged the cliff face to avoid being blown about. The clouds masked the sky overhead completely, building on themselves. A few stray drops of rain began to fall.

She gritted her teeth. She did not fancy being caught out in the open like this if the storm broke. She had to finish her exploration and climb up again quickly.

She backed down into a pocket of scrub. Thorns raked her legs and arms, and she pushed away angrily. Working through the brush, she continued down. Glancing over her shoulder, she could see something that had not been apparent before, a darkness against the wall, a depression. She fought to contain her excitement. She signaled Garth to give her more slack and dropped quickly along the rock. The darkness grew closer. It was larger than she had believed, a great black hole in the face. She peered through the gloom. She couldn't see what lay inside, but there were others as well, there, off to the side, two of them, and there, another, partially obscured by the brush, hidden by the rock . . .

Caves!

She signaled for more slack. The rope released, and she slid slowly toward the closest of the openings, eased toward its blackness, her eyes squinting . . .

Then she heard the sound, a rustling, from just below and within. It startled her, and for a moment she froze. She peered down again. Shadows shrouded everything, layers of darkness. She could see nothing. The wind blew shrilly, muffling other sounds.

Had she been mistaken?

She dropped another few feet, uncertain.

There, something . . .

She jerked frantically on the rope to halt her descent, hanging inches above the dark opening.

The Roc burst into view beneath her, exploding from the blackness as if shot from a catapult. It seemed to fill the air, wings stretched wide against the gray waters of the Blue Divide, across the shadows and clouds. It passed so close that its body brushed her feet and sent her spinning like a web-tangled piece of cotton. She curled into a ball instinctively, clinging to the rope as she would a lifeline, bouncing against the rough surface of the rock and fighting not to cry out, all the while praying the bird wouldn't see her. The Roc lifted away, oblivious to her presence or uncaring of it, a golden-hued body with a head the color of fire. It looked wild and ferocious, its plumage in disarray, its wings marked and scarred. It soared into the storm-filled skies west and disappeared.

And that's why there are no seabirds about, Wren confirmed to herself in a frightened daze.

She hung paralyzed against the cliff face for long moments, waiting to be certain that the Roc would not return, then gave a cautious tug on the rope and let Garth haul her to safety.

It BEGAN TO RAIN shortly after she regained the summit of the cliffs. Garth wrapped her in his cloak and hustled her back to the valley where they found temporary shelter in a stand of fir. Garth built a fire and made soup to warm her. She stayed cold for a long time, shivering with the memory of hanging there helplessly as the Roc swept underneath, close enough to snatch her away, to make an end of her. Her mind was numb. She had thought to find the Roc caves in making her descent. She had never dreamed she would find the Rocs as well.

After she had recovered sufficiently to move again, after the soup had chased the chill from within her stomach, she began conversing with Garth.

"If there are Rocs, there might be Elves as well," she said, fingers translating. "What do you think?"

Garth made a face. *I think you almost got yourself killed.*

"I know," she admitted grudgingly. "Can we let that pass for now? I feel foolish enough."

Good, he indicated impassively.

"If the Addershag was right about the caves of the Rocs, don't you think there is a pretty fair chance she was right about the Elves as well?" Wren forged ahead. "I think so. I think someone will come if we light a signal fire. Right up on that ledge. In that pit. There have been fires there before. You saw. Maybe this valley was home to the Elves once. Maybe it still is. Tomorrow we'll build that signal fire and see what happens."

She ignored his shrug and settled back comfortably, her blankets wrapped close, her eyes bright with determination. The incident with the Roc was already beginning to recede into the back corners of her mind.

She slept until well after midnight, taking watch late because Garth chose not to wake her. She was alert for the remainder of the night, keeping her mind active with thoughts of what was to come. The rain ended, and by daybreak the summer heat was back, steamy and thick. They foraged for dry wood, cut pieces small enough to load, built a sled, and used the horses to haul their cuttings to the cliff edge. They worked steadily through the heat, careful not to overexert themselves or their animals, taking frequent rests, and drinking sufficient water to prevent heat stroke. The day stayed clear and sultry, the rains a distant memory. An occasional breeze brew in off the water but did little to cool them. The sea stretched away from the land in a smooth, glassy surface that from the cliff heights seemed as flat and hard as iron.

They saw nothing further of the Rocs. Garth believed them to be night birds, hunters that preferred the cover of darkness before venturing forth. Once or twice Wren thought she might have heard their call, faint and muffled. She would have liked to know how many nested in the caves and whether there were babies. But one brush with the giant birds was enough, and she was content to let her curiosity remain unsatisfied.

They built their signal fire in the stone depression on the rock ledge overlooking the Blue Divide. When sunset approached, Garth used his flint to ignite the kindling, and soon the larger pieces of wood were burning as well. The flames soared skyward, a red and gold glare against the fading light, crackling in the stillness. Wren glanced about in satisfaction. From this height, the fire could be seen for miles in every direction. If there were anyone out there looking, they would see it.

They ate dinner in silence, seated a short distance from the signal fire, their eyes on the flames, their minds elsewhere. Wren found herself thinking about her cousins, Par and Coll, and about Walker Boh. She wondered whether they had been persuaded, as she had, to take up the charges of Allanon. Find the Sword of Shannara, the shade had told Par. Find the Druids and lost Paranor, it had told Walker. And to her, find the missing Elves. If they did not, if any of them failed, then the vision it had shown them of a world turned barren and empty would come to pass, and the people of the races would become the playthings of the Shadowen. Her lean face tightened, and she brushed absently at a loose curl. The Shadowen—what were they? Cogline had spoken of them, she reflected, without actually revealing much. The history he had given them that night at the Hadeshorn was surprisingly vague. Creatures formed in the vacuum left with the failing of the magic at Allanon's death. Creatures born out of stray magic. What did that mean?

She finished her meal, rose, and walked out to the cliff edge. The night was clear and the sky filled with a thousand stars, their white light shimmering on the surface of the ocean to form a glittering tapestry of silver. Wren lost herself in the beauty of it for a time, basking in the evening cool, freed momentarily of her darker thoughts. When she came back to herself, she wished she knew better where she was going. What had once been a very certain, structured existence had turned surprisingly quixotic.

She moved back to the fire and rejoined Garth. The big man was arranging bedrolls carried up from the valley. They were to sleep by the fire and tend it until the three days elapsed or until someone came. The horses were tethered back in the trees at the edge of the valley. As long as it didn't rain, they would be comfortable enough sleeping in the open.

Garth offered to stand the first watch, and Wren agreed. She wrapped herself in her blankets at the edge of the fire's warmth and lay back. She watched the flames dance against the darkness, losing herself in their hypnotic motion, letting herself drift. She thought again of her mother, of her face and voice in the dream, and wondered if any of it was real.

Remember me.

Why couldn't she?

She was still mulling it over when she fell asleep.

SHE CAME AWAKE AGAIN with Garth's hand on her shoulder. He had woken her hundreds of times over the years, and she had learned to tell from his touch alone what he was feeling. His touch now told her he was worried.

She rolled to her feet instantly, sleep forgotten. It was early yet; she could tell that much by a quick glance at the night sky. The fire burned on beside them, its glow undiminished. Garth was facing away, back toward the valley. Wren could hear something approaching—a scraping, a clicking, the sound of claws on rock. Whatever was out there wasn't bothering to hide its coming.

Garth turned to her and signed that everything had been completely still until just moments before. Their visitor must have drawn close at first on cat's feet, then changed its mind. Wren did not question what she was being told. Garth heard with his nose and his fingers and mostly with his instincts. Even deaf, he heard better than she did. *A Roc?* she suggested quickly, reminded of their clawed feet. Garth shook his head. *Then perhaps it was whoever the Addershag had promised would come?* Garth did not respond. He didn't have to. What approached was something else, something dangerous . . .

Their eyes locked, and abruptly she knew.

It was their shadow, come to reveal itself at last.

The scraping grew louder, more prolonged, as if whatever approached was dragging itself. Wren and Garth moved away from the fire a few steps, trying to put some of the light between themselves and their visitor, trying to put some of the darkness at their backs.

Wren felt for the long knife at her waist. Not much of a weapon. Garth gripped his hardened quarter staff. She wished she had thought to gather up hers, but she had left it with the horses.

Then a misshapen face pushed into the light, shoving out of the darkness as if tearing free of something. A muscled body followed. Wren went cold in the pit of her stomach. What stood before her wasn't real. It had the look of a huge wolf, all bristling gray hair, dark muzzle, and eyes that glittered with the fire's light. But it was grotesquely human, too. It had a human's forelegs with hands and fingers, though the hair grew everywhere, and the fingers ended in claws and were misshapen and thick with callouses. The head had something of a human cast to it as well—as if someone had fitted it with a wolf's mask and worked it like clay to make it fit.

The creature's head swung toward the fire and away again. Its hard eyes locked on them.

So this was their shadow. Wren took a slow breath. This was the thing that had tracked them relentlessly across the

Westland, the thing that had followed after them for weeks. It had stayed hidden all that time. Why was it showing itself now?

She watched the muzzle draw back to reveal long rows of hooked teeth. The glittering eyes seemed to brighten. It made no sound as it stood before them.

It is showing itself now because it has decided to kill us, Wren realized, and was suddenly terrified.

Garth gave her a quick glance, a look that said everything. He had no illusions as to what was about to happen. He took a step toward the beast.

Instantly it came at him, a lunge that carried it into the big Rover almost before he could brace himself. Garth jerked his head back just in time to keep it from being ripped from his shoulders, whipped the quarter staff around, and flung his attacker aside. The wolf creature landed with a grunt, regained its footing in a scramble of clawed feet, and wheeled about, teeth bared. It came at Garth a second time, ignoring Wren completely. Garth was ready this time and slammed the end of the heavy quarter staff into the gnarled body. Wren heard the sound of bone cracking. The wolf thing tumbled away, came to its feet again, and began to circle. It continued to pay no attention to Wren, other than to make certain it could see what she was doing. It had apparently decided that Garth was the greater threat and must be dealt with first.

What are you? Wren wanted to scream. *What manner of thing?*

The beast tore into Garth again, barreling recklessly into the waiting staff. Pain did not seem to faze it. Garth flung it away, and it attacked again instantly, teeth snapping. Back it came, time after time, and nothing Garth did seemed to slow it. Wren crouched and watched, helpless to intervene without risking her friend. The wolf thing allowed her no opening and gave her no opportunity to strike. And it was quick, so swift that it was never down for more than an instant, moving with a fluid grace that suggested the agility of both man and beast. Certainly no wolf had ever moved like this, Wren knew.

The battle wore on. There were wounds to both combatants, but while Garth's blood streamed from the cuts he had suffered, the damage to the wolf creature seemed to heal almost instantly. Its cracked ribs should have slowed it, should have hampered its movements, but they did not. The blood from its cuts disappeared in seconds. Its injuries appeared not to concern it, almost as if . . .

And suddenly Wren remembered the story Par had told her of the Shadowen that he and Coll and Morgan Leah had encountered during their journey to Culhaven—that monstrous man thing, reattaching its severed arm as if pain meant nothing to it.

This wolf thing was a Shadowen!

The realization impelled her forward almost without thinking. She came at the creature with her long knife drawn, angry and determined as she bounded toward it. It turned, a hint of surprise reflected in its hard eyes, distracted momentarily from Garth. She reached it at the same instant that Garth did, and they had the beast trapped between them. Garth's staff hammered down across its skull, splintering with the force of the impact. Wren's blade buried itself in the bristling chest, sliding in smoothly. The creature jerked up and back, and for the first time made a sound. It shrieked, the cry of a woman in pain. Then it wheeled sharply and launched itself at Wren, bearing her down. It was enormously strong. Wren tumbled back, kicking up with her feet as she struggled to keep the hooked teeth from tearing her face. The wolf thing's momentum saved her, carrying it head over heels into the darkness. Wren scrambled to her feet. The long knife was gone, still buried in the beast's body. Garth's staff was ruined. He was already gripping a short sword.

The wolf thing came back into the light. It moved without pain, without effort, teeth bared in a terrifying grin.

The wolf thing.

The Shadowen.

Wren knew suddenly that they would not be able to kill it—that it was going to kill them.

She backed quickly to stand with Garth, frantic now, fighting to keep her reason. He withdrew his long knife and passed it to her. She could hear the ragged sound of his breathing. She could not bring herself to look at him.

The Shadowen came for them, hurtling forward in a rush. It shifted at the last instant toward Garth. The big Rover met its rush and turned it, but the force of the attack knocked him from his feet. Instantly the Shadowen was on him, snarling. Garth forced the sword between them, holding the wolf jaws back. Garth was stronger than any man Wren had ever known. But not stronger than this monster. Already she could see him weakening.

Garth!

She launched herself at the wolf thing, slamming the long knife into its body. It did not seem to notice. She clutched at the beast, struggling to dislodge it. Beneath, she could glimpse Garth's dark face, sweat stained and rigid. She screamed in fury.

Then the Shadowen shook itself, and she was thrown clear. She sprawled in a heap, weaponless, helpless. She hauled herself to her knees, aware suddenly that she was burning from the heat of the fire. The burning was intense—how long had it been there?—centered in her chest. She clawed at herself, thinking she had caught fire somehow. No, there were no flames, she realized, nothing at all except . . .

Her fingers flinched as they found the little leather bag with its painted rocks. The burning was there!

She yanked the bag free and almost without thinking about what she was doing poured the rocks into her palm.

Instantly they exploded into light, dazzling, terrifying. She found that she could not release them. The paint covering the rocks disappeared, and the rocks became . . . She could not bring herself to think the word, and there was no time for thinking in any case. The light flared and gathered like a living thing. From across the clearing, she saw the Shadowen's wolfish head jerk up. She saw the glitter of its eyes. She and Garth might still have a chance to survive, if . . .

She acted out of instinct, sending the light hurtling ahead with only a thought. It launched itself with frightening speed and hammered into the Shadowen. The wolf creature was flung away from Garth, twisting and shrieking. The light wrapped it about, fire everywhere, burning, consuming. Wren held her hand forth, commanding the fire. The magic terrified her, but she forced her terror down. Power coursed through her, dark and exhilarating, both at once. The Shadowen fought back, wrestling with the light, fighting to break free. It could not. Wren howled triumphantly as the Shadowen died, watching it explode and turn to dust and disappear.

Then the light disappeared as well, and she and Garth were alone.

4

REN WORKED SWIFTLY to bind Garth's wounds. No bones were broken, but he had suffered a series of deep lacerations on his forearms and chest, and he was cut and bruised from head to foot. He lay back against the earth as she knelt above him applying the healing salves and herbs that Rovers carried everywhere, his dark face calm. Iron Garth. The great, muscular body flinched once or twice as she cleaned and bandaged, stitched and bound, but that was all. Nothing showed on his face or revealed in his eyes the trauma and pain he had endured.

Tears came to her eyes momentarily, and she bent her head so he would not see. He was her closest friend, and she had very nearly lost him.

If not for the Elfstones . . .

And they were Elfstones. Real Elfstones.

Don't think about it!

She concentrated harder on what she was doing, blocking out her anxious, frightened thoughts. The signal fire burned on, flames leaping at the darkness, and wood crackling as it disintegrated with the heat. She labored in silence, yet she could hear everything about her—the fire's roar, the whistle of the wind across the rocks, the lapping of waves against the shore, the hum of insects far back in the valley, and the hiss of her own breathing. It was as if all of the night sounds had been magnified a hundredfold—as if she had been placed in a great, empty canyon where even the smallest whisper had an echo.

She finished with Garth and for a moment felt faint, a swarm of images swimming before her eyes. She saw again the wolf thing that was a Shadowen, all teeth and claws and bristling hair. She saw Garth, locked in combat with the monster. She saw herself as she rushed to help him, a vain attempt. She saw the fire's glow spread across them all like blood. She saw the Elfstones come to life, flaring with white light, with ancient power, filling the night with their brilliance, lancing out and striking the Shadowen, burning it as it struggled to break free . . .

She tried to rise and fell back. Garth caught her in his arms, having risen somehow to his knees, and eased her to the ground. He held her for a moment, cradled her as he might a child, and she let him, her face buried against his body. Then she pushed gently away, taking slow, deep breaths to steady herself. She rose and moved over to their cloaks, retrieved them and brought them back to where Garth waited. They wrapped themselves against the night's chill and sat staring at each other wordlessly.

Finally Wren lifted her hands and began to sign. *Did you know about the Elfstones?* she asked.

Garth's gaze was steady. *No.*

Not that they were real, not what they could do, nothing?

No.

She studied his face for a moment without moving. Then she reached into her tunic and drew out the leather bag that hung about her neck. She had slipped the Elfstones back inside when she had gone to help Garth. She wondered if they had transformed again, if they had returned to being the painted rocks they once were. She even wondered if she had somehow been mistaken in what she had seen. She turned the bag upside down and shook it over her hand.

Three bright blue stones tumbled free, painted rocks no longer, but glittering Elfstones—the Elfstones that had been given to Shea Ohmsford by Allanon over five hundred years ago and had belonged to the Ohmsford family ever since. She stared at them, entranced by their beauty, awed that she should be holding them. She shivered at the memory of their power.

"Garth," she whispered. She placed the Elfstones in her lap. Her fingers moved. "You must know something. You must. I was given into your care, Garth. The Elfstones were with me even then. Tell me. Where did they really come from?"

You already know. Your parents gave them to you.

My parents. She felt a welling up of pain and frustration. "Tell me about them. Everything. There are secrets, Garth. There have always been secrets. I have to know now. Tell me."

Garth's dark face was frozen as he hesitated, then signed to her that her mother had been a Rover and that her father had been an Ohmsford. They brought her to the Rovers when she was a baby. He was told that the last thing they did before leaving was to place the leather bag with its painted rocks about her neck.

"You did not see my mother. Or my father?"

Garth shook his head. He was away when they came and when he returned they were gone. They never came back. Wren was taken to Shady Vale to be raised by Jaralan and Mirianna Ohmsford. When she was five, the Rovers took her back again. That was the agreement the Ohmsfords had made. It was what her parents had insisted upon.

"But why?" Wren interrupted, bewildered.

Garth didn't know. He had never even been told who had made the bargain on behalf of the Rovers. She was given into his care by one of the family elders, a man who had died shortly after. No one had ever explained why he was to train her as he did—only what was to be done. She was to be quicker, stronger, smarter, and better able to survive than any of them. Garth was to make her that way.

Wren sat back in frustration. She already knew everything that Garth was telling her. He had told it all to her before. Her jaw tightened angrily. There must be something more, something that would give her some insight into where she had come from and why she was carrying the Elfstones.

"Garth," she tried again, insistent now. "What is it that you haven't told me? Something about my mother? I dreamed of her, you know. I saw her face. Tell me what you are hiding!"

The big man was expressionless, but there was hurt in his eyes. Wren almost reached out to reassure him, but her need to know kept her from doing so. Garth stared at her for long moments without responding. Then his fingers signed briefly.

I can tell you nothing that you cannot see for yourself.

She flinched. "What do you mean?"

You have Elven features, Wren. More so than any Ohmsford. Why do you think that is?

She shook her head, unable to answer.

His brow furrowed. *It is because your parents were both Elves.*

Wren stared in disbelief. She had no memory at all of her parents looking like Elves and she had always thought of herself as simply a Rover girl.

"How do you know this?" she asked, stunned.

I was told by one who saw them. I was also told that it would be dangerous for you to know.

"Yet you choose to tell me now?"

Garth shrugged, as much as if to say, What difference does it make after what has happened? How much more danger can you be in by knowing? Wren nodded. Her mother a Rover. Her father an Ohmsford. But both of them Elves. How could that be? Rovers weren't Elves.

"You're sure about this?" she repeated. "Elves, not humans with Elven blood, but Elves?"

Garth nodded firmly and signed, *It was made very clear.*

To everyone but her, she thought. How had her parents come to be Elves? None of the Ohmsfords had been Elves, only of Elven descent with some percentage of Elven blood. Did this mean that her parents had lived with the Elves? Did it mean that they had come from them and that this was why Allanon had sent her in search of the Elves, because she herself was one?

She looked away, momentarily overwhelmed by the implications. She saw her mother's face again as she had seen it in her dream—a girl's face, of the race of Man, not Elf. That part of her that was Elf, those more distinctive features, had not been evident. Or had she simply missed seeing them? What about her father? Funny, she thought. He had never seemed very important in her musings of what might have been, never as real, and she had no idea why. He was faceless to her. He was invisible.

She looked back again. Garth was waiting patiently. "You did not know that the painted rocks were Elfstones?" she asked one final time. "You knew nothing of what they were?"

Nothing.

What if she had discarded them? she asked herself peevishly. What then of her parent's plans—whatever they were—for her? But she knew the answer to that question. She would never have given up the painted rocks, her only link to her past, all she had to remind her of her parents. Had they relied on that? Why had they given her the Elfstones in the first place? To protect her? Against what? Shadowen? Something more? Something that hadn't even existed when she was born?

"Why do you think I was given these Stones?" she asked Garth, genuinely confused.

Garth looked down a moment, then up again. His great body shifted. He signed. *Perhaps to protect you in your search for the Elves.*

Wren stared, blank faced. She had not considered that possibility. But how could her parents have known she would go in search of the Elves? Or had they simply known she would one day seek out her own heritage, that she would insist on knowing where she had come from and who her people were?

"Garth, I don't understand," she confessed to him. "What is this all about?"

But the big man simply shook his head and looked sad.

They kept watch together through the night, one dozing while the other stayed awake, until finally dawn's light brightened the eastern skies. Then Garth fell asleep until noon, his strength exhausted. Wren sat staring out at the vast expanse of the Blue Divide, pondering the implications behind her discovery of the Elfstones. They were the Elfstones of Shea Ohmsford, she decided. She had heard them described often enough, listened to stories of their history. They belonged to whomever they were given and they had been given to the Ohmsford family—and then lost again, supposedly. But perhaps not. Perhaps they had been simply taken away at some point. It was possible. There had been many Ohmsfords after Brin and Jair and three hundred years in which to lose track of the magic—even a magic as personal and powerful as the Elfstones. There had been a time when no one could use them, she reminded herself. Only those with sufficient Elven blood could invoke the magic with impunity. Wil Ohmsford had been damaged that way. His use of the Stones had caused him to absorb some of their magic. When his children were born, Brin and Jair, the magic had transformed itself into the wishsong. So perhaps one of the Ohmsfords had decided to take the Elfstones back to those who could use them safely—to the Elves. Was that how they had found their way to her parents?

The questions persisted, overwhelming, insistent, and unanswerable. What was it that Cogline had said to her when he had found her that first time in the Tirfing and persuaded her to come with him to the Hadeshorn to meet with Allanon? *It is not nearly so important to know who you are as who you might be.* She was beginning to see how that might be true in a way she had never envisioned.

Garth rose at noon and ate the vegetable stew and fresh bread she had prepared. He was stiff and sore, and his strength had not yet returned. Nevertheless, he thought it necessary that he make a sweep of the area to make certain that there wasn't another of the wolf things about. Wren had not considered the possibility. Both of them had recognized their attacker as a Shadowen—a thing once human that had become part beast, a thing that could track and hunt, that could hide and stalk, and that could think as well as they and kill without compunction. No wonder it had tracked them so easily. She had assumed it had come alone. It was an assumption she could not afford to make. She told Garth that she was the one who would go. She was better suited at the moment than he, and she had the Elfstones. She would be protected.

She did not tell him how frightened she was of the Elven magic or how difficult she would find it if she were required to invoke it again.

As she backtracked the country south and east, searching for prints, for signs, or for anything out of place, relying mostly on her instincts to warn her of any danger, she thought about what it meant to be in possession of such magic. She remembered when Par had kidded her about the dreams, saying that she had the same Elven blood as he and perhaps some part of the magic. She had laughed. She had only her painted rocks, she had said. She remembered the Addershag's touch at her breast where the Elfstones hung in their leather bag and the unbidden cry of "Magic!" She hadn't even thought of the painted rocks that time. All her life she had known of the Ohmsford legacy, of the magic that had belonged to them as the descendants of the Elven house of Shannara. Yet she had never thought to have use of the magic herself, never even desired it. Now it was hers as the Elfstones were hers, and what was she to do about it? She did not want the responsibility of the Stones or their magic. She wanted nothing of the legacy. The legacy was a millstone that would drag her down. She was a Rover, born and raised free, and that was what she knew and was comfortable with being—not any of this other. She had accepted her Elven looks without questioning what they might imply. They were part of her, but a lesser part, and nothing at all of the Rover she was. She felt as if she had been turned inside out by the discovery of the Elfstones, as if the magic by coming into her life was somehow taking life out of her and making her over. She did not like the feeling. She was not anxious to be changed into someone other than who she was.

She pondered her discomfort all that day and had not come close to resolving it on her return to the camp. The signal fire was a guiding beacon, and she followed its glow to where Garth waited. He was anxious for her—she could see it in his eyes. But he said nothing, passing her food and drink and sitting back quietly to watch her eat. She told him she had not found any trace of other Shadowen. She did not tell him that she was beginning to have second thoughts about this whole business. She had asked herself once before, once right at the beginning when she had decided she would try to learn something about who she was, What would happen if she did not like what she discovered? She had dismissed the possibility. She was worried now that she had made a very big mistake.

The second night passed without incident. They kept the signal fire burning steadily, feeding it new wood as the old was consumed, patiently waiting. Another day began and ended, and still no one appeared. They searched the skies and the land from horizon to horizon, but there was no sign of anyone. By nightfall, both were edgy. Garth, his superficial wounds already healed and the deeper ones beginning to close, prowled the campsite like a caged animal, repeating meaningless tasks to keep from having to sit. Wren sat to keep from prowling. They slept as often as they could, resting themselves because they needed to and because it was something to do. Wren found herself doubting the Addershag, questioning the old woman's words. How long had the Addershag been a captive of those men, chained and imprisoned in that cellar? Perhaps her memory had failed her in some way. Perhaps she had become confused. But she had not sounded feeble or confused. She had sounded dangerous. And what about the Shadowen that had tracked them the length and breadth of the Westland? All those weeks it had kept hidden, following at a distance. It had shown itself only after the signal fire had been lit. Then it had come forth to destroy them. Wasn't it reasonable to assume that its appearance had been brought about by what it was seeing them do, that it believed the signal fire posed some sort of threat and so must be stopped? Why else would it have chosen that moment to strike?

So don't give up, Wren kept telling herself, the words a litany of hope to keep her confidence from failing completely. *Don't give up.*

The third night dragged away, minutes into hours. They changed the watch frequently because by now neither could sleep for more than a short time without waking. More often than not they kept watch together—uneasy, anxious, worried. They fed deadwood into the flames and watched the fire dance against the night. They stared out over the black void above the Blue Divide. They sifted through the night sounds and their scattered thoughts.

Nothing happened. No one came.

It was nearing morning when Wren dozed off in spite of herself, some time during the final hour of her watch. She was still sitting up, her legs crossed, her arms about her knees, and her head dipped forward. It seemed only moments had passed when she jerked awake again. She glanced about warily. Garth was asleep a few feet away, wrapped in his great cloak. The fire continued to burn fiercely. The land was cloaked in a frost-tipped blanket of shadows and half-light, the sunrise no more than a faint silver lightening at the rim of the mountains east. A scattering of stars still brightened the sky west, although the moon had long since disappeared. Wren yawned and stood up.

Clouds were moving in from out on the ocean, low-hanging, dark . . .

She started. She was seeing something else, she realized, something blacker and swifter, moving out of the darkness for the bluffs, streaking directly for her. She blinked to make certain, then stepped back hurriedly and reached down for Garth. The big Rover was on his feet at once. Together they faced out across the Divide, watching the black thing take shape. It was a Roc, they realized after a few seconds more, winging its way toward the fire like a moth drawn by the flames. It swept across the bluff and wheeled back again, its outline barely visible in the faint light. It flew over them twice, turning each time, crossing and recrossing as if studying what lay below. Wren and Garth watched wordlessly, unable to do anything else.

Finally, the Roc plummeted toward them, its massive body whistling overhead, so close it might have snatched them up with its great claws if it had wished. Wren and Garth flattened themselves against the rocks protectively and stared as the bird settled comfortably down at the edge of the cliffs, a giant, black-bodied creature with a head as scarlet as fire and wings greater than those on the bird that Wren had barely escaped days earlier.

Wren and Garth climbed back to their feet and brushed themselves off.

There was a man seated astride the Roc, held in place by straps from a leather harness. They watched as the man released the straps and slid smoothly to the ground. He stood next to the bird and studied them momentarily, then started forward. He was small and bent, wearing a tunic, pants, boots, and gloves made of leather. He walked with an oddly rolling gait, as if not altogether comfortable with the task. His features were Elven, narrow and sharp, and his face was deeply lined. He wore no beard, and his brown hair was short cropped and peppered with gray. Fierce black eyes blinked at them with alarming rapidity.

He came to a stop when he was a dozen feet away.

"Did you light that fire?" he demanded. His voice was high-pitched and rough about the edges.

"Yes," Wren answered him.

"Why did you do that?"

"Because I was told to."

"Were you now? By whom, if you don't mind my asking?"

"I don't mind at all. I was told to light it by the Addershag."

The eyes blinked twice as fast. "By the what?"

"An old woman, a seer I spoke with in Grimpen Ward. She is called the Addershag."

The little man grunted. "Grimpen Ward. Ugh! No one in his right mind goes there." His mouth tightened. "Well, why did this Addershag tell you to light the fire, eh?"

Wren sighed impatiently. She had waited three days for someone to come and she was anxious to discover if this gnarled little fellow was the person she had been expecting or not. "Let me ask you something first," she replied. "Do you have a name?"

The frown deepened. "I might. Why don't you tell me yours first?"

Wren put her hands on her hips challengingly. "My name is Wren Ohmsford. This is my friend Garth. We're Rovers."

"Hah, is that so now? Rovers, are you?" The little man chuckled as if enjoying some private joke. "Got a bit of Elf in you, too, it looks."

"Got a bit in you as well," she replied. "What's your name?"

"Tiger Ty," the other said. "At least, that's what everyone calls me. All right now, Miss Wren. We've introduced ourselves and said hello. What are you doing out here, Addershag and what-all notwithstanding? Why'd you light that fire?"

Wren smiled. "Maybe to bring you and your bird, if you're the one who can take us to the Elves."

Tiger Ty grunted and spit. "That bird is a Roc, Miss Wren. He's called Spirit. Best of them all, he is. And there aren't any Elves. Everyone knows that."

Wren nodded. "Not everyone. Some think there are Elves. I've been sent to see if that's so. Can you and Spirit help?"

There was a long silence as Tiger Ty scrunched his face into a dozen different expressions. "Big fellow, your friend Garth, isn't he? I see you telling him what we're saying with your hands. Bet he hears better than we do, push come to shove." He paused. "Who are you, Miss Wren, that you would care to know whether there are Elves or not?"

She told him, certain now that he was the one for whom

the signal fire was intended and that he was simply being cautious about what he revealed until he found out whom he was dealing with. She disclosed her background, revealing that she was the child of an Elf and a Rover, searching for some link to her past. She advised him of her meeting with the shade of Allanon and the Druid's charge that she go in search of the missing Elves, that she discover what had become of them, and that she return them to the world of Men so that they could take part in the battle against the Shadowen.

She kept quiet about the Elfstones. She was not yet ready to trust anyone with that information.

Tiger Ty shifted and fidgeted as she talked, his face worrying itself into a dozen different expressions. He seemed heedless of Garth, his attention focused on Wren. He carried no weapons save for a long knife, but with Spirit standing watch she supposed he had no need of weapons. The Roc was clearly his protector.

"Let's sit," Tiger Ty said when she had finished, pulling off his leather gloves. "Got anything to eat?"

They seated themselves beside the now-forgotten signal fire, and Wren produced a collection of dried fruit, a little bread, and some ale. They ate and drank in silence, Wren and Garth exchanging occasional glances, Tiger Ty ignoring them both, absorbed in the task of eating.

When they were finished, Tiger Ty smiled for the first time. "A good start to the day, Miss Wren. Thanks very much."

Wren nodded. "You're welcome. Now tell me. Was our fire meant for you?"

The leathery face furrowed. "Well, now. Depends, you know. Let me ask you, Miss Wren. Do you know anything of Wing Riders?"

Wren shook her head no.

"Because that's what I am, you see," the other explained. "A Wing Rider. A flyer of the skylanes, a watcher of the Westland coast. Spirit is my Roc, trained by my father, given to me when I became old enough. One day he'll go to my son, if my son proves out. There's some question about it just now. Fool boy keeps winging about where he's not supposed to. Doesn't pay attention to what I tell him. Impetuous. Anyway, Wing Riders have flown their Rocs along the Blue Divide for hundreds of years. This very spot, right here—and back there in the valley—was our home once. It was called the Wing Hove. That was in the time of the Druid Allanon. You see, I know a few things."

"Do you know the Ohmsford name?" Wren asked impulsively.

"There was a tale about an Ohmsford some several hundred years ago when the Elves fought demons released out of the Forbidding. Wing Riders fought in that war, too, they say. But there was an Ohmsford, I'm told. Relation of yours?"

"Yes," she said. "Twelve generations removed."

He nodded thoughtfully. "So that's you, is it? A child of the house of Shannara?"

Wren nodded. "I suppose that's why I've been sent to find the Elves, Tiger Ty."

Tiger Ty looked doubtful. "Wing Riders are Elves, you know," he said carefully. "But we're not the Elves you're looking for. The Elves you're looking for are Land Elves, not Sky Elves. Do you understand the difference?"

She shook her head no once more. He explained then that the members of the Wing Hove were Sky Elves and considered themselves a separate people. The majority of the Elves were called Land Elves because they had no command of the Rocs and therefore could not fly.

"That's why they didn't take us with them when they left," he finished, eyebrows arched. "That's why we wouldn't have gone with them in any case."

Wren felt her pulse quicken. "Then there are still Elves, aren't there? Where are they, Tiger Ty?"

The gnarled little man blinked and squinched up his leathery face. "Don't know if I should tell you that," he opined. "Don't know if I should tell you anything. You might be who you say. Then again, you might not. Even if you are, maybe it's not for you to know about the Elves. The Druid Allanon sent you, you say? Told you to find the Elves and bring them back? Tall order, if you ask me."

"I could use a little help," Wren admitted. "What would it hurt you to give it to me, Tiger Ty?"

He ceased his ruminations and rocked back thoughtfully.

"Well, now, you've got a point there, Miss Wren," he replied, nodding in agreement with himself. "Besides, I sort of like what I see in you. My son could use a little of what you've got. On the other hand, maybe that's what he's already got too much of! Humph!"

He cocked his head and his sharp eyes fixed her. "Out there," he said, pointing to the Blue Divide. "That's where they are, the ones that are left." He paused, scowling. "It's a long story, so make certain you listen close because I don't intend to repeat myself. You, too, big fellow." He indicated Garth with a menacing finger.

Then he took a deep breath and sat back. "Long time ago, better than a hundred years, the Land Elves held a council and decided to migrate out of the Westland. Don't ask me why; I don't pretend to know. The Federation, mostly, I'd guess. Pushing in, taking over, pretending everything that ever was or ever would be belonged to them. And blaming everything on the magic and saying it was all the fault of the Elves. Lot of nonsense. Land Elves didn't like it in any case and decided to leave. Problem was, where could they go? Wasn't as if there was anywhere a whole people could move to without upsetting someone already settled in. Eastland, Southland, Northland—all taken. So they asked us. Sky Elves get around more than most, see places others don't even know exist. So we said to them, well, there's some islands out there in the Blue Divide that no one lives on, and they thought it over, talked about it, took a few flights out on the Rocs with Wing Riders, and came to a decision. They picked a gathering spot, built boats—hundreds of them, all in secret—and off they went."

"All of them?"

"Every last one, so I'm told. Sailed away."

"To live on the islands?" Wren asked, incredulous.

"One island." Tiger Ty held up a single finger for emphasis. "Morrowindl."

"That was its name? Morrowindl?"

The other nodded. "Biggest of all the islands, better than two hundred miles across, ideal for farming, something like the Sarandanon already planted. Fruits, vegetables, trees, good soil, shelter—everything. Hunting was good, too. The Land Elves had some notion about starting over, taking themselves out of the old world, and beginning again in the new. Isolate themselves all over again, let the other races do what they wanted with themselves. Wanted their magic back, too—that was part of it."

He cleared his throat. "As I said, that was a long time ago. After a while, we migrated, too. Not so far, you understand— just to the islands offshore, just far enough away to keep the Federation from hunting us. Elves are Elves to them. We'd had enough of that kind of thinking. Not so many of us to make the move, of course; not like the Land Elves. We needed less space and could settle for the smaller islands. That's where we still are, Miss Wren. Out there, couple miles offshore. Only come back to the mainland when it's necessary—like when someone lights a signal fire. That was the agreement we made."

"Agreement with whom?"

"With the Land Elves. A few who remained behind of the other races knew to light the fire if there was need to talk to us. And a few of the Elves came back over the years. So some knew about the fire. But most have long since died. This Addershag—I don't know how she found out."

"Back up a moment, Tiger Ty," Wren requested, holding out her hands placatingly. "Finish your story about the Land Elves first. What happened to them? You said they migrated more than a hundred years ago. What became of them after that?"

Tiger Ty shrugged. "They settled in, made a home, raised their families, and were happy. Everything worked out the way they thought it would—at first. Then about twenty years ago, they started having trouble. It was hard to tell what the problem was; they wouldn't discuss it with us. We only saw them now and again, you see. Still didn't mix much, even after we'd migrated out, too. Anyway, everything on Morrowindl began to change. It started with Killeshan, the volcano. Dormant for hundreds of years and suddenly it came awake again. Started smoking, spitting, erupted once or twice. Clouds of vog—you know, volcanic ash—started filling the skies. The air, the land, the water about—it was all different." He paused, a hard look darkening his face. "They changed, too—the Land Elves. Wouldn't admit it, but we saw that something was different. You

could see it in the way they behaved when we were about—
guarded, secretive about everything. Armed to the teeth everywhere they went. And strange creatures began appearing on the
island, monstrous things, things that had never been there before. Just appeared, just out of nothing. And the land began to
grow sick, changing like everything else."

He sighed. "The Land Elves began to die off then, a few at
a time, more after a while. They had lived all over the island
once; they quit doing that and moved into their city, all jammed
together like rats in a sinking ship. They built fortifications and
reinforced them with magic. Old magic, you know, brought
back out of time and the old ways. Sky Elves want nothing to
do with it, but we've never used the magic anyway like them."

He sat back. "Ten years ago, they disappeared completely."

Wren started. "Disappeared?"

"Vanished. Still on Morrowindl, mind. But gone. Island was
a mass of ash and mist and steamy heat by then, of course.
Changed so completely it might have been a different place
entirely." He tightened his frown. "We couldn't get in to find
out what had happened. Sent half a dozen Wing Riders. Not a
one came back. Not even the birds. And no one came out. No
one, Miss Wren. Not in all that time."

Wren was silent for a moment, thinking. The sun was up
now, warm light cascading down from atop the Irrybis, the
cloudless morning sky bright and friendly. Spirit remained
perched on the cliff edge, oblivious to them. The Roc was a
statue frozen in place. Only his sharp, searching eyes registered
life.

"So if there are any Elves left," Wren said finally, "any Land
Elves, that is, they're still on Morrowindl somewhere. You're
sure about that, Tiger Ty?"

The Wing Rider shrugged. "Sure as I can be. I suppose they
could have disappeared to somewhere else, but it's odd that they
didn't get word to us."

Wren took a deep breath. "Can you take us to Morrowindl?"
she asked.

It was an impulsive request, born out of a fierce and quixotic
determination to discover a truth that was apparently hidden
not only from herself but from everyone else as well. She rec-

ognized how selfish she was being. She had not even considered asking Garth for his thoughts; she had not even bothered to remember how badly he had been injured in their fight with the Shadowen. She couldn't bring herself to look at him now. She kept her eyes fastened on Tiger Ty.

There was no mistaking what he thought of the idea. The little man scowled fiercely. "I *could* take you to Morrowindl," he said. "But I won't."

"I have to know if there are any Elves left," she insisted, trying to keep her voice level. Now she risked a quick glance at Garth. The big Rover's face registered nothing of what he was thinking. "I have to discover if they can be brought back into the world of Men. It was Allanon's charge to me, and I guess I believe it important enough to carry it out."

"Allanon, again!" Tiger Ty snapped irritably. "You'd risk your life on the word of a shade? Do you have any idea what Morrowindl is like? No, of course you don't! Why do I even ask? You didn't hear a word I said, did you? You think you can just walk in and look around and walk out again? Well, you can't! You wouldn't get twenty feet, Miss Wren—you or your big friend! That whole island is a death trap! Swamp and jungle, vog choking off everything, Killeshan spitting fire. And the things that live there, the monsters? What sort of chance do you think you'll have against them? If a Wing Rider and his Roc couldn't land and come out again, you sure as demon's blood can't either!"

"Maybe," Wren agreed. "But I have to try." She glanced again at Garth, who signed briefly, not a rebuke, but a caution. *Are you certain about this?* She nodded resolutely, saying to Tiger Ty "Don't you want to know what's happened to them? What if they need help?"

"What if they do?" he growled. "What are the Sky Elves supposed to do? There's only a handful of us. There were thousands of them. If they couldn't deal with what's there, what chance would we have? Or you, Miss Rescuer?"

"Will you take us?" she repeated.

"No, I will not! Forget the whole business!" He rose in a huff.

"Very well. Then we'll build a boat and reach Morrowindl that way."

"Build a boat! What do you know about building boats! Or sailing them for that matter!" Tiger Ty was incensed. "Of all the foolish, pigheaded . . . !"

He stormed off toward Spirit, then stopped, kicked at the earth, wheeled, and came back again. His seamed face was crimson, his hands knotted into fists.

"You mean to do this thing, don't you?" he demanded. "Whether I help you or not?"

"I have to," she answered calmly.

"But you're just . . . You're only . . ." He sputtered, seemingly unable to complete the thought.

She knew what he was trying to say and she didn't like it. "I'm stronger than you think," she told him, a hard edge to her voice now. "I'm not afraid."

Tiger Ty stared long and hard at her, glanced briefly at Garth, and threw up his hands. "All right, then!" He leveled a scorching glare at her. "I'll take you! Just to the shoreline, mind, because unlike you I'm good and scared and I don't fancy risking my neck or Spirit's just to satisfy your curiosity!"

She met his gaze coolly. "This doesn't have anything to do with satisfying my curiosity, Tiger Ty. You know that."

He dropped down in front of her, his sun-browned face only inches from her own. "Maybe. But you listen. I want your promise that after you see what you're up against, you'll rethink this whole business. Because despite the fact that you're a bit short of common sense, I kind of like you and I'd hate to see anything bad happen to you. This isn't going to turn out the way you think. You'll see that soon enough. So you promise me. Agreed?"

Wren nodded solemnly. "Agreed."

Tiger Ty stood up, hands on hips, defiant to the end. "Come on, then," he muttered. "Let's get this over with."

5

TIGER TY WAS ANXIOUS to be off, but he was forced to wait almost an hour while Wren and Garth went back down into the valley to gather up the gear and weapons they would carry with them on their journey and to provide for their horses. The horses were tethered, and Garth released them so that they could graze and drink as they needed. The valley provided grass and water enough on which to survive, and the horses were trained not to wander. Wren sorted through their provisions, choosing what they would need and be able to carry. Most of their supplies were too cumbersome, and she stashed them for when they returned.

If they returned, she thought darkly.

What had she done? Her mind spun with the enormity of the commitment she was making, and she was forced to wonder, if only in the privacy of her own thoughts, whether she would have cause to regret her brashness.

When they regained the cliffs, Tiger Ty was waiting impatiently. Bidding Spirit to stand, he helped Wren and Garth climb atop the giant bird and fasten themselves in place with the straps of the harness. There were foot loops, knotted hand grips, and a waist restraint, all designed to keep them safely in place. The Wing Rider spent long moments telling them how the Roc would react once in flight and how flying would make them feel. He gave them each a bit of bitter-tasting root to chew on, advising that it would keep them from being sick.

"Not that a couple of seasoned veterans of the Rover life should be bothered by any of this," he chided, managing a grin that was worse than his scowl.

He clambered aboard in front of them, settled himself comfortably, pulled on his heavy gloves, and without warning gave a shout and whacked Spirit on the neck. The giant bird shrieked in response, spread his wings, and lifted into the air. They cleared the edge of the cliffs, dipped sharply downward, caught a current of wind, and rose skyward. Wren felt her stomach lurch. She closed her eyes against what she was feeling, then opened them again, aware that Tiger Ty was looking over his shoulder at her, chuckling. She smiled back bravely. Spirit flattened out above the Blue Divide, wings barely moving, letting the wind do the work. The coastline behind them grew small, then lost definition. Soon it was nothing more than a thin dark line against the horizon.

Time slipped away. They saw nothing below them save for a scattering of rocky atolls and the occasional splash of a large fish. Seabirds wheeled and dived in small white flashes, and clouds lay along the western horizon like strips of gauze. The ocean stretched away, a vast, flat blue surface streaked with the foaming crests of waves that rolled endlessly toward distant shores. After a time Wren was able to dismiss her initial uneasiness and settle back. Garth was less successful in adjusting. He was seated immediately behind her, and whenever she glanced back at him she found his dark face rigid and his hands clutched about the restraining straps. Wren quit looking at him and concentrated on the sweep of the ocean ahead.

She soon began thinking about Morrowindl and the Elves. Tiger Ty did not seem the sort to exaggerate the danger she faced if she persisted in trying to penetrate the island. It was true enough that she was determined to discover what had become of the Elves; it was also true that her discovery would serve little purpose if she didn't survive to do something about it. And what exactly did she expect to do? Suppose the Elves were still there on Morrowindl? Suppose they were alive? If no one had gotten in or out in ten years, how was her appearance going to change anything? Why, whatever their present circumstances, would the Elves even consider what Allanon had sent her to propose—that they abandon life outside the Four Lands and return?

She had no answers to these questions, of course. It was pointless to try to find any. She had made her decisions up to now based strictly on instinct—to search for the Elves in the first place, to seek out the Addershag in Grimpen Ward and then to follow her directions, to persuade Tiger Ty to convey them to Morrowindl. She could not help but wonder if her instincts had misled her. Garth had stayed with her, virtually without argument, but Garth could be doing so out of loyalty or friendship. He might have resolved to see this matter through, but that didn't mean he had any better sense of what they were about than she did. She scanned the empty expanse of the Blue Divide, feeling small and vulnerable. Morrowindl was an island in the middle of the ocean, a tiny speck of earth amid all that water. Once she and Garth were there, they would be isolated from everything familiar. There would be no way off again without the aid of a Roc or a boat, nor was it certain there would be anyone on the island who could help them. There might no longer be any Elves. There might be only the monsters . . .

Monsters. She considered for a moment the question of what sort of monsters were there. Tiger Ty had failed to say. Were they as dangerous as the Shadowen? If so, then that would explain why the Elves had disappeared. Enough of these monsters could have trapped them, she supposed, or even destroyed them. But how had the Elves let such a thing happen? And if the monsters hadn't trapped them, then why did the Elves still remain on Morrowindl? Why hadn't even one of them escaped to seek help?

There were so many questions once again. She closed her eyes and willed them away.

It was approaching noon when they passed over a cluster of small islands that looked like emeralds floating in the sea, brilliant green against the blue. Spirit circled for a moment under Tiger Ty's direction, then descended toward the largest, choosing a narrow bluff thick with grasses to land upon. Once the great bird was settled, his riders released their safety straps and climbed down. Wren and Garth were stiff and sore already, and it took a few moments for them to get their limbs working again. Wren rubbed her aching joints and glanced around. The island appeared to be formed of a dark, porous rock on which vegetation grew as if on rich soil. The rock lay everywhere, crunching beneath their feet when they walked on it. Wren reached down and picked up a piece, finding it surprisingly light.

"Lava rock," Tiger Ty said with a grunt, seeing the puzzled look on her face. "All these islands are part of a chain formed by volcanoes sometime in the past, hundreds, maybe thousands of years ago." He paused, made a face, and then pointed. "The islands the Sky Elves live upon are just south. Course, we're not going there, you understand. I don't want anyone to discover I'm taking you to Morrowindl. I don't want them finding out how stupid I am."

He moved over to a grassy knoll and seated himself. After pulling off his gloves and boots, he began massaging his feet. "We'll have something to eat and drink in a minute," he muttered.

Wren said nothing. Garth had stretched out full length in the grass and his eyes were closed. He was happy, she thought, to be on the ground again. She put down the rock she had been examining and moved over to sit with Tiger Ty.

"You spoke of monsters on Morrowindl," she said after a minute. A soft breeze ruffled her hair, blowing curls across her face. "Can you tell me anything about them?"

The sharp eyes fastened on her. "There's all kinds, Miss Wren. Big and little, four-legged and two, flying, crawling, and stalking. There's those with hair, those with scales, and those with skin. Some come out of your worst nightmares. Some, they say, aren't living things. They hunt in packs, some of them. Some burrow in the earth and wait." He shook his gray-peppered head. "I've only seen one or two myself. Most I've just heard described. But they're there right enough." He paused, considering. "Odd though, isn't it, that there's so many different kinds? Odd, too, that there weren't any at first and then all of a sudden they just started to appear."

"You think the Elves had something to do with it." She made it a statement of fact.

Tiger Ty pursed his lips thoughtfully. "I have to think that.

It has to have something to do with their recovery of the magic—their return to the old ways. They wouldn't say so, wouldn't admit to a thing, the few I talked to. Ten years ago, that was. More, I guess. They claimed it all had something to do with the volcano and the changes in the earth and climate. Imagine that."

He smiled disarmingly. "That's the way it is, you know. Nobody wants to tell you the truth. Everybody wants to keep secrets." He paused to rub his chin. "Take yourself, for instance. I don't suppose you want to tell me what happened back there at the Wing Hove, do you? While you were waiting for me to spy your fire?" He watched her face. "See, I'm pretty quick to pick up on things. I don't miss much. Like your big friend over there, all bandaged up the way he is. Scratched and marked from a fight, a recent one, a bad one. You have a few marks yourself. And there was a dark scar on the rocks, the kind made from a very hot fire. Wasn't where the signal fire usually burns and it was new. And the rock was scraped pretty bad a place or two. From iron dragging, I'd guess. Or claws."

Wren had to smile in spite of herself. She regarded Tiger Ty with newfound admiration. "You're right—you don't miss much. There was a fight, Tiger Ty. Something tracked us for weeks, a thing we call a Shadowen." She saw recognition in his eyes instantly. "It attacked us when we lit the signal fire. We destroyed it."

"Did you now?" the little man sniffed. "Just the two of you. A Shadowen. I know a little of the Shadowen. Way I understand it, it would take something special to destroy one of them. Fire, maybe. The kind that comes from Elven magic. That would account for the burn on the rock, wouldn't it?"

He waited. Wren nodded slowly. "It might."

Tiger Ty leaned forward. "You're like the rest of them somehow, aren't you, Miss Wren. You're an Ohmsford like the others. You have the magic, too."

He said it softly, speculatively, and there was a curiosity mirrored in his eyes that hadn't been there before. He was right again, of course. She did have the magic, a discovery she had pointedly avoided thinking about since she had made it because to do otherwise would be to acknowledge that she had some responsibility for its possession and use. She continued to tell herself that the Elfstones did not really belong to her, that she was merely a caretaker and an unwilling one at that. Yes, they had saved Garth's life. And her own. And yes, she was grateful. But their magic was dangerous. Everyone knew that. She had been taught all of her life to be self-sufficient, to rely upon her instincts and her training, and to remember that survival was dependent principally on your own abilities and thought. She did not want a reliance on the magic of the Elfstones to undermine that.

Tiger Ty was still looking at her, waiting to see if she was going to respond. Wren met his gaze boldly and did not.

"Well," he said finally, and shrugged his disinterest. "Time to get a bite to eat."

The island was thick with fruit trees, and they made a satisfactory meal from what they picked. Afterward, they drank from a freshwater stream they found inland. Flowers grew everywhere—bougainvillea, oleander, hibiscus, orchids, and many more—massive bushes filled with their blooms, the colors bright through the green, the scents wafting on the air at every turn. There were palms, acacia, banyan, and something called a ginkgo. Strange birds perched in the branches of armored, spiny recops, their plumage a rainbow's blend. Tiger Ty described it all as they walked, pointing, identifying and explaining. Wren stared about in amazement, not permitting her gaze to linger anywhere for more than a few seconds, anxious that she not miss anything. She had never seen such beauty, a profusion of incredibly wonderful living things. It was almost overpowering.

"Was Morrowindl like this?" she asked Tiger Ty at one point.

He gave her a brief glance. "Once," he replied, and did not elaborate.

They climbed back atop Spirit shortly afterward and resumed their flight. It was easier now, a bit more familiar, and even Garth seemed to have discovered a way to make the journey bearable. They flew west and north, angling away from the sun as it passed overhead. There were other islands, small and mostly rocky, though all sustained at least a sprinkling of growth. The air was warm and soothing against their skin, and the sun burned down out of a cloudless sky, brightening the Blue Divide until it glistened. They saw massive sea animals that Tiger Ty called whales and claimed were the largest creatures in the ocean. There were birds of all sizes and shapes. There were fish that swam in groups called schools and leapt from the water in formation, silver bodies arcing against the sun. The journey became an incredible learning experience for Wren, and she immersed herself in its lessons.

"I have never seen anything like this!" she shouted enthusiastically at Tiger Ty.

"Wait until we reach Morrowindl," he grunted back.

THEY DESCENDED A SECOND TIME for a brief rest at midafternoon, choosing a solitary island with wide, white-sand beaches and coves so shallow the water was a pale turquoise. Wren noticed that Spirit had not eaten all day and asked about it. Tiger Ty said the Roc consumed meat and hunted on its own. It required food only once every seven days.

"A very self-sustaining bird, the Roc," the Wing Rider said with undisguised admiration. "Doesn't ask much more than to be left alone. More than you can say about most people."

They continued their journey in silence, both Wren and Garth beginning to tire now, stiff from sitting in the same position all day, worn from the constant rocking motion of the flight, and from gripping the knotted hand restraints until their fingers cramped. The waters of the Blue Divide passed steadily beneath, an endless progression of waves. They had been out of sight of the mainland for hours, and the ocean seemed to stretch away forever. Wren felt dwarfed by it, reduced by its size to something so insignificant she threatened to disappear. Her earlier sense of isolation had increased steadily with the passing of the hours, and she found herself wondering for the first time if she would ever see her home again.

It was nearing sunset when at last they came in sight of Morrowindl. The sun had drifted west to the edge of the horizon, its light growing soft, changing from white to pale orange. A streaking of purple and silver laced a long line of odd-shaped clouds that paraded across the sky like strange animals. Silhouetted against this panorama was the island, dark and misted and forbidding. It was much larger than any other landmass they had encountered, rising up like a wall as they approached. Killeshan lifted its jagged mouth skyward, steam seeping from its throat, slopes dropping away into a thick blanket of fog and ash, disappearing for hundreds of feet until they surfaced again at a shoreline formed of rocky projections and ragged cliffs. Waves crashed against the rocks, white foaming caldrons that threw their spray skyward.

Spirit flew closer, winging down toward the shroud of vog. A stench filled the air, the smell of sulfur escaped from beneath the earth where the volcano's fire burned rock to ash. Through the clouds and mist they could see valleys and ridges, passes and defiles, all heavily forested, a thick, strangling jungle. Tiger Ty glanced back over his shoulder and gestured. They were going to circle the island. Spirit wheeled right at his command. The north end of the island was engulfed in driving rain, a monsoon that inundated everything, creating vast waterfalls that tumbled down cliffs thousands of feet high. West the island was as barren as a desert, all exposed lava rock except for a scattering of brightly flowering shrubs and stunted, gnarled, wind-blown trees. South and east the island was a mass of singular rock formations and black-sand beaches where the shoreline met the waters of the Blue Divide before rising to disappear into jungle and mist.

Wren stared down at Morrowindl apprehensively. It was a forbidding, inhospitable place, a sharp contrast to the other islands they had seen. Weather fronts collided and broke apart. Each side of the island offered a different set of conditions. The whole of it was shadowed and clouded, as if Killeshan were a demon that breathed fire and had wrapped itself in the cloak of its own choking breath.

Tiger Ty wheeled Spirit about one final time, then took him down. The Roc settled cautiously at the edge of a broad, black-sand beach, claws digging into the crushed lava rock, wings folding reluctantly back. The giant bird turned to face the jungle, and his piercing eyes fixed on the mist.

Tiger Ty ordered them to dismount. They released their harness straps and slid to the beach. Wren looked inland. The island rose before her, all rock and trees and mist. They could no longer see the sun. Shadows and half-light lay over everything.

The Wing Rider faced the girl. "I suppose you're still set on this? Stubborn as ever?"

She nodded wordlessly, unwilling to trust herself to speak.

"You listen, then. And think about changing your mind while you do. I showed you all four sides of Morrowindl for a reason. North, it rains all the time, every day, every hour of the day. Sometimes it rains hard, sometimes drizzles. But the water is everywhere. Swamps and pools, falls and drops. If you can't swim, you drown. And there's nests of things waiting to pull you down in any case."

He gestured with his hand. "West is all desert. You saw. Nothing but open country, hot and dry and barren. You could walk it all the way to the top of the mountain, you probably think. Trouble is, you wouldn't get a mile before you ran cross-wise of the things that live under the rock. You'd never see them; they'd have you before you could think. There's thousands of them, all sizes and shapes, most with poison that will kill you quick. Nothing gets through."

His frown etched the lines of his seamed face even deeper. "That leaves south and east, which it happens are pretty much the same. Rock and jungle and vog and a lot of very unpleasant things that live within. Once off this beach, you won't be safe again until you're back. I told you once that it was a death trap in there. I'll tell you again in case you didn't hear me.

"Miss Wren," he said softly. "Don't do this. You don't stand a chance."

She reached out impulsively and took his gnarled hands in her own. "Garth and I will look out for each other," she promised. "We've been doing so for a long time."

He shook his head. "It won't be enough."

She tightened her grip. "How far must we travel to find the Elves? Can you give us some idea?"

He released himself and pointed inland. "Their city, if it's still there, sits halfway down the mountain in a niche that's protected from the lava flows. Most of the flows run east and some of those tunnel under the rock to the sea. From here, it's maybe thirty miles. I don't know what the land's like in there anymore. Ten years changes a lot of things."

"We'll find our way," she said. She took a deep breath to

steady herself, aware of how impossible this effort was likely to prove. She glanced at Garth, who stared back at her stone-faced. She looked again at Tiger Ty. "I need to ask one thing more of you. Will you come back for us? Will you give us sufficient time to make our search and then come back?"

Tiger Ty folded his arms across his chest, his leathery face managing to look both sad and stern. "I'll come, Miss Wren. I'll wait three weeks—time enough for you to make it in and get out again. Then I'll look for you once a week four weeks running." He shook his head. "But I have to tell you that I think it will be a waste of time. You won't be back. I won't ever see you again."

She smiled bravely. "I'll find a way, Tiger Ty."

The Wing Rider's eyes narrowed. "Only one way. You better be meaner and stronger than anything you run up against. And—" He jabbed at her with a bony finger. "—you better be prepared to use your magic!"

He wheeled abruptly and stalked to where Spirit waited. Without pausing, he pulled himself up the harness loops and settled into place. When he had finished fastening the safety straps, he looked back at them.

"Don't try going in at night," he advised. "The first day, at least, travel when it's light. Keep Killeshan's mouth to your right as you climb." He threw up his hands. "Demon's blood, but this is a foolish thing you're doing!"

"Don't forget about us, Tiger Ty!" Wren called in reply.

The Wing Rider scowled at her for an instant, then kicked Spirit lightly. The Roc lifted into the air, wings spreading against the wind, rising slowly, wheeling south. In seconds, the giant bird had become nothing more than a speck in the fading light.

Wren and Garth stood silently on the empty beach and watched until the speck had disappeared.

CHAPTER

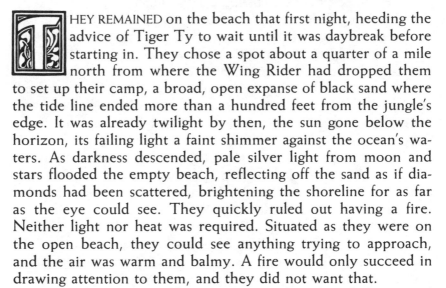

6

THEY REMAINED on the beach that first night, heeding the advice of Tiger Ty to wait until it was daybreak before starting in. They chose a spot about a quarter of a mile north from where the Wing Rider had dropped them to set up their camp, a broad, open expanse of black sand where the tide line ended more than a hundred feet from the jungle's edge. It was already twilight by then, the sun gone below the horizon, its failing light a faint shimmer against the ocean's waters. As darkness descended, pale silver light from moon and stars flooded the empty beach, reflecting off the sand as if diamonds had been scattered, brightening the shoreline for as far as the eye could see. They quickly ruled out having a fire. Neither light nor heat was required. Situated as they were on the open beach, they could see anything trying to approach, and the air was warm and balmy. A fire would only succeed in drawing attention to them, and they did not want that.

They ate a cold meal of dried meat, bread, and cheese and washed it down with ale. They sat facing the jungle, their backs to the ocean, listening and watching. Morrowindl lost definition as night fell, the sweep of jungle and cliffs and desert disappearing into blackness until at last the island was little more than a silhouette against the sky. Finally even that disappeared, and all that remained was a steady cacophony of sounds. The sounds were indistinguishable for the most part, faint and muffled, a scattering of calls and hoots and buzzings, of birds and insects and animals, all lost deep within the sheltering dark. The waters of the Blue Divide rolled in steady cadence against the island's shores, washing in and retreating again, a slow and steady lapping. A breeze sprang up, soft and fragrant, washing away the last of the day's lingering heat.

When they had finished their meal, they stared wordlessly ahead for a time—at the sky and the beach and the ocean, at nothing at all.

Already Morrowindl made Wren feel uneasy. Even now, cloaked in darkness, invisible and asleep, the island was a presence that threatened. She pictured it in her mind, Killeshan rising up against the sky with its ragged maw open, a patchwork of jungled slopes, towering cliffs, and barren deserts, a chained giant wrapped in vog and mist, waiting. She could feel its breath on her face, anxious and hungry. She could hear it hiss in greeting.

She could sense it watching.

It frightened her more than she cared to admit, and she could not seem to dispel her fear. It was an insidious shadow that crept through the corridors of her mind, whispering words whose meanings were unintelligible but whose intent was clear. She felt oddly bereft of her skills and her training, as if all had been stripped from her at the moment she had arrived. Even her instincts seemed muddled. She could not explain it. It made no sense. Nothing had happened, and yet here she was, her confidence shredded and scattered like straw. Another woman might have been able to take comfort from the fact that she possessed the legendary Elfstones—but not Wren. The magic was foreign to her, a thing to be mistrusted. It belonged to a past she had only heard about, a history that had been lost for generations. It belonged to someone else, someone she did not know. The Elfstones, she thought darkly, had nothing to do with her.

The words brought a chill to the pit of her stomach. They, of course, were a lie.

She put her hands over her face, hiding herself away. Doubts crowded in on every side, and she wondered briefly, futilely, whether her decision to come to Morrowindl had been wrong.

Finally she took her hands away and edged forward until she was close enough in the darkness to see clearly Garth's bearded face. The big man watched unmoving as she lifted her hands and began to sign.

Do you think I made a mistake by insisting we come here? she asked him.

He studied her for a moment, then shook his head. *It is never a mistake to do something you feel is necessary.*

I did feel it necessary.

I know.

"But I did not come just to discover if the Elves are still alive," she said, fingers moving. "I came to find out about my parents, to learn who they were and what became of them."

He nodded without replying.

"I didn't use to care, you know," she went on, trying to explain. "It didn't use to make any difference. I was a Rover, and that was enough. Even after Cogline found us and we went east to the Hadeshorn and met with the Shade of Allanon, even when I began asking about the Elves, hoping to learn something of what had happened to them, I wasn't thinking about my parents. I didn't have any idea where it was all leading. I just went along, asking my questions, learning finally of the Addershag, then of the signal fire. I was just following a trail, curious to see where it would lead."

She paused. "But the Elfstones, Garth—that was something I hadn't counted on. When I discovered that they were real—that they were the Elfstones of Shea and Wil Ohmsford—everything changed. So much power—and they belonged to my parents. Why? How did my parents come by them in the first place? What was their purpose in giving them to me? You see, don't you? I won't ever have any answers unless I find out who my parents were."

Garth signed, *I understand. I wouldn't be here with you if I didn't.*

"I know that," she whispered, her throat tightening. "I just wanted to hear you say it."

They were silent for a moment, eyes turned away. Something huge splashed far out in the water. The sound reverberated momentarily and disappeared. Wren pushed at the rough sand with her boot.

Garth, she signed, catching his eye. *Is there anything about my parents that you haven't told me?*

Garth said nothing, his face expressionless.

"Because if there is," she signed, "you have to tell me now. You cannot let me continue with this search not knowing."

Garth shifted, his head lowering into shadow. When he lifted it again, his fingers began to move. *I would not keep anything from you that was not necessary. I keep nothing from you now about your parents. What I know, I have told you. Believe me.*

"I do," she affirmed quietly. Yet the answer troubled her. Was there something else he kept from her, something he considered necessary? Did she have the right to demand to know what it was?

She shook her head. He would never hurt her. That was the important thing. Not Garth.

We will discover the truth about your parents, he signed suddenly. *I promise.*

She reached out briefly to take his hands, then released them. "Garth," she said, "you are the best friend I shall ever have."

She kept watch then while he slept, feeling comforted by his words, reassured that she was not alone after all, that they were united in their purpose. Hidden by the darkness, Morrowindl continued to brood, sinister and threatening. But she was not so intimidated now, her resolve strengthened, her purpose clear. It would be as it had been for so many years—she and Garth against whatever waited. It would be enough.

When Garth woke at midnight, she went quickly to sleep.

SUNRISE BRIGHTENED THE SKIES with pale silver, but Morrowindl was a black wall that shut that light away. The island stood between the dawn on the one hand and Garth and Wren on the other as if seeking to lock the Rovers permanently in shadow. The beach was still and empty, a black line that stretched away into the distance like a scattered bolt of mourning crepe. Rocks and cliffs jutted out of the green tangle of the jungle, poking forth like trapped creatures seeking to breathe. Killeshan thrust skyward in mute silence, steam curling from fissures down the length of its lava-rock skin. Far distant to the north, a glimpse of the island's desert side revealed a harsh, broken surface over which a blanket of sulfuric mist had been thrown and on which nothing moved.

The Rover girl and her companion washed and ate a hurried breakfast, anxious to be off. The day's heat was already beginning to settle in, chasing the ocean's breezes back across her waters. Seabirds glided and swooped about them, casting for food. Crabs scuttled about the rocks cautiously, seeking shelter in cracks and crevices. All about, the island was waking up.

Wren and Garth shouldered their packs, checked the readiness of their weapons, glanced briefly at each other, and started in.

The beach faded into a short patch of tall grass that in turn gave way to a forest of towering acacia. The trunks of the ancient trees rose skyward like pillars, running back until distance gave them the illusion of being a wall. The floor of the forest was barren and cleared of scrub; storms and risen tides had washed away everything but the giant trees. Within the acacia, all was still. The sun was masked yet in the east, and shadows lay over everything. Wren and Garth walked slowly, steadily ahead, watchful for any form of danger. They passed out of the acacia and into a stand of bamboo. They skirted it until they found a narrowing of the growth and used short swords to hack their way through. From there they proceeded along a meadow where the grasses were waist-high and wildflowers grew in colorful profusion amid the green. Ahead, the forest rose along the slopes of Killeshan, trees and brush amid odd formations of lava rock, all of it disappearing finally into the vog.

The first day passed without incident. They traveled through open country whenever they could find it, choosing a path that let them see what they were walking into. They camped that night in a meadow, comfortably settled on high ground that again gave them a clear view in all directions. The second day passed in the same manner as the first. They made good progress, navigating rivers and streams and climbing ravines and foothills without difficulty. There was no sign of the monsters that Tiger Ty had warned them about. There were brightly colored snakes and spiders that were most certainly poisonous, but the Rovers had dealt with their cousins in other parts of the world and knew enough to avoid any contact. They heard the harsh cough of moor cats, but saw nothing. Once or twice predatory birds flew overhead, but after a series of cursory passes these hunters soon sped away in search of easier prey. It rained frequently and heavily, but never for very long at one time, and except for threatening to trap them in dry riverbeds with an unexpected flash flood or to drop them into newly formed sinkholes, the rain did little more than cool them off.

All the while the haze blanketing Killeshan's slopes drew closer, a promise of harsher things to come.

The third day began in the same way as the two before, shadowed and still and brooding. The sun rose and was visible briefly through the trees ahead, a warm and inviting beacon. Then abruptly it disappeared as the lower edges of the vog descended. The haze was thin and untroubling at first, not much more than a thickening of the air, a graying of the light. But slowly it began to deepen, gathering in patches that screened away everything more than thirty feet from where they walked. The country grew rougher as the shoreline lowlands and grassy foothills gave way to slides and drops, and the lava rock turned crumbly and loose. Footing grew uncertain and the pace slowed.

They ate a hurried, troubled, silent lunch and started out again cautiously. They tied thick hides about their legs above the boot tops and below the knees to protect against snakes. They pulled on their heavy cloaks and wrapped them close. The heat of the lower slopes was absent here, and the air—which they had thought would turn warm as they moved closer to Killeshan—grew cold. Garth took the lead, deliberately shielding Wren. Shadows moved all about them in the mist, things that lacked shape and form but were there nevertheless. The familiar sounds of birds and insects died away, fading into an expectant hush. Dusk fell early, a draining away of light, and rain began to fall in steady sheets.

They made their camp at the foot of an ancient koa that fronted a small clearing. With their backs to the tree, they ate their dinner and watched the light deepen from smoke to charcoal. The rain slowed to an intermittent drizzle, and mist began to creep down the mountainside in probing tendrils. Already the forest was beginning to turn to jungle, the trees thickly grown and tangled with vines, the ground damp and soft and yielding.

Slugs and beetles crawled through brush and rotting logs. The ground was dry beneath the koa, but the dampness in the air seemed to penetrate everywhere. There was no possibility of a fire. Wren and Garth hunched within their cloaks and pushed closer to each other. The night settled down about them, turning the world an inky black.

Wren offered to stand the first watch, too edgy to sleep. Garth acquiesced without comment. He pulled up his knees, put his head on his crossed arms, and was asleep almost immediately.

Wren sat staring into the blackness. The trees and mist screened away any light from moon and stars, and even after her eyes had adjusted it was impossible to see more than a dozen feet from where she kept watch. Shadows drifted at the periphery of her vision, brief, quick, and suggestive. Sounds darted out of the haze to challenge and tease—the shrill call of night birds, the click of insects, scrapes and rustlings, huffings and snarls. The low cough of hunting cats came from somewhere distant. She could smell faintly the sulfur fumes of Killeshan, wafting on the air, mingling with the thicker, more pungent scents of the jungle. All around her an invisible world was waking up.

Let it, she thought defiantly.

The air grew still as even the drizzle faded away and only fog remained. Time slipped away. The sounds slowed and softened, and there was a sense that everything out there in the blackness lay in wait, that everything watched. She was aware that the shadows at the edge of the encroaching mist had faded away. Garth was snoring softly. She shifted her cramped body but made no effort to rise. She liked the feel of the tree against her back and Garth pressing close. She hated how the island made her feel—exposed, vulnerable, unprotected. It was the newness, she told herself. It was the unfamiliarity of the terrain, the isolation from her own country, the memory of Tiger Ty's warning that there were monsters here. It would take time to adjust . . .

She left the thought unfinished as she saw the silhouette of something huge appear at the edge of the mist. It walked upright on two legs momentarily, then dropped down on four. It stopped and she knew it was looking at her. The hair on the back of her neck prickled, and she edged her hand down until her fingers closed about the long knife at her waist.

She waited.

The thing that watched did not move. It seemed to be waiting with her.

Then she saw another of the shadows appear, similar to the first. And another. And a fourth. They gathered in the darkness and went still, invisible eyes glittering. Wren took slow, deep breaths. She thought about waking Garth, but told herself over and over that she would wait just one more minute, just long enough to see what would happen.

But nothing happened. The minutes crawled past, and the shadows stayed where they were. Wren wondered how many were out there. Then she wondered if they were behind her where she couldn't see them, sneaking up until they were close enough to . . .

She turned quickly and looked. There was nothing there. At least, nothing within the limited range of her vision.

She turned back again. She knew suddenly that the things in the darkness were waiting to see what she would do, trying to ascertain how dangerous she might be. If she sat there long enough they would grow impatient and decide to test her. She wondered how much time she had. She wondered what it would take to discourage them. If the monsters were here already, only three nights off the beach, they would be there every night from here on in, watching and waiting. And there would be others. There were bound to be.

Wren's blood pumped through her, racing as quickly as her thoughts. Together, Garth and she were a match for most things. But they could not afford to fight everything they came across.

The shadows had begun to move again, restless. She heard murmurings, not words exactly, but something. She could feel movement all about her, something other than the shadows, things she could not see. The inhabitants of the jungle had discovered them and were gathering. She heard a growl, low and menacing. Beside her, Garth shifted in his sleep, turning away.

Wren's face felt hot.

Do something, she whispered to herself. *You have to do something.*

She knew without looking that the shadows were behind her now.

She felt a burning against her breast.

Almost without thinking, she reached down into her tunic and removed the leather bag with the Elfstones. Swiftly, unwilling to think about what she was doing, she shook the Stones into her hand and quickly closed her fingers about them. She could feel the shadows watching.

Just a hint of what they can do, she told herself. *That should be enough.*

She stretched forth her hand and let her fingers open slightly. The blue light of the Elfstones brightened. It gathered, a cold fire, and issued forth in thin streamers to probe the darkness.

Instantly the shadows were gone. They disappeared so swiftly and so completely that they might never have been there. The sounds died into a hush. The world became a vacuum, and she and Garth were all that remained within it.

She closed her fingers tightly again and withdrew her hand. The shadows, whatever they were, knew something of Elven magic.

Her instincts had told her that they would.

She was filled with a sudden bitterness. The Elfstones were not a part of her life, she had insisted. Oh, no—not her life. They belonged to someone else, not to her. How quick she had been to tell herself so. And how quick to turn to them the moment she felt threatened.

She slipped the Stones back into their container and shoved it within her tunic again. The night was peaceful and still; the mist was empty of movement. The things that lived on Morrowindl had gone in search of easier prey.

It was after midnight when she woke Garth. Nothing further had appeared to threaten them. She did not tell Garth what had happened. She wrapped herself in her cloak and leaned back against him.

It was a long time before she fell asleep.

THEY SET OUT AGAIN AT DAWN. Vog lay thick across the slopes of Killeshan, and the light was thin and gray. Dampness filled the air; it seeped up through the ground on which they walked, penetrated the clothing they wore, and left them shivering. After a time, the sun began to burn through the mist, and some of the chill faded. Travel was slow and difficult, the land uneven and broken, a series of ravines and ridges choked by the jungle's growth. Last night's hush persisted, a sullen still- ness that isolated the pair and spun webs of uneasiness all about them.

At the edge of their vision, the shadows persisted, furtive, cautious, a gathering of quick and formless ghosts that were there until the instant you looked for them and then were gone. Garth seemed oblivious to their presence, but Wren knew he was not. As she stole a furtive glance at his dark face from time to time she could see the calm that reflected in his eyes. She marveled that her giant friend could keep everything so care- fully closed away. Her own eyes searched the haze relentlessly, for even now she was unsure how much the things that hid there feared the Elfstones, how long the magic would continue to keep them at bay. Her fingers strayed constantly to her tunic and the leather bag beneath, seeking reassurance that her protection was still there.

The day wore slowly down. They passed through forests of koa and banyan, old and shaggy with moss and vines, along slides where the lava rock was crusted and broken off into loose pieces that crumbled and skidded away as they tried to find footing, down ravines where the brush was thorny and across the sweep of valleys over which heavy clouds stretched in an impenetrable blanket of gray. All the while they continued to climb, working their way up Killeshan's slopes, catching brief glimpses of the volcano through breaks in the vog, the summit lifting away, seemingly never closer.

They began to recognize more and more of the dangers of the island. There were certain plants, bright colored and intri- cately formed, that snared and trapped anything that came within reach. There were sinkholes that could swallow you up in a moment's time if you were unfortunate enough to step in one. There were strange animals that showed themselves briefly and disappeared again, hunters all, scaled and spiked, clawed and sharp-toothed. No monsters appeared, but Wren suspected they were there, watching and waiting, the specters that whispered from the mist.

Night came and they slept, and this time the shadows did not approach, but stayed carefully hidden. A moor cat prowled close, but Garth blew into a thick stalk of grass, producing a whistling sound the big cat apparently did not care for, and it faded back into silence. Wren dreamed of home, of the Westland when she was young and everything was new, and she woke with the memories clear and bright.

"Garth, I used the Elfstones again," she told him at breakfast, the two of them huddled close against the chill gloom. "Two nights ago when the shadows first appeared."

I know, he replied, his eyes fixing her as he signed. *I was awake.*

"How much did you see?" she whispered, shaking her head in disbelief.

Enough. The magic frightens you, doesn't it?

She smiled wistfully. "Everything we do frightens me."

They walked through the silence of the dawn, lost in thought. The land flattened out before them and the jungle stretched away. The vog was thicker here, steady and unmoving before them. The air was still. They crossed an open space and found themselves at the edge of a swamp. Cautiously they skirted its reed-lined borders, searching for firmer ground. When they were successful, they started ahead again. The swamp persisted. Time after time, they were forced to change direction, seeking safer passage. The bog was a dull, flat shimmer of dampness stretched across masses of grass and weeds, and trees poked out of it like the limbs of drowned giants. Winged insects buzzed about, glittering and iridescent. Garth produced an ill-smelling salve that they used to coat their faces and arms, a shield against bites and stings. Snakes slithered in the mud. Spiders crawled everywhere, some larger than Garth's fist. Webs and moss and vines trailed from branches and brush, clinging and deadly. Bats flew through the cathedral ceilings of the trees, their squeaking sharp and chilling.

At one point they encountered a giant web concealed overhead and set like a snare to fall on whatever passed beneath. A less skilled pair of hunters might have missed it and been caught, but Garth spotted the trap at once. The strands of the webbing were as thick as Wren's fingers, and so close to transparent that they were invisible if you were not looking for them. She poked at one with a reed, and the reed was instantly stuck fast. Wren and Garth peered about cautiously for a long time without moving. Whatever it was that had spun that webbing was not something they wanted to meet.

Satisfied at last that the webmaker was not about, they pressed on.

It was nearing noon when they heard the scraping sound. They slowed and then stopped. The sound was rough and frantic, much too loud for the stillness of the swamp, almost a thrashing. It came from their left where shadows lay across a thicket of scrub with brilliant red flowers. With Garth leading, they skirted the scrub right, following a ridge of solid ground to a clearing of koa, moving silently, listening as the scraping sound continued. Almost immediately they saw strands of the clear webbing trailing earthward from the tops of the trees. The strands shook as something tugged against them from within the brush. It was apparent what had happened. Garth beckoned to Wren, and they continued cautiously on.

Amid the koa, they stopped again. A series of snares had been laid through the trees, one large and several small. One of the smaller snares had been tripped, and the scraping sound came from the creature it had entangled as it struggled to break free. The creature was unlike anything either Wren or Garth had ever seen. As large as a small hunting dog, it appeared to be a cross between a porcupine and a cat, its barrel-shaped body covered with black and tan ringed quills and supported by four short, thick legs while its squarish head, hunched virtually neckless between its shoulders, narrowed abruptly into the blunt, furry countenance of a feline. Wrinkled paws ended in powerful clawed fingers that dug at the earth, and its stubby, quilled tail whipped back and forth in a frantic effort to snap the lines of webbing that had wrapped about it.

The effort was futile. The more it thrashed, the more the webbing caught it up. Finally the creature paused, its head lifted, and it saw them. Wren was astonished by the creature's eyes.

They had lids and lashes and were colored a brilliant blue. They were not the eyes of an animal; they were eyes like her own.

The creature's body sagged, exhausted from its struggle. The quills laid back sleekly, and the strange eyes blinked.

"Pfftttt!" The creature spit—very like the cat it in part, at least, resembled. "Don't suppose you would consider helping me," the creature softly rasped. "After all, you share some—arrgggh—responsibility for my predicament."

Wren stared, then glanced hurriedly over at Garth, who for once appeared as surprised as she was. How could this creature talk? She turned back again. "What do you mean, I share some responsibility?"

"Rrrowwwggg. I mean, you're an Elf, aren't you?"

"Well, no, as a matter of fact I'm not. I'm a . . ." She hesitated. She had been about to say she was a Rover. But the truth was she was at least part Elf. Wasn't that how the creature had identified her—by her Elven features? She frowned. How did it know of Elves anyway?

"Who are you?" she asked.

The creature appraised her silently for a moment, blue eyes unblinking. When he spoke, its voice was a low growl. "Stresa."

"Stresa," she repeated. "Is that your name?"

The creature nodded.

"My name is Wren. This is my friend Garth."

"Hssttt. You are an Elf," Stresa repeated, and the cat face furrowed. "But you are not from Morrowindl."

"No," she responded. She put her hands on her hips, puzzled. "How did you know that?"

The blue eyes squinted slightly. "You don't recognize me. You don't know what I am. Hrrrrowwl. If you lived on Morrowindl, you would."

Wren nodded. "What are you, then?"

"A Splinterscat," the creature answered. He growled deep in its throat. "That is what we are called, the few of us who remain. Part of this and part of that, but mostly something else altogether. Puurrft."

"And how is it that you know about Elves? Are there still Elves living here?"

The Splinterscat regarded her coolly, patient within his

snare. "If you help me get free," he replied, his rough voice a low purr, "I will answer your questions."

Wren hesitated, undecided.

"Fffppht! You had better hurry," he advised. "Before the Wisteron comes."

Wisteron? Wren glanced again at Garth, signing to indicate what Stresa had said. Garth made a brief response.

Wren turned back. "How do we know you won't hurt us?" she asked the Splinterscat.

"Harrrwl. If you are not from Morrowindl and you have come this far, then you are more dangerous than I," he answered, coming as close as he probably could to laughing. "Hurry, now. Use your long knives to cut the webbing. The edge of the blade only; keep the flat turned away." The strange creature paused, and for the first time she saw a hint of desperation in its eyes. "There isn't much time. If you help me— hrroww—perhaps I can help you in return."

Wren signed to Garth, and they moved over to where the Splinterscat was bound, careful to avoid triggering any of the snares still in place. Working quickly, they sliced through the strands entangling the creature and then backed away. Stresa stepped over the fallen webbing gingerly and eased past them to where the ground was firm. He spread his quills and shook himself violently. Both Wren and Garth flinched at the sudden movement, but no quills flew at them. The Splinterscat was merely shaking loose the last of the webbing clinging to his body. He began preening himself, then stopped when he remembered they were watching.

"Thank you," he said in his low, rough voice. "If you had not freed me, I would have died. Grrwwll. The Wisteron would have eaten me."

"The Wisteron?" Wren asked.

The Splinterscat laid back its quills, ignoring the question. "You should already be dead yourself," he declared. The cat face furrowed once more. "Pffftt!" he spit. "You are either very lucky or you have the protection of magic. Which is it?"

Wren took a moment to respond. "You promised to answer my questions, Stresa. Tell me of the Elves."

The Splinterscat bunched itself up and sat down. He was

bigger than he had looked in the snare, more the size of a dog than the cat or porcupine he looked. "The Elves," he said, the growl creeping back into his voice, "live inland, high on the slopes of Killeshan in the city of Arborlon—hrrowggh—where the demons have them trapped."

"Demons?" Wren asked, immediately thinking of those that had been shut away within the Forbidding by the Ellcrys. They had already broken free once in the time of Wil Ohmsford. Had they done so again? "What do these demons look like?" she pressed.

"Sssssttt! Like lots of different things. What difference does it make? The point is, the Elves made them and now they can't get rid of them. Pfft! Too bad for the Elves. The magic of the Keel fails now. It won't be long before everything goes."

The Splinterscat waited while Wren wrestled with this latest news. There was still too much she didn't understand. "The Elves *made* the demons?" she repeated in confusion.

"Years ago. When they didn't know any better."

"But . . . made them from what?"

Stresa's tongue licked out, a dark violet against its brown face. "Why did you come here—grrwll? Why are you looking for the Elves?"

Wren felt Garth's cautionary hand on her shoulder. She turned and saw him gesture off into the jungle.

"Hssttt, yes, I hear it, too," Stresa announced, rising hurriedly. "The Wisteron. It begins to hunt, to check its snares for food. We have to get away from here quickly. Once it discovers I've escaped, it will come looking for me." The Splinterscat shook out its quills. "Hhgggh. Since you don't appear to know your way, you had better follow me."

He started off abruptly. Wren hurried to catch up, Garth trailing. "Wait a moment! What sort of creature is this Wisteron?" she asked.

"Better for you if you never find out," Stresa replied enigmatically, and all of his quills stood on end. "This swamp is called the In Ju. The Wisteron makes its home here. The In Ju stretches all the way to Blackledge—and that is a long way off. Phffaghh."

He shambled away, moving far more quickly than Wren would have expected. "I still don't understand how you know so much about the Elves," she said, hastening after. "Or how it is that you can talk, for that matter. Does everything on Morrowindl talk?"

Stresa glanced back, a cat look, sharp and knowing. "Rraarggh—did I forget to tell you? The reason I can talk is that the Elves made me, too. Hsssstt." The Splinterscat turned away. "Enough questions for now. Better if we keep still for a while."

He moved rapidly into the trees, as silent as smoke, leaving Wren with Garth to follow, pondering her confusion and disbelief.

7

THEY FLED SWIFTLY, silently through the In Ju. The Splinterscat led, his brownish quilled body shambling through brush and into grasses, under brambles and over logs as if they were all one, a single obstacle that required the same amount of effort to surmount. Wren and Garth followed, forced to skirt the heavier undergrowth, to pick their way more cautiously, to test the ground before they walked upon it. They managed to keep pace only because Stresa had sufficient presence of mind to look back for them now and again and wait until they caught up.

None of them spoke as they hastened on, but they all listened carefully for sounds of the Wisteron's pursuit.

The jungle grew darker and webs began to appear everywhere. Many were trailers from snares long since sprung or worn away, yet an equal number were triggers to nets stretched through the treetops, across brush, even over pits in the earth. The webbing was clear and invisible except where leaves or dirt had become attached and gave color and definition, and even then it was hard to detect. Wren soon gave up searching for anything else, concentrating solely on the dangerous nets. A spider would spin webs such as these, she thought to herself, and pictured the Wisteron so in her mind.

They had been fleeing for only a handful of minutes when she finally heard it moving. The sound reached her clearly— brush and scrub thrashing, the limbs of trees snapping, bark scraping, and water splashing and churning. The Wisteron was big and it was making no effort to hide its coming. It sounded as if a juggernaut were rolling over everything, implacable, inescapable. The In Ju was a monstrous green cathedral in which the silence had been snatched away. Wren was suddenly very afraid.

They passed through a broad clearing in which a lake had formed, forcing them to change direction. After a moment's hesitation, they skirted right along a low ridge on which a thick patch of brambles grew. Stresa tunneled ahead, oblivious. Wren and Garth followed bravely, ignoring the scrapes and cuts they received, the sounds of the Wisteron's coming growing louder behind them.

Then abruptly the sounds disappeared.

Stresa stopped instantly, freezing in place. The Rovers did so as well. Wren listened, motionless. Garth put his hands against the earth. All was still. The trees hovered motionless about them, the misted half-light a curtain of gauze. The only sound was a rustling of the wind . . . Except that there was no wind. Wren went cold. The air was as still as death. She looked quickly at Stresa. The Splinterscat was looking up.

The Wisteron was moving through the trees.

Garth was on his feet again, his long knife sliding free. Wren searched the canopy of limbs and branches overhead in a frantic, futile effort to catch sight of something. The rustling was closer, more recognizable, no longer the whisper of wind against leaves but the movement of something huge.

Stresa began to run, an odd-shaped chunk of prickly earth skimming toward a stand of koa, silent somehow, but frantic as well. Wren and Garth went, too, unbidden, unquestioning. Wren was sweating freely beneath her clothes, and her body ached from the effort to remain still. She moved in a crouch, afraid now to look back, to look up, or to look anywhere but ahead to where the Splinterscat raced. The rustling of leaves filled her ears, and there was a snapping of branches. Birds darted through the cavernous forest, spurts of color and movement that were gone in the blink of an eye. The jungle shimmered damp and frozen about her, a still life in which only they moved. The koa rose ahead, massive trunks trailing yards of mossy vines, great hoary giants rooted in time.

Wren started unexpectedly. Nestled against her breast, the Elfstones had begun to burn.

Not again, she thought desperately, *I won't use the magic again,* but knew even as she thought it she would.

They reached the shelter of the koa, moving hurriedly within, down a hall formed of trunks and shadows. Wren looked up, searching for snares. There were none to be seen. She watched Stresa scurry to one side toward a gathering of brush and push within. She and Garth followed, stooping to make their way past the branches, pulling their packs after them, clutching them close to mask any sound.

Crouched in blackness and breathing heavily, they knelt against the jungle floor and waited. The minutes slipped by. The leafy branches of their shelter muffled any sound from without, so they could no longer hear the rustling. It was close within their concealment, and the stench of rotting wood seeped up from the earth. Wren felt trapped. It would be better to be out in the open where she could run, where she could see. She felt a sudden urge to bolt. But she glanced at Garth and saw the calm set of the big man's face and held her ground. Stresa had eased back toward the opening, flattened against the earth, head cocked, stubby cat's ears pricked.

Wren eased down next to the creature and peered out.

The Splinterscat's quills bristled.

In that same instant she saw the Wisteron. It was still in the trees, so distant from where they hid that it was little more than a shadow against the screen of vog. Even so, there was no mistaking it. It crept through the branches like some massive wraith . . . No, she corrected. It wasn't creeping. It was stalking. Not like a cat, but something far more confident, far more determined. It stole the life out of the air as it went, a shadow that swallowed sound and movement. It had four legs and a tail and it used all five to grasp the branches of the trees and pull itself along. It might have been an animal once; it still had the look of one. But it moved like an insect. It was all misshapen and distorted, the parts of its body hinged like giant grapples that allowed it to swing freely in any direction. It was sleek and sinewy and grotesque beyond even the wolf thing that had tracked them out of Grimpen Ward.

The Wisteron paused, turning.

Wren's breath caught in her throat, and she held it there with a single-mindedness that was heartstopping. The Wisteron hung suspended against the gray, a huge, terrifying shadow. Then abruptly it swung away. It passed before her like the promise of her own death, hinting, teasing, and whispering silent threats. Yet it did not see her; it did not slow. On this afternoon, it had other victims to claim.

Then it was gone.

THEY EMERGED FROM HIDING after a time to continue on, edgy and furtive, traveling mostly because it was necessary to do so if they ever wanted to get clear of the In Ju. Even so, they had not succeeded when darkness fell and so spent that night within the swamp. Stresa found a large hollow in the trunk of a dead banyan, and the Rovers reluctantly crawled in at the Splinters-cat's urging. They were not anxious to be confined, but it was better than sleeping out in the open where the creatures of the swamp could creep up on them. In any event, it was dry within the trunk, and the chill of night was less evident. The Rovers wrapped themselves in their heavy cloaks and sat facing the opening, staring out into the murky dark, smelling rot and mold and damp, watching the ever-present shadows flit past.

"What is it that's moving out there?" Wren asked Stresa finally, unable to contain her curiosity any longer. They had just finished eating. The Splinterscat seemed capable of devouring just about anything—the cheese, bread, and dried meats they carried in equal measure with the grubs and insects he foraged on his own. At the moment he was sitting just to one side of the opening in the banyan, gnawing on a root.

He glanced up alertly. "Out there?" he repeated. The words were so guttural Wren could barely understand them. "Grrrsssst. Nothing much, really. Some ugly, little creatures that wouldn't dare show their faces in other circumstances. They creep about now—hhhrrgg—because all the really dangerous things—except the wwwssst Wisteron—are at Arborlon, waiting for the Keel to give out."

"Tell me about the Keel," she urged. Her fingers signed to Garth, translating the Splinterscat's words.

Stresa put down the root. The purr was back in his rough voice. "The Keel is the wall that surrounds the city. It was formed of the magic, and the magic keeps the demons out. Hggghhhh. But the magic weakens, and the demons grow stronger. The Elves don't seem to be able to do anything about either." The Splinterscat paused. "How did you find out about the demons? Hssttt. What is your name again? Grrllwren? Wren? Who told you about Morrowindl?"

Wren leaned back against the banyan trunk. "It's a long story, Stresa. A Wing Rider brought us here. He was the one who warned us about the demons, except that he called them monsters. Do you know about Wing Riders?"

"Ssttppft! The Elves with the giant birds—yes, I know. They used to come here all the time. Not anymore. Now when they come, the demons are waiting. They pull them down and kill them. Fffftt—quick. That's what would have happened to you as well if they weren't all at Arborlon—or at least most of them. The Wisteron doesn't bother with such things."

Arborlon, Wren was thinking, had been the home city of the Elves when they had lived in the Westland. It had disappeared when they did. Had they rebuilt it on Morrowindl? What had they done with the Ellcrys? Had they brought it with them? Or had it died out once again as it had in the time of Wil Ohmsford? Was that why there were demons on Morrowindl?

"How far are we from the the city?" she asked, pushing the questions aside.

"A long way yet," Stresa answered. The cat face cocked. "The In Ju runs to a mountain wall called Blackledge that stretches all the way across the south end of the island. Beyond that lies a valley where the Rowen flows. Rrwwwn. Beyond that sits Arborlon, high on a bluff below Killeshan's mouth. Is that where you are trying to go?"

Wren nodded.

"Ppffahh! Whatever for?"

"To find the Elves," Wren answered. "I have been sent to give them a message."

Stresa shook his head and fanned his quills away from his body an inch or so. "I hope the message is important. I don't see how you will ever manage to deliver it with demons all about the city—if the city is even there anymore. Ssstt."

"We will find a way." Wren wanted to change the subject. "You said earlier that the Elves made you, Stresa. And the demons. But you didn't explain how."

The Splinterscat gave her an impatient look. "Magic, of course!" he rasped. "Hrrrwwll! Elven magic allows you to do just about anything. I was one of the first, long before they decided on the demons or any of the others. That was almost fifty years ago. Splinterscats live a long time. Ssppptt. They made me to guard the farms, to keep away the scavengers and such. I was very good at it. We all were. Pfftt. We could live off the land, required very little looking after, and could stay out for weeks. But then the demons came and killed most of us off, and the farms all failed and were abandoned, and that was that. We were left to fend for ourselves—grrrsssst—which was all right because we had gotten pretty used to it by then. We could survive on our own. Actually, it was better that way. I would hate to be shut up inside that city with demons—hssstt—all about." The creature gave a low growl. "I hate even to think about it."

Wren was still trying to figure out what the Elves were doing using magic again. Where had the magic come from? They hadn't had the use of magic when they had lived in the Westland—hadn't had it since the time of faerie except for their healing powers. The real magic had been lost for years. Now, somehow, they had gotten it back again. Enough, it appeared, to allow them to create demons. Or to summon them, perhaps. A black choice, if ever there was one. What could have possessed them to do such a thing?

She wondered suddenly what her parents had to do with all of this. Were they involved in using the magic? If they were, then why had they given the Elfstones—the most powerful magic of all—to her?

"If the Elves . . . created these demons with their magic, why can't they destroy them?" she asked, curious still about where these so-called demons had come from and whether they were really demons at all. "Why can't they use their magic to free themselves?"

Stresa shook his head and picked up the root again. "I haven't any idea. No one has ever explained any of it to me. I never go to the city. I haven't spoken to an Elf in years. You are the first—and you're not wholly elf, are you? Prruufft. Your blood is mixed. And your friend is something else altogether."

"He is human," she said.

"Ssspttt. If you say so. I haven't seen anyone like him before. Where does he come from?"

Wren realized for the first time that Stresa probably didn't know that there was anyone out there other than Elves and Wing Riders or any place other than the islands.

"We both come from the Westland, which is part of a country called the Four Lands, which is where all the Elves came from years ago. There are lots of different kinds of people there. Garth and I are just one of them."

Stresa studied her thoughtfully. His quilled body bunched as his legs inched together. "After you find the Elves— rrrgggghh—and deliver your message, what will you do then? Will you go back to where you came from?"

Wren nodded.

"The Westland, you called it. Is it anything like—grwwl— Morrowindl?

"No, Stresa. There are things that are dangerous, though. Still, the Westland is nothing like Morrowindl." But even as she finished speaking, she thought, Not yet anyway, but for how long with the Shadowen gaining strength?

The Splinterscat chewed on the root for a moment, then remarked, "Pfftt. I don't think you can get to Arborlon on your own." The strange blue eyes fixed on Wren.

"No?" she replied.

"Pft, pft. I don't see how. You haven't any idea how to scale Blackledge. Whatever happens you have to avoid the hrrrwwll Harrow and the Drakuls. Below, in the valley, there's the Revenants. Those are just the worst of the demons; there are dozens of others as well. Ssspht. Once they discover you . . ."

The quilled body bristled meaningfully and smoothed out again. Wren was tempted to ask about the Draculs and the Revenants. Instead, she glanced at Garth for an opinion. Garth merely shrugged his indifference. He was used to finding his own way.

"Well, what do you suggest we do?" she asked the Splinterscat.

The eyes blinked. The purr lifted from the creature's throat. "I would suggest that we make a bargain. I will guide you to the city. If you get past the demons and deliver your message and get out again, I will guide you back. Hrrrwwll." Stresa paused. "In return, you will take me with you when you leave the island."

Wren frowned. "To the Westland? You want to leave Morrowindl?"

The Splinterscat nodded. "Spppptt. I don't like it here much anymore. You can't really blame me. I have survived for a long time on wits and experience and instinct, but mostly on luck. Today my luck ran out. If you hadn't happened along, I would be dead. I am tired of this life. I want to go back to the way things were before. Perhaps I can do that where you live."

Perhaps, Wren thought. Perhaps not.

She looked at Garth. The big man's fingers moved swiftly in response. *We don't know anything about this creature. Be careful what you decide.*

Wren nodded. Typical Garth. He was wrong, of course—they did know one thing. The Splinterscat had saved them from the Wisteron as surely as they had saved him. And he might prove useful to have along, particularly since he knew the dangers of Morrowindl far better than they did. Agreeing to take him with them when they left the island was a small enough trade-off.

Unless Garth's suspicions should prove correct and the Splinterscat was playing some sort of game.

Don't trust anyone, the Addershag had warned her.

She hesitated a moment, thinking the matter through. Then she shrugged the warning aside. "We have a bargain," she announced abruptly. "I think it is a good idea."

The Splinterscat spread his quills with a flourish. "Hrrwwll. I thought you would," he said, and yawned. Then he stretched out full length before them and placed his head comfortably on his paws. "Don't touch me while I'm sleeping," he advised. "If you do, you will end up with a face full of quills. I would feel badly if our partnership ended that way. Phfftt."

Before Wren could finish communicating the warning to Garth, Stresa's eyes were closed, and the Splinterscat was asleep.

WREN TOOK THE EARLY WATCH, then slept soundly until dawn. She woke to Stresa's stirrings—the rustle of quills, the scrape of claws against wood. She rose, her mind fuzzy and her eyes dry and scratchy. She felt weak and unsettled, but ignored her discomfort as Garth passed her the aleskin and some bread. Their food was being depleted rapidly, she knew; much of it had simply gone bad. They would have to forage soon. She hoped that Stresa, despite his odd eating habits, might be of some help in sorting out what was edible. She chewed a bit of the bread and spit it out. It tasted of mold.

Stresa lumbered outside, and the Rovers followed, crawling from the hollow trunk and pushing themselves to their feet, muscles cramped and aching. Daybreak was a faint gray haze seeping through the treetops, barely able to penetrate the darkness beneath. Vog swirled through the jungle as if soup stirred within a cooking pot, but the air at ground level was still and lifeless. Things moved in the fetid waters of the bogs and sinkholes and on the deadwood that bridged them, a shifting of shapes and forms against the gloom. Sounds wafted dully from the shadows and hung waiting in challenge.

They started walking through the half-light, Stresa in the lead, a shambling, rolling mass of spikes. They continued slowly, steadily through the morning hours, the vog enfolding them at every turn, a colorless damp wrapper smelling of death. The light brightened from gray to silver, but remained faint and diffuse as it hovered about the edges of the trees. Strands of the the Wisteron's webbing wrapped about branches and vines, and snares hung everywhere, waiting to fall. The monster itself did not appear, but its presence could be felt in the hush that lay over everything.

Wren's discomfort increased as the morning wore on. She felt queasy now and she had begun to sweat. At times she could not see clearly. She knew she had contracted a fever, but she told herself it would pass. She walked on and said nothing.

The jungle began to break apart shortly after midday, the ground turning solid again, the swamp fading back into the earth, and the canopy of the trees opening up. Light shone in bold patches through sudden rifts in the screen of the vog. The hush faded in an undercurrent of buzzings and clicks. Stresa mumbled something, but Wren couldn't make out what it was. She had been unable to focus her thoughts for some time now, and her vision was so clouded that even the Splinterscat and Garth were just shadows. She stopped, aware that someone was talking to her, turned to find out who, and collapsed.

She remembered little of what happened next. She was carried for a short time, barely conscious of the motion, burdened with a lethargy that threatened to suffocate her. The fever burned through her, and she knew somehow that she would not be able to shake it off. She fell asleep, woke to discover she was lying wrapped in blankets, and promptly fell asleep again. She came awake thrashing, and Garth held her and made her drink something bitter and thick. She vomited it up and was forced to drink it again. She heard Stresa say something about water, felt a cool cloth on her forehead, and slept once more.

She dreamed this time. Tiger Ty was there, standing next to Stresa, the two of them looking down on her, bluff and craggy Wing Rider and sharp-eyed Splinterscat. They spoke in a similar voice, rough and guttural, commenting on what they saw, speaking of things she didn't understand at first, and then finally of her. She had the use of magic, they said to each other. It was clear she did. Yet she refused to acknowledge it, hiding it as if it were a scar, pretending it wasn't there and that she didn't need it. Foolish, they said. The magic was all she had. The magic was the only thing she could trust.

She awakened reluctantly, her body cool again, and the fever gone. She was weak, and so thirsty it felt as if all the liquids in her body had been drained away. Pushing back the covers that wrapped her, she tried to rise. But Garth was there instantly, pressing her down again. He brought a cup to her lips. She drank a few swallows—it was all she could manage—and lay back. Her eyes closed.

When she came awake next, it was dark. She was stronger now, her vision unclouded, and her sense of what was happening about her clear and certain. Gingerly she pushed herself up on one elbow and found Garth staring into her eyes. He sat cross-legged beside her, his dark, bearded face creased and worn from lack of sleep. She glanced past him to where Stresa lay curled in a ball, then looked back again.

Are you better? he signed.

"I am," she answered. "The fever is gone."

He nodded. *You have been asleep for almost two days.*

"So long? I didn't realize. Where are we?"

At the foot of Blackledge. He gestured into the darkness. *We left the In Ju after you collapsed and made camp here. The Splinterscat recognized the sickness that infected you and found a root that would cure it. I think without his help, you might have died.*

She grinned faintly. "I told you it was a good idea to have him come along."

Go back to sleep. There are several hours still until dawn. If you are well enough, we'll go on then.

She lay back obediently, thinking that Garth must have kept watch by himself for the entire time she was sick, that Stresa would not have bothered, comfortable within the protection of his own armor. A sense of gratitude filled her. Garth was always there for her. She resolved that her giant friend would have the sleep he deserved when it was night again.

She slept well and woke rested, anxious to resume their journey. She changed clothes, although nothing she carried was clean by now, washed, and ate breakfast. At Garth's insistence, she took a few moments to exercise her muscles, testing her strength for what lay ahead. Stresa looked on, by turns curious and indifferent. She stopped long enough to thank the Splinterscat for his help in chasing the fever. He claimed not to know what she was talking about. The root he had provided for her did nothing more than to help her sleep. What had saved her was her Elven magic, he growled, and spread his quills and trundled off to find something to eat.

It took them all of that day and most of the next to climb Blackledge, and it would have taken them much longer—if indeed they could have done it at all—without Stresa. Blackledge was a towering wall of rock that ran along the Southwest slope of Killeshan. It lay midway up the ascent and appeared to have been formed when an entire section of the volcano had split away and then dropped several thousand feet into the jungle. The cliff face, once sheer, had eroded over the years, turned pitted and craggy, and grown thick with scrub and vines. There were only a few places where Blackledge could be scaled, and Stresa knew them all. The Splinterscat chose a section of the cliff where the rock wall had separated, and a fissure sliced down to less than a thousand feet above the jungle floor. Within the fissure lay a pass that ran back into a valley. It was there, across the Rowen, Stresa announced, that the Elves would be found.

Resolutely he led them up.

The climb was hard and slow and seemingly endless. There were no passes or trails. There were, in fact, very few places that presented any kind of purchase at all, none of them offering more than a brief respite. The lava rock was knife-edge sharp beneath their hands and feet and would break away without warning. The Rovers wore heavy gloves and cloaks to protect their skin and to keep the spiders from biting and the scorpions from stinging. The vog rolled down the rock face as if poured from its edge, thick and stinking of sulfur and soot. Most of what grew on the rock was thorny and tough and had to be cut away. Every inch of the climb was a struggle that drained their strength. Wren had felt rested when she began. Before it was even midday, she was exhausted. Even Garth's incredible stamina was quickly depleted.

Stresa had no such problem. The Splinterscat was tireless, lumbering up the cliff face at a slow, steady pace, powerful claws finding adequate footing, digging into the rock, pulling the bulky body ahead. Spiders and scorpions did not seem to affect Stresa; if one got close enough, he simply ate it. He led the way, choosing the approaches that would be easiest for his human companions, frequently stopping to wait until they could catch up. He detoured briefly to bring back a branch laden with a sweet red berry that they quickly and gratefully consumed. When it was nightfall and they were still only halfway up the slope, he found a ledge on which they could spend the night, clearing it first of anything that might threaten them and then, to their utter astonishment, offering to keep watch while they slept. Garth, having spent the previous two nights standing guard over the feverish Wren, was too exhausted to argue. The girl slept the better portion of the night, then relieved the Splinterscat several hours before dawn, only to discover that Stresa preferred talk to sleep in any event. He wanted to know about the Four Lands. He wanted to hear of the creatures that lived within them. He told Wren more about life on Morrowindl, a harrowing account of the daily struggle to survive in a world where everything was always hunting or being hunted, where there were no safe havens, and where life was usually short and bitter.

"Rrrwwll. Wasn't like that in the beginning," he growled softly. "Not until the Elves made the demons and everything turned bad. Phhhfft. Foolish Elves. They made their own prison."

He sounded so bitter that she decided not to pursue the matter. She was still uncertain as to whether or not the Splinterscat knew what he was talking about. The Elves had always been healers and caretakers—never creators of monsters. She found it hard to believe they could have turned a paradise into a quagmire. She kept thinking there must be more to this story than what Stresa knew and she must reserve judgment until she had learned it all.

They resumed their climb at daybreak, pulling themselves up the rocks, scrambling and clawing against the cliff face, and peering up through the swirling mist. It rained several times, and they were left drenched. The heat lessened as they worked their way higher, but the dampness persisted. Wren was still weak from her bout with the swamp fever, and it took all of her strength and concentration to continue putting one foot in front of the other and to reach out with her hand for one more pull up. Garth helped her when he could, but there was seldom room to maneuver, and they were forced to make the ascent one behind the other.

They saw caves in the cliffs from time to time, dark openings that yawned silent and empty. Stresa pointedly steered his charges away from them. When Wren questioned him about what lay within, the Splinterscat hissed and declared rather pointedly that she didn't want to know.

Midafternoon finally brought them to the bottom of the fissure and the narrow defile that lay beyond. They stood on flat, solid ground again, aching and worn, and looked back across the south end of the island to where it dropped away in a rolling, misted carpet of green jungle and black lava rock to the azure-blue sweep of the ocean. Blackledge rose above them to either side, craggy and misted, stretching in an unbroken wall until it disappeared into the horizon. Seabirds circled against the sky. Sunlight appeared momentarily through a break in the clouds, blinding in its intensity, turning the muted colors of the land below vibrant and bright. Wren and Garth squinted against its glare, enjoying the warmth of it against their faces. Then it faded, gone as suddenly as it had appeared; the chill and damp returned, and the island's colors became dull again.

Turning away into the shadow of the fissure, they began to climb toward the mouth of the narrow pass. Then they were inside. The cliff rock rose all about them, a hulking, brooding presence, and wind blew down out of Killeshan's heights in rough, quick gusts like the sound of something breathing. It was cold in the pass, and the Rovers wrapped themselves tightly in their cloaks. Rain descended in sudden bursts and was gone again, and the vog spilled down off the rocks in opaque waves.

Twilight had descended by the time they reached the fissure's end. They stood at the rim of a valley that stretched away toward the final rise of Killeshan, a green-etched bowl settled beneath a distant stretch of forestline that lifted to the barren lava rock of the high slopes beyond. The valley was broad and misted, and it was difficult to see what lay within. The faint shimmer of a ribbon of water was visible east, winding through stands of acacia-dotted hills and ridgelines laced with black streamers of pitted rock. Across the sweep of the valley, all was still.

They made camp in the shelter of the pass under an overhang that fronted the valley. Night fell quickly, and with the sky so completely screened away the world about them turned frighteningly black. The silence of dusk slowly gave way to a jumble of rough sounds—the intermittent, barely perceptible rumble of Killeshan, the hiss of steam from cracks in the earth where the heat of the volcano's core broke through, the grunts and growls of hunting things, the sudden screams as something died, and the frantic whispers as something else fled. Stresa curled into a ball and lay facing out at the blackness, less quick to sleep this night. Wren and Garth sat next to him, anxious, uneasy, wondering what lay ahead. They were close now; the Rover girl could sense it. The Elves were not far. She would find them soon. Sometimes, through the black and the haze, she thought she could catch the glimmer of fires like eyes winking in the night. The fires were distant, across the valley, high on the slopes below the treeline's final stretch. They looked lonely and isolated, and she wondered if the perception was an accurate one. How far had the Elves come in their move away from the Four Lands? Too far, perhaps? So far that they could not get back again?

She fell asleep finally with the questions still on her mind.

They set out again at daybreak. Morrowindl had become a gray, misted world of shadows and sounds. The valley fell away sharply below them as they walked, and it was as if they were descending into a pit. The trail was rocky and slick with damp, and the green that had seemed so predominant in the previous night's uncertain light revealed itself now as nothing more than small patches of beleaguered moss and grass crouched amid long stretches of barren rock. Tendrils of steam laced with the stench of sulfur rose skyward to blend with the vog, and pockets of intense heat burned through the soles of their boots and seared the skin of their faces. Stresa set a slow pace, picking his way carefully, lumbering from side to side amid the rocks and their islands of green. Several times he stopped and turned back again altogether, choosing a different way. Wren could not tell what it was that the Splinterscat saw; everything was invisible to her. She felt bereft of her skills once more, a stranger in a hostile, secretive world. She tried to relax herself. Ahead, Stresa's bulky form rolled with the motion of his walk, daggerlike quills rising and falling rhythmically. Behind, Garth stalked as if at hunt, dark face intense, unreadable, hard. How very alike they were, she thought in surprise.

They had come down off a small rise into a stand of brush when the thing attacked. It launched itself out of the haze with a shriek, a bristling horror with claws and teeth bared, slashing in a desperate frenzy. It had legs and a body and a head—there was no time to tell more. It bypassed Stresa and came for Wren, who barely managed to bring her arms up before it was upon her. Instinctively she rolled, taking the weight of the thing as she did and then thrusting it away. It slashed and bit, but the heavy gloves and cloak protected her. She saw its eyes, yellow and maddened; she felt its fetid breath. Shaking free, she scrambled to her feet, seeing the thing wheel back again out of the corner of her eye.

Then Garth was there, short sword cutting. A glitter of iron and the creature's arm was gone. It fell, screaming, tearing at the earth. Garth stepped in swiftly and severed its head, and it went still.

Wren stood there shaking, still uncertain what the thing was. A demon? Something else? She looked down at the bloodied, shapeless husk. It had all happened so fast.

"Phfftt! Listen!" Stresa sharply hissed. "Others come! Ssstttfttp. This way! Hurry!"

He lumbered swiftly off. Wren and Garth were quick to follow, tunneling after him into the gloom.

Already they could hear the sounds of pursuit.

CHAPTER

8

THE CHASE BEGAN SLOWLY, gathering momentum as it careened downward into the valley. Wren, Garth, and the Splinterscat were alone at first, sought after but not yet found, and their hunters were nothing more than scattered bits of noise still distant and indistinct. They slipped ahead swiftly, watchfully, without panic or fear. The landscape about them was dreamlike, by turns barren and empty where black lava had buried the foliage beneath its glistening rocky carpet and lush where patches of acacia and heavy grass fought from small islands within the wilderness to reclaim what had been taken. Vog hung over everything, a vast, loosely woven shroud, swirling and shifting, creating the illusion that everything it touched was alive. Overhead, visible in small patches through the haze, the skies were iron-gray and sunless.

Stresa chose a rambling, circuitous route, taking them first one way and then the other, his thick quilled body rolling and lurching so that it constantly seemed as if he were about to tip over. He favored neither the open sweep of the lava rock nor the canopied cover of the brush-grown forest, veering from one to the other impartially, whether selecting his path from intuition or experience, it was impossible to tell. Wren could hear his heavy breathing, a growl in his throat that turned to a hiss when he came across something he didn't like. Once or twice he looked back at them as if to make certain they were still there. He did not speak, and they kept silent as well.

It was chance alone that led to their discovery. They had come upon a stretch of open rock, and the creature was lying in wait. It rose up almost in front of them, thrusting out of the earth where it had burrowed, hissing and shrieking, a sort of birdlike thing on legs with a great hooked beak and claws at its wing tips. Talons swept downward to rip at Stresa, but the Splinterscat's backside hunched and rippled instantly and a flurry of razor-sharp quills flew into the attacker. The creature screamed in pain and tumbled back, tearing at its face.

"Sssttt! Quick!" the Splinterscat snapped, hurrying away.

They fled swiftly, the cries of their attacker fading behind them. But now others were alerted and began to close. The sounds were all about, snarls and growls and huffings, slicing through the haze, out of the shadows. Garth drew his short sword. They slipped down a shallow ravine and something flung itself out of the brush. Wren ducked as the thing flew past and saw the glitter of Garth's blade as it swept up. The thing fell away and was still. They climbed from the ravine onto a new stretch of lava rock, then raced for a cluster of trees. A flurry of small, four-legged creatures that resembled boars tore from the cover and bore down on them. Stresa crouched and shivered, and a shower of quills flew into the attackers. Squeals filled the air, and clawed forefeet tore at the earth. Stresa veered past them, quills lifting like spikes. One or two made a vain attempt to rise, but Garth kicked them aside.

Then they were into the trees, pushing through damp grasses and vines, feeling the wet slap of the foliage against their faces and arms. *Just give us a few minutes more,* Wren was thinking when a coiled body dropped out of the trees, wrapped about Garth, and lifted him away. She wheeled back, her sword drawn, and caught a final glimpse of the big man as he was pulled from view, half carried, half dragged, thrashing powerfully to break free.

"Garth!" she cried out.

She started after him instantly, but had only taken a dozen steps before Stresa slammed into her from behind, sweeping her legs from beneath her, knocking her to the ground, crying "Down, girl! Ssstt. Stay!"

She heard a hissing sound like dozens of snakes, then a ripping as the foliage overhead was sliced apart. Stresa pushed forward until he was next to her.

"That was foolish!" he spit roughly. "Look. Phffttt! See what almost got you?"

Wren looked. There was an odd-shaped bush that was as quilled as the Splinterscat, needles pointing in every direction. As she stared in disbelief, leaves folded about the needles to hide them, and the bush took on a harmless look once more.

"Hsssst! That's a Darter!" Stresa breathed. "Poisonous! Touch it, disturb it in any way, and it flings its needles! Death, if they prick you!"

The Splinterscat fixed her with his bright eyes. Wren could no longer see or hear Garth. Anger and frustration filled her, their bitter heat churning in her stomach. Where was he? What had been done to him? She had to find him! She had to . . .

Then Stresa was up and moving again, and she was moving with him. They pushed through the heavy foliage, searching the haze, listening. And suddenly she could hear struggling sounds again, and ahead there was a flash of movement. Stresa lumbered forward, bristling; Wren was a step behind. There was a grunt of pain and a thrashing. Garth rose up momentarily and then disappeared from view.

"Garth!" Wren shouted, and rushed forward heedlessly.

The big Rover was sprawled on the earth when she reached him, scratched and bruised, but otherwise unhurt. Whatever it was that had latched onto him had apparently tired of the struggle. Garth permitted the girl a momentary hug, then gently disentangled himself and stumbled back to his feet.

Stresa got them moving again at once, back through the trees, through the heavy undergrowth and out onto the lava rock. A cluster of shadows passed overhead and disappeared, silent, formless. The sounds of pursuit continued to build around them, rough and anxious. They scurried along a flat to a ridge that dropped into a pit of swirling mist. Stresa took them quickly past, down a slide to the streambed that had gone almost dry.

A new horror lumbered out of the mist, a being vaguely

manlike, but with multiple limbs and a face that seemed all jaws and teeth. Stresa curled into a ball, quills jutting out in every direction, and the monster lurched past without slowing. Wren swung her sword defensively and jumped aside, barely avoiding a clutch of anxious fingers. Garth stood his ground and let the thing come to him, then cut at it so fast Wren could barely follow the movement of his blade. Blood flew from the beast, but it barely slowed. Grunting, it reached for Garth. The giant Rover leapt back and aside, then came at it again. Wren attacked from the rear, but one monstrous arm swung about and sent her flying. She kept her grip on the sword, rose, and saw the thing almost on top of her. Garth swept under it in a rush, caught her up and yanked her away. They were running again, flying along the glistening black rock, the crunch of it sharp beneath their boots. Garth slowed without stopping and swung her down. Her feet struck and instantly she was running with him. She saw Stresa ahead, somehow back in the lead. She heard the growling and huffing of the creature behind.

Then something exploded out of the shadows on her left and struck at her. Pain rushed along her arm, and she saw blood stain her sleeve. There was a tearing of teeth and claws. She screamed and pushed at whatever was clinging to her. It was too close for her to use her sword. Garth materialized out of nowhere, grasping her attacker with his bare hands and tearing it free. She saw its ugly, twisted face and gnarled body as it dropped. With a howl, she swung at it with her sword, and it flew apart.

"Grrrlll!" Stresa was next to them. "We have to hide! Sssttt! They are too many!"

Behind, too close to consider, the monster tracking them gave a triumphant roar. They fled from it again, back into the mist, through the tangle of shadows and half-light, stumbling and clawing their way across the rock. Wren was bleeding heavily. She could see blood on Garth as well, but wasn't sure if it was his or her own. Her mouth was dry and her chest burned as she gulped in air. Her strength was beginning to fail.

They topped a rise and suddenly Stresa, still leading, tumbled abruptly from view. Hurrying to where he had fallen, they found him sprawled awkwardly at the bottom of a short drop.

"Here! A hiding place!" he called out suddenly, spitting and hissing as he regained his feet.

They scrambled down the open side of the drop—the other was a mass of boulders—and saw where he was looking. Beneath an overhang was a split in the rock leading back into darkness.

"Sssstttppp! Inside, quickly. Go, it's safe enough!" the Splinterscat urged. When they failed to respond, he rushed at them threateningly. "Hide! I'll lead the thing away and come back for you! Hrrgggll! Go! Now!"

He whirled about and disappeared. Garth hesitated only a moment, then plunged into the cleft. Wren was a step behind. They brought up their hands awkwardly as the darkness closed about, groping to find their way. The split opened back into the lava for some distance, burrowing down into the earth. When they were inside far enough that they could barely see the light from without, they crouched down to wait.

Seconds later they heard the sounds of their pursuer. The monster approached without slowing and lumbered past. The sounds faded.

Wren reached for Garth and squeezed his arm. Her eyes were beginning to adjust, and she could just barely make him out in the dark. She sheathed her short sword, removed her leather jacket, and tore away the sleeve of her tunic. She could see the dark streaks of the claw marks down her arm. She medicated the wounds with a healing salve and bound them with the last clean scarf she carried. The stinging disappeared after a time, turning to a dull, throbbing ache. She sat back wearily, listening to the sound of her own breathing mesh with Garth's in the silence.

Time slipped away. Stresa did not return. Wren allowed her eyes to close and her thoughts to drift. How far were they from the river now? she wondered. The Rowen lay between themselves and Arborlon, and once they had crossed it they would reach the Elves. She considered momentarily what that meant. She had barely allowed herself time to think about the fact that the Elves even existed, that they were not simply rumor or legend, but real and alive, and that against all odds, she had found them. Or almost found them, at least. Another day, two at the most . . .

She let her eyes open again and that was when she saw the creature.

At first she thought she must be mistaken, that the shadows were playing tricks on her. But there was sufficient light for her to trust what she was seeing. It crouched motionless on a shelf of rock several feet behind Garth. It was small, barely a dozen inches high, she guessed, although it was hard to be certain when it was hunched down that way. It had large, round eyes that stared fixedly and huge ears pointing off a tiny head with a fox face. It had a spindly body and looked vaguely spiderlike at first glance—so much so that Wren had to fight down a moment's revulsion as she recalled the encounter with the Wisteron. But it was small and helpless looking, and it had tiny hands and feet like a human. It stared at her, and she stared back. She knew instinctively that the odd creature had chosen this cleft as a hiding place just as they had. It had frozen in place to avoid being seen, but now it was discovered and was trying to decide what to do.

Wren smiled and kept still. The creature watched, eyes searching. Casually Wren caught Garth's attention, brought her hands up slowly, and told him what was going on. She asked him to ease over next to her. He did so, and they sat together studying the creature. After a while, Wren reached into her pack and extracted a few scraps of food. She took a bite of some cheese and passed what remained to Garth. The big man finished it. The creature's tongue licked out.

"Hello, little one," Wren said softly. "Are you hungry?"

The tongue reappeared.

"Can you talk?"

No response. Wren leaned forward with a bit of cheese. The creature did not move. She eased a little closer. The creature stayed motionless. She hesitated, not certain what to do next. When the creature still did not move, she stretched out her hand cautiously and gently tossed the cheese toward the ledge.

Faster than the eye could follow, the creature's hand shot out and caught the cheese in midair. After hauling in its catch, the creature sniffed it, then gobbled it down.

"Hungry indeed, aren't you?" Wren whispered.

There was a shuffling at the entrance to their hiding place.

The creature on the rock vanished instantly into the shadows. Wren and Garth turned, swords drawn.

"Hhrrrrgghh," Stresa muttered as he eased slowly into view, puffing and grunting. "Demon wouldn't give up the hunt. Ffphtt. Took much longer than I thought to lose it." He shook his quills until they rattled.

"Are you all right?" Wren asked.

The Splinterscat bristled. "Of course I'm all right. Do you see anything wrong with me? Ssstttt! I'm winded, that's all."

Wren glanced furtively at the ledge. The strange creature was back again, watching.

"Can you tell me what that is?" she asked, nodding in the direction of the creature.

Stresa peered into the gloom and then snorted. "Ssspptt. That's just a Tree Squeak! Completely harmless."

"It looks frightened."

The Splinterscat blinked. "Tree Squeaks are frightened of everything. That's what keeps them alive. That and their quickness. Fastest things on Morrowindl. Smart, too. Smart enough not to let themselves get trapped. You can be certain there is another way out of this crevice or this one wouldn't even be here. Rrrwwlll. Look at it stare. Seems to have taken an interest in you."

Wren kept her eyes on the little creature. "Did the Elves make the Tree Squeaks, too?"

Stresa settled himself comfortably in place, paws tucked in. "The Tree Squeaks were always here. But the magic has changed them like everything else. See the hands and feet? Used to be paws. They communicate, too. Watch."

He made a small chirping sound. The Tree Squeak cocked its head. Stresa tried again. This time the Tree Squeak responded, a soft, low squeaking.

Stresa shrugged. "It's hungry." The Splinterscat lost interest, his blunt head lowering onto its forepaws. "We'll rest until midday, then go on. The demons sleep when its hottest. Best time for us to be about."

His eyes closed, and his breathing deepened. Garth glanced purposefully at Wren and settled back as well, finding a smooth spot amid the rough edges of the lava rock. Wren was not ready to sleep. She waited a bit, then reached into her pack for another chunk of cheese. She nibbled at it while the Tree Squeak watched, then gently eased across the floor of the crevice until she had closed the distance between them. When she was no more than an arm's length away, she broke off a bit of the cheese and held it out to the Tree Squeak. The little creature took it gingerly and ate it.

A short time later the Tree Squeak was curled up in her lap. It was still there when she finally fell asleep.

GARTH'S HAND ON HER SHOULDER, firm and reassuring, brought her awake again. She blinked and glanced about. The Tree Squeak was back on its ledge, watching. Garth signed that it was time to go. She rose cautiously in the cleft's narrow confines and pulled on her pack. Stresa waited by the entrance, quills spread, sniffing the air. It was hot within their shelter, the air still and close.

She looked around briefly to where the Tree Squeak crouched. "Good-bye, little one," she called softly.

Then they moved out of the darkness and into the misty light. Midday had come and gone while they slept. The vog that shrouded the valley seemed denser than before, its smell sulfuric and rank, and its taste gritty with ash and silt. Heat from Killeshan's core rose through the porous rock and hung stubborn and unmoving in the air, trapped within the valley's windless expanse as if captured in a kettle. The mist reflected whitely the diffused sunlight, causing Wren to squint against its glare. Shadowy stands of acacia rose against the haze, and ribbons of black lava rock disappeared into other worlds.

Stresa took them forward, making his way cautiously through the vog's murk, angling from one point to the next, sniffing as he went. The day had gone uncomfortably silent. Wren listened suspiciously, remembering that Stresa had said the demons would sleep now, mistrusting the information all the same. They worked their way deeper into the valley's bowl, past islands of jungle grown thick with vines and grasses, down ridges and drops carpeted with scrub, and along the endless strips of barren, crusted lava rock that unraveled like black bands through the mist.

The afternoon wore quickly on. In the haze about them, nothing moved. There were things out there, Wren knew—she could feel their presence. There were creatures like the one that had almost caught them that morning and others even worse. But Stresa seemed aware of where they were and made certain to avoid them, leading his charges on, confident in his choice of paths as he picked his way through the treacherous maze. Everything shifted and changed as they went, and there was a sense of nothing being permanent, of the whole of Morrowindl being in continual flux. The island seemed to break apart and reform about them, a surreal landscape that could be anything it wished and was not bound by the laws of nature that normally governed. Wren grew increasingly uneasy, used to the dependable terrain of plains and mountains and forests, to the sweep of country not hemmed about by water and settled upon a furnace that could open on a whim and consume everything that lived on it. Killeshan's breath steamed through fissures in the lava rock, small eruptions that stank of burning rock and gases and left shards of debris to drift upon the air. Incongruous amid the lava rock and weeds, isolated clusters of flowering bushes grew, fighting to survive against the heat and ash. Once, Wren thought to herself, this island must have been very beautiful, but it was difficult to imagine it so now.

It was late in the day when they finally reached the Rowen, the light gone gray and faint. The creatures within the haze had begun to stir again, their rumblings and growls causing the three companions to grow increasingly more watchful. They came upon the river at a point where its far shore was hidden by a screen of mist and its near fell sharply away to a rush of waters that were murky and rough, choked with silt and debris, clouded so thick that nothing of what lay beneath the surface showed.

Stresa stopped at the shore's edge, casting left and right uncertainly, sniffing the heavy air.

Wren knelt next to the Splinterscat. "How do we get across?" she asked.

"At the Narrows," the other answered with a grunt. "Ssspptt.

The trouble is, I'm not sure where they are. I haven't been this way in a long time."

Wren glanced back at Garth, who watched impassively. The light was failing rapidly now, and the sound of the demons rising from their sleep was growing louder. The air remained still and thick as the heat of midday cooled to a damp swelter.

"Rrrwwll. Downstream, I think," Stresa ventured, sounding none too sure.

Then Wren saw something move in the mist behind them and started. Garth had his short sword out instantly. A small figure inched into view, and Wren came to her feet in surprise. It was the Tree Squeak. It circled away from Garth and came up to her, taking hold of her arm tentatively.

"What are you doing here, little one?" she murmured, and stroked its furry head.

The Tree Squeak pulled itself up on her shoulder and chittered softly at Stresa.

The Splinterscat grunted. "It says the crrrwwwll crossing is upstream, just a short distance from here. Phffttt. It says it will show us the way."

Wren frowned doubtfully. "It knows what we're looking for?"

"Ssssttt. Seems to." Stresa hunched his quills anxiously. "I don't like standing about in the open like this. Let's take a chance and do what it says. Maybe it knows something."

Wren nodded. With Stresa still leading, they started upstream, following the ragged curve of the Rowen's bank. Wren carried the Tree Squeak, who clung to her possessively. It must have followed them all the way from that cleft in the lava rock, she realized. Apparently it hadn't wanted to be left behind. Perhaps the small kindnesses she had shown had won it over. She stroked the wiry body absently and wondered how much kindness anything encountered on Morrowindl.

Moments later Stresa stopped abruptly and drew them back into the concealment of a cluster of rocks. Something huge and misshapen passed before them on its way to the river, a silent shadow in the haze. Patiently they waited. The volume of coughs and grunts continued to grow as the dusk deepened. When they went forward again, even their breathing had slowed to a whisper.

Then the shoreline moved away from where they walked, sloping downward into the river's swift waters, turning the swirling surface to broken rapids. The haze lifted sufficiently to reveal a narrow bridge of rocks. Quickly they crossed, crouched low against the water, darting for the cover of the mist beyond. When they were safely gathered on the far shore, the Tree Squeak again chittered to Stresa.

"Go left, it says," the Splinterscat translated, the words a low growl in its throat.

They did as the Tree Squeak advised, moving into the vog. The last of the daylight faded away and darkness closed about. The only light came from far ahead, an odd white glow that shimmered faintly through the haze. They were forced to slow, to grope ahead in the darker pockets, to pause and listen and then judge where it was safe to venture. The demons seemed to be ahead of them—massed, Wren was willing to bet, between themselves and their destination.

She discovered soon enough that she had guessed right. The company crested a rise on a slide of lava rock thick with withered scrub, and abruptly the mist cleared. Quickly they flattened themselves into the brush. Hunched close together in the shadows, they stared out at what lay before them.

Arborlon stood on a rise less than a mile ahead and was itself the source of the strange glow. The glow emanated from a massive wall that ringed the city, pulsing faintly against the mist and clouds. All about, the demons pressed close, shadows that slipped in and out of the vog and mist, faceless, formless wraiths caught momentarily in the glare of fires that burned from fissures in the earth where spouts of molten lava had broken through. Jets of steam filled the air with ash and heat and turned the charred earth into a ghostly, fiery netherworld. Demon growls disappeared into rumblings that rose from deep within the earth where the volcano's molten core churned and tossed. In the distance, looming high above the city and the wraiths that besieged it, Killeshan's maw steamed, jagged and threatening, a fire monster waiting to feast.

Wren's eyes shifted from the besieged city to the ruined landscape in shock. That the Elves could have allowed themselves to be trapped in a world such as this was beyond belief.

She felt herself go hollow with fear and loathing. How could this have come about? The Elves were healers, trained from the moment of their birth to restore life, to keep the land and its living things whole. What had prevented that here? Arborlon was an island within its walls—its people somehow preserved, somehow still able to sustain themselves—while the world without had become a nightmare.

She bent close to Stresa. "How long have things been like this?"

The Splinterscat hissed. "Fffpphtt! Years. The Elves have been barricaded away for as long as any of us can remember, hiding behind their magic. Sssttttppp! See the light that rises from the wall that shields them? Mmssst. That is their protection!"

The Tree Squeak chittered softly, causing her to turn. Stresa grunted. "Hwrrrll. The Squeak says the light weakens and the magic fails. Not much time left before it goes out completely."

Wren stared out again at the carnage. Not much time, she repeated to herself. Shades, there could be little doubt of that. She experienced a sudden sense of futility. What was the point of her search now? She had come to Morrowindl to find the Elves and return them to the world of Men—Allanon's charge to her at the Hadeshorn. But how could the Elves ever return out of this? Surely they would have done so long ago if it were at all possible. Yet here they remained, ringed all about. She took a deep breath. Why had Allanon sent her here? What was she supposed to do?

A great sadness filled her. What if the Elves were lost? The Elves were all that was left of the world of faerie, all that remained of the first people, of the magic that had given life when life began. They had done so much to bring the Four Lands into being when the Great Wars ended and the old ways were lost. All of the children of Shannara had come from Elven blood; all of the struggles that had been waged to preserve the Races had been won by them. It seemed impossible that it could all be relegated to history's scroll, that nothing would remain of the Elves but the stories.

Myths and legends, she reflected—*the way it is now.*

She thought again of the promise she had made to herself

to learn the truth about her parents, to find out who they were and why they had left her. And what of the Elfstones? She had vowed to discover why they had been given to her. Her fingers lifted to trace the outline of the leather bag about her neck. She had not thought of the Elfstones since they had begun their ascent of Blackledge. She had not even thought to use the magic when they were threatened. She shook her head. But then why should she? Look how much good the magic had done the Elves.

She felt Garth's hand on her shoulder and saw the questioning look in his eyes. He was wondering what she intended to do. She found herself wondering the same thing.

Go home, a voice whispered inside her. *Give this madness up.*

Part of her agreed. It was madness, and she had no reason to be here beyond foolish curiosity and stubborn insistence. Look at how little her skills and her training could help her in this business. She was lucky she had gotten this far. She was lucky even to be alive.

But here she was nevertheless. And the answers to all her questions lay just beyond the light.

"Stresa," she whispered, "is there a way to get into the city?"

The Splinterscat's eyes shone in the dark. "Wrroowwll, Wren of the Elves. You are determined to go down there, are you?" When she failed to respond, he said, "Within a ravine that—hrrwwll—lies close to where the demons prowl, there are tunnels hidden. Sssstttpht. The tunnels lead into the city. The Elves use them to sneak away—or did once upon a time. That was how they let us out to keep watch for them. Phhffft. Perhaps there is still one in use, do you think?"

"Can you find it?" she asked softly.

The Splinterscat blinked.

"Will you show it to me?"

"Hssstttt. Will you remember your promise to take me with you when this is finished?"

"I will."

"Very well." The cat face furrowed. "The tunnels, then. Which of us goes? Ssttpht."

"Garth, you, and me.

The Tree Squeak chittered instantly.

Stresa purred. "I thought as much. The Squeak plans on going, too. Rwwwll. Why not? It's only a Squeak."

Wren hesitated. She felt the Tree Squeak's fingers clutch tightly at her arm. The Squeak chittered once more.

"Sssttt." Stresa might have been laughing. "She says to tell you that her name is Faun. She has decided to adopt you."

"Faun." Wren repeated the name and smiled faintly. "Is that your name, little one?" The round eyes were fixed on her, the big ears cocked forward. It seemed odd that the Tree Squeak should even have a name. "So you would adopt me, would you? And go where I go?" She shook her head ruefully. "Well, it is your country. And I probably couldn't keep you from going if I tried."

She glanced at Garth to make certain he was ready. The rough face was calm and the dark eyes fathomless. She took a last look down at the madness below, then pushed back the fear and the doubt and told herself with as much conviction as she could muster that she was a Rover girl and that she could survive anything.

Her fingers passed briefly across the hard surface of the Elfstones.

If it becomes necessary . . .

She blocked the thought away. "Lead us in, Stresa," she whispered. "And keep us safe."

The Splinterscat didn't bother to reply.

CHAPTER

9

REN OHMSFORD COULD NOT remember a time when she had been afraid of much of anything. It simply wasn't her nature. Even when she was small and the world was still new and strange and virtually everyone and everything in it was either bigger and stronger or quicker and meaner, she was never frightened. No matter the danger, whatever the uncertainty, she remained confident that somehow she would find a way to protect herself. This confidence was innate, a mix of iron-willed determination and self-assurance that had given her a special kind of inner strength all her life. As she grew, particularly after she went to live with the Rovers and began her training with Garth, she acquired the skill and experience needed to make certain that her confidence was never misplaced, that it never exceeded her ability.

All that had changed when she had come in search of the Elves. Twice since she had begun that search she had found herself unexpectedly terrified. The first time had been when the Shadowen that had tracked them all through the Westland had finally shown itself on the first night of the signal fire, and she had discovered to her horror that she was powerless against it. All of her training and all of her skill availed her nothing. She should have known it would be like that; certainly Par had warned her when he had related the details of his own encounter with the dark creatures. But for some reason she had thought it would be different with her—or perhaps she simply hadn't considered what it would be like at all. In any case, there she had been, bereft of Garth—Garth, whom she had believed stronger and quicker than anything!—face to face with something against which no amount of confidence and ability could prevail.

She would have died that night if she had not been able to call upon the magic of the Elfstones. The magic alone had been able to save them both.

Now, as she made her way forward with the others of her little company through the darkness and vog of Morrowindl, as they crept slowly ahead into a nightmare world of shadows and monsters, she found herself terrified anew. She tried to rationalize it away; she tried to argue against it. Nothing helped. She knew the truth of things, and the truth was the same as it had been that night at the ruins of the Wing Hove when she had confronted the Shadowen. Confidence, skill, experience, and Garth's protective presence, however formidable in most instances, were of little reassurance here. Morrowindl was a cauldron of unpredictable magic and unreasoning evil, and the only weapon she possessed that was likely to prove effective against it was the Elfstones. Magic alone kept the Elves alive inside the walls of Arborlon. Magic, however misguided, had apparently summoned the evil that besieged them. Magic had changed forever the island and the things that lived upon it. There was no reason for Wren to think that she could survive on Morrowindl for very long without using magic of her own.

Yet use of the Elfstones was as frightening to her as the monsters the magic was intended to protect against. Look at her; as a Rover girl, she had spent her entire life learning to depend upon her own skills and training and to believe that there was nothing they could not overcome. That was how Garth had schooled her and what life with the Rovers had taught her, but more important it was what she had always believed. The world and the things in it were governed by a set of behavioral laws; learn those laws and you could withstand anything. Reading trail signs, understanding habits, knowing another's weaknesses and strengths, using your senses to discover what was there—those were the things that kept you alive. But magic? What was magic? It was invisible, a force beyond nature's laws, an unknown that defied understanding. It was power without discernible limits. How could you trust something like that? The history of her family, of Ohmsfords ten generations gone, suggested you could not. Look what the magic had done to Wil and Brin and Jair. What certainty was there if she was forced to rely on something so unpredictable? What would using the magic do to her? True, it had been summoned easily enough in her confrontation with the Shadowen. It had flowed ever so smoothly from the Stones, come almost effortlessly, striking at the mere direction of her thoughts. There had been no sense of wrongness in its use—indeed, it was as if the power had been waiting to be summoned, as if it belonged to her.

She shivered at the recognition of what that meant. She had been given the Elfstones, she knew, in the belief that one day she would need them. Their power was intended to be hers.

She tightened her resolve against such an idea. She didn't want it. She didn't want the magic. She wanted her life to stay as it was, not to be irrevocably changed—for it would be so—by power that exceeded her understanding and, she believed, her need.

Except, of course, now—here on Killeshan's slopes, surrounded by demons, by things formed of magic and dark intention, set upon a landscape of fire and mist, where in a second's time she could be lost, unless . . .

She cut the thought short, refusing to complete it, focusing instead on Stresa's quilled bulk as the Splinterscat tunneled his way through the gloom. Shadows wafted all about as the vog shifted and reformed, cloaking and lifting clear from islands of jungle scrub and bare lava rock, as if the substance of a kaleidoscopic world that could not decide what it wanted to be. Growls sounded, disembodied and directionless, low and threatening as they rose and fell away again. She crouched down in the haze, a frantic inner voice shrieking at her to disappear, to burrow into the rock, to become invisible, to do anything to escape. She ignored the voice, looking back for Garth instead, finding him reassuringly close, then thinking in the next instance that it made no difference, that he was not enough, that nothing was.

Stresa froze. Something skittered away through the shadows ahead, claws clicking on stone. They waited. Faun hung expectantly upon her shoulder, head stretched forward, ears cocked, listening. The soft brown eyes glanced at her momentarily, then shifted away.

What phase of the moon was it? she wondered suddenly. How long had it been since Tiger Ty had left them here? She realized that she didn't know.

Stresa started forward again. They topped a rise stripped of everything but stunted, leafless brush and angled downward into a ravine. Mist pooled on the rocky floor, and they groped their way ahead uncertainly. Stresa's quills shimmered damply, and the air turned chill. There was light, but it was difficult to tell where it was coming from. Wren heard a cracking sound, as if something had split apart, then a hiss of trapped steam and gases being released. A shriek rose and disappeared. The growls quieted, then started again. Wren forced her breathing to slow. So much happening and she could see none of it. Sounds came from everywhere, but lacked identity. There were no signs to read, no trails to follow, only an endless landscape of rock and fire and vog.

Faun chittered softly, urgently.

At the same moment, Stresa came to a sudden halt. The Splinterscat's quills fanned out, and the bulky form hunched down. Wren dropped into a crouch and reached for her short sword, starting as Garth brushed up against her. There was something dark in the haze ahead. Stresa backed away, half turned, and looked for another way to go. But the ravine was narrow here, and there was no room to maneuver. He wheeled back, bristling.

The dark image coalesced and began to take on form. Something on two legs walked toward them. Garth fanned out to one side, as silent as the shadows. Wren eased her sword clear of its sheath and quit breathing.

The figure emerged from the haze and slowed. It was a man, clad all in close-fitting, earth-colored clothes. The clothes were wrinkled and worn, streaked with ash and grime, and free of any metal clasps or buckles. Soft leather boots that ended just above the ankle were scuffed and had the tops folded down one turn. The man himself was a reflection of his clothes, of medium height but appearing taller than otherwise because he was so angular. His face was narrow with a hawk nose and a seamed, beardless face, and his dark hair was mostly captured in an odd, stockinglike cap. Overall, he had the appearance of something that was hopelessly creased and faded from having been folded up and put away for so long.

He didn't seem surprised to see them. Nor did he seem afraid. Saying nothing, he put a finger to his lips, glanced over his shoulder momentarily, and then pointed back the way they had come.

For a minute, no one moved, still not certain what to do. Then Wren saw what she had missed before. Beneath the cap and the tousled hair were pointed ears and slanted brows.

The man was an Elf.

After all this time, she thought. *After so much effort.* Relief flooded through her and at the same time a strangeness that she could not identify. It seemed odd somehow to finally come face to face with what she had worked so hard to find. She stood there, staring, caught up in her emotions.

He gestured again, a bit more insistent than before. He was older than he had first appeared, but so weathered that it was impossible for Wren to tell how much of his aging was natural and how much the result of hard living.

Coming back to herself at last, she caught Garth's attention and signed for him to do as the Elf had asked. She rose and started back the way she had come, the others following. The Elf passed them a dozen steps along the way, a seemingly effortless task, and beckoned for them to follow. He took them back down the ravine and out again, drawing them across a bare stretch of lava rock and finally into a stand of stunted trees. There he crouched down with them in a circle.

He bent close, his sharp gray eyes fixing on Wren. "Who are you?" he whispered.

"Wren Ohmsford," she whispered back. "These are my friends—Garth, Stresa, and Faun." She indicated each in turn.

The Elf seemed to find this humorous. "Such odd company. How did you get here, Wren?"

He had a gentle voice, as seamed and worn as the rest of him, as comfortable as old shoes.

"A Wing Rider named Tiger Ty brought Garth and me here

from the mainland. We've come to find the Elves." She paused. "And you look to me to be one of them."

The lines on the other's face deepened with a smile. "There are no Elves. Everyone knows that." The joke amused him. "But if pressed, I suppose that I would admit to being one of them. I am Aurin Striate. Everyone calls me the Owl. Maybe you can guess why?"

"You hunt at night?"

"I can see in the dark. That is why I am out here, where no one else cares to go, beyond the walls of the city. I am the queen's eyes."

Wren blinked. "The queen?"

The Owl dismissed the question with a shake of his head. "You have come all this way to find the Elves, Wren Ohmsford? Whatever for? Why should you care what has become of us?" The eyes crinkled above his smile. "You are very lucky I found you. You are lucky for that matter that you are even still alive. Or perhaps not. You are Elven yourself, I see." The smile faded. "Is it possible . . . ?"

He trailed off doubtfully. There was something in his eyes that Wren could not make out. Disbelief, hope, what? She started to say something, but he gestured for her to be silent. "Wren, I will take you inside the city, but your friends will have to wait here. Or more accurately, back by the river where it is at least marginally safe."

"No," Wren said at once. "My friends come with me."

"They cannot," the Owl explained, his voice staying patient and kind. "I am forbidden to bring any but the Elven into the city. I would do otherwise if I could, but the law cannot be broken."

"Phfft. I can wait at the—hrwwll—river," Stresa growled. "I've done what I promised in any case."

Wren ignored him. She kept her gaze fixed on the Owl. "It is not safe out here," she insisted.

"It is not safe anywhere," the other replied sadly. "Stresa and Faun are used to looking after themselves. And your friend Garth seems fit enough. A day or two, Wren—that would be all. By then, perhaps you can persuade the Council to let them come inside. Or you can leave and rejoin them."

Wren didn't know what sort of Council he was talking about, but irrespective of what was decided about Stresa and Faun she was not going to leave Garth. The Splinterscat and the Tree Squeak might be able to survive on their own, but this island was as foreign and treacherous for Garth as it was for her and she was not about to abandon him.

"There has to be another . . ." she started to say.

And suddenly there was a shriek and a wave of multilimbed things came swarming out of the mist. Wren barely had time to look up before they were upon her. She caught a glimpse of Faun streaking into the night, of Stresa's quilled body flexing, and of Garth as he rose to defend her, and then she was knocked flying. She got her sword up in time to cut at the closest attacker. Blood flew and the creature tumbled away. There were bodies everywhere, crooked and black, bounding about as they ripped and tore at the members of the little company. Stresa's quills flew into one and sent it shrieking away. Garth threw back another and battled to her side. She stood back to back with him and fought as the things came at them. She couldn't see them clearly, only glimpses of their misshapen bodies and the gleaming eyes. She looked for the Owl, but he was nowhere to be found.

Then abruptly she caught sight of him, a shadow rising from the earth as he cut two of the attackers down before they knew what was happening. In the next instant he was gone again, then back at another place, a pair of long knives in his hands, though Wren couldn't remember having seen any weapons on him before. The Elf was like smoke as he slipped among the attackers, there and gone again before you could get a fix on him.

Garth pressed forward, his massive arms flinging the attackers aside. The demons held their ground momentarily, then fell back, bounding away to regroup. Howls rose out of the darkness all about.

Aurin Striate materialized at Wren's side. His words were harsh, urgent. "Quick. This way, all of you. We'll worry about the Council later."

He took them across the stretch of lava rock and back into the ravine. Sounds of pursuit came from everywhere. They ran in a low crouch along the rocky basin, angling through boulders and cuts, the Owl leading, a phantom that threatened at every turn to disappear into the night.

They had gone only a short distance when something small and furry flung itself onto Wren's shoulder. She gasped, reeled away protectively, then straightened as she realized it was Faun, returned from wherever she had run off to. The Tree Squeak burrowed into her shoulder, chittering softly.

Seconds later the demons caught up with them, swarming out of the haze once more. They swept past Stresa, who curled into a ball instantly, quills pointing every which way, and flung themselves on the humans. Garth took the brunt of the attack, a wall that refused to buckle as he flung the creatures back one after another. Wren fought next to him, quick and agile, the blade of the short sword flicking left and right.

Against her chest, nestled in their leather bag, the Elfstones began to burn.

Again the attackers drew back, but not so far this time and not so readily. The night and the fog turned them to shadows, but their howls were close and anxious as they waited for others to join them. The Elf and his charges gathered in a knot, fighting for breath, their weapons glistening damply.

"We have to keep running," the Owl insisted. "It is not far now."

A dozen feet away, Stresa uncurled, hissing. "Ssssttppht! Run if you must, but this is enough for me! Phhfft!" He swung his cat head toward Wren. "I'll be waiting—rwwwll—Wren when you return. At the river I'll be. Don't forget your promise!"

Then abruptly he was gone, slipping away into the dark, having become one of the shadows about him.

The Owl beckoned, and Wren and Garth began to run once again, still following the curve of the ravine. There was movement all about them in the mist, swift and furtive. Jets of steam gushed from the earth through cracks in the lava, and the stench of sulfur filled the air. A slide of rocks blocked their way, and they scrambled past it hurriedly. Ahead, Arborlon glowed behind its protective wall, a shimmer of buildings and towers amid forest trees. In the mixed light of the city's magic and the volcano's fire, Killeshan's barren, ravaged slope was dotted with islands of scrub and trees that had somehow escaped the initial devastation and were now reduced to a slow suffocation from the heat. Vog hung across the landscape in a ragged curtain, and the monsters that hid within it passed through its ashen haze like bore worms through earth.

A depression lay ahead, a continuation of the ravine they had been following. The Owl had them hurrying toward it when the demons attacked again. They flew at them from both sides this time, materializing out of the gloom as if risen from the earth. The Owl was knocked sprawling, and Wren went down in a flurry of claws and teeth. Only Garth remained standing, and there were demons all over him, clinging, tearing, trying to bring him down. Wren kicked out violently and freed herself. Faun had already disappeared, quick as a thought, back into the night. Wren's sword slashed blindly, cut into something, held momentarily, then jerked free. She scrambled up and was borne back again, hammered against the rock. She could feel gashes open on the back of her head and neck. Pain brought tears to her eyes. She rolled clear and came to her feet, demons circling all about. Night and mist had swallowed up the Owl. Garth was down, the demons atop him a writhing mass of black limbs. She screamed and struggled to reach him, but crooked hands clutched roughly at her and held her back.

The Elfstones seared her chest like fire.

Burdened by the weight of her attackers, she began to fall. She knew instinctively that this time she would not be able to get back up, that this was the end for all of them.

She could hear herself scream soundlessly somewhere deep inside.

Reason fled before her need, and fear gave way to rage. There were bodies all about her, claws and teeth ripping, and fetid breath against her skin. Her fingers plunged into her tunic and yanked the Stones free.

They flared to life instantly, an eruption of light and fire. The leather bag disintegrated. The magic exploded through cracks in the Rover girl's fingers, too impatient and too willful to wait for her hand to open. It swept the air like a scattering of knives, cutting apart the black things, turning them to dust almost before their screams died away. Wren was suddenly free again. She stumbled to her feet, with the Elfstones stretched forth now, the fire and the light racing from within her, joining with the magic until there was no distinction. She threw back her head as the power ripped through her—harsh, defiant, and exhilarating. She was transformed, and her fears of what would become of her in the wake of the magic's use dissipated and were lost. It made no difference who or what she had been or how she had lived her life. The magic was everything. The magic was all that mattered.

She turned its power on the mass of bodies atop Garth and it hammered into them. In seconds, they disintegrated. Some withstood the fury of the attack a few moments longer than the others—those that were larger and more hardened—but in the end they all died. Garth rose, bloodied, his clothes in tatters, and his dark, bearded face ashen. What was he staring at? she wondered vaguely. She marveled at the look on his face as she used the power of the Stones to sweep the landscape clean. The Owl reappeared out of the haze, and there was awe etched on his leathery face as well. And fear. They were both so afraid . . .

Suddenly she understood. She closed her fingers in shock, and the magic was gone. The exhilaration and the fire left her, draining away in an instant, and it was as if she had been stripped naked and set out for everyone to see. Weariness flooded through her. She felt ashamed. The magic had snared her, taken her for its own, destroyed her resolution to withstand its lure, and buried all her promises that she would not give way to it, that she would not become another of the Ohmsfords it had claimed.

Ah, but she had needed its power, hadn't she? Hadn't it kept her alive—kept them all alive? Hadn't she wanted it, even gloried in it? What else could she have done?

Garth was next to her, holding her by the shoulders, keeping her upright, his dark eyes intense as he looked into her own. She nodded vaguely that she was aware of him, that she was all right. But she wasn't, of course. The Owl was there as well, saying "Wren, you are the one that she has waited for, the one who was promised. You are welcome indeed. Come quickly now, before the dark things regroup and attack again. Hurry!"

She followed obediently, wordlessly, her body a foreign thing that swept her along as she watched from somewhere just without. Heat and exhaustion worked through her, but she felt detached from them. She saw the landscape revert to a sea of vog through which a strange array of shadows floated. Trees lifted skyward in clusters, leafless and bare, brittle stalks waiting to crumble away. Ahead, glistening like something trapped behind a rain-streaked window, was the city of the Elves, a jeweled treasure that shimmered with promise and hope.

A lie, the thought struck her suddenly, incongruously, and she was surprised with the intensity of it. It is all a lie.

Then the Owl led them through a tangle of brush and down a narrow defile where the shadows were so thick it was all but impossible to see. He crouched down, worked at a gathering of rocks, and a trapdoor lifted. Swiftly they scrambled inside, the air hot and stifling. The Elf reached up and pulled the trapdoor back into place and secured it. The darkness lasted only a moment, and then there was a hint of the city's strange light through the tunnel that lay ahead. The Owl took them down its length, saying nothing, lean and shadowy against the faint wash of brightness. Wren felt the sense of detachment fading now; she was back inside herself, returned to who and what she was. She knew what had happened, what she had done, but she would not let herself dwell on it. There was nothing to do but to go forward and to complete the journey she had set herself. The city lay ahead—Arborlon. And the Elves, whom she had come to find. That was what she must concentrate on.

She realized suddenly that Faun had not come back to her. The Tree Squeak was still outside, fled into that fiery netherworld . . . She shut her eyes momentarily. The Stresa was there as well, gone of his own choice. She feared for them both. But there was nothing she could do.

They worked their way down the tunnel for what seemed an endless amount of time, crouched low in the narrow passageway, wordless as they went. The light brightened the farther they went until it was as clear as daylight within the rock. The world without faded entirely—the vog, the heat, the ash, and the stench—all gone. Suddenly the rock disappeared as well, turning abruptly to earth, black and rich, a reminder for Wren of the forests of the Westland, of her home. She breathed the smell in deeply, wondering that it could be. The magic, she thought, had preserved it.

The tunnel ended at a set of stone stairs that led upward to a heavy, iron-bound door set in a wall of rock. As they reached the door, the Owl turned suddenly to face them.

"Wren," he said softly, "listen to me." The gray eyes were intense. "I know I am a stranger to you, and you have no particular reason to trust anything I say. But you must rely on me at least this once. Until you speak with the queen, and only when you are alone with her, should you reveal that you have possession of the Elfstones. Tell no one else before. Do you understand?"

Wren nodded slowly. "Why do you ask this of me, Aurin Striate?"

The Owl smiled sadly, the creases in his worn face deepening. "Because, Wren, though I would wish it otherwise, not everyone will welcome your coming."

Then, turning, he tapped sharply on the door, waited, and tapped again—three and then two, three and then two. Wren listened. There was movement on the other side. Heavy locks released, sliding free.

Slowly the door swung open, and they stepped through.

CHAPTER

10

I HAVE COME HOME.

It was Wren's first thought—vivid, startling, and unexpected.

She was inside the city walls, standing in an alcove that opened beneath the shadow of the parapets. Arborlon stretched away before her, and it was as if she had returned to the Westland, for there were oaks, hickories and elm, green bushes and grass, and earth that smelled of growing things and changes of season, streams and ponds, and life at every turn. An owl hooted softly, and there was a flutter of wings close at hand as a smaller bird darted away from its hidden perch. Some others sang. Whippoorwills! Fireflies glimmered in a stand of hemlock and crickets chirped. She could hear the soft rush of water from a river where it tumbled over the rocks. She could feel the whisper of a gentle night wind against her cheek. The air smelled clean, free of the stench of sulfur.

And there was the city itself. It nestled within the greenery—clusters of homes and shops, streets and roadways below and skypaths overhead, wooden bridges that connected across the tangle of streams, lamps that lit windows and flickered in welcome, and people—a handful not yet gone to sleep—walking perhaps to ease their restlessness or to marvel at the sky. For there was sky again, clear and cloudless, brilliant with stars and a three-quarter moon as white as new snow. Beneath its canopy, everything glimmered faintly with the magic that emanated from the walls. Yet the glow was not harsh as it had seemed to Wren from without, and the walls, despite their height and thickness, were so softened by it that they appeared almost ephemeral.

Wren's eyes darted from place to place, finding flower gardens set out in well-tended yards, hedgerows that lined walkways, and street lamps of intricately wrought iron. There were horses, cows, chickens, and animals of all sorts in pens and barns. There were dogs curled up asleep in doorways and cats on sills. There were colored flags and umbrellas astride entries and awnings hung from shop fronts and barter carts. The houses and shops were white and clean, edged with fresh-painted borders in a myriad of colors. She could not see it all, of course, only the closest parts of the city. Yet there was no mistaking where she was or how it made her feel.

Home.

Yet as quickly as the pleasing rush of familiarity and sense of belonging swept over her, it disappeared. How could she come home to a place she had never been, had never seen, and hadn't even been certain existed until this moment?

The vision blurred then and seemed to shrink back into the night's shadows as if seeking to hide. She saw what she had missed before—or perhaps simply what she had not allowed herself to see in her excitement. The walls teemed with men, Elves in battle dress with weapons in hand, their lines of defense stretched across the battlements. An attack was under way. The struggle was oddly silent, as if the magic's glow muffled somehow the sounds. Men fell, some to rise again, and some to disappear. The shadows that attacked suffered casualties as well, some burned by the light that sparked and fizzled as a dying fire might, and some cut down by the defenders. Wren blinked. Within the walls, the city of the Elves seemed somehow less bright and more worn. The houses and shops were a little darker, a little less carefully tended than she had first imagined, the trees and bushes not as lush, and the flowers paler. The air she breathed was not so clean after all—there was a hint of sulfur and ash. Beyond the city, Killeshan loomed dark and threatening, and its mouth glowed blood-red against the night.

She was aware suddenly of the Elfstones still clenched tightly in her hand. Without looking down at them, she slipped them into her pocket.

"Come this way, Wren," Aurin Striate said.

There were guards at the door through which they had entered, hard-faced young men with distinctly Elven features and eyes that seemed tired and old. Wren glanced at them as she passed and was chilled by the way they stared back at her. Garth edged close against her shoulder and blocked their view.

The Owl took them out from beneath the parapets and over a rampway bridging a moat that encircled the city inside its walls. Wren looked back, squinting against the light. There was no water in the moat; there seemed to be no purpose in having dug it. Yet it was clearly meant to be some sort of defense for the city, bridged at dozens of points by ramps that led to the walls. Wren glanced questioningly at Garth, but the big man shook his head.

A roadway opened through the trees before them, winding ahead into the center of the city. They started down it, but had gone only a short distance when a large company of soldiers hurried past, led by a man with hair so sun-bleached it was almost white. The Owl pulled Wren and Garth aside into the shadows, and the man went past without seeing them.

"Phaeton," the Owl said, looking after him. "The queen's anointed on the field of battle, her savior against the dark things." He said it ironically, without smiling. "An Elven Hunter's worst nightmare."

They went on wordlessly, turning off the roadway to follow a series of side streets that took them through rows of darkened shops and cottages. Wren glanced about curiously, studying, considering, taking everything in. Much was as she had imagined it would be, for Arborlon was not so different, apart from its size, from Southland villages like Shady Vale—and except, of course, for the continuing presence of the protective wall, still a shimmer in the distance, a reminder of the struggle being waged. When, after a time, the glow disappeared behind a screen of trees, it was possible to think of the city as it must have once been, before the demons, before the beginning of the siege. It would have been wonderful to live here then, Wren thought, the city forested and secluded as it had been above the Rill Song, reborn out of its Westland beginnings into this island paradise, its people with a chance to begin life anew, free of the threat of oppression by the Federation. No demons then, Killeshan dormant, and Morrowindl at peace—a dream come out of imagining.

Did anyone still remember that dream? she wondered.

The Owl took them through a grove of ash and willowy birch where the silence was a cloak that wrapped comfortably about. They reached an iron fence that rose twenty feet into the air, its summit spiked and laced with sharpened spurs, and turned left along its length. Beyond its forbidding barrier, tree-shaded grounds stretched away to a sprawling, turreted building that could only be the palace of the Elven rulers. The Elessedils, in the time of her ancestors, Wren recalled. But who now? They skirted the fence to where the shadows were so deep it was difficult to see. There the Owl paused and bent close. Wren heard the rasp of a key in a lock, and a gate in the fence swung open. They stepped inside, waited until the Owl locked the gate anew, and then crossed the dappled lawn to the palace. No one appeared to challenge them. No one came into view. There were guards, Wren knew. There must be. They reached the edge of the building and stopped.

A figure detached itself from the shadows, lithe as a cat. The Owl turned and waited. The figure came up. Words were exchanged, too low for Wren to hear. The figure melted away again. The Owl beckoned, and they slipped through a gathering of spruce into an alcove. A door was already ajar. They stepped inside into the light.

They stood in an entry with a vaulted ceiling and wood-carved lintels and jams that shone with polish. Cushioned benches had been placed against facing walls and oil lamps bracketed arched double doors opened to a darkened hallway beyond. From somewhere down that hallway, deep within the bowels of the palace, Wren could hear movement and the distant sound of voices. Following the Owl's lead, Wren and Garth seated themselves on the benches. In the light Wren could see for the first time how ragged she looked, her clothing ripped and soiled and streaked with blood. Garth looked even worse. One sleeve of his tunic was gone entirely and the other was in shreds. His massive arms were clawed and bruised. His bearded face was swollen. He caught her looking at him and shrugged dismissively.

A figure approached, easing silently out of the hallway, coming slowly into the light. It was an Elf of medium height and build, plain looking and plainly dressed, with a steady, penetrating gaze. His lean, sun-browned face was clean-shaven, and his brown hair was worn shoulder length. He was not much older than Wren, but his eyes suggested that he had seen and endured a great deal more. He came up to the Owl and took his hand wordlessly.

"Triss," Aurin Striate greeted, then turned to his charges. "This is Wren Ohmsford and her companion Garth, come to us from out of the Westland."

The Elf took their hands in turn, saying nothing. His dark eyes locked momentarily with Wren's, and she was surprised at how open they seemed, as if it would be impossible for them ever to conceal anything.

"Triss is Captain of the Home Guard," the Owl advised.

Wren nodded. No one spoke. They stood awkwardly for a moment, Wren remembering that the Home Guard was responsible for the safety of the Elven rulers, wondering why Triss wasn't wearing any weapons, and wondering in the next instant why he was there at all. Then there was movement again at the far end of the darkened hallway, and they all turned to look.

Two women appeared out of the shadows, the most striking of the two small and slender with flaming red hair, pale clear skin, and huge green eyes that dominated her oddly triangular face. But it was the other woman, the taller of the two, who caught Wren's immediate attention, who brought her to her feet without even being aware that she had risen, and who caused her to take a quick, startled breath. Their eyes met, and the woman slowed, a strange look coming over her face. She was long-limbed and slender, clothed in a white gown that trailed to the floor and was gathered about her narrow waist. Her Elven features were finely chiseled with high cheekbones and a wide, thin mouth. Her eyes were very blue and her hair flaxen, curling down to her shoulders, tumbled from sleep. Her skin was smooth across her face, giving her a youthful, ageless appearance.

Wren blinked at the woman in disbelief. The color of the
eyes was wrong, and the cut of the hair was different, and she
was taller, and a dozen other tiny things set them apart—but
there was no mistaking the resemblance.

Wren was seeing herself as she would look in another thirty
years.

The woman's smile appeared without warning—sudden, brilliant, and effusive. "Eowen, see how closely she mirrors Alleyne!" she exclaimed to the red-haired woman. "Oh, you were
right!"

She came forward slowly, reaching out to take Wren's hands
in her own, oblivious to everyone else. "Child, what is your
name?"

Wren stared at her in bewilderment. It seemed somehow as
if the woman should already know. "Wren Ohmsford," she answered.

"Wren," the other breathed. The smile brightened even
more, and Wren found herself smiling in response. "Welcome,
Wren. We have waited a long time for you to come home."

Wren blinked. What had she said? She glanced about hurriedly. Garth was a statue, the Owl and Triss impassive, and the
red-haired woman intense and anxious. She felt suddenly abandoned. The light of the oil lamps flickered uncertainly, and the
shadows crept close.

"I am Ellenroh Elessedil," the woman said, hands tightening,
"Queen of Arborlon and the Westland Elves. Child, I barely
know what to say to you, even now, even after so much anticipation." She sighed. "Here, what am I thinking? Your wounds
must be washed and treated. And those of your friend as well.
You must have something to eat. Then we can talk all night if
we need to. Aurin Striate." She turned to the Owl. "I am in your
debt once again. Thank you, with all my heart. By bringing
Wren safely into the city, you give me fresh hope. Please stay
the night."

"I will stay, my Lady," the Owl replied softly.

"Triss, see that our good friend is well looked after.
And Wren's companion." She looked at him. "What is your
name?"

"Garth," Wren answered at once, suddenly frightened by the

speed with which everything was happening. "He doesn't speak."
She straightened defensively. "Garth stays with me."

The sound of boots in the hall brought them all about once
again. A new Elf appeared, dark-haired, square-faced, and rather
tall, a man whose smile was as ready and effortless as that of the
queen's. He came into the room without slowing, self-assured
and controlled. "What's all this? Can't we enjoy a few hours'
sleep without some new crisis? Ah, Aurin Striate is here, I see,
come in from the fire. Well met, Owl. And Triss is up and about
as well?"

He stopped, seeing Wren for the first time. There was an
instant's disbelief mirrored on his face, and then it disappeared.
His gaze shifted to the queen. "She has returned after all, hasn't
she?" The gaze shifted back to Wren. "And as pretty as her
mother."

Wren flushed, conscious of the fact that she was doing so,
embarrassed by it, but unable to help herself. The Elf's smile
broadened, unnerving her further. He crossed quickly and put
his arm protectively about her. "No, no, please, it is true. You
are every bit your mother." He gave her a companionable
squeeze. "If a bit dusty and tattered about the edges."

His smile drew her in, warming her and putting her instantly
at ease. There might not have been anyone else in the room. "It
was a rather rough journey up from the beach," she managed,
and was gratified by his quick laugh.

"Rough indeed. Very few others would have made it. I am
Gavilan Elessedil," he told her, "the queen's nephew and your
cousin." He cut himself short when he saw her bewildered look.
"Ah, but you don't know about that yet, do you?"

"Gavilan, take yourself off to sleep," Ellenroh interrupted,
smiling at him. "Time enough to introduce yourself later. Wren
and I need to talk now, just the two of us."

"What, without me?" Gavilan assumed an injured look. "I
should think you would want to include me, Aunt Ell. Who was
closer to Wren's mother than I?"

The queen's gaze was steady as it fixed on him. "I was." She
turned again to Wren, moving Gavilan aside, placing herself
next to the girl. Her arms came about Wren's shoulders. "This
night should be for you and I alone, Wren. Garth will be waiting

for you when we are done. But I would like it if we spoke first, just the two of us."

Wren hesitated. She was reminded of the Owl telling her that she must say nothing of the Elfstones except to the queen. She glanced over at him, but he was looking away. The red-haired woman, on the other hand, was looking intently at Gavilan, her face unreadable.

Garth caught her attention, signing, *Do as she asks.*

Still Wren did not reply. She was on the verge of learning the truth about her mother, about her past. She was about to discover the answers she had come seeking. And suddenly she did not want to be alone when it happened.

Everyone was waiting. Garth signed again. *Do it.* Rough, uncompromising Garth, harborer of secrets.

Wren forced a smile. "We'll speak alone," she said.

THEY LEFT THE ENTRYWAY and went down the hall and up a set of winding stairs to the second floor of the palace. Garth remained behind with Aurin Striate and Triss, apparently untroubled that he was not going with her, comfortable with their separation even knowing Wren was clearly not. She caught Gavilan staring after her, saw him smile and wink and then disappear another way, a sprite gone back to other amusing games. She liked him instinctively, just as she had the Owl, but not in the same way. She wasn't really sure yet what the difference was, too confused at the moment by everything happening to be able to sort it out. She liked him because he made her feel good, and that was enough for now.

Despite the queen's admonishment to the others about wanting to speak with Wren alone, the red-haired woman trailed after them, a wraith white faced against the shadows. Wren glanced back at her once or twice, at the strangely intense, distant face, at the huge green eyes that seemed lost in other worlds, at the flutter of slender hands against a plain, soft gown. Ellenroh did not seem to notice she was there, hastening along the darkened corridors of the palace to her chosen destination, forgoing light of any sort save the moon's as it flooded through long, glassed windows in silver shafts. They passed down one hallway and turned into another, still on the second floor, and finally approached a set of double doors at the hall's end. Wren started at a hint of movement in the darkness to one side—one that another would not have seen but did not escape her. She slowed deliberately, letting her eyes adjust. An Elf stood deep in the shadows against the wall, still now, watchful.

"It is only Cort," the queen softly said. "He serves the Home Guard." Her hand brushed Wren's cheek. "You have our Elf eyes, child."

The doors led into the queen's bedchamber, a large room with a domed ceiling, latticed windows curved in a bank along the far wall, a canopied bed with the sheets still rumpled, chairs and couches and tables in small clusters, a writing desk, and a door leading off to a wash chamber.

"Sit here, Wren," the queen directed, leading her to a small couch. "Eowen will wash and dress your cuts."

She looked over at the red-haired woman, who was already pouring water from a pitcher into a basin and gathering together some clean cloths. A minute later she was back, kneeling beside Wren, her hands surprisingly strong as she loosened the girl's clothes and began to bathe her. She worked wordlessly while the queen watched, then finished by applying bandages where they were needed and supplying a loose-fitting sleeping gown that Wren gratefully accepted and slipped into—the first clean clothes she had enjoyed in weeks. The red-haired woman crossed the room and returned with a cup of something warm and soothing. Wren sniffed at it tentatively, discovered traces of ale and tea and something more, and drank it without comment.

Ellenroh Elessedil eased down on the couch beside her and took her hand. "Now, Wren, we shall talk. Are you hungry? Would you like something to eat first?" Wren shook her head, too tired to eat, too anxious to discover what the queen had to tell her. "Good, then." The queen sighed. "Where shall we begin?"

Wren was suddenly conscious of the red-haired woman moving over to sit down across from them. She glanced at the woman doubtfully—Eowen, the queen had called her. She had assumed that Eowen was the queen's personal attendant and had been brought along solely for the purpose of seeing to their comfort and would then be dismissed as the others had. But the queen had not dismissed her, appearing barely aware of her presence in fact, and Eowen gave no indication that she thought she was expected to leave. The more Wren thought about it the less Eowen seemed simply an attendant. There was something about the way she carried herself, the way she reacted to what the queen said and did. She was quick enough to help when asked, but she did not show the deference to Ellenroh Elessedil that the others did.

The queen saw where Wren was looking and smiled. "I'm afraid I've gotten ahead of myself again. And failed to show proper manners as well. This is Eowen Cerise, Wren. She is my closest friend and advisor. She is the reason, in fact, that you are here."

Wren frowned slightly. "I don't understand what you mean. I am here because I came in search of the Elves. That search came about because the Druid Allanon asked me to undertake it. What has Eowen to do with that?"

"Allanon," the Elf Queen whispered, momentarily distracted. "Even in death, he keeps watch over us." She released Wren's hand in a gesture of confusion. "Wren, let me ask you a question first. How did you manage to find us? Can you tell us of your journey to reach Morrowindl and Arborlon?"

Wren was anxious to learn about her mother, but she was not the one in control here. She concealed her impatience and did as the queen asked. She told of the dreams sent by Allanon, the appearance of Cogline and the resulting journey to the Hadeshorn, the charges of the Druid shade to the Ohmsfords, her return with Garth to the Westland and search for some hint of what had become of the Elves, their subsequent arrival at Grimpen Ward and talk with the Addershag, their escape to the ruins of the Wing Hove, the coming of Tiger Ty and Spirit, and the flight to Morrowindl and the journey in. She left out only two things—any mention of the Shadowen that had tracked them or the fact that she possessed the Elfstones. The Owl had been quite clear in his warning to say nothing of the Stones until she was alone with the queen, and unless she spoke of the Stones she could say nothing of the Shadowen.

She finished and waited for the queen to say something.

Ellenroh Elessedil studied her intently for a moment and then smiled. "You are a cautious girl, Wren, and that is something you must be in this world. Your story tells me exactly as much as it should—and nothing more." She leaned forward, her strong face lined with a mix of feelings too intricate for Wren to sort out. "I am going to tell you something now in return and when I am done there will be no more secrets between us."

She picked up Wren's hands once more in her own. "Your mother was called Alleyne, as Gavilan told you. She was my daughter."

Wren sat without moving, her hands gripped tightly in the queen's, surprise and wonder racing through her as she tried to think what to say.

"My daughter, Wren, and that makes you my grandchild. There is one thing more. I gave to Alleyne, and she in turn was to give to you, three painted stones in a leather bag. Do you have them?"

Wren hesitated, trapped now, not knowing what she was supposed to do or say. But she could not lie. "Yes," she admitted.

The queen's blue eyes were penetrating as they scanned Wren's face, and there was a faint smile on her lips. "But you know the truth of them now, don't you? You must, Wren, or you would never have gotten here alive."

Wren forced her face to remain expressionless. "Yes," she repeated quietly.

Ellenroh patted her hands and released them. "Eowen knows of the Elfstones, child. So do a few of the others who have stood beside me for so many years—Aurin Striate, for one. He warned you against saying anything, didn't he? No matter. Few know of the Elfstones, and none have seen them used—not even I. You alone have had that experience, Wren, and I do not think you are altogether pleased, are you?"

Wren shook her head slowly, surprised at how perceptive the queen was, at her insight into feelings Wren had thought carefully hidden. Was it because they were family and therefore much alike, their heredity a bonding that gave each a window into the other's heart? Could Wren, in turn, perceive when she chose what Ellenroh Elessedil felt?

Family. She whispered the word in her mind. *The family I came to find. Is it possible? Am I really the grandchild of this queen, an Elessedil myself?*

"Tell me the rest of how you came to Arborlon," the queen said softly, "and I will tell you what you are so anxious to know. Do not be concerned with Eowen. Eowen already knows everything that matters."

So Wren related the balance of what had occurred on her journey, all that involved the wolf thing that was Shadowen and the discovery of the truth about the painted stones that her mother had given her as a child. When she was done, when she had told them everything, she folded her arms protectively, feeling chilled by her own words, at the memories they invoked. Then, impulsively, she rose and walked to where her discarded clothing lay. Searching hurriedly through the tattered pieces, she came upon the Elfstones, still tucked inside where she had left them after entering the city. She carried them to the queen and held them forth. "Here," she offered. "Take them."

But Ellenroh Elessedil shook her head. "No, Wren." She closed Wren's fingers over the Elfstones and guided her hand to a pocket of the sleeping gown. "You keep them for me," she whispered.

For the first time, Eowen Cerise spoke. "You have been very brave, Wren." Her voice was low and compelling. "Most would not have been able to overcome the obstacles you faced. You are indeed your mother's child."

"I see so much of Alleyne in her," the queen agreed, her eyes momentarily distant. Then she straightened, fixing her gaze on Wren once more. "And you have been brave indeed. Allanon was right in choosing you. But it was predetermined that you should come, so I suppose that he was only fulfilling Eowen's promise."

She saw the confusion in Wren's eyes and smiled. "I know, child. I speak in riddles. You have been very patient with me, and it has not been easy. You are anxious to hear of your mother and to discover why it is that you are here. Very well."

The smile softened. "Three generations before my own birth, while the Elves still lived within the Westland, several members of the Ohmsford family, direct descendants of Jair Ohmsford, decided to migrate to Arborlon. Their decision, as I understand it, was prompted by the encroachment of the Federation on Southland villages like Shady Vale and the beginnings of the witch hunt to suppress magic. There were three of these Ohmsfords, and they brought with them the Elfstones. One died childless. Two married, but when the Elves chose to disappear only one of the two went with them. The second, I was told, a man, returned to Shady Vale with his wife. That would have been Par and Coll Ohmsfords' great-grandparents. The Ohmsford who remained was a woman, and she kept with her the Elfstones."

Ellenroh paused. "The Elfstones, Wren, as you know, were formed in the beginning by Elven magic and could be used only by those with Elven blood. The Elven blood had been bred out of the Ohmsfords in the years since the death of Brin and Jair, and they were of no particular use to those Ohmsfords who kept custody of them. They decided therefore at some point and by mutual agreement that the Stones belonged back with the people who had made them—or, more properly, I suppose, with their descendants. So when the three who came from Shady Vale married and began their new lives, it was natural enough for them to decide that the Elfstones, a trust to the Ohmsford family from Allanon since the days of their ancestor Shea, should remain with the Elves no matter what became of them personally.

"In any case, the Elfstones disappeared when the Elves did, and I suppose I need to say a word or two about that." She shook her head, remembering. "Our people had been receding farther into the Westland forests for years. They had become increasingly isolated from the other Races as the Federation expansion worked its way north. Some of that was their own doing, but an equal share was the result of a growing belief, fostered by the Federation's Coalition Council, that the Elves were different and that different was not good. The Elves, after all, were the descendants of faerie people and not really human. The Elves were the makers of the magic that had shaped the world since the advent of the First Council at Paranor, and no one had ever much trusted either the magic or its users. When the things you call Shadowen began to appear—there was no name for them then—the Federation was quick to place the blame for the sickening of the land on the Elves. After all, that was where the magic had originated, and wasn't it magic that was causing all the problems? If not, why were the Elves and their homeland not affected? It all multiplied as such things do until finally our people had had enough. The choice was simple. Either stand up to the Federation, which meant giving them the war they were so actively seeking, or find a way to sidestep them completely. War was not an attractive prospect. The Elves would stand virtually alone against the strongest army in the Four Lands. Callahorn had already been absorbed and the Free Corps disbanded, the Trolls were as unpredictably tribal as ever, and the Dwarves were hesitant to commit.

"So the Elves decided simply to leave—to migrate to a new territory, resettle, and wait the Federation out. This decision wasn't arrived at easily; there were many who wanted to stand and fight, an equal number who thought it better to wait and see. After all, this was their homeland they were being asked to abandon, the birthplace of Elves since the cataclysm of the Great Wars. But, in the end, after much time and deliberation, it was agreed that the best choice was to leave. The Elves had survived moves before. They had established new homelands. They had perfected the art of seeming to disappear while in fact still being there."

She sighed. "It was so long ago, Wren, and I wasn't there. I can't be certain now what their motives were. The move began a slow gathering together of Elves from every corner of the Westland so that villages simply ceased to exist. Meanwhile, the Wing Riders found this island, and it suited the needs of the Land Elves perfectly. Morrowindl. When it was settled that this is where they would come, they chose a time and just disappeared."

She seemed to deliberate as to whether to explain further, then shook her head. "Enough of what brought us here. As I said, one among the Ohmsfords stayed. Two generations passed with children being born, and then my mother married the King of the Elessedils, and the Ohmsford and Elessedil families merged. I was born and my brother Asheron after me. My brother was chosen to be king, but he was killed by the demons—one of the first to die. I became queen then instead. I married and your mother was born, Alleyne, my only child. Eventually the demons killed my husband as well. Alleyne was all I had left."

"My mother," Wren echoed. "What was she like?"

The queen smiled anew. "There was no one like her. She was smart, willful, pretty. She believed she could do anything—some part of her wanted to try, at least." She clasped her hands and the smile faded. "She met a Wing Rider and chose him for her husband. I didn't think it a good idea—the Sky Elves have never really bonded with us—but what I thought didn't really matter, of course. This was nearly twenty years ago, and it was a dangerous time. The demons were everywhere and growing stronger. We were being forced back into the city. Contact with the outside world was becoming difficult.

"Shortly after she was married, Alleyne became pregnant with you. That was when Eowen told me of her vision." She glanced at the other woman, who sat watching impassively, green eyes huge and depthless. "Eowen is a seer, Wren, perhaps the best that ever was. She was my playmate and confidante when I was a child, even before she knew she had the power. She has been with me ever since, advising and guiding me. I told you that she was the reason you are here. When Alleyne became pregnant, Eowen warned me that if my daughter did not leave Morrowindl before you were born, both of you would die. She had seen it in a vision. She told me as well that Alleyne could never return, but that one day you must and that your coming would save the Elves."

She took a deep breath. "I know. I felt as you must now. How can this be true? I did not want Alleyne to go. But I knew that Eowen's visions were never wrong. So I summoned Alleyne and had Eowen repeat what she had told to me. Alleyne did not hesitate, although I know she was inwardly reluctant. She said she would go, that she would see to it that the baby was kept safe. She never mentioned herself. That was your mother. I still had possession of the Elfstones, passed down to me through the union of my parents. I gave them to Alleyne to keep her safe, first changing their appearance with a bit of my own magic to see to it that they would not be immediately recognizable or appear to have any value.

"Alleyne was to return to the Westland with her husband. She was to journey from there to Shady Vale and reestablish contact with the descendants of the Ohmsfords who had gone back when the Elves had come to Morrowindl. I never knew if she did. She disappeared from my life for nearly three years. Eowen could only tell me that she—and you—were safe.

"Then, a little more than fifteen years ago now, Alleyne decided to return. I don't know what prompted that decision, only that she came. She gave you the leather bag with the Elfstones, placed you in the care of the Ohmsfords in Shady Vale, and flew back with her husband to us."

She shook her head slowly, as if the idea of her daughter's return were incomprehensible even now. "By then, the demons had overrun Morrowindl; the city was all that was left to us. The Keel had been formed of our magic to protect us, but the demons were everywhere without. Wing Riders were coming in less and less frequently. The Roc Alleyne and her husband were riding came down through the vog and was struck by some sort of missile. He landed short of the city gates. The demons . . ."

She stopped, unable to continue. There were tears in her eyes. "We could not save them," she finished.

Wren felt a great hollowness open within. In her mind, she saw her mother die. Impulsively she leaned forward and put her arms around her grandmother, the last of her family, the only tie that remained to her mother and her father, and hugged her close. She felt the queen's head lower to her shoulder and the slender arms come about her in reply. They sat in silence for a long time, just holding each other. Wren tried to conjure up images of her mother's face in her mind and failed. All she could see now was her grandmother's face. She was conscious of the fact that however deep her own loss, it would never match the queen's.

They pulled away from each other finally, and the queen smiled once more, radiant, bracing. "I am so glad you have come, Wren," she repeated. "I have waited a very long time to meet you."

"Grandmother," Wren said, the word sounding odd when she spoke it. "I still don't understand why I was sent. Allanon told me that I was to find the Elves because there could be no healing of the Lands until they returned. And now you tell me Eowen has foretold that my coming will save the Elves. But what difference does my being here make? Surely you would have returned long ago if you were able."

The smile faded slowly. "It is more complicated than that, I am afraid."

"How can it be more complicated? Can't you leave, if you choose?"

"Yes, child, we can leave."

"If you can leave, why don't you? What is it that keeps you? Do you stand because you must? Are these demons come from the Forbidding? Has the Ellcrys failed again?"

"No, the Ellcrys is well." She paused, uncertain.

"Then where did these demons come from?"

There was a barely perceptible tightening of the queen's smooth face. "We are not certain, Wren."

She was lying. Wren knew it instinctively. She heard it in her grandmother's voice and saw it in the sudden lowering of Eowen's green eyes. Shocked, hurt, angry as well, she stared at the queen in disbelief. *No more secrets between us?* she thought, repeating the other's own words. *What are you hiding?*

Ellenroh Elessedil seemed not to notice her grandchild's distress. She reached out again and embraced her warmly. Though tempted, Wren did not push away, thinking there must be a reason for this secrecy and it would be explained in time, thinking as well that she had come too far to discover the truth about her family and give up on finding it out because some part of it was slow in coming. She forced her feelings aside. She was a Rover girl, and Garth had trained her well. She could be patient. She could wait.

"Time enough to speak more of this tomorrow, child," the queen whispered in her ear. "You need sleep now. And I need to think."

She drew back, her smile so sad that it almost brought tears to Wren's eyes. "Eowen will show you to your room. Your friend Garth will be sleeping right next door, should you need him. Rest, child. We have waited a long time to find each other and we must not rush the greeting."

She came to her feet, bringing Wren up with her. Across

from them, Eowen Cerise rose as well. The queen gave her grandchild a final hug. Wren hugged her back, masking the doubts that crowded within. She was tired now, her eyes heavy, and her strength ebbing. She felt warm and comforted and she needed to rest.

"I am glad to be here, Grandmother," she said quietly, and meant it.

But I will know the truth, she added to herself. *I will know it all.*

She let Eowen Cerise lead her from the bedchamber and into the darkened hallway beyond.

CHAPTER

11

HEN WREN AWOKE the following morning she found herself in a room of white-painted walls, cotton bedding with tiny flowers sewn into the borders, and tapestries woven of soft pastel threads that shimmered in the wash of brilliant light flooding through breaks in lace curtains that hung in folds across the floor-to-ceiling windows.

Sunlight, she marveled, in a land where beyond the walls of the city and the power of the Elven magic there was only darkness.

She lay back, drowsy still, taking time to gather her thoughts. She had not seen much of the room the night before. It had been dark, and Eowen had used only candlelight to guide her. She had collapsed into the down-stuffed bed and been asleep almost immediately.

She closed her eyes momentarily, trying to connect what she was seeing to what she remembered, this dreamlike, translucent present to the harsh, forbidding past. Had it all been real—the search to find where the Elves had gone, the flight to Morrowindl, the trek through the In Ju, the climb up Blackledge, the march to the Rowen and then Arborlon? Lying there as she was, swathed in sunlight and soft sheets, she found it hard to believe so. Her memory of what lay without the city's walls— the darkness and fire and haze, the monsters that came from everywhere and knew only how to destroy—seemed dim and far away.

Her eyes blinked open angrily, and she forced herself to

remember. Events paraded before her, vivid and harsh. She saw Garth as he stood with her against the Shadowen at the edge of the cliffs above the Blue Divide. She pictured once more how it had been that first night on the beach when Tiger Ty and Spirit had left them. She thought of Stresa and Faun, forced herself to remember how they looked and talked and acted, and what they had endured in helping her travel through this monstrous world, friends who had helped her only to be left behind.

Thinking of the Splinterscat and the Tree Squeak was what finally brought her awake. She pushed herself into a sitting position and looked slowly around. She was here, she assured herself, in Arborlon, in the palace of the Elf Queen, in the home of Ellenroh Elessedil, her grandmother. She took a deep breath, wrestling with the idea, working to make it be real. It was, of course—yet at the same time it didn't yet seem so. It was too new, she supposed. She had come looking to find the truth about her parents; she could not have guessed the truth would prove so startling.

She remembered what she had said to herself when Cogline had first approached her about the dreams: What she learned by agreeing to travel to the Hadeshorn to speak with Allanon might well change her life.

She could not have imagined how much.

It both intrigued and frightened her. So much had happened to bring her to Morrowindl and the Elves, and now she was faced with confronting a world and a people she did not really know or understand. She had discovered last night just how difficult things might prove to be. If even her own grandmother would choose to lie to her, how much trust could she put in any of the others? It rankled still that there were secrets being kept from her. She had been sent to the Elves for a purpose, but she still didn't know what it was. Ellenroh, if she knew, wasn't saying—at least not yet. And she wasn't saying anything about the demons either—only that they hadn't come through the Forbidding and that the Ellcrys hadn't failed. But they had come from somewhere, and the queen knew where that was, Wren was certain. She knew a lot of things she wasn't telling.

Secrets—there was that word again.

Secrets.

She let the matter drop with a shake of her head. The queen was her grandmother, the last of her family, the giver of life to her mother, and a woman of accomplishment and beauty and responsibility and love. Wren shook her head. She could not bring herself to think ill of Ellenroh Elessedil. She could not disparage her. She was too like her, perhaps—physically, emotionally, and in word and thought and act. She had seen it for herself last night; she had felt it in their conversation, in the glances they exchanged, and in the way they responded to each other.

She sighed. It was best that she do as she had promised, that she wait and see.

After a time, she rose and walked to the door that led to the adjoining chamber. Almost immediately the door opened and Garth was there. He was shirtless, his muscled arms and torso wrapped in bandages, and his dark bearded face cut and bruised. Despite the impressive array of injuries, the big Rover looked rested and fit. When she beckoned him in, he reached back into his own room for a tunic and hastily slipped it on. The clothes that had been provided him were too small and made him look decidedly outsized. She hid her smile as they moved over to sit on a bench by the lace-curtained window, happy just to see him again, taking comfort from his familiar presence.

What have you learned? he signed.

She let him see her smile now. Good, old, dependable Garth—right to the point every time. She repeated her previous night's conversation with the queen, relating what she had been told of the history of the Elessedils and Ohmsfords and of her mother and father. She did not voice her suspicion that Ellenroh was shading the truth about the demons. She wanted to keep that to herself for now, hoping that given a little time her grandmother would choose to confide in her.

Nevertheless, she wanted Garth's opinion about the queen.

"What did you notice about my grandmother that I missed?" she asked him, fingers translating as she spoke.

Garth smiled faintly at the implication that she had missed anything. His response was quick. *She is frightened.*

"Frightened?" Wren had indeed missed that. "What do you think frightens her?"

Difficult to say. Something that she knows and we don't, I would guess. She is very careful with what she says and how she says it. You saw as much.

He paused. *She may be frightened for you, Wren.*

"Because my mother was killed by coming back here, and now I am at risk as well? But I was supposed to return according to Eowen's vision. They have been expecting me. And what do you make of this vision anyway? How am I supposed to save the Elves, Garth? Doesn't that seem silly to you? After all, it was all we could do just to stay alive long enough to reach the city. I don't see what difference my being here can make."

Garth shrugged. *Keep your eyes and ears open, Rover girl. That's how you learn things.*

He smiled, and Wren smiled in return.

He left her then so that she could dress. As he closed the door separating their rooms, she stood staring after him for a moment. It occurred to her suddenly that there were enormous inconsistencies in the stories told by her grandmother and Garth concerning her parents. Admittedly, Garth's version was secondhand and the queen's based entirely on events that had taken place before the departure from Arborlon, so perhaps inconsistencies were to be expected. Still, neither had commented on what each must have viewed as the other's obvious mistakes. There was no mention of Wing Riders by Garth. There was no mention of Rovers by the queen. There was nothing from either about why her parents had not traveled first to Shady Vale and the Ohmsfords but had gone instead to the Westland.

She wondered if she should say anything about it to Garth. Given the importance of her other concerns, she wondered if this one really mattered.

She found clothing set out for her to wear, garments that fit better than Garth's—pants, a tunic, stockings, a belt, and a pair of fine-worked leather ankle boots. She slipped the clothing on, going over in her mind as she did so the revelations of the night before, considering anew what she had learned. The queen seemed decided on the importance of Wren's arrival in Arborlon, certain in her own mind at least that Eowen's vision would prove accurate. Aurin Striate, too, had mentioned that they had been waiting for her. Yet no one had said why, if, in fact, anyone knew. There hadn't been any mention in the dream of what it was that Wren's presence was supposed to accomplish. Maybe it would take another vision to find out.

She grinned at her own impudence and was pulling on her boots when the grin abruptly faded.

What if the importance of her return was that she carried with her the Elfstones? What if she was expected to use the Stones as a weapon against the demons?

She went cold with the thought, remembering anew how she had been forced to use them twice now despite her reluctance to do so, remembering the feeling of power as the magic coursed through her, liquid fire that burned and exhilarated at the same time. She was aware of their addictive effect on her, of the bonding that took place each time they were employed, and of how they seemed so much a part of her. She kept saying she would not use them, then found herself forced to do so anyway—or persuaded, perhaps. She shook her head. The choice of words didn't matter; the results were the same. Each time she used the magic, she drifted a little farther from who and what she was and a little closer to being someone she didn't know. She lost power over herself by using the power of the magic.

She jammed her feet into the boots and stood up. Her thinking was wrong. It couldn't be the Elfstones that were important. Otherwise, why hadn't Ellenroh simply kept them here instead of giving them to Alleyne? Why hadn't the Stones been used against the demons long ago if they could really make a difference?

She hesitated, then reached over to her sleeping gown and extracted the Elfstones from the pocket in which she had placed them the night before. They lay glittering in her hand, their magic dormant, harmless, and invisible. She studied them intently, wondering at the circumstances that had placed them in her care, wishing anew that Ellenroh had agreed last night to take them back.

Then she brushed aside the bad feelings that thinking of the Elfstones conjured up and shoved the troublesome talismans deep into her tunic pocket. After slipping a long knife into her belt, she straightened confidently and walked from the room.

An Elven Hunter had been posted outside her door, and after pausing to summon Garth, the sentry escorted them downstairs to the dining hall and breakfast. They ate alone at a long, polished oak table covered in white linen and decorated with flowers, seated in a cavernous room with an arched ceiling and stained-glass windows that filtered the sunlight in prismatic colors. A serving girl stood ready to wait upon them, making the self-sufficient Wren feel more than a little uncomfortable. She ate in silence, Garth seated across from her, wondering what she was supposed to do when she was finished.

There was no sign of the queen.

Nevertheless, as the meal was being completed, the Owl appeared. Aurin Striate looked as gaunt and faded now as he had in the shadows and darkness of the lava fields without, his angular body loose and disjointed as he moved, nothing working quite as it should. He was wearing clean clothes and the stocking cap was gone, but he still managed to look somewhat creased and rumpled—it seemed that was normal for him. He came up to the dining table and took a seat, slouching forward comfortably.

"You look a whole lot better than you did last night," he ventured with a half smile. "Clean clothes and a bath make you a pretty girl indeed, Wren. Rest well, did you?"

She smiled back at him. She liked the Owl. "Well enough, thanks. And thanks again for getting us safely inside. We wouldn't have made it without you."

The Owl pursed his lips, glanced meaningfully at Garth, and shrugged. "Maybe so. But we both know that you were the one who really saved us." He paused, stopped short of mentioning the Elfstones, and settled back in his chair. His aging Elven features narrowed puckishly. "Want to take a look around when you're done? See a little of what's out there? Your grandmother has put me at your disposal for a time."

Minutes later, they left the palace grounds, passing through the front gates this time, and went down into the city. The palace was settled on a knoll at the center of Arborlon, deep in the sheltering forests, with the cottages and shops of the city all around. The city was alive in daylight, the Elves busy at their work, the streets bustling with activity. As the three edged their way through the crowds, glances were directed toward them from every quarter—not at the Owl or Wren, but at Garth, who was much bigger than the Elves and clearly not one of them. Garth, in typical fashion, seemed oblivious. Wren craned her neck to see everything. Sunlight brightened the greens of the trees and grasses, the colors of the buildings, and the flowers that bordered the walkways; it was as if the vog and fire without the walls did not exist. There was a trace of ash and sulfur in the air, and the shadow of Killeshan was a dark smudge against the sky east where the city backed into the mountain, but the magic kept the world within sheltered and protected. The Elves were going about their business as if everything were normal, as if nothing threatened, and as if Morrowindl outside the city might be exactly the same as within.

After a time they passed through the screen of the forest and came in sight of the outer wall. In daylight, the wall looked different. The glow of the magic had subsided to a faint glimmer that turned the world beyond to a soft, hazy watercolor washed of its brightness. Morrowindl—its mountains, Killeshan's maw, the mix of lava rock and stunted forest, the fissures in the earth with their geysers of ash and steam—was misted almost to the point of invisibility. Elven soldiers patroled the ramparts, but there were no battles being fought now, the demons having slipped away to rest until nightfall. The world outside had gone sullen and empty, and the only audible sounds came from the voices and movement of the people within.

As they neared the closest bridgehead, Wren turned to the Owl and asked, "Why is there a moat inside the wall?"

The Owl glanced over at her, then away again. "It separates the city from the Keel. Do you know about the Keel?"

He gestured toward the wall. Wren remembered the name now. Stresa had been the first to use it, saying that the Elves were in trouble because its magic was weakening.

"It was built of the magic in the time of Ellenroh's father, when the demons first came into being. It protects against them, keeps the city just as it has always been. Everything is the same as it was when Arborlon was brought to Morrowindl over a hundred years ago."

Wren was still mulling over what Stresa had said about the

magic growing weaker. She was about to ask Aurin Striate if it was so when she realized what he had just said.

"Owl, did you say when Arborlon was *brought* to Morrow-indl? You mean when it was built, don't you?"

"I mean what I said."

"That the buildings were brought? Or are you talking about the Ellcrys? The Ellcrys is here, isn't it, inside the city?"

"Back there." He gestured vaguely, his seamed face clouded. "Behind the palace."

"So you mean—"

The Owl cut her short. "The city, Wren. The whole of it and all of the Elves that live in it. That's what I mean."

Wren stared. "But . . . It was rebuilt, you mean, from timbers the Elves ferried here . . ."

He was shaking his head. "Wren, has no one told you of the Loden? Didn't the queen tell you how the Elves came to Mor-rowindl?"

He was leaning close to her now, his sharp eyes fixed on her. She hesitated, saying finally, "She said that it was decided to migrate out of the Westland because the Federation—"

"No," he cut her short once more. "That's not what I mean."

He looked away a moment, then took her by the arm and walked her to a stone abutment at the foot of the bridge where they could sit. Garth trailed after them, his dark face expressionless, taking up a position across from them where he could see them speak.

"This isn't something I had planned on having to tell you, girl," the Owl began when they were settled. "Others could do the job better. But we won't have much to talk about if I don't explain. And besides, if you're Ellenroh Elessedil's grandchild and the one she's been waiting for, the one in Eowen Cerise's vision, then you have a right to know."

He folded his angular arms comfortably. "But you're not going to believe it. I'm not sure I do."

Wren smiled, a trifle uncomfortable with the prospect. "Tell me anyway, Owl."

Aurin Striate nodded. "This is what I've been told, then—not what I necessarily know. The Elves recovered some part of their faerie magic more than a hundred years back, before Morrowindl, while they were still living in the Westland. I don't know how they did it; I don't really suppose I care. What's important to know is that when they made the decision to migrate, they supposedly channeled what there was of the magic into an Elfstone called the Loden. The Loden, I think, had always been there, hidden away, kept secret for the time when it would be needed. That time didn't come for hundreds of years—not in all the time that passed after the Great Wars. But the Elessedils had it put away, or they found it again, or something, and when the decision was made to migrate, they put it to use."

He took a steadying breath and tightened his lips. "This Elfstone, like all of them, I'm told, draws its strength from the user. Except in this case, there wasn't just a single user but an entire race. The whole of the strength of the Elven nation went into invoking the Loden's magic." He cleared his throat. "When it was done, all of Arborlon had been picked up like . . . like a scoop of earth, shrunk down to nothing, and sealed within the Stone. And that's what I mean when I say Arborlon was brought to Morrowindl. It was sealed inside the Loden along with most of its people and carried by just a handful of caretakers to this island. Once a site for the city was found, the process was reversed and Arborlon was restored. Men, women, children, dogs, cats, birds, animals, houses and shops, trees, flowers, grass—everything. The Ellcrys, too. All of it."

He sat back and the sharp eyes narrowed. "So now what do you say?"

Wren was stunned. "I say you're right, Owl. I don't believe it. I can't conceive of how the Elves were able to recover something that had been lost for thousands of years that fast. Where did it come from? They hadn't any magic at all in the time of Brin and Jair Ohmsford—only their healing powers!"

The Owl shrugged. "I don't pretend to know how they did any of it, Wren. It was long before my time. The queen might know—but she's never said a word about it to me. I only know what I was told, and I'm not sure if I believe that. The city and its people were carried here in the Loden. That's the story. And that's how the Keel was built, too. Well, it was actually constructed of stone by hand labor first, but the magic that protects it came out of the Loden. I was a boy then, but I remember the old king using the Ruhk Staff. The Ruhk Staff holds the Loden and channels the magic."

"You've seen this?" Wren asked doubtfully.

"I've seen the Staff and its Stone many times," the Owl answered. "I saw them used only that once."

"What about the demons?" Wren went on, wanting to learn more, trying to make sense of what she was hearing. "What of them? Can't the Loden and the Ruhk Staff be used against them?"

The Owl's face darkened, changing expression so quickly that it caught Wren by surprise. "No," he answered quietly. "The magic is useless against the demons."

"But why is that?" she pressed. "The magic of the Elfstones I carry can destroy them. Why not the magic of the Loden?"

He shook his head. "It's a different kind of magic, I guess."

He didn't sound very sure of himself. Quickly Wren said, "Tell me where the demons came from, Owl?"

Aurin Striate looked uncomfortable. "Why ask me, Wren Elessedil?"

"Ohmsford," she corrected at once.

"I don't think so."

There was a strained silence as they faced each other, eyes locked. "They came out of the magic, too, didn't they?" Wren said finally, unwilling to back off.

The Owl's sharp gaze was steady. "You ask the queen, Wren. You talk with her."

He rose abruptly. "Now that you know how the city got here, according to legend at least, let's finish looking around. There's three sets of gates in the Keel, one main and two small. See over there . . ."

He started off, still talking, explaining what they were seeing, steering the conversation away from the questions no one seemed to want to answer. Wren listened halfheartedly, more interested in the tale of how the Elves had come to Morrowindl. It required such incredible magic to gather up an entire city, reduce it to the size of an Elfstone, and seal it inside for a journey that would carry it over an ocean. She still could not conceive of it. Elven magic recovered from out of faerie, from a time that was barely remembered—it was incredible. All that power, and still no way to break free of the demons, no way to destroy them. Her mouth tightened against a dozen protestations. She really didn't know what to believe.

They spent the morning and the early part of the afternoon walking through the city. They climbed to the ramparts and looked out over the land beyond, dim and hazy, empty of movement save where Killeshan's steam erupted and the vog swirled. They saw Phaeton again, passing from the city to the Keel, oblivious to them, his strong features scarred and rough beneath his sun-bleached hair. The Owl watched stone faced and was turning to continue their walk when Wren asked him to tell her about Phaeton. The queen's field commander, Aurin Striate answered, second in command only to Barsimmon Oridio and anxious to succeed him.

"Why don't you like him?" Wren asked bluntly.

The Owl cocked one eyebrow. "That's a hard one to explain. It's a fundamental difference between us, I suppose. I spend most of my time outside the walls, prowling the night with the demons, taking a close look at where they are and what they're about. I live like them much of the time, and when you do that you get to know them. I know the kinds and their habits, more about them than anyone. But Phaeton, he doesn't think any of that matters. To him, the demons are simply an enemy that need to be destroyed. He wants to take the Elven army out there and sweep them away. He's been after Barsimmon Oridio and the queen to let him do exactly that for months. His men love him; they think he's right because they want to believe he knows something they don't. We've been shut away behind the Keel for almost ten years. Life goes on, and you can't tell by just looking or even by talking to the people, but they're all sick at heart. They remember how they used to live and they want to live that way again."

Wren considered momentarily bringing up the subject of how the demons got there and why they couldn't simply be sent back again, but decided against it. Instead she said, "You think that there isn't any hope of the army winning out there, I gather."

The Owl fixed her with a hard stare. "You were out there with me, Wren—which is more than Phaeton can say. You traveled up from the beach to get here. You faced the demons time and again. What do you think? They're not like us. There's a hundred different kinds, and each of them is dangerous in a different way. Some you can kill with an iron blade and some you can't. Down along the Rowen there's the Revenants—all teeth and claws and muscle. Animals. Up on Blackledge there's the Draculs—ghosts that suck the life out of you, like smoke, nothing to fight, nothing to put a sword to. And that's only two kinds, Wren." He shook his head. "No, I don't think we can win out there. I think we'll be lucky if we can manage to stay alive in here."

They walked on a bit farther and then Wren said, "The Splinterscat told me that the magic that shields the city is weakening."

She made it a statement of fact and not a question and waited for an answer. For a long time the Owl did not respond, his head lowered toward his stride, his eyes on the ground before him.

Finally, he looked over, just for a moment, and said, "The Scat is right."

They went down into the city proper for a time, wandering into the shops and poring over the carts that dominated the marketplace, perusing the wares and studying the people buying and selling them. Arborlon was a city that in all respects but one might have been any other. Wren gazed at the faces about her, seeing her own Elven features reflected in theirs, the first time she had ever been able to do that, pleased with the experience and with the idea that she was the first person to be able to do so in more than a hundred years. The Elves were alive; the Elves existed. It was a wondrous discovery, and it still excited her to have been the one to have made it.

They had a quick meal in the marketplace—some thin-baked bread wrapped about seared meat and vegetables, a piece of fresh fruit that resembled a pear, and a cup of ale, and then continued on. The Owl took them behind the palace into the Gardens of Life. They walked the pathways in silence, losing themselves in the fragrance of the flower beds and in the scents of the hundreds of colorful blooms that lay scattered amid the plants and bushes and trees. They came upon a white-robed Chosen, one of the caretakers of the Ellcrys, who nodded and passed by. Wren found herself thinking of Par Ohmsford's tale of the Elven girl Amberle, the most famous Chosen of all. They climbed to the summit of the hill on which the Gardens had been planted and stood before the Ellcrys, the tree's scarlet leaves and silver branches vibrant in the sunlight, so striking that it seemed they could not be real. Wren wanted to touch the tree, to whisper something to it, and to tell it perhaps that she knew and understood who and what it had endured. She didn't, though; she just stood there. The Ellcrys never spoke to anyone, and it already knew how she felt. So she simply stared at it, thinking as she did how terrible it would be if the Keel failed completely and the demons overran the Elves and their city. The Ellcrys would be destroyed, of course, and when that happened all of the monsters imprisoned within the Forbidding, the things out of faerie shut away for all these years, would be released into the world of mortal Men once more. Then, she thought darkly, Allanon's vision of the future would truly come to pass.

They went back to the palace after that to rest until dinner. The Owl left them inside the front entry, saying he had business to attend to, offering nothing more.

"I know you have more questions than you know what to do with, Wren," he said in parting, his lean face creasing solemnly. "Try to be patient. The answers will come all too soon, I'm afraid."

He went back down the walkway and out the gates. Wren stood with Garth and watched him go, saying nothing. The big Rover turned to her after a moment, signing. He was hungry again and wanted to go back to the dining hall to see if he could find the kitchen and a bite to eat. Wren nodded absently, still thinking about the Elves and their magic, thinking as well that the Owl never had answered her question about why there was a moat inside the Keel. Garth disappeared down the hallway, footsteps echoing into silence. After a moment she wheeled about and started for her room. She wasn't sure what she would do once she got there other than to think matters through, but maybe that was enough. She climbed the main stairs, listening to the silence, caught up in the spin of her thoughts, and was starting down the hallway at their head when Gavilan Elessedil appeared.

"Well, well, cousin Wren," he greeted brightly, flamboyant in a yellow and blue cross-hatch weave with a silver chain belt. "Been up and about the city, I understand. How are you today?"

"Fine, thanks," Wren answered, slowing to a halt as he came up to her.

He reached for her hand and lifted it to his lips, kissing softly. "So tell me. Are you glad you came or do you wish you had stayed home?"

Wren smiled, blushing in spite of her resolve not to. "A little of each, I suppose." She took her hand away.

Gavilan's eyes twinkled. "That sounds as it should be. Some sour and some sweet. You came a long way to find us, didn't you? It must have been a very compelling search, Wren. Have you learned what you came to discover?"

"Some of it."

The handsome face turned grave. "Your mother, Alleyne, was someone you would have liked very much. I know that the queen has told you about her, but I want to say something, too. She cared for me as a sister would when I was growing up. We were very close. She was a strong and determined girl, Wren— and I see that in you."

Wren smiled anew. "Thank you, Gavilan."

"It is the truth." The other paused. "I hope you will think of me as your friend rather than simply your cousin. I want you to know that if you ever need anything, or want to know anything, please come to me. I will be happy to help if I can."

Wren hesitated. "Gavilan, could you describe my mother for me? Could you tell me what she looked like?

Her cousin shrugged. "Easily done. Alleyne was small like you. Her hair was colored the same. And her voice . . ." He trailed off. "Hard to describe. It was musical. She was quick-witted and she laughed a lot. But I suppose I remember her eyes best. They were just like yours. When she looked at you, you felt as if there wasn't anyone or anything more important in all the world."

Wren was thinking of the dream, the one in which her

mother was bending close to her, looking very much as Gavilan had described her, saying *Remember me. Remember me.* It no longer seemed just a dream to her now. She felt that once, long ago, it must have really happened.

"Wren?"

She realized that she was staring off into space. She looked back at Gavilan, wondering all at once if she should ask him about the Elfstones and the demons. He seemed willing enough to talk with her, and she was drawn to him in a way that surprised her. But she didn't really know him yet, and her Rover training made her cautious.

"These are difficult times for the Elves," Gavilan offered suddenly, bending close. Wren felt his hands come up to take her shoulders. "There are secrets of the magic that—"

"Good day, Wren," Eowen Cerise greeted, appearing at the head of the stairs behind her. Gavilan went still. "Did you enjoy your walk about the city?"

Wren turned, feeling Gavilan's hands drop away. "I did. The Owl was an excellent guide."

Eowen approached, her green eyes shifting to fix Gavilan. "How do you find your cousin, Gavilan?"

The Elf smiled. "Charming, strong-minded—her mother's daughter." He glanced at Wren. "I have to be on my way. Lots to do before dinner. I will talk with you then."

He gave a short nod and walked away, loose, confident, a bit jaunty. Wren watched him go, thinking that he masked a lot with his well-met attitude, but that what lay beneath was rather sweet.

Eowen met her gaze as she turned back. "Gavilan makes us all feel like young girls again." Her flaming red hair was tucked within a netting, and she was wearing a loose, flower-embroidered shift. Her smile was warm, but her eyes, as always, seemed cool and distant. "I think we are all in love with him."

Wren flushed. "I don't even know him."

Eowen nodded. "Well, tell me about your walk. What have you learned of the city, Wren? What did Aurin Striate tell you about it?"

They began to walk the length of the hallway toward Wren's

bedchamber. Wren told Eowen what the Owl had said, hoping secretly that the seer would reveal something in return. But Eowen simply listened, nodded encouragingly, and said nothing. She seemed preoccupied with other things, although she paid close enough attention to what Wren was saying that she did not lose the threads of the conversation. Wren finished her narrative as they reached the door to her sleeping room and turned so that they were facing each other.

A smile flickered on Eowen's solemn face. "You have learned a great deal for someone who has been in the city less than a day, Wren."

Not nearly as much as I would like to learn, Wren thought. "Eowen, why is it that no one will tell me where the demons come from?" she asked, throwing caution to the winds.

The smile disappeared, replaced by a palpable sadness. "The Elves don't like to think about the demons, much less talk about them," she said. "The demons came out of the magic, Wren— out of misunderstanding and misuse. They are a fear and a shame and a promise." She paused, saw the disappointment and frustration mirrored in Wren's eyes, and reached out to take her hands. "The queen forbids me, Wren," she whispered. "And perhaps she is right. But I promise you this. Some day soon, if you still wish it, I will tell you everything."

Wren met her gaze, saw honesty reflected in her eyes, and nodded. "I will hold you to that, Eowen. But I would like to think my grandmother would choose to tell me first."

"Yes, Wren. I would like to think so, too." Eowen hesitated. "We have been together a long time, she and I. Through childhood, first love, husbands, and children. All are gone. Alleyne was the worst for both of us. I have never told your grandmother this—though I think she suspects—but I saw in my vision that Alleyne would try to return to Arborlon and that we could not stop her. A seer is blessed and cursed with what she sees. I know what will happen; I can do nothing to change it."

Wren nodded, understanding. "Magic, Eowen. Like that of the Elfstones. I wish I could be shed of it. I don't trust what it does to me. Is it any different for you?"

Eowen tightened her grip, her green eyes locking on Wren's

face. "We are given our destiny in life by something we can neither understand nor control, and it binds us to our future as surely as any magic."

She released Wren's hands and stepped away. "As we speak the queen determines the fate of the Elves, Wren. It is your coming that prompts this. You would know what difference your being here makes? Tonight, I think, you shall."

Wren started in sudden realization. "You have had a vision, haven't you, Eowen? You've seen what is to be."

The seer brought up her hands as if not knowing whether to ward the accusation off or to embrace it. "Always, child," she whispered. "Always." Her face was anguished. "The visions never leave."

She turned away then and disappeared back down the hall. Wren stood watching after her as she had watched after the Owl, prophets wandering toward an uncertain future, visions themselves of what the Elves were destined to be.

DINNER THAT NIGHT was a lengthy, awkward affair marked by long periods of silence. Wren and Garth were summoned at dusk and went down to find Eowen and the Owl already waiting. Gavilan joined them a few minutes later. They were seated close together at one end of the long oak table, an impressive array of food was laid out before them, serving people were placed at their beck and call, and the dining hall was brightly lit against the coming night. They spoke little, working hard when they did to avoid wandering into those areas that had already been designated as swampy ground. Even Gavilan, who did most of the talking, chose his topics carefully. Wren could not tell whether her cousin was intimidated by the presence of Eowen and the Owl or whether something else was bothering him. He was as bright and cheerful as before, but he lacked any real interest in the meal and seemed preoccupied. When they spoke, it was mostly to discuss Wren's childhood with the Rovers and Gavilan's memories of Alleyne. The meal passed tediously, and there was an unmistakable sense of relief when it was finally finished.

Although everyone kept looking for her, Ellenroh Elessedil did not appear.

The five were rising and preparing to go their separate ways when an anxious messenger burst into the room and held a hurried conversation with the Owl.

The Owl dismissed him with a scowl and turned to the others. "The demons have mounted an attack against the north wall. Apparently they've succeeded in breaking through."

They scattered quickly then, Eowen to find the queen, Gavilan to arm himself, the Owl, Wren and Garth to discover for themselves what was happening. The Owl led as the latter three rushed through the palace, out the front gates, and down into the city. Wren watched the ground fly beneath her feet as she ran. The dusk had turned to darkness, and the Keel's light flared wildly through the screen of the trees. They passed down a series of side streets, Elves running in every direction, shouting and calling out in alarm, the whole of the city mobilizing at the news of the assault. The Owl avoided the crowds that were already forming, skirting the heart of the city, hastening east along its backside until the trees broke apart and the Keel loomed before them. The wall was swarming with Elven soldiers as hundreds more crossed the bridges to join them, all rushing toward a place in the glow where the light had dimmed to almost nothing and a massive knot of fighters battled in near darkness.

Wren and her companions continued on until they were less than two hundred yards from the wall. There they were stopped as lines of soldiers surged forward in front of them.

Wren gripped Garth's arm in shock. The magic seemed to have failed completely where the Keel had been breached, and the stone of the wall had been turned to rubble. Hundreds of dark, faceless bodies jammed into the gap, fighting to break through as the Elves fought to keep them out. The struggle was chaotic, bodies twisting and writhing in agony as they were crushed by those pressing from behind. Shouts and screams filled the air, and there was no muffling of the sounds of battle between Elf and demon on this night. Swords hacked and claws rent, and the dead and wounded lay everywhere about the break.

For a time the demons seemed to have succeeded, their numbers so great that those in the vanguard were actually inside the city. But the Elves counterattacked ferociously and drove them back again. Back and forth the battle surged about the breach with neither side able to gain an advantage.

Then the cry of "Phaeton, Phaeton" sounded, and the white-blond head of the Elven commander appeared at the forefront of a newly arrived company of soldiers. Sword arm raised, he led a rush for the wall. The demons were thrust back, shrieking and howling, as the Elves hammered into them. Phaeton stood foremost in the attack, miraculously untouched as his men fell all around him. The Elves on the ramparts joined the counter-attack, striking from above, and spears and arrows rained down. The Keel's glow brightened, knitting together momentarily across the gap in the damaged wall.

Then the demons mounted yet another assault, a huge mass of them, scrambling through at every turn. The Elves held momentarily, then started to fall back once more. Phaeton leapt before them, sword lifted. The battle stalled as the combatants on each side struggled to take control. Wren watched in horror as the carnage mounted, the dead and dying and injured lying everywhere, the struggle so intense that no one could reach them. Crowds of Elves had formed all about Wren and her companions, old people, women and children, all who were not soldiers in the Elven army, and a curious silence hung over them as they watched, their voices stunned into silence by what they were seeing.

What if the demons break through? Wren thought suddenly. *No one will have a chance. There is no place for these people to run. Everyone will be killed.*

She glanced about frantically. *Where is the queen?*

And suddenly she was there, surrounded by a dozen of her Home Guard, the crowd parting before her. Wren caught sight of Triss, hard-faced and grim as he led his Elven Hunters. The queen walked straight and tall in their midst, seemingly uncon-cerned by the turmoil raging about her, smooth face calm, and eyes directed ahead. She moved past the edges of the crowd toward the nearest bridge spanning the moat. In one hand she carried the Ruhk Staff, the Loden shimmering white hot at its tip.

What is she going to do? Wren wondered, and was suddenly frightened for her.

The queen walked to the center of the bridge, where it arched above the waters of the moat, and stood where she could be seen by all. Shouts rose, and the soldiers at the wall began to cry out her name, taking heart. The Elves who fought with Phaeton in the breach renewed their efforts. The defense gathered strength and surged forward. Again the demons were pushed back. The clang and rasp of iron weapons rose and with it the screams of the dying.

Then suddenly Phaeton went down. It was impossible to see what had happened—one moment he was there, leading the way, and the next he was gone. The Elves cried out and charged forward to protect him. The demons gave way grudgingly, thrown back by the rush. The battle surged into the gap once more, and this time went beyond as the demons were pushed down the other side and back through the light. Again the magic that protected the Keel began to knit, the lines of the magic weaving together.

Then the demons started back a third time. The Elves, exhausted, reeled away.

Ellenroh Elessedil raised the Ruhk Staff and pointed. The Loden flared abruptly. Warnings were shouted, and the Elves poured back through the breach. Light exploded from the Loden, lancing toward the Keel as the magic of the Elfstone gathered force. It reached the wall as the last of the Elven soldiers threw themselves clear. Stone rubble lifted piece by piece, grinding and scraping as it came, and the wall began to rebuild itself. Demons were caught in the whirlwind and buried. Stones layered themselves one on top of the other and mortar filled the gaps, the magic working and guiding, the power of the Loden reaching out. Wren caught her breath in disbelief. The wall rose, closing off the black hole that had been hammered through it, reconstructing itself until it was whole again.

In seconds the magic had done its work, and the demons were shut without once more.

THE QUEEN STOOD MOTIONLESS at the center of the bridge while new companies of Elven soldiers raced past her to man the battlements. She waited until a messenger she had dispatched returned from the carnage. The messenger knelt briefly and rose to speak. Wren watched the queen nod once, turn and come back across the bridge. The Home Guard cleared a path for her once more, but this time she came directly toward Wren, able to find her somehow in the swelling crowds. The Rover girl was frightened by what she saw in her grandmother's face.

Ellenroh Elessedil swept up to her, robes billowing out like banners flown from the Ruhk Staff she held pressed to her body, the Loden still glimmering with wicked white light.

"Aurin Striate," the queen called out as she reached them, her eyes fixing momentarily on the Owl. "Go ahead of us, if you will. Summon Bar and Eton from their chambers—if they are still there. Tell them . . ." Her breath seemed to catch in her throat, and her hand tightened about the Ruhk Staff. "Tell them that Phaeton died in the attack, an accident, killed by an arrow from his own bowmen. Tell them that I wish a meeting in the chambers of the High Council at once. Go now, quickly."

The Owl melted into the crowd and was gone. The queen turned to Wren, one arm coming up to encircle the girl's slender shoulders, the other gesturing with the Staff toward the city. They began to walk, Garth a step behind, the Home Guard all around.

"Wren," the Elf Queen whispered, bending near. "This is the beginning of the end for us. We go now to determine if we can be saved. Stay close to me, will you? Be my eyes and ears and good right arm. It is for this that you have come to me."

Saying no more, she clutched Wren to her and hurried on into the night.

CHAPTER

12

THE CHAMBERS OF the Elven High Council were situated not far from the palace within an ancient grove of white oak. The building was framed by massive timbers and walled with stone, and the council room itself, which formed the principal part of the structure, was a cavernous chamber shaped like a hexagon, its ceiling braced with beams that rose from the joinder of the walls to a center point like a sheltering star. Heavy wooden doors opened from one wall and faced a three-step dais on which rested the throne of the Elven Kings and Queens, and flanking the throne were standards from which pennants hung that bore the personal insignia of the ruling houses. To either side, set against the remaining walls, were rows of benches, a gallery for observers and participants in public meetings. At the center of the room was a broad stretch of flooring dominated by a round table and twenty-one seats. When the High Council was in session, it sat here, and the king or queen sat with it.

Ellenroh Elessedil entered the chamber with a flourish, robes sweeping out behind here, the Ruhk Staff carried before her, and Wren, Garth, Triss, and a handful of the Home Guard trailing after. Gavilan Elessedil was already seated at the council table and rose hurriedly as the queen appeared. He wore chain mail and his broadsword hung from the back of his chair. The queen went to him, embraced him warmly, and moved on to the head of the table.

"Wren," she said, turning. "Sit next to me."

Wren did as she was asked. Garth drifted off to one side and made himself comfortable in the gallery. The chamber doors closed again, and two of the Home Guard took up positions to either side of the entry. Triss moved over to sit at the table next to Gavilan, his lean, hard face distant. Gavilan straightened in his chair, smiled uneasily at Wren, smoothed out his tunic sleeves nervously, and looked away. Ellenroh folded her hands before her and did not speak, clearly waiting for whoever else was expected. Wren surveyed the chamber, peering into dark corners where the lamplight failed to penetrate. Polished wood gleamed faintly in the gloom behind Garth, and images cast by the flames of the lamp danced at the edges of the light. At her back, the pennants hung limp and unmoving, their insignia cloaked in heavy folds. The chamber was still, and only the soft scrape of boots and the rustle of clothing disturbed the silence.

Then she saw Eowen, seated far back in the gallery opposite Garth, nearly invisible in the shadows.

Wren's eyes shifted instantly to the queen, but Ellenroh gave no indication that she knew the seer was there, her gaze fastened on the council chamber doors. Wren looked back at Eowen momentarily, then off into the shadows. She could feel the tension in the air. Everyone seated in that room knew something was going to happen, but only the queen knew what. Wren took a deep breath. It was for this moment, the queen had told her, that she had come to Arborlon.

Be my eyes and ears and good right arm.

Why?

The doors to the council chamber opened and Aurin Striate entered with two other men. The first was old and heavyset, with graying hair and beard and slow, ponderous movements that suggested he was not a man to let things stand in his way. The second was of average size, clean-shaved, his eyes hooded but alert, his movements light and easy. He smiled as he entered. The first scowled.

"Barsimmon Oridio," the queen greeted the first. "Eton Shart. Thank you both for coming. Aurin Striate, please stay."

The three men seated themselves, eyes fastened on the queen. They were all looking at her now, waiting.

"Cort, Dal," she addressed the guards at the door. "Wait outside, please."

The Elven Hunters slipped through the doors and were gone. The doors closed softly.

"My friends." Ellenroh Elessedil sat straight backed in her chair, her voice carrying easily through the silence as she spoke. "We can't pretend any longer. We can't dissemble. We can't lie. What we have struggled for more than ten years to prevent is upon us."

"My Lady," Barsimmon Oridio began, but she silenced him with a glance.

"Tonight the demons broke through the Keel. The magic has been failing now for months—probably for years—and the things without have been stealing its strength for themselves. Tonight the balance shifted sufficiently to enable them to create a breach. Our hunters fought valiantly to prevent it, doing everything they could to throw back the assault. They failed. Phaeton was killed. In the end, I was forced to use the Ruhk Staff. If I had not done so, the city would have fallen.

"My Lady, that is not so!" Barsimmon Oridio could keep silent no longer. "The army would have rallied. It would have prevailed. Phaeton took too many chances or he would still be alive!"

"He took those chances to save us!" Ellenroh was stone faced. "Do not speak unkindly of him, Commander. I forbid it." The big man's scowl deepened. "Bar." the queen spoke gently now, the warmth in her voice evident. "I was there. I saw it happen."

She waited until his fierce eyes lowered, then turned her gaze again to the table at large. "The Keel will not protect us much longer. I have used the Ruhk Staff to strengthen it, but I cannot do so again or we risk losing its power altogether. And that, my friends, I cannot allow. I have called you together then to tell you that I have decided on another course of action."

She turned to Wren. "This is my granddaughter, Wren, the child of Alleyne, sent to us out of the old world as Eowen Cerise foresaw. She appears, the foretelling promises, in order that the Elves should be saved. I have waited for her to come for many years, not really believing that she would or that if she did she could do anything for us. I did not want her to come, in truth, because I was afraid that I would lose her as I lost Alleyne."

She reached over and touched Wren's cheek softly with her fingers. "I am still afraid. But Wren is here despite my fears, having crossed the vast expanse of the Blue Divide and braved the terrors of the demons to sit now with us. I can no longer doubt that she is meant to save us, just as Eowen foretold." She paused. "Wren neither fully believes nor understands this yet." Her eyes were warm as they found Wren's own. "She has come to Arborlon for reasons of her own. The shade of Allanon summoned her and dispatched her to find us. The Four Lands, it seems, are beset by demons of their own, creatures called Shadowen. We are needed, the shade insists, if the Four Lands are to be preserved."

"What happens in the Four Lands is not our problem, my Lady," Eton Shart advised calmly.

She turned to face him. "Yes, First Minister, that is exactly what we have said for more than a hundred years, haven't we? But what if we are wrong? What if our problem is also theirs? What if, contrary to what we have believed, the fates of all are linked together and survival depends on the forging of a common bond? Wren, tell those gathered how you came to find me. Tell them everything that was told to you by the Druid's shade and the old man. Tell them as well of the Elfstones. It will be all right now. It is time they knew."

So Wren related once more the story of how she and Garth had come to Arborlon, beginning with the dreams and ending with her discovery of who she was. She spoke hesitantly of the Elfstones, uncertain still that she should reveal their presence. But the queen nodded encouragingly when she began, so she left nothing out. When she was finished, there was silence. Those seated at the table exchanged uncertain glances. Gavilan stared at her as if seeing her for the first time.

"Now do you understand why I think it impossible to ignore any longer what takes place beyond Morrowindl?" the queen asked quietly.

"My Lady, I believe we understand," the Owl said, "but we need to hear now what you propose to do."

Ellenroh nodded. "Yes, Aurin Striate, you do." The room

went still once more. "There is nothing left for us here on Mor-rowindl," she said finally. "Therefore, it is time for us to leave, to return to the old world, and to become a part of it once again. Our days of disappearance and isolation are finished. It is time to use the Loden."

Gavilan was on his feet instantly. "Aunt Ell, no! We can't just give up! How do we know the Loden even works after all this time? It's just a story! And what about the Keel's magic? If we leave, it's lost! We can't do such a thing!"

Wren heard Barsimmon Oridio growl in agreement.

"Gavilan!" Ellenroh was furious. "We are in council. You will address me properly!"

Gavilan flushed. "I apologize, my Lady."

"Now sit down!" the queen snapped. Gavilan sat. "It seems to me that we owe our present predicament to indecision. We have failed to act for too long. We have allowed fate to dictate our choices for us. We have struggled with the magic even after it became apparent to all of us that we could no longer depend upon it."

"My Lady!" a pale-faced Eton Shart cautioned hurriedly.

"Yes, I know," Ellenroh responded. She did not look directly at Wren, but there was a flicker of movement in her eyes that told the girl that the warning had been given because of her.

"My Lady, you are asking that we give up the magic en-tirely?"

The queen's nod was curt. "It no longer serves much purpose to retain it, does it, First Minister?"

"But, as young Gavilan says, we have no way of knowing if the Loden will do as we expect."

"If it fails, we have lost nothing. Except, perhaps, any chance of escape."

"But escape, my Lady, is not necessarily the answer we are looking for. Perhaps help from another source . . ."

"Eton." The queen cut him short. "Consider what you are suggesting. What other source is there? Do you propose to sum-mon more magic still? Do we use what we have in another way, convert it to some further horror, perhaps? Or are we to seek help from the very people we abandoned to the Federation years ago?"

"We have the army, my Lady," a glowering Barsimmon Oridio declared.

"Yes, Bar, we do. For the moment. But we cannot regenerate
those lives that are lost. That magic we lack. Every new assault
takes more of our Hunters. The demons materialize out of the
very air, it seems. If we stay, we won't have an army much
longer."

She shook her head slowly, her smile ironic. "I know what
I am asking. If we return Arborlon and the Elves to the world
of Men, to the Four Lands and their Races, the magic will be
lost. We will be as we were in the old days. But maybe that is
enough. Maybe it will have to be."

Those seated about the table regarded her in silence, their
faces a mix of anger, doubt, and wonder.

"I don't understand about the magic," Wren said finally, unable just to continue sitting there while the questions piled up
inside. "What do you mean when you say the magic will be lost
if you leave Morrowindl?"

Ellenroh turned to face her. "I keep forgetting, Wren, that
you are not versed in Elven lore and know little yet of the
origins of the magic. I will try to make this simple. If I invoke
the Loden, as I intend to do, Arborlon and the Elves will be
gathered within the Elfstone for the journey back to the Westland. When that happens, the magic that shields the city falls
away. The only magic left then is that which comes from the
Loden and protects what is carried within. When Arborlon is
restored, that magic ceases as well. The Loden, you see, has
only one use, and once put to that use, its magic fades."

Wren shook her head in confusion. "But what about the way
it restored the Keel where the demons breached it? What of
that?"

"Indeed. I appropriated some of the same magic that the
Loden requires to transport the city and its people. In short, I
stole some of its power. But using that power to shore up the
Keel drains what is needed for the Elfstone's primary use." Ellenroh paused. "Wren, you are aware by now that the Elves
recaptured some of the magic they had once wielded in the time
of faerie. They did so after discovering that the magic had its
source in the earth and its elements. Even before we came to

Morrowindl, years ago, long before my time, a decision was made to attempt a recovery." She paused. "That effort was not entirely successful. Eventually it was abandoned completely. What magic was left went into the formation of the Keel. But the magic exists only so long as there is need. Once the city is gone, the need is gone. When that happens, the magic disappears."

"And cannot be reinstated once you return to the Westland?"

Ellenroh's face turned to stone. "No, Wren. Never again."

"You assume . . ." Gavilan began.

"Never!" Ellenroh snapped, and Gavilan went still.

"My Lady." Eton Shart drew her attention gently. "Even if we do what you suggest and invoke the power of the Loden, what chance do we have of getting back to the Westland? The demons are all about. As you say, we have barely been able to hold our own within the walls of the city. What happens when those walls are gone? Will even our army be enough to get us to the beaches? And what happens to us then without boats and guides?"

"The army cannot hold the beaches for long, my Lady," Barsimmon Oridio agreed.

"No, Bar, it can't," the queen said. "But I don't propose to use the army. I think our best chance is to leave Morrowindl as we came to it—just a handful of us carrying the Loden and the rest safely captured inside."

There was stunned silence.

"A handful, my Lady?" Barsimmon Oridio was aghast. "They won't stand a chance!"

"Well, that's not necessarily true," Aurin Striate quietly mused.

The queen smiled. "No, Aurin, it isn't. After all, my granddaughter is proof of that. She came through the demons with no one to help her but her friend Garth. The truth of the matter is that a small party stands a far better chance of getting clear than an entire army. A small party can travel quickly and without being seen. It would be a hazardous journey, but it could be done. As for what would happen once that party reached the beaches, Wren has already made those arrangements for us. The

Wing Rider Tiger Ty will be there with his Roc to convey at least one of us and the Loden to safety. Other Wing Riders can remove the rest. I have thought this through carefully and I believe it is the answer to our problem. I think, my friends, it is the only answer."

Gavilan shook his head. He was calm now, his handsome face composed. "My Lady, I know how desperate things have become. But if this gamble you propose fails, the entire Elven nation will be lost. Forever. If the party carrying the Loden is killed, the power of the Elfstone cannot be invoked and the city and its people will be trapped inside. I don't think it is a risk we can afford to take."

"Isn't it, Gavilan?" the queen asked softly.

"A better risk would be to summon further magic from the earth," he replied. His hands lifted to ward off her sharp protest. "I know the dangers. But this time we might be successful. This time the magic might be strong enough to keep us safe within the Keel, to keep the dark things locked without."

"For how long, Gavilan? Another year? Two? And our people still imprisoned within the city?"

"Better that than their extinction. A year might give us the time we need to find a method to control the earth magic. There must be a way, my Lady. We need only discover it."

The queen shook her head sadly. "We have been telling ourselves that for more than a hundred years. No one has found the answer yet. Look at what we have done to ourselves. Haven't we learned anything?"

Wren did not comprehend entirely what was being said, but she understood enough to realize that somewhere along the line the Elves had run into problems with the magic they had summoned. Ellenroh was saying they should have nothing further to do with it. Gavilan was saying they needed to keep trying to master it. Without being told as much, Wren was certain that the demons were at the heart of the dispute.

"Owl." The queen addressed Aurin Striate suddenly. "What do you think of my plan?"

The Owl shrugged. "I think it can be done, my Lady. I have spent years outside the city walls. I know that it is possible for a single man to go undetected by the demons, to travel among them. I think a handful could do the same. As you say, Wren and Garth came up from the beaches. I think they could go down again as well."

"Are you saying that you would give the Loden to this girl and her friend?" Barsimmon Oridio exclaimed in disbelief.

"A good choice, don't you think?" Ellenroh replied mildly. She glanced at Wren, who was thinking that she was the last person the queen should consider. "But we would have to ask them first, of course," Ellenroh continued, as if reading her mind. "In any case, I think more than two are needed."

"How many, then?" the Elven commander demanded.

"Yes, how many?" Eton Shart echoed.

The queen smiled, and Wren knew what she was thinking. She had them considering the proposal now, not simply arguing against it. They hadn't agreed to anything, but they were at least weighing the merits.

"Nine," the queen said. "The Elven number for luck. Just enough to make sure the job is done right."

"Who would go?" Barsimmon Oridio asked quietly.

"Not you, Bar," the queen replied. "Nor you either, Eton. This is a journey for young men. I wish you to stay with the city and our people. This will all be new for them. The Loden is only a story, after all. Someone must keep order in my absence, and you will do best."

"Then you intend to be one of those who makes the journey?" Eton Shart said. "This journey for young men?"

"Don't look so disapproving, First Minister," Ellenroh chided gently. "Of course I must go. The Ruhk Staff is in my charge and the power of the Loden mine to invoke. More to the point, I am Queen. It is up to me to see to it that my people and my city are brought safely back into the Westland. Besides, the plan is mine. I cannot very well advocate it and then leave it for someone else to carry out."

"My Lady, I don't think . . ." Aurin Striate began doubtfully.

"Owl, please do not say it." Ellenroh's frown left the other silent. "I am certain I can repeat word for word every objection you are about to make, so don't bother making them. If you feel it necessary, you can relate them to me as we go along since I expect you to make the journey as well."

"I wouldn't have it any other way." The Owl's seamed face was clouded with doubt.

"There is no one better able to survive outside the walls than you, Aurin Striate. You will be our eyes and ears out there, my friend."

The Owl nodded wordlessly in acknowledgment.

Ellenroh glanced about. "Triss, I'll need you and Cort and Dal to safeguard the Loden and the rest of us. That's five. Eowen will go. We may have need of her visions if we are to survive. Gavilan." She looked hopefully at her nephew. "I would like you to go as well."

Gavilan Elessedil surprised them all with a brilliant smile. "I would like that, too, my Lady."

Ellenroh beamed. "You can go back to calling me 'Aunt Ell,' Gavilan, after tonight."

She turned finally to Wren. "And you, child. Will you go with us, too? You and your friend Garth? We need your help. You have made the journey from the beach and survived. You know something of what is out there, and that knowledge is valuable. And you are the one the Wing Rider has promised to come back for. Am I asking too much?"

Wren was silent for a moment. She didn't bother looking over at Garth. She knew that he would go along with whatever she decided. She knew as well that she had not come all the way to Arborlon to be shut away, that Allanon had not dispatched her here to hide, and that she had not been given possession of the Elfstones only to forbear any use of them. The reality was harsh and demanding. She had been sent as more than a messenger, to do more than simply learn about who she was and from where she had come. Her part in this business— whether she liked it or not—was just beginning.

"Garth and I will come," she answered.

She believed her grandmother wanted to reach over and hug her then, but the queen remained straight backed in her chair and simply smiled instead. What Wren saw in her eyes, though, was better than any hug.

"Are we really agreed on doing this, then?" Eton Shart asked suddenly from the other end of the table.

The room was silent as Ellenroh Elessedil rose. She stood before them, pride and confidence reflected in her finely sculpted features, in the way she held herself, and in the glitter of her eyes. Wren thought her grandmother beautiful at that moment, the ringlets of her flaxen hair tumbling to her shoulders, the robes falling to her feet, and the lines of her face and body smooth and soft against the mix of shadows and light.

"We are, Eton," she replied softly. "I asked you to meet with me to hear what I had decided. If I could not persuade you, I told myself, I would not proceed. But I think I would have gone ahead in any case—not out of arrogance, not out of a sense of certainty in my own vision of what must be, but out of love for my people and fear that if they were lost the fault would be mine. We have a chance to save ourselves. Eowen foretold in her vision that this would be. Wren by coming has said that now is the time. All that we are and would ever be is at risk whatever choice we make, but I would rather the risk be taken in doing something than nothing. The Elves will survive, my friends. I am certain of it. The Elves always do."

She looked from face to face, her smile radiant. "Do you stand with me in this?"

They rose then, one by one, Aurin Striate first, Triss, Gavilan, Eton Shart, and Barsimmon Oridio after a brief hesitation and with obvious misgiving. Wren came to her feet last of all, so caught up in what she was seeing that she forgot for a moment that she was a part of it.

The queen nodded. "I could not ask for better friends. I love you all." She gripped the Ruhk Staff before her. "We will not delay. One day to advise our people, to prepare ourselves, and to make ready for what lies ahead. Sleep now. Tomorrow is already here."

She turned away from them then and walked from the room. In silence, they watched her go.

WREN WAS STANDING just outside the High Council doors, staring absently at patches of bright, star-filled sky and thinking that she could barely remember her life before the beginning of her search for the Elves, when Gavilan came up to her. The others had already gone, all but Garth, who lounged against a tree some distance off, looking out at the city. Wren had searched for Eowen, hoping to speak with her, but the seer had disappeared. Now she turned as Gavilan approached, thinking to speak with him instead, to ask him the questions she was still anxious to have answered.

The ready smile appeared immediately. "Little Wren," he greeted, ironic, a bit wistful. "Do you see our future as Eowen Cerise does?"

She shook her head. "I'm not sure I want to see it just now."

"Hmmm, yes, you might be right. It doesn't promise to be as soft and gentle as this night, does it?" He folded his arms comfortably and looked into her eyes. "What will we see once we're outside these walls, can you tell me? I've never been out there, you know."

Wren pursed her lips. "Demons. Vog, fire, ash, and lava rock until you reach the cliffs, then swamp and jungle, and then there's mostly vog. Gavilan, you shouldn't have agreed to come."

He laughed. "And you should? No, Wren, I want to die a whole man, knowing what's happened, not wondering from within the shield of the Loden's magic. If it even works. I wonder. No one really knows, not even the queen. Perhaps she'll invoke it and nothing will happen."

"You don't believe that, though, do you?"

"No. The magic always works for Ellenroh. Almost always, at least." The hands dropped away wearily.

"Tell me about the magic, Gavilan," she asked impulsively. "What is it about the magic that doesn't work? Why is it that no one wants to talk about it?"

Gavilan shoved his hands in the pockets of his coat, seeming to hunch down within himself as he did so. "Do you know, Wren, what it will be like for the Elves if Aunt Ell invokes the Loden's magic? None of them were alive when Arborlon was brought out of the Westland. None of them have ever seen the Four Lands. Only a few remember what it was like when Morrowindl was clean and free of the demons. The city is all they know. Imagine what it will be like for them when they are taken away from the island and put back into the Westland. Imagine what they will feel. It will terrify them."

"Perhaps not," she ventured.

He didn't seem to hear her. "We will lose everything we know when that happens. The magic has sustained us for our entire lives. The magic does everything for us. It cleans the air, shelters against the weather, keeps our fields fertile, feeds the plants and animals of the forest, and provides us with our water. Everything. What if these things are lost?"

She saw the truth then. He was terrified. He had no concept of life beyond the Keel, of a world without demons where nature provided everything for which the Elves now relied upon the magic.

"Gavilan, it will be all right," she said quietly. "Everything you enjoy now was there once before. The magic only provides you with what will be there again if nature's balance is restored. Ellenroh is right. The Elves will not survive if they remain on Morrowindl. Sooner or later, the Keel will fail. And it may be that the Four Lands, in turn, cannot survive without the Elves. Perhaps the destiny of the Races is linked in some way, just as Ellenroh suggested. Perhaps Allanon saw that when he sent me to find you."

His eyes fixed on hers. The fear was gone, but his look was intense and troubled. "I understand the magic, Wren. Aunt Ell thinks it is too dangerous, too unpredictable. But I understand it and I think I could find a way to master it."

"Tell me why she fears it." Wren pressed. "What is it that causes her to think it dangerous?"

Gavilan hesitated, and for a moment he seemed about to answer. Then he shook his head. "No, Wren. I cannot tell you. I have sworn I wouldn't. You are an Elf, but . . . It is better if you never find out, believe me. The magic isn't what it seems. It's too . . ."

He brought up his hands as if to brush the matter aside, frustrated and impatient. Then abruptly his mood changed, and he was suddenly buoyant. "Ask me something else, and I will answer. Ask me anything."

Wren folded her arms angrily. "I don't want to ask you anything else. I want to know about this."

The dark eyes danced. He was enjoying himself. He stepped so close to her that they were almost touching. "You are Alleyne's child, Wren. I'll give you that. Determined to the end."

"Tell me, then."

"Won't give it up, will you?"

"Gavilan."

"So caught up in wanting an answer you won't even see what's right in front of your face."

She hesitated, confused.

"Look at me," he said.

They stared at each other without speaking, eyes locked, measuring in ways that transcended words. Wren could feel the warmth of his breath and could see the rise and fall of his chest.

"Tell me," she repeated stubbornly.

She felt his hands come up to grip her arms, their touch light but firm. Then his face lowered to hers, and he kissed her.

"No," he whispered, gave her a quick, uncertain smile, and disappeared into the night.

CHAPTER

13

BY NOON OF THE FOLLOWING DAY everyone in Arborlon knew of Ellenroh Elessedil's decision to invoke the power of the Loden and return the Elves and their home city to the Westland. The queen had sent word at first light, dispatching select messengers to every quarter of her besieged kingdom—Barsimmon Oridio to the officers and soldiers of the army, Triss to the Elven Hunters of the Home Guard, Eton Shart to the remainder of the High Council and from there to the officials who served in the administrative bureaus of the government, and Gavilan to the market district to gather together the leaders in the business and farming communities. By the time Wren had awakened, dressed, eaten breakfast, and gone out into the city, the talk was of nothing else.

She found the Elves' response remarkable. There was no panic, no sense of despair, and no threats or accusations against the queen for making her decision. There was uncertainty, of course, and a healthy measure of doubt. None among the Elves had been alive when Arborlon had been carried out of the Westland, and while all had heard the story of the migration to Morrowindl, few had given much thought to migrating out again. Even with the city ringed by the demons and life drastically altered from what it was in the time of Ellenroh's father, concern for the future had not embraced the possibility of employing the Loden's magic. As a result the people talked of leaving as if the idea was an entirely new one, a prospect freshly conceived, and for the most part the conversations that Wren listened in on suggested that if Ellenroh Elessedil believed it best, then certainly it must be so. It was a tribute to the confidence that the Elves placed in their queen that they would accept her proposal so readily—especially when it was as drastic as this one.

"It will be nice to be able to go out of the city again," more than one said. "We've lived behind walls for too long."

"Travel the roads and see the world," others agreed. "I love my home, but I miss what lies beyond."

There was more than one mention of life without the constant threat of demons, of a world where the dark things were just a memory and the young could grow without having to accept that the Keel was all that allowed them to survive and there could never be any kind of existence beyond. Some expressed concern about how the magic worked, or if it even would, but most seemed satisfied with the queen's assurance that life within the city would go on as always during the journey, that the magic would protect and insulate against whatever happened without, and that it would be as before except that in place of the Keel there would be a darkness that none could pass through until the magic of the Loden was recalled.

She ran across Aurin Striate in the market center. The Owl had been up since dawn gathering together the supplies the company of nine would require to make the journey down Killeshan's slopes to the beaches. His task was made difficult mostly by the queen's determination that they would take only what they could carry on their backs and that stealth and quickness would serve them best in their efforts to elude the demons.

"The magic, as I understand it, works like this," he explained as they walked back toward the palace. "There's both a wrapping about and a carrying away when it is invoked. Once in place, it protects against intrusions from without, like a shell. At the same time, it removes you to another place—city and all—and keeps you there until the spell is released. There is a kind of suspension in time. That way you don't feel anything of what's happening during the journey; you don't have any sense of movement."

"So everything just goes on as before?" Wren queried, trying to envision how that could happen.

"Pretty much. There isn't any day or night, just a grayness

as if the skies were cloudy, the queen tells me. There's air and water and all the things you need to survive, all wrapped carefully away in this sort of cocoon."

"And what happens once you get to where you are going?"

"The queen removes the Loden's spell, and the city is restored."

Wren's eyes shifted to find the Owl's. "Assuming, of course, that what Ellenroh has been told about the magic is the truth."

The Owl sighed. "So young to be so skeptical." He shook his head. "If it isn't the truth, Wren, what does any of this matter? We are trapped on Morrowindl without hope, aren't we? A few might save themselves by slipping past the dark things, but most would perish. We have to believe the magic will save us, girl, because the magic is all we have."

She left him as they neared the palace gates, letting him go on ahead, tired eyed and stoop shouldered, his thin, rumpled shadow cast against the earth, a mirror of himself. She liked Aurin Striate. He was comfortable and easy in the manner of old clothes. She trusted him. If anyone could see them through the journey that lay ahead, it was the Owl.

She turned away from the palace and wandered absently toward the Gardens of Life. She had not looked for Garth when she had risen, slipping from her room instead to search out the queen. But Ellenroh was nowhere to be found once again, and so she had decided to walk out into the city by herself. Now, her walk completed, she found that she still preferred to be alone. She let her thoughts stray as she entered the deserted Gardens, making her way up the gentle incline toward the Ellcrys, and her thoughts, as they had from the moment she had come awake, gravitated stubbornly toward Gavilan Elessedil. She stopped momentarily, picturing him. When she closed her eyes she could feel him kissing her. She took a deep breath and let it out slowly. She had only been kissed once or twice in her life—always too busy with her training, aloof and unapproachable, caught up in other things, to be bothered with boys. There had been no time for relationships. She had had no interest in them. Why was that? she wondered suddenly. But she knew that she might as well inquire as to why the sky was blue as to question who she had become.

She opened her eyes again and walked on.

When she reached the Ellcrys, she studied it for a time before seating herself within its shade. Gavilan Elessedil. She liked him. Maybe too much. It seemed instinctual, and she distrusted the unexpected intensity of her feelings. She barely knew him, and already she was thinking of him more than she should. He had kissed her, and she had welcomed it. Yet it angered her that he was hiding what he knew about the magic and the demons, a truth he refused to share with her, a secret so many of the Elves harbored—Ellenroh, Eowen, and the Owl among them. But she was bothered more by Gavilan's reticence because he had come to her to proclaim himself a friend, he had promised to answer her questions when she asked them, he had kissed her and she had let him, and despite everything he had gone back on his word. She smoldered inwardly at the betrayal, and yet she found herself anxious to forgive him, to make excuses for him, and to give him a chance to tell her in his own time.

But was it any different with Gavilan than it had been with her grandmother? she asked herself suddenly. Hadn't she used the same reasoning with both?

Perhaps her feelings for each were not so very different.

The thought troubled her more than she cared to admit, and she shoved it hastily away.

It was still and calm within the Gardens, secluded amid the trees and flower beds, cool and removed beneath the silken covering of the Ellcrys. She let her eyes wander across the blanket of colors that formed the Gardens, studying the way they swept the earth like brush strokes, some short and broad, some thin and curving, borders of brightness that shimmered in the light. Overhead, the sun shone down out of a cloudless blue sky, and the air was warm and sweet smelling. She drank it in slowly, carefully, savoring it, aware as she did so that it would all be gone after tonight, that when the magic of the Loden was invoked she would be cast adrift once more in the wilderness dark of Morrowindl. She had been able to forget for a time the horror that lay beyond the Keel, to block away her memories of the stench of sulfur, the steaming fissures in the crust of lava rock, the swelter of Killeshan's heat rising off the earth, the darkness and the vog, and the rasps and growls of the demons at hunt. She shivered and hugged herself. She did not want to go back out into it. She felt it waiting like a living thing, crouched down patiently, determined it would have her, certain she must come.

She closed her eyes again and waited for the bad feelings to subside, gathering her determination a little at a time, calming herself, reasoning that she would not be alone, that there would be others with her, that they would all protect one another, and that the journey down out of the mountains would pass quickly and then they would be safe. She had climbed unharmed to Arborlon, hadn't she? Surely she could go back down again.

And yet her doubts persisted, nagging whispers of warning that echoed in the Addershag's warning at Grimpen Ward. *Beware, Elf-girl. I see danger ahead for you, hard times, and treachery and evil beyond imagining.*

Trust no one.

But if she did as the Addershag had advised, if she kept her own counsel and gave heed to no one else, she would be paralyzed. She would be cut off from everyone and she did not think she could survive that.

How much had the Addershag seen of her future? she wondered grimly. How much had she failed to reveal?

She pushed herself to her feet, took a final look at the Ellcrys, and turned away. Slowly she descended the Gardens of Life, stealing as she went faint memories of their comfort and reassurance, brightness and warmth, tucking them away for the time when she would need them, for when the darkness was all about and she was alone. She wanted to believe it would not happen that way. She hoped the Addershag was wrong.

But she knew she could not be certain.

GARTH CAUGHT UP WITH HER shortly after that and she remained with him for what was left of the day. They spoke at length about what lay ahead, listing the dangers they had already encountered and debating what they would require to make a journey back through the madness that lay without. Garth seemed relaxed and confident, but then he always seemed that way. They agreed that whatever else happened, they would stay close to each other.

She saw Gavilan only once and only for a moment. It was late that afternoon and he was leaving the palace on yet another errand as she came across the lawn. He smiled at her and waved as if everything was as it should be, as if the whole world were set right, and in spite of her irritation at his casual manner she found herself smiling and waving back. She would have spoken with him if she could have managed it, but Garth was there and several of Gavilan's companions as well, and there was no opportunity. He did not reappear after that, although she made it a point to look for him. As dusk approached she found herself alone in her room once more, staring out the windows at the dying light, thinking that she ought to be doing something, feeling as if she were trapped and wondering if she should be fighting to get free. Garth was secluded once again in the adjoining room, and she was about to seek out his company when her door opened and the queen appeared.

"Grandmother," she greeted, and she could not mask entirely the relief in her voice.

Ellenroh swept across the room wordlessly and took her in her arms, holding her close. "Wren," she whispered, and her arms tightened as if she were afraid that Wren might flee.

She stepped back finally, smiled past a momentary mask of sadness, then took Wren's hand and led her to the bed where they seated themselves. "I have ignored you shamefully all day. I apologize. It seemed that every time I turned around I was remembering something else that needed doing, some small task I had forgotten that had to be completed before tonight." She paused. "Wren, I am sorry to have gotten you involved in this business. The problems we made for ourselves should not be yours as well. But there is no help for it. I need you, child. Do you forgive me?"

Wren shook her head, confused. "There is nothing to forgive, Grandmother. When I decided to bring Allanon's message to you I chose to involve myself. I knew that if you heeded that message I would be coming with you. I never thought of it in any other way."

"Wren, you give me such hope. I wish that Alleyne was here to see you. She would have been proud. You have her strength and her determination." The smooth brow furrowed. "I miss her so much. She has been gone for years, and still it seems that she has only stepped away for a moment. I sometimes find myself looking for her even now."

"Grandmother," Wren said quietly, waiting until the other's eyes were locked on her own. "Tell me about the magic. What is it that you and Gavilan and Eowen and the Owl and everyone else knows that I don't? Why does it frighten everyone so?"

For a moment Ellenroh Elessedil did not respond. Her eyes went hard, and her body stiffened. Wren could see in that instant the iron resolve that her grandmother could call upon when she was in need, a casting that belied the youthful face and slender form. A silence settled between them. Wren held her gaze steady, refusing to look away, determined to put an end to the secrets between them.

The queen's smile, when it came, was unexpected and bitter. "As I said, you are like Alleyne." She released Wren's hands as if anxious to establish a boundary between them. "There are some things I would like to tell you that I cannot, Wren. Not yet, in any case. I have my reasons, and you will have to accept my assurance that they are good ones. So I will tell you what I can and there the matter must rest."

She sighed and let the bitterness of her smile drift away. "The magic is unpredictable, Wren. It was so in the beginning; it remains so now. You know yourself from the tales of the Sword of Shannara and the Elfstones that the magic is not a constant, that it does not always do what is expected, that it reveals itself in surprising ways, and that it evolves with the passage of time and use. It is a truth that seems to continually elude us, one that must be constantly relearned. When the Elves came into Morrowindl, they decided to recover the magic, to rediscover the old ways, and to model themselves after their forefathers. The problem, of course, was that the model had long since been broken and no one had kept the plans. Recovery of the magic was accomplished more easily than expected, but mastering it once in hand was something else again. Attempts were made; many failed. In the course of those attempts, the demons were let into being. Inadvertent and unfortunate, but a fact just the same. Once here, they could not be dispatched. They flourished and reproduced and despite every effort employed to destroy them, they survived."

She shook her head, as if seeing those efforts parade before her eyes. "You would ask me why they cannot be sent back to wherever they came from, wouldn't you? But the magic doesn't work that way; it will not permit so easy a solution. Gavilan, among others, believes that further experimentation with the magic will produce better results, that trial and error will eventually give us a way to defeat the creatures. I do not agree. I understand the magic, Wren, because I have used it and I know the extent of its power. I am afraid of what it can do. There are no limits, really. It dwarfs us as mortal creatures; it lacks the restraints of our humanity. It is greater than we are; it will survive after we are all long dead. I have no faith in it beyond that which has been gleaned out of experience and is required by necessity. I believe that if we continue to test it, if we continue to believe that the solution to our problems lies in what it can do, then some new horror will find its way into our lives and we will wish that the demons were all that we had to deal with."

"What of the Elfstones?" Wren asked her quietly.

Ellenroh nodded, smiled, and looked away. "Yes, child, what of the Elfstones? What of their magic? We know what it can do; we have seen its results. When Elven blood fails, when it is not strong enough as it was not strong enough in Wil Ohmsford, it creates unexpected results. The wishsong. Good and bad, both." She looked back again. "But the magic of the Elfstones is known and it is contained. No one believes or suggests that it could be subverted to another use. Nor the Loden. We have some understanding of these magics and will employ them because we must if we are to survive. But there is much greater magic waiting to be discovered, child—magic that lives beneath the earth, that can be found in the air, and that cries out for recognition. That is the magic that Gavilan would gather. It is the same magic that the Druid called Brona sought to harness more than a thousand years ago—the same magic that convinced him to become the Warlock Lord and then destroyed him."

Wren understood her grandmother's fear of the magic, could

TERRY BROOKS

see the dangers as she saw them, and could share with her as could no one else the feelings that invocation of the magic aroused—in the Elfstones, in the Loden—power that could overwhelm, that could subvert, and that could swallow you up until you were lost.

"You said that you wanted the Elves to go back to the way they were before they recovered the magic," she said, thinking back to the previous night when Ellenroh had addressed the High Council. "But can that happen? Won't some among the Elves simply bring it back again, perhaps find it in another way?"

"No." Ellenroh's eyes were suddenly distant. "Not again. Not ever again."

She was leaving something out. Wren sensed it immediately—sensed as well that it was not something Ellenroh would discuss. "And what of the magic you have already invoked, that which protects the city?"

"It will all disappear once we leave—all but that required to fulfill the Loden's use and to carry the Elves and Arborlon back into the Westland. All but that."

"And the Elfstones?"

The queen smiled. "There are no absolutes, Wren. The Elfstones have been with us for a long time."

"I could cast them away once we are safe."

"Yes, child, you could—should you choose to do so."

Wren felt something unspoken pass between them, but she could not identify its meaning. "Will the magic of the Loden really do as you believe, Grandmother? Will it carry the Elves safely out of Morrowindl?"

The queen's smooth face lowered momentarily, shaded with doubt and something more. "Oh, the magic is there, certainly. I have felt it in my use of the staff. I have been told its secret and I know it to be the truth." Her face lifted abruptly. "But it is we, Wren, who must do the carrying. It is we who must see to it that those who have been gathered up by the Loden's spell—our people—are restored to the world again, that they are given a new chance at life. Magic alone is not enough. It is never enough. Our lives, and ultimately the lives of all those who depend upon us, are forever our responsibility. The magic is only a tool. Do you understand?"

Wren nodded somberly. "I will do anything I can to help," she said softly. "But I tell you now that I wish the magic dead and gone, all of it, every last bit, everything from Shadowen to demons to Loden to Elfstones. I would see it all destroyed."

The queen rose. "And if it were, Wren, what then would take its place? The sciences of the old world, come back to life? A greater power still? It would be something, you know. It will always be something."

She reached down and pulled Wren up with her. "Call Garth now and come with me to dinner. And smile. Whatever else might come of this, we have found each other. I am very glad that you are here."

She hugged Wren close once more, holding her. Wren hugged her back and said, "I'm glad, too, Grandmother."

ALL OF THE MEMBERS of the inner circle of the High Council were in attendance at dinner that night—Eton Shart, Barsimmon Oridio, Aurin Striate, Triss, Gavilan, and the queen, together with Wren, Garth, and Eowen Cerise—all those who had been present when the decision was made to invoke the Loden's power and abandon Morrowindl. Even Cort and Dal were there, standing watch in the halls beyond, barring any from entering, including the service staff once the food was on the table. Comfortably secluded, those gathered discussed the arrangements for the coming day. Talk was animated and direct with discussions about equipment, supplies, and proposed routes dominating the conversation. Ellenroh, after consulting with the Owl, had decided that the best time to attempt an escape was just before dawn when the demons were weary from the night's prowl and anxious for sleep and a full day's light lay ahead for travel. Night was the most dangerous time to be out, for the demons always hunted then. It would take the company of nine a bit more than a week to reach the beaches if all went smoothly. If any of them doubted that it would really happen that way, at least they kept it to themselves.

Gavilan sat across from Wren, one place removed, and smiled at her often. She was aware of his attention and politely acknowledged it, but directed her talk to her grandmother and the Owl and Garth. She ate something, but later she couldn't remember what, listening to the others talk, glancing frequently at Gavilan as if studying him might somehow reveal the mystery of his attraction, and thinking distractedly about what the queen had told her earlier.

Or, more to the point, what she hadn't told her.

The queen's revelations, on close examination, were a trifle threadbare. It was all well and good to say that the magic had been recovered; but where had it been recovered from? It was fine to admit that recovery had somehow triggered the release of the demons that besieged them; but what was it about the magic that had freed them? And from where? Wren still hadn't heard a word about what had gone wrong with usage of the magic or why it was that no magic was available to undo the wrong that had been done. What her grandmother had given her was a sketch without shadings or colors or background of any kind. It wasn't enough by half.

And yet Ellenroh had insisted that it must be.

Wren sat with her thoughts buzzing inside like gnats. The conversations flowed heatedly about her as faces turned this way and that, the light failed without as the darkness closed down, and time passed by with silent footsteps, a retreat from the past, a stealthy approach toward a future that might change them all forever. She felt disconnected from everything about her, as if she had been dropped into place at the dinner table quite un-expectedly, an uninvited guest, an eavesdropper on the lives of those about her. Even Garth's familiar presence failed to comfort her, and she said little to him.

When dinner ended, she went straight to her room to sleep, stripped off her clothing, slipped beneath the bed coverings, and lay waiting in the dark for things to change back again. They refused. Her breathing slowed, her thoughts scattered, and at last she fell asleep.

Even so, she was awake again and dressed before the knock on the door that was meant to rouse her. Gavilan stood there, clothed in drab hunter's garb with weapons strapped all about, the familiar grin shelved, looking like someone else entirely.

"I thought you might like to walk down to the wall with me," he said simply.

Her smile in response brought a trace of his own. "I would," she agreed.

With Garth in tow, they departed the palace and moved through the dark, deserted streets of the city. Wren had thought the people would be awake and watchful, anxious to observe what would happen when the magic of the Loden was invoked. But the homes of the Elves were dark and silent, and those who watched did so from the shadows. Perhaps Ellenroh had not told them when the transformation would occur, she thought. She became aware of someone following them and glanced back to find Cort a dozen paces behind. Triss must have dispatched him to make certain they reached their appointed gathering spot on time. Triss would be with the queen or Eowen Cerise or Aurin Striate—or Dal would. All of them shepherded down to the Keel, to the door that led out into the desolation beyond, into the harsh and barren emptiness that they must traverse in order to survive.

They arrived without incident, the darkness unbroken, the dawn's light still hidden beneath the horizon. All were gathered—the queen, Eowen, the Owl, Triss, Dal, and now the four of them. Only nine, Wren thought, suddenly aware of how few they were and how much depended on them. They exchanged hugs and hand clasps and furtive words of encouragement, a handful of shadows whispering into the night. All wore hunter's garb, loose fitting and hardy, protection against the weather and, to some small measure, the dangers that waited without. All carried weapons, save for Eowen and the queen. Ellenroh carried the Ruhk Staff, its dark wood glimmering faintly, the Loden a prism of colors that winked and shimmered even in the near black. Atop the Keel, the magic was a steady glow that illuminated the battlements and reached heavenward. Elven Hunters patrolled the walls in groups of half a dozen, and sentries stood at watch within their towers. From without, the growls and hissings were sporadic and distant, as if the things emitting them lacked interest and would as well have slept.

"We'll give them a surprise before this night is over, won't we?" Gavilan whispered in her ear, a tentative smile on his face.

"Just so long as they're the ones who end up being surprised," she whispered back.

She saw Aurin Striate by the door leading down into the tunnels and moved over to stand beside him. His rumpled body shifted in the gloom. He glanced at her and nodded.

"Eyes and ears sharp, Wren?"

"I guess so."

"Elfstones handy?"

Her mouth tightened. The Elfstones were in a new leather bag strung about her neck—she could feel their weight resting against her chest. She had managed to avoid thinking about them until now. "Do you think I'll need them?"

He shrugged. "You did last time."

She was silent for a moment, considering the prospect. Somehow she had thought she might escape Morrowindl without having to call on the magic again.

"It seems quiet out there," she ventured hopefully.

He nodded, his slender frame draping itself against the stone. "They won't be expecting us. We'll have our chance."

She leaned back next to him, shoulders touching. "How good a chance will it be, Owl?"

He laughed tonelessly. "What difference does it make? It is the only chance we have."

Barsimmon Oridio materialized out of the blackness, went directly to the queen, spoke to her in hushed tones for a few minutes, and then disappeared again. He looked haggard and worn, but there was determination in his step.

"How long have you been going out there?" she asked the Owl suddenly, not looking at him. "Out with them."

There was a hesitation. He knew what she meant. She could feel his eyes fixing on her. "I don't know anymore."

"What I want to know, I guess, is how you made yourself do it. I can barely make myself go even this once, knowing what's out there." She swallowed against the admission. "I mean, I can do it because it's the only choice, and I won't have to do it again. But you had a choice each time, before this. You must have thought better of it more than once. You must not have wanted to go."

"Wren." She turned when he spoke her name and faced him. "Let me tell you something you haven't learned yet, something you learn only by living awhile. As you get older, you find that life begins to wear you down. Doesn't matter who you are or what you do, it happens. Experience, time, events—they all conspire against you to steal away your energy, to erode your confidence, to make you question things you wouldn't have given a second thought to when you were young. It happens gradually, a chipping away that you don't even notice at first, and then one day it's there. You wake up and you just don't have the fire anymore."

He smiled faintly. "Then you have a choice. You can either give in to what you're feeling, just say 'okay, enough is enough' and be done with it, or you can fight it. You can accept that every day you're alive you're going to have to face it down, that you're going to have to say to yourself that you don't care what you feel, that it doesn't matter what happens to you because sooner or later it is going to happen anyway, that you're going to do what you have to because otherwise you're defeated and life doesn't have any real purpose left. When you can do that, little Wren, when you can accept the wearing down and the eroding, then you can do anything. How did I manage to keep going out nights? I just told myself I didn't matter all that much—that those in here mattered more. You know something? It's not so hard really. You just have to get past the fear."

She thought about it a minute and then nodded. "I think you make it sound a lot easier than it is."

The Owl lifted off the wall. "Do I?" he asked. Then he smiled anew and walked away.

Wren drifted back over to stand with Garth. The big Rover pointed to the ramparts of the Keel. Elven Hunters were coming down off the heights—furtive, silent figures easing out of the light and down into the shadows. Wren glanced eastward and saw the first faint tinge of dawn against the black.

"It is time," Ellenroh said suddenly, and motioned them toward the wall.

They moved quickly, Aurin Striate in the lead, pulling open the doorway that led down into the tunnels, pausing at the entry to look back at the queen. Ellenroh had moved away from the wall to the bridgehead, stopping just before she reached its ramp to plant the butt end of the Ruhk firmly in the earth. From somewhere within Arborlon a bell tolled, a signal, and those few

Elven Hunters who remained atop the Keel slipped hurriedly away. In seconds, the wall was deserted.

Ellenroh Elessedil glanced back at the eight who waited just once, then turned to face the city. Her hands clasped the polished shaft of the Ruhk, and her head lowered.

Instantly the Loden began to glow. The brightness grew rapidly to white fire, flaring outward until the queen was enveloped. Steadily the light continued to spread, rising up against the darkness, filling the space within the walls until all of Arborlon was lit as bright as day. Wren tried to watch what was happening, but the intensity of the light grew until it blinded her and she was forced to look away. The white fire flooded to the parapets of the Keel and began to churn. Wren could feel it happen more than she could see it, her eyes closed against the glare. Without, the demons began to shriek. There was a rush of wind that came out of nowhere and grew into a howl. Wren dropped to her knees, feeling Garth's strong arm come up about her shoulders and hearing Gavilan's voice call to her. Images formed in her mind, triggered by Ellenroh's summoning, wild and erratic visions of a world in chaos. The magic was racing past her, a brushing of fingers that whispered and sang.

It ended in a shriek, a sound that no voice could have made, and then the light rushed away, whipping back into the black, withdrawing as if sucked down into a whirlpool. Wren's eyes jerked up, following the motion, trying to see. She was just quick enough to catch the last of it as it disappeared into the Loden's brilliant orb. She blinked once, and it was gone.

The city of Arborlon was gone as well—the people, the buildings, the streets and walkways, the gardens and lawns, the trees, everything from wall to wall within the Keel, disappeared. All that remained was a shallow crater in the earth—as if a giant hand had simply scooped Arborlon up and spirited it away.

Ellenroh Elessedil stood alone at the edge of what had once been the moat and was now the lip of the crater, leaning heavily on the Ruhk Staff, her own energy drained. Above her, the Loden was a prism of many-colored fire. The queen stirred herself, tried to move and failed, stumbled, and fell to her knees. Triss raced back for her instantly, lifted her as if she were a weary child, and started back again. It was then that Wren realized that the magic that had protected the Keel had faded as well, just as her grandmother had forewarned, its glow vanished completely. Overhead, the sky was enveloped in a haze of vog and the sunrise was a sullen lightening of the eastern skies barely able to penetrate the night's blackness. Wren drew a breath and found the stench of sulfur had returned. All that had been of Arborlon's shelter had vanished.

The silence of a moment earlier gave way to a cacophony of demon howls and shrieks as the realization of what had happened set in. The sound of bodies scrambling onto the walls and of claws digging in rose from every quarter.

Triss had reached them, the queen and the Ruhk Staff clutched in his arms.

"Inside, quickly!" the Owl shouted, hurrying ahead.

Hastening to follow after him, the others of the little company charged with the safe delivery of Arborlon and its Elves disappeared through the open door and down into the black.

14

N A WORLD OF LIGHT and shadows where truths were a shimmer of inconsistency, of life stolen out of substance and made over into transparency, of nonbeing and mist, Walker Boh was brought face to face with the impossible.

"I have been waiting a long time, Walker, hoping you would come," the ghost before him whispered.

Cogline—he had been dead weeks now, killed by the Shadowen at Hearthstone, destroyed by Rimmer Dall—and Rumor with him. Walker had seen it happen, sick almost beyond recovery from the poison of the Asphinx, crouched helplessly in his bedroom as the old man and the moor cat fought their last battle. He had seen it all, the final rush of the monsters created of the dark magic, the fire of the old man's magic as it flared in retaliation, and the explosion that had consumed everyone within reach. Cogline and Rumor had disappeared in the conflagration along with dozens of their attackers. None had survived save Rimmer Dall and a handful who had been thrown clear.

Yet here was Cogline and the cat, come somehow into Paranor, shades out of death.

Except that Walker Boh found them as real as he was, a reflection of himself in this twilight world into which the Black Elfstone had dispatched him, ghostlike and yet alive when they should not have been. Unless he was dead as well and a reflection of them instead. The contradictions overwhelmed him. His breath caught sharply in his throat and he could not speak. Who was alive and who was not?

"Walker." The old man spoke his name, and the sound of it drew him back from the precipice on which he was poised.

Cogline approached, slowly, carefully, seeming to realize the fear and confusion that his presence had generated in his pupil. He spoke softly to Rumor, and the moor cat sat back on his haunches obediently, his luminous eyes bright and interested as they fixed on Walker. Cogline's body was as fragile and sticklike as ever beneath the gathering of worn robes, and the gray, hazy light passed through him in narrow streamers. Walker flinched as the old man reached out to touch him on the shoulder, the skeletal fingers trailing down to grip his arm.

The grip was warm and firm.

"I am alive, Walker. And Rumor, too. We are both alive," he whispered. "The magic saved us."

Walker Boh was silent a moment, staring without comprehension into the other's eyes, searching for something that would give meaning to the other's words. Alive? How could it be? He nodded finally, needing to respond in some fashion, to get past the fear and confusion, and asked hesitantly, "How did you get here?"

"Come sit with me," the other replied.

He led Walker to a stone bench that rested against a wall, both an odd glimmer of hazy relief against the shadows, wrapped in mist and gloom. Sound was muffled within the Keep, as if an unwelcome guest forced to tread lightly in order not to draw attention. Walker glanced about, disbelieving still, searching the maze of walkways that disappeared ahead and behind, catching glimpses of stone walls and parapets and towers rising up about him, as empty of life as tombs set within the earth. He sat beside the old man, feeling Rumor rub up against him as he did.

"What has happened to us?" he asked, a measure of steadiness returning, his determination to discover the truth pushing back the uncertainty. "Look at us. We are like wraiths."

"We are in a world of half-being, Walker," Cogline replied softly. "We are somewhere between the world of mortal men and the world of the dead. Paranor rests there now, brought back out of nonbeing by the magic of the Black Elfstone. You found it, didn't you? You recovered it from wherever it was hidden and carried it here. You used it, as you knew you must, and brought us back.

"Wait, don't answer yet." He cut short Walker's attempt to speak. "I get ahead of myself. You must know first what happened to me. Then we will speak of you. Rumor and I have had an adventure of our own, and it has brought us to this. Here is what happened, Walker. Some weeks earlier when I spoke with the shade of Allanon, I was warned that my time within the world of mortal men was almost gone, that death would come for me when next I saw the face of Rimmer Dall. When that happened, I was to hold the Druid History to me and not to give it up. I was told nothing more. When the First Seeker and his Shadowen appeared at Hearthstone, I remembered Allanon's words. I managed to slow them long enough to retrieve the book from its hiding place. I stood with it clasped to my breast on the porch of the cottage, Rumor pressed back up against me, as the Shadowen reached to tear me apart.

"You thought it was my magic that enveloped me. It was not. When the Shadowen closed about me, a magic contained within the Druid History came to my defense. It released white fire, consuming everything about it, destroying everything that was not a part of me, except for Rumor, who sought to protect me. It did not harm us, but instead caught us up and carried us away as quick as the blink of an eye. We fell unconscious, a sleep that was as deep as any I have ever known. When we came awake again, we were here within Paranor, within the Druid's Keep."

He bent close. "I cannot know for certain what happened when the magic was triggered, Walker, but I can surmise. The Druids would never leave their work unprotected. Nothing of what they created would ever be left for use by those who lacked the right and the proper intent. It was so, I am certain, of their Histories. The magic that protected them was such that any threat would result in their return to the vault within the Keep that had sheltered them all those years. That was what happened to the History I held. I have looked within the vaults and found the History back among the others, safely returned. Allanon must have known this would happen—and known that anyone holding the History would be carried away as well—back into Paranor, back into the Druid's sanctuary.

"But not," he finished, "back into the world of mortal men."

"Because the Keep had been sent elsewhere three hundred years ago," Walker murmured, beginning to understand now.

"Yes, Walker, because the Keep had been sent from the Four Lands by Allanon and would remain gone until the Druids brought it back again. So the book was returned to it and Rumor and I sent along as well." He paused. "It appears that the Druids are not done with me yet."

"Are you trapped here, then?" Walker asked softly.

The other's smile was tight. "I am afraid so. I lack the magic to free us. We are a part of Paranor now, just as the Histories are, alive and well, but ghosts within a ghost castle, caught in some twilight time and place until a stronger magic than mine sets us free. And that is why I have been waiting for you." The bony fingers tightened about Walker's arm. "Tell me now. Have you brought the Black Elfstone? Will you show it to me?"

Walker Boh remembered suddenly that he still had hold of the Stone, the talisman clasped so tightly in his hand that the edges had embedded themselves in the flesh of his palm. He held his hand out tentatively, and his fingers slipped open one by one. He was cautious, afraid that the magic would overwhelm him. The Black Elfstone gleamed darkly in the hollow of his palm, but the magic lay dormant, the nonlight sealed away.

Cogline peered down at the Stone wordlessly for long moments, not attempting more, his narrow, seamed face reflecting wonder and hesitation. Then he looked up again and said, "How did you find it, Walker? What happened after Rumor and I were taken away?"

Walker told him then of the coming of Quickening, the daughter of the King of the Silver River, and of how she had healed his arm. He related all that had happened on the journey north to Eldwist, of the struggle of Quickening and her companions to survive in that land of stone, of the search for Uhl Belk, of the encounters with the Rake and the Maw Grint, and of the ultimate destruction of the city and those who sought to preserve it.

"I came here alone," he concluded, his gaze distant as the

memories of what had befallen him recalled themselves. "I knew what was expected of me. I accepted that the trust Allanon had bequeathed to Brin Ohmsford had been meant for me." He glanced over. "You always told me that I first needed to accept in order to understand, and I suppose I have done as you advised. And as Allanon charged. I used the Black Elfstone and brought back the Druid's Keep. But look at me, Cogline. I appear as you do, a ghost. If the magic has achieved what was intended, then why—"

"Think, Walker," the other interrupted quickly, a pained look in his ancient eyes. "What was your charge from Allanon? Repeat it to me."

Walker took a deep breath, his pale face troubled. "To bring back Paranor and the Druids."

"Yes, Paranor and the Druids—both. You realize what that means, don't you? You understand?"

Walker's brow knotted with frustration and reluctance. "Yes, old man." He breathed harshly in response. "I must become a Druid if Paranor is to be restored. I have accepted that, though it shall be as I wish it and not as a shade three hundred years dead intends." His words were angry now and quick. "I will not be as they were, those old men who—"

"Walker!" Cogline's anger was as intense as his own, and he went still immediately. "Listen to me. Do not proclaim what you will do and how you will be until you understand what is required of you. This is not simply a matter of accepting a charge and carrying it out. It was never that. Acceptance of who you are and what you must do is just the first of many steps your journey requires. Yes, you have recovered the Black Elfstone and summoned its magic. Yes, you have gained entry into disappeared Paranor. But that is only the beginning of what is needed."

Walker stared. "What do you mean? What else is there?"

"Much, I am afraid," the other whispered. A sad smile eased across the wrinkled features, seamed wood splitting with age. "You came to Paranor much in the same way as Rumor and I. The magic brought you. But the magic gives you entry on its own terms. We are here at its sufferance, alive under the conditions it dictates. You have already noted how you seem—

almost a ghost, having substance and life yet not enough of either to be as other mortal men. That should tell you something, Walker. Look about you. Paranor appears the same—here and yet not here, vague in its form, not come fully to life."

The thin mouth tightened. "Do you see? We are none of us—Rumor, you and I, Paranor—returned yet to the world of men. We are still in a limbo existence, somewhere between being and nonbeing, and we are waiting. We are waiting, Walker, for the magic to restore us fully. Because it has not done that yet, despite your use of the Black Elfstone and your entry into the Keep. Because it has not yet been mastered."

He reached down and gently closed Walker's fingers back around the Black Elfstone, then slowly sat back, a frail bundle of sticks against the shadows.

"In order for Paranor to be restored to the world of men, the Druids must come again. More precisely, one Druid, Walker. You. But acceptance of what this means is not enough to let you become a Druid. You must do more if the magic is to be yours, if it is to belong to you. You must become what you are charged with being. You must transform yourself."

"Transform myself?" Walker was aghast. "It would seem that I have done so already! What further transformation is required? Must I disappear altogether? No, don't answer that. Let me puzzle this through a moment on my own. I have the legacy of Allanon, possession of the Black Elfstone, and still I must do more if any of this is to mean anything. Transform myself, you say? How?"

Cogline shook his head. "I don't know. I know that if you do not do so you will not become a Druid and Paranor will not be restored to the world of men."

"Am I trapped here if I fail?" Walker demanded furiously.

"No. You can leave whenever you choose. The Black Elfstone will see you clear."

There was an uncertain moment of angry silence as the two men faced each other, vague shadows seated on the stone bench beneath the castle walls. "And you?" Walker asked finally. "And Rumor? Can you come away with me?"

Cogline smiled faintly. "We gained life at a cost, Walker. We are tied to the magic of the Druid Histories, irrevocably bound. We must remain with them. If they are not restored into the world of men, then we cannot be brought back either."

"Shades." Walker breathed the word like a curse. He felt the weight of Paranor's stone settle down about him. "So I can gain my own freedom, but not yours. I can leave, but you must stay." His own smile was hard and ironic. "I would never do that, of course. Not after you gave up your own life so that I could keep mine. You knew that, didn't you? You knew it from the start. And Allanon surely knew. I am trapped at every turn, aren't I? I posture about who I will be and what I will do, how I will control my own destiny, and my words are meaningless."

"Walker, you are not bound to us," Cogline interjected quickly. "Rumor and I fought to save you because we wished to."

"You fought because it was necessary if I was to carry out Allanon's charge, Cogline. There is no escaping why I am alive. And if I refuse to carry it out now, or if I fail, everything that has gone before will have been pointless!" He fought to control himself as his voice threatened to become a shout. "Look at what is being done to me!"

Cogline waited a moment, then said quietly, "Is it really so bad, Walker? Have you been so misused?"

There was a pause as Walker glared at him. "Because I have nothing to say about what is to become of me? Because I am fated to be something I despise? Because I must act in ways I would not otherwise act? Old man, you astonish me."

"But not sufficiently to provoke you to answer?"

Walker shook his head in disgust. "Answers are pointless. Any answer I might give would only come back to haunt me later. I feel I am betrayed by my own thoughts in this business. Better to deal with what is given than what might be, isn't it?" He sighed. The cold of the stone seeped into him, felt now for the first time. "I am as trapped here as you are," he whispered.

Cogline leaned back against the castle wall, looking momentarily as if he might disappear into it. "Then make your escape, Walker," he said quietly. "Not by running from your fate, but by embracing it. You have insisted from the beginning that you would not allow yourself to be manipulated by the Druids. Do you suppose that I feel any different? We are both victims of circumstances set in motion three hundred years ago, and we would neither of us be so if we had the choice. But we don't. And it does no good to rail against what has been done to us. So, Walker, do something to turn things to your advantage. Do as you are fated, become what you must, and then act in whatever ways you perceive to be right."

Walker's smile was ironic. "So you would have me transform myself. How do I do that, Cogline? You have yet to tell me."

"Begin with the Druid Histories. All of the secrets of the magic are said to be contained within." The old man's hand gripped his arm impulsively. "Go up into the Keep and take the Histories from their vault, one by one, and see for yourself what they can teach. The answers you need must lie therein. It is a place to start, at least."

"Yes," Walker agreed, inwardly mulling over the possibility that Cogline was right, that he might gain what he sought not by pushing his fate away but by turning it to his own use. "Yes, it is a start."

He rose then, and Cogline with him. Walker faced the old man in silence for a moment, then reached out with his good arm and gently embraced him. "I am sorry for what has been done to you," he whispered. "I meant what I said back at Hearthstone before Rimmer Dall came—that I was wrong to blame you for any of what has happened, that I am grateful for all you have done to help me. We shall find a way to get free, Cogline. I promise."

Then he stepped back, and Cogline's answering smile was a momentary ray of sunlight breaking through the gloom.

So WALKER BOH WENT up into the keep, following the lead of Cogline and Rumor, three specters at haunt in a twilight world. The castle of the Druids was dark and heavy, shimmering like an image reflected in a pool of water adrift with shadows. The stone of the walls and floors and towers was cold and empty of life, and the hallways wound about like tunnels beneath the earth, dark and dank. There were bones scattered here and there along the carpeted, tapestried halls, the remains of those Gnomes who had died when Allanon had invoked the magic that sent the Keep out of the Four Lands three hundred years earlier. Piles of dust marked the end of the Mord Wraiths trapped there, and all that remained of what they had been was a whisper of a memory sealed away by the walls.

Passageways came and went, stairways that ran straight and curved about, a warren of corridors burrowing back into the stone. The silence was pervasive, thick and deep as leaves in late autumn in the forest, rooted in the castle walls and inexorable. They did not challenge it, wordless as they passed through its curtain, focusing instead on what lay ahead, on the path they followed to the paths that waited. Doors and empty chambers came and went about them, stark and uninviting within their trappings of gloom. Windows opened into grayness, a peculiar haze that shaded everything beyond so that the Keep was an island. Walker searched for something of the forestland that ringed the empty hill on which Paranor had stood, but the trees had disappeared; or he had, he amended—come out of the Four Lands into nothingness. Color had been drained from the carpets and tapestries and paintings, from the stone itself, and even from the sky. There was only the gloom, a kind of gray that defied any brightening, that was empty and dead.

Yet there was one thing more. There was the magic that held Paranor sealed away. It was present at every turn, at once invisible and suddenly revealed, a kind of swirling, greenish mist. It hovered in the shadows and along the edges of their vision, wicked and certain, the hiss of its being a whisper of killing need. It could not touch them, for they were protected by other magic and were at one with the Keep itself. But it could watch. It could tease and taunt and threaten. It could wait with the promise of what would happen when their protection was gone.

It was odd that it should be such an obvious presence; Walker Boh felt it immediately. It was as if the magic were a living thing, a guard dog set at prowl through the Keep, searching out intruders and hunting them down so that they might be destroyed. Its presence reminded him of the Rake in Eldwist, a Creeper that scoured its master's grounds and swept them clean of life. The magic lacked the substance of the Rake, but its feel was the same. It was an enemy, Walker sensed, that would eventually have to be faced.

Within the Druid library, behind the bookcases where the vault was concealed, they found the Histories, banks of massive, leather-bound books set within the walls of the Keep, the magic that had once hidden them from mortal eyes faded with the passing of the Keep from the world of men. Walker studied the books for a time, deliberating, then chose one at random, seated himself, and began to read. Cogline and Rumor kept him company, silent and unobtrusive. Time passed, but the light did not change. There was no day or night in Paranor. There was no past or future. There was only the here and now.

Walker did not know how long he read. He did not grow tired and did not find himself in need of sleep. He did not eat or drink, being neither hungry nor thirsty. Cogline told him at one point that in the world into which Paranor had been dispatched, mortal needs had no meaning. They were ghosts as much as they were two men and a moor cat. Walker did not question. There was no need.

He read for hours or days or even weeks; he did not know. He read at first without comprehending, simply seeing the words flow in front of his eyes, a narrative that was as distant and removed as the life he had known before the dreams of Allanon. He read of the Druids and their studies, of the world they had tried to make after the cataclysm of the Great Wars, of the First Council at Paranor, and of the coming together of the Races out of the holocaust. What should it mean to him? he wondered. What difference did any of it make now?

He finished one book and went on to another, then another, working his way steadily through the volumes, constantly searching for something that would tell him what he needed to know. There were recitations of spells and conjurings, of magics that could aid in small ways, of healings by touch and thought, of the succor of living things, and of the work that was needed to make the land whole again. He read them, and they told him nothing. How was he supposed to transform himself from what he was into what he was expected to be? Where did it say what he was supposed to do? The pages turned, the words ran on, and the answers stayed hidden.

He did not finish in one sitting, even though he was free of the distractions of his mortal needs and did not sleep or eat or drink. He left to walk about periodically, to think of other things, and to let his mind clear itself of all that the Histories related. Sometimes Cogline went with him, his shadow; sometimes it was Rumor. They might have been back at Hearthstone, walking its trails, keeping each other company, living in the seclusion of the valley once more. But Hearthstone was gone, destroyed by the Shadowen, and Paranor was dark and empty of life, and no amount of wishing could change what had gone before. There was no returning to the past, Walker thought to himself more than once. Everything that had once been was lost.

After a time, he began to despair. He had almost finished reading the Druid Histories and still he had discovered nothing. He had learned everything of who and what the Druids were, of their teachings and their beliefs, and of how they had lived and what they they had sought to accomplish, and none of it told him anything about how they acquired their skills. There was no indication of where Allanon had come from, how he had learned to be a Druid or who had taught him, or what the subject matter of his teachings had been. The books were devoid of any reference to the conjuring that had sealed away the Keep or what it might require to reverse the spell.

"I cannot fathom it, Cogline," Walker Boh admitted finally, frustrated beyond hope as the last of the volumes sat open on his lap before him. "I have read everything, and none of it has helped. Is it possible that there are volumes missing? Is there something more to be tried?"

But Cogline shook his head. The answers, if they existed in written form, would be found here. There were no other books, no other sources of reference. Everything was contained in the Histories. All of the Druid studies began and ended there.

Walker went out alone then for a time, stalking the halls in anger, feeling betrayed and cheated, a victim of Druid whim and conceit. He thought bitterly of all that had been done to him because of who he was, of all that he had been forced to endure. His home had been destroyed. He had lost an arm and barely escaped with his life. He had been lied to and tricked repeatedly. He had been made to feel responsible for the fate of an entire world. Self-pity washed through him, and then his mouth tightened in admonishment. Enough, he chided himself. He was alive, wasn't he? Others had not been so fortunate. He was still haunted by Quickening's face; he could not forget how she had looked when he had let her fall. *Remember me,* she had pleaded with Morgan Leah—but she had been speaking to him as well. *Remember me*—as if anyone who had known her could ever forget.

Absently he turned down a corridor that led toward the center of the Keep and the entrance to the black well that had given birth to the magic that sealed away Paranor. His mind was still on Quickening, and he recalled once again the vision the Grimpond had shown him of her fate. Bitterness welled up within him. The vision had been right, of course. The Grimpond's visions were always right. First the loss of his arm, then the loss of Quickening, then . . .

He stopped suddenly, startled into immobility, a statue staring blankly into space at the center of the cavernous passageway. *He had forgotten. There was a third vision.* He took a steadying breath, picturing it in his mind. He stood within an empty, lifeless castle fortress, stalked by a death he could not escape, pursued relentlessly . . .

He exhaled sharply. *This castle?* He closed his eyes, trying to remember. Yes, it might have been Paranor.

He felt his pulse quicken. In the vision, he felt a need to run, but could not. He stood frozen as Death approached. A dark-robed figure stood behind him, holding him fast, preventing his escape.

Allanon.

He felt the silence grow oppressive. What had become of this third vision? he wondered. When was it supposed to happen? Was it meant to happen here?

And suddenly he knew. The certainty of it shocked him, but he did not doubt. The vision would come to pass, just as the others had, and it would come to pass here. Paranor was the castle, and the death that stalked him was the dark magic called forth to seal the Keep. Allanon did indeed stand behind him, holding him fast—not physically, but in ways stronger still.

But there was more, some part of things that he had not yet divined. It was not foreordained that he should die. That was the obvious meaning of the Grimpond's vision, what the Grimpond wanted Walker to think. The visions were always deceptive. The images were cleverly revealed, lending themselves to more than one interpretation. Like pieces to a puzzle, you had to play with them to discover how they fit.

Walker's eyes prowled the dark shadows that lay all about, hunting. What if he could find a way to turn the Grimpond's cleverness to his own use? What if this time he could decipher the vindictive spirit's foretelling in advance of its happening? And suppose—he hardly dared let himself hope—deciphering the vision could provide him with the key to understanding his fate within the Druid's Keep?

A fire began to build within him—a burning determination. He did not have the answers he needed yet, but he had something just as good. He had a way to discover what they were.

He thought back to his entry into Paranor, to his meeting with Cogline and Rumor. The missing pieces were there, somewhere. He retraced his reading of the Druid Histories, seeing again the words on the pages, feeling anew the weight of the books, the texture of the bindings. Something was there, something he had missed. He closed his eyes, picturing himself, following all that had happened, relating it to himself in his mind, a sequence of events. He searched it, standing solitary in that hall, wrapped in shadows and silence, feeling the edges of his confusion begin to draw away, hearing sounds that were new and welcome begin to whisper to him. He went down inside himself, reaching for the darker places where the secrets hid themselves. His magic rose to greet him. He could see anything if he searched hard and long enough, he told himself. He dropped away into the stillest, calmest part of himself, letting everything fall away.

What had he overlooked?

Whosoever shall have the cause and the right shall wield it to its proper end.

His eyes snapped open. His hand came up slowly along his body, groping. His fingers found what they were seeking, carefully tucked within his clothing, and they closed tightly about it.

The Black Elfstone.

Clutching the talisman protectively, his mind awash with new possibilities, he hurried away.

CHAPTER

15

WREN OHMSFORD CROUCHED wordlessly with her companions in the darkness of the tunnels beneath the Keel while the Owl worked in silence somewhere ahead, striking flint against stone to produce a spark that would ignite the pitch-coated torch he balanced on his knees. The magic that had illuminated the tunnel when Wren had come into the city was gone now, disappeared with Arborlon and the Elves into the Loden. Triss had been the last to enter, carrying Ellenroh from the bridge, and he had closed the door tightly behind, shutting them away from the madness that raged without, but trapping them as well with the heat and the stench of Killeshan's fire.

A spark caught in the darkness ahead, and a dark orange flame flared to life, casting shadows everywhere. Heads turned to where the Owl was already starting away.

"Be quick," he whispered back to them, his voice rough and urgent. "It won't take long for the dark things to find that door."

They crept swiftly after him, Eowen, Dal, Gavilan, Wren, Garth, Triss carrying Ellenroh, and Cort trailing. Beyond, burrowing down into the earth with the tenacity of moles, the howls and shrieks of the demons tracked them. Sweat beaded on Wren's skin, the heat of the tunnels intense and stifling. She brushed at her eyes, blinked away the stinging moisture, and worked to keep pace. Her thoughts strayed as she labored, and she remembered Ellenroh, standing at the center of the bridge-head, invoking the Loden, calling forth the light that would sweep up all of Arborlon and carry it down into the gleaming depths of the Stone. She could see the city disappear, vanishing as if it never were—buildings, people, animals, trees, grass, everything. Now Arborlon was their responsibility, theirs to protect, cradled within a magic that was only as strong as the nine men and women to whom it had been entrusted.

She pushed past trailing roots and spider's webs, and the enormity of the task settled on her like a weight. She was only one, she knew, and not the strongest. Yet she could not escape the feeling that the responsibility was inevitably hers alone, an extension of Allanon's charge, the reason for which she had come in search of the Elves.

She shook the feeling aside, crowding up against Gavilan in her haste to keep moving.

Then abruptly the earth shuddered.

The line stopped, and heads lowered protectively as silt broke free of the tunnel roof in a shower. The ground shook again, the tremors building steadily, rocking the earth as if some giant had seized the island in both hands and was struggling to lift it free.

"What's happening?" Wren heard Gavilan demand. She dropped to her knees to keep from being thrown off balance, feeling Garth's steadying hand settle on her shoulder.

"Keep moving!" the Owl snapped. "Hurry!"

They ran now, crouched low against a pall of loose dirt that hung roiling in the air. The tremors continued, a rumbling from beneath, the sound rising and falling, a quaking that tossed them against the tunnel walls and left them struggling to remain upright. The seconds sped away, fleeing as quickly as they did, it seemed, from the horror following. A part of the tunnel collapsed behind them, showering them with dirt. They could hear a cracking of stone, a splitting apart of the lava rock, as if the earth's crust were giving way. There was a heavy thud as a great boulder dropped through a crevice and struck the tunnel floor.

"Owl, get us out of here!" Gavilan called out frantically.

Then they were climbing free again, scrambling from the tunnel through an opening in the earth, clawing their way into the weak morning light. Behind them, the tunnel collapsed completely, falling away in a rush of air, silt exploding through the opening they had fled. The tremors continued to roll across Morrowindl's heights, ripping its surface, causing the rock to grate and crumble. Wren hauled herself to her feet with the others and stood in the shelter of a copse of dying acacia, looking back at where they had been.

The Keel was swarming with demons, their black bodies everywhere as they sought to scale the hated barrier. The magic was gone, but the tremors that had replaced it proved an even more formidable obstacle. Demons flew from the heights, screaming as they fell, shaken free like leaves from an autumn tree in a windstorm. The Keel cracked and split as the mountainside shuddered beneath it, chunks of stone tumbling away, the whole of it threatening to collapse. Fires spurted out of the earth from within, the crater from which Arborlon had been scooped by the magic become a cauldron of heat and flames. Steam hissed and spurted in geysers. High on Killeshan's slopes, the crust of the mountain's skin had ruptured and begun to leak molten rock.

"Killeshan comes awake," Eowen said softly, causing them all to turn. "The disappearance of Arborlon shifted the balance of things on Morrowindl; a void was created in the magic. The disruption reaches all the way to the core of the island. The volcano is no longer dormant, no longer stable. The fires within will burn more fiercely, and the gases and heat will build, until they can no longer be contained."

"How long?" the Owl snapped.

Eowen shook her head. "Hours here on the high slopes, days farther down." Her eyes were bright. "It is the beginning of the end."

There was an instant of uncertain silence.

"For the demons, perhaps, but not for us." It was Ellenroh Elessedil who spoke, back on her feet again, recovered from the strain of invoking the Loden's magic. She freed herself from Triss's steadying grip and walked through them, drawing them after in her wake until she turned to face them. She looked calm and assured and unafraid. "No hesitation now," she admonished.

"We go quickly, quietly, down to the shores of the Blue Divide and off the island, back to where we belong. Keep together, keep your eyes sharp. Owl, take us out of here."

Aurin Striate turned away at once, and the others went with him. There were no questions asked—Ellenroh Elessedil's presence was that strong. Wren glanced back once to see her grandmother come up beside Eowen, who seemed to have lapsed into a trance, put her arms about the seer, and lead her gently away. Behind them, the glare of the volcano's fire turned the Keel and the demons the color of blood. It seemed as if everything had disappeared in a wash of red.

Shadows against the hazy light, the company crept down off the slopes of Killeshan through the rugged mix of lava rock, deadwood, and scrub. All of the sounds were behind them now where the demons converged on an enemy that they were just beginning to discover was no longer there. Ahead there was only the steady rush of the Rowen as its gray waters churned toward the sea. The tremors chased after, shudders that rippled along the stretches of lava rock and shook the trees and brush; but their impact diminished the farther the company went. Vog clouded the air before them, turning the brightness of early-morning haze and the shape of the land indistinct. Wren's breathing steadied, and her body cooled. She no longer felt trapped as she had in the tunnel, and the intensity of the heat had lessened. She began to relax, to feel herself merge with the land, her senses reaching out like invisible feelers to search out what was hidden.

Even so, she failed to detect the demons that lay in wait for them before the attack. There were more than a dozen, smallish and gnarled, crooked like deadwood, rising up with a rending of brush and sticks to seize at them. Eowen went down, and the Owl disappeared in a flurry of limbs. The others rallied, striking out at their attackers with whatever came to hand, bunching together about Eowen protectively. The Elven Hunters fought with grim ferocity, dispatching the demons as if they were nothing more than shadows. The fight was over almost before it began. One of the black things escaped; the rest lay still upon the ground.

The Owl reappeared from behind a ridge, one sleeve shredded, his thin face clawed. He beckoned them wordlessly, turning away from the path they had been following, taking them swiftly down from the summit of a rise to a narrow gully that wound ahead into the fog. They watched closely now, alert for further attacks, reminded that the demons would be everywhere, that not all of them would have gone to the Keel. The sky overhead turned a peculiar yellow as the sun ascended the sky yet struggled unsuccessfully to penetrate the vog. Wren crept ahead with long knives in both hands, her eyes sweeping the shadows cautiously for any sign of movement.

They were nearing the Rowen when Aurin Striate brought them to a sudden halt. He dropped into a crouch, motioning them down with him, then turned, gestured for them to remain where they were, and disappeared ahead into the haze. He was gone for less than five minutes before reappearing. He shook his head in warning and motioned them left. Keeping low, they slipped along a line of rocks to where a ridge hid them from the Rowen. From there they worked their way parallel to the river for more than a mile, then resurfaced cautiously atop a rise. Wren peered out at the sluggish gray surface of the river, empty and broad before her as it stretched away into the distance.

Nothing moved.

The Owl rejoined them, his leathery face furrowed. "The shallows are filled with things we don't want anything to do with. We'll cross here instead. It's too broad and too wide to swim. We'll have to ferry over. We'll build a raft big enough to hold on to—that will have to do."

He took the Elven Hunters with him to gather wood, leaving Gavilan and Garth with the women. Ellenroh came over to Wren and gave her a brief hug and a reassuring smile. All was well, she was saying, but there were worry lines etched in her brow. She moved quietly away.

"Feel the earth with your hands, Wren," Eowen whispered suddenly, crouching next to her. Wren reached down and let the tremors rise into her body. "The magic comes apart all about us—everything the Elves sought to build. The fabric of our arrogance and our fear begins to unravel." The rust-colored hair tumbled wildly about the distant green eyes, and Eowen had the look of someone awakening from a nightmare. "She will have to tell you sometime, Wren. She will have to let you know."

Then she was gone as well, moving over to join the queen. Wren was not sure exactly what she had been talking about, but assumed she was referring to Ellenroh, and that, as the Rover girl already knew, there were secrets still unrevealed.

The vog swirled about, screening off the Rowen, snaking through the cracks and crevices of the land, changing the shape of everything as it passed. Cort and Dal returned hauling lengths of deadwood, then disappeared again. The Owl passed through the gloom heading toward the river, stick-thin and bent as if at hunt. Everything moved as if not quite there, a shading of some half-forgotten memory that could trick you into believing things that never were.

A sudden convulsion rocked the earth underfoot, causing Wren to gasp in spite of herself and to reach down hurriedly to regain her balance. The waters of the Rowen seemed to surge sharply, gathering force in a wave that crashed against the shore-line and rolled on into the distance.

Garth touched her shoulder. *The island shakes itself apart.*

She nodded, thinking back to Eowen's declaration that the impending cataclysm was the result of a disruption in the magic. She had thought the seer was referring solely to Ellenroh's use of the Loden, but now it occurred to her that the seer meant something more. The implication of what she had just told Wren was that the disruption of the magic was broader than simply the taking away of Arborlon, that at some time in the past the Elves had sought to do something more and failed and that what was happening now was a direct result.

She stored the information away carefully for a time when she could make use of it.

Garth moved down to help the Elven Hunters, who were beginning to lash together the logs for the raft. Gavilan was speaking in low tones with Ellenroh, and there was a restless anger reflected in his eyes. Wren watched him carefully for a moment, measuring what she saw now against what she had seen before, the hard-edged tension and the careless disregard, two images in sharp contrast. She found Gavilan intriguing, a complex mix of possibilities and enticements. She liked him; she wanted him close. But there was something hidden in him that bothered her, something she had yet to define.

"Just a few more minutes," the Owl advised, passing by her like a shadow and fading back into the mist.

She started to climb to her feet, and something small and quick darted from the undergrowth and threw itself on her. She tumbled back, flailing desperately, then realized in shock that the thing clinging to her was Faun. She laughed in spite of herself and hugged the Tree Squeak close.

"Faun," she cooed, nuzzling the odd little creature. "I thought something terrible had happened to you. But you're all right, aren't you? Yes, little one, you're just fine."

She was aware of Ellenroh and Gavilan looking over, puzzlement registered on their faces, and she quickly climbed to her feet again, waving to them reassuringly, smiling in spite of herself.

"Hrrwwwll. Have you forgotten your promise?"

She turned abruptly to find Stresa staring up at her from the edge of the gloom, quills all on end.

She knelt hurriedly. "So you are all right as well, Mr. Splinterscat. I was worried for you both. I couldn't come out to see if you were safe, but I hoped you were. Did you find each other after I left?"

"Yes, Wren of the Elves," the Splinterscat replied, his words cool and measured. "Pfftt. The Squeak came scampering back at dawn, fur all wild and ragged, chittering about you. It found me down by the river where I was waiting. So, now—your promise. You remember your promise, don't you?"

Wren nodded solemnly. "I remember, Stresa. When I left the city, I was to take you with me to the Westland. I will keep that promise. Did you worry I would not?"

"Hssst, pfftt!" The Splinterscat flattened its quills. "I hoped you were someone whose word meant something. Not like—" He cut himself short.

"Grandmother," Wren called out to the queen, and Ellenroh moved over to join her, curly hair blowing across her face like a veil. "Grandmother, these are my friends, Stresa and Faun. They helped Garth and me find our way to the city."

"Then they are friends of mine as well," Ellenroh declared.

"Lady," Stresa replied stiffly, not altogether charmed, it seemed.

"What's this?" Gavilan came up next to them, amusement dancing in his eyes. "A Scat? I thought they were all gone."

"There are a few of us—sssttt—no thanks to you," Stresa announced coldly.

"Bold fellow, aren't you?" Gavilan couldn't quite conceal his disapproval.

"Grandmother," Wren said quickly, putting an end to the exchange, "I promised Stresa I would take him with us when we left the island. I must keep that promise. And Faun must come as well." She hugged the furry Tree Squeak, who hadn't even looked up yet from her shoulder, still burrowed down against her, clinging like a second skin.

Ellenroh looked doubtful, as if taking the creatures along presented some difficulty that Wren did not understand. "I don't know," she answered quietly. The wind whistled past her, gathering force in the gloom. She gazed off at the Elven Hunters, at work now on loading backpacks and supplies onto the raft, then said, "But if you gave your promise . . ."

"Aunt Ell!" Gavilan snapped angrily.

The queen's gaze was icy as it fixed on him. "Keep silent, Gavilan."

"But you know the rules . . ."

"Keep silent!"

The anger in Gavilan's face was palpable. He avoided looking at either her or Wren, shifting his gaze instead to Stresa. "This is a mistake. You should know best, Scat. Remember who made you? Remember why?"

"Gavilan!" The queen was livid. The Elven Hunters stood up abruptly from their work and looked back at her. The Owl reappeared from out of the mist. Eowen moved to stand next to the queen.

Gavilan held his ground a moment longer, then wheeled away and stalked down to the raft. For a moment, no one else moved, statues in the mist. Then Ellenroh said, to no one in particular, her voice sounding small and lost, "I'm sorry."

She walked off as well, sweeping Eowen up in her wake, her

youthful features so stricken that it kept Wren from following after.

She looked instead at Stresa. The Splinterscat's laugh was bitter. "She doesn't want us off the island. Fffttt. None of them do."

"Stresa, what is going on here?" Wren demanded, angry herself now, bewildered at the animosity Stresa's appearance had generated.

"Rrrwwll. Wren Ohmsford. Don't you know? Hssst. You don't, do you? Ellenroh Elessedil is your grandmother, and you don't know. How strange!"

"Come, Wren," the Owl said, passing by once more, touching her lightly on the shoulder. "Time to be going. Quick, now."

The Elven Hunters were shoving the raft down to the water's edge, and the others were hastening after. "Tell me!" she snapped at Stresa.

"A ride down the rwwlll Rowen is not my idea of a good time," the Splinterscat said, ignoring her. "I'll sit directly in the middle, if you please. Hsssttt. Or if you don't, for that matter."

A renewed series of shudders shook the island, and in the haze behind them Killeshan erupted in a shower of crimson fire. Ash and smoke belched out, and a rumbling rose from deep within the earth.

They were all calling for Wren now, and she ran to them, Stresa a step ahead, Faun draped about her neck. She was furious that no one would confide in her, that arguments could be held in her presence about things of which she was being kept deliberately ignorant. She hated being treated this way, and it was becoming apparent that unless she forced the issue no one was ever going to tell her anything about the Elves and Morrowindl.

She reached the raft as they were pushing it out into the Rowen, meeting Gavilan's openly hostile gaze with one of her own, shifting deliberately closer to Garth. The Elven Hunters were already in water up to their knees, steadying the raft. Stresa hopped aboard without being asked and settled down squarely in the middle of the backpacks and supplies, just as he had threatened he would do. No one objected; no one said anything. Eowen and the queen were guided to their places by Triss, the queen clutching the Ruhk Staff tightly in both hands. Wren and Garth followed. Together, the members of the little company eased the raft away from the shoreline, leaning forward so that its logs could bear the weight of their upper bodies, their hands grasping the rope ties that had been fashioned to give them a grip.

Almost immediately the current caught them up and began to sweep them away. Those closest to the shore kicked in an effort to move clear of the banks, away from the rocks and tree roots that might snag them. Killeshan continued to erupt, fire and ash spewing forth, the volcano rumbling its discontent. The skies darkened with this new layer of vog, clouding farther against the light. The raft moved out into the center of the channel, rocking with the motion of the water, picking up speed. The Owl shouted instructions to his companions, and they tried in vain to maneuver the raft toward the far bank. Geysers burst through the lava rock on the shoreline behind them, rupturing the stone skin of the high country, sending steam and gas thrusting skyward. The Rowen shuddered with the force of the earth's rumblings and began to buck. The waters turned choppy and small whirlpools began to form. Debris swirled past, carried on the crest of the river. The raft was buffeted and tossed, and those clinging to it were forced to expend all of their efforts just to hang on.

"Tuck in your legs!" the Owl shouted in warning. "Tighten your grip!"

Downriver they swept, the shoreline passing in a blur of jagged trees and scrub, rugged lava fields, and mist and haze. The volcano disappeared behind them, screened away by a bend in the river and the beginnings of the valley into which it poured. Wren felt things jab and poke at her, slam up against her and spin away, and whip past as if yanked by an invisible rope. Her hands and fingers began to ache with the strain of holding on to the rope stays, and her body was chilled numb by the icy mountain waters. The river's rush drowned out the roar of the volcano, but she could still feel it shudder beneath her, waking up, recoiling with sickness, and splitting apart with convulsions. Cliffs appeared in front of them, rising like impassable walls. Then they were in their midst, the rock miraculously dividing to let the Rowen tumble through a narrow defile. For a few minutes the rapids were so severe that it seemed they must break apart on the rocks. Then they were clear again, the channel broadening out once more, the cliffs receding into the distance. They spun through a series of wide, sluggish riffs and emerged in a lake that stretched away into the green haze of a jungle.

The river slowed and quieted. The raft quit spinning and began to float lazily toward the center of the lake. Mist hung thick upon its gleaming surface, screening the shoreline to either side, transforming it into a deep green mask of silence. From somewhere distant, Killeshan's angry rumble sounded.

At the center of the raft, Stresa lifted his head tentatively and looked about. The Splinterscat's sharp eyes shifted quickly to find Wren. "Sssppptt! We must get away from here!" he urged. "This is not a good—ssspp—place to be! Over there is Eden's Murk!"

"What are you muttering about, Scat?" Gavilan growled irritably.

Ellenroh shifted her grip on the Ruhk Staff where it lay across the raft. "Owl, do you know where we are?"

Aurin Striate shook his head. "But if the Splinterscat says it is unsafe . . ."

The waters behind him erupted thunderously, and a huge, crusted black head reared into view. It rose into the brume slowly, almost languorously, balanced atop a thick, sinuous body of scales and bumps that rippled and flexed against the half-light. Tendrils trailed from its jaws like feelers twisting to find food. Teeth bared as its greenish mouth widened, crooked and double rowed. It coiled until it towered over them, no more than fifty feet away, and then it hissed like a snake that has been stepped upon.

"A serpent!" Eowen cried softly.

The Elven Hunters were already moving, hastily changing positions so that they were bunched between the monster and their charges. Weapons drawn, they began to scull the raft toward the opposite shore. It was a futile attempt. The serpent swam soundlessly in pursuit, expending almost no effort to overtake them, dipping its head threateningly, jaws agape. Wren worked next to Garth to help push the raft ahead, but the riverbank seemed a long way off. At the center of the raft, Stresa's spines stuck out in all directions, and his head disappeared.

The serpent hit them with its tail when they were still a hundred yards from shore, swinging it up into them from underneath, lifting the raft and the nine who clung to it clear of the water, spinning them into the air. They flew for a short distance and landed with a *whump* that knocked the breath from their bodies. Grips loosened, and people and packs tumbled away. Eowen splashed frantically, went under, and was pulled back to the surface by Garth. The raft had begun to come apart from the force of the landing, ties loosening, logs splitting. The Owl yelled at them to kick, and they did, frantically, furiously, for there was nothing else they could do.

The serpent came at them again, sliding out of the Rowen with a huffing that sprayed water everywhere. Its cry was a deep, booming cough as it launched itself, body flexing and coiling, huge and monstrous as it descended. Wren and Garth broke free of the raft as the beast struck, dragging Ellenroh and Faun with them. Wren saw Gavilan dive, watched the others scatter, and then the serpent struck and everything disappeared in an explosion of water. The raft flew apart, hammered into kindling. Wren went under, Faun clinging desperately to her. She resurfaced, sputtering for air. Heads bobbed in the water, waves generated by the attack washing over them. The serpent's head reared into the haze once more, but this time Triss and Cort had hold of it, swords stabbing and hacking furiously. Scales and dark blood flew, and the monster cried out in fury. Its body thrashed in an effort to shake loose its attackers, and then it dove. As it went under, Triss buried his sword in the scaly head and broke away. Cort was still attacking, his youthful face grimly set.

The serpent's body convulsed, scattering everyone. Stray logs from the shattered raft were sent spinning.

One flew at Wren and caught her a glancing blow along the side of her head. She had a momentary vision of the serpent diving, of Garth hauling Eowen toward the shore, and of Ellenroh and the Owl clinging to other stray bits of the raft, and then everything went black.

She drifted, unfeeling, unfettered, numb to her soul. She could tell that she was sinking, but she didn't seem to be able to do anything about it. She held her breath as the water closed over her, then exhaled when she could hold it no longer and felt the water rush in. She cried out soundlessly, her voice lost to her. She could feel the weight of the Elfstones about her neck; she could feel them begin to burn.

Then something caught hold of her and began to pull, something that fastened first on her tunic, then slipped down about her body. A hand first, then an arm—she was in the grip of another person. Slowly she began to ascend again.

She surfaced, sputtering and choking, struggling to breathe as she coughed out the water in her lungs. Her rescuer was behind her, pulling her to safety. She laid back weakly and did not resist, still stunned from the blow and the near drowning. She blinked away the water in her eyes and looked back across the Rowen. It spread away in a choppy silver sheen, empty now of everything but debris, the serpent disappeared. She could hear voices calling—Eowen's, the Owl's, and one or two more. She heard her own name called. Faun was no longer clinging to her. What had become of Faun?

Then the shore came into view on either side, and her rescuer ceased swimming and stood up, hauling her up as well and turning her about. She was face to face with Gavilan.

"Are you all right, Wren?" he asked breathlessly, worn from the strain of hauling her. "Look at me."

She did, and the anger she had felt toward him earlier faded when she saw the look on his face. Concern and a trace of fear were mirrored there, genuine and unforced.

She gripped his hand "It's okay. Everything's fine." She took a deep, welcome breath of air. "Thank you, Gavilan."

He looked surprisingly uncomfortable. "I said I was here to help you if you needed it, but I didn't expect you to take me up on my offer so soon."

He helped her from the water to where Ellenroh was waiting to fold her into her arms. She hugged Wren anxiously and whispered something barely audible, words that didn't need to be heard to be understood. Garth was there as well, and the Owl, drenched and sorry-looking, but unharmed. She saw most of their supplies stacked at the water's edge, soaked through but salvaged. Eowen sat disheveled and worn beneath a tree where Dal was looking after her.

"Faun!" she called, and immediately heard a chittering. She looked out across the Rowen and saw the Tree Squeak clinging to a bit of wood several dozen yards away. She charged back out into the water until she was almost up to her neck, and then her furry companion abandoned its float and swam quickly to reach her, scrambling up on her shoulder as she hauled it to shore. "There, there, little one, you're safe as well now, aren't you?"

A moment later Triss stumbled ashore, one side of his sun-browned face scraped raw, his clothing torn and bloodied. He sat long enough for the Owl to check him over, then rose to walk back down to the river with the others. Standing together, they looked out over the empty water.

There was no sign of either Cort or Stresa.

"I didn't see the Scat after the serpent struck the raft that last time," Gavilan said quietly, almost apologetically. "I'm sorry, Wren. I really am."

She nodded without answering, unable to speak, the pain too great. She stood rigid and expressionless as she continued to search futilely for the Splinterscat.

Twice now I've left him, she was thinking.

Triss reached down to tighten the stays on the sword he had picked up from the supplies they had salvaged. "Cort went down with the serpent. I don't think he was able to get free."

Wren barely heard him, her thoughts dark and brooding. *I should have looked for him when the raft sank. I should have tried to help.*

But she knew, even as she thought it, that there was nothing she could have done.

"We have to go on," the Owl said quietly. "We can't stay here."

As if to emphasize his words, Killeshan rumbled in the distance, and the haze swirled sluggishly in response. They hesitated a moment longer, bunched close at the riverbank, water dripping from their clothing, silent and unmoving. Then slowly, one after another, they turned away. After picking up the backpacks and supplies and checking to be certain that their weapons were in place, they stalked off into the trees.

Behind them, the Rowen stretched away like a silver-gray shroud.

CHAPTER

16

THE COMPANY HAD GONE less than a hundred yards from the Rowen's edge when the trees ended and the nightmare began. A huge swamp opened before them, a collection of bogs thick with sawgrass and weeds and laced through with sparse stretches of old-growth acacia and cedar whose branches had grown tight about one another in what appeared to be a last, desperate effort to keep from being pulled down into the mud. Many were already half fallen, their root systems eroded, their massive trunks bent over like stricken giants. Through the tangle of dying trees and stunted scrub, the swamp spread away as far as the eye could see, a vast and impenetrable mire shrouded in haze and silence.

The Owl brought them to an uncertain halt, and they stood staring doubtfully in all directions, searching for even the barest hint of a pathway. But there was nothing to be found. The swamp was a clouded, forbidding maze.

"Eden's Murk," the Owl said tonelessly.

The choices available to the company were limited. They could retrace their steps to the Rowen and follow the river upstream or down until a better route showed itself, or they could press on through the swamp. In either case, they would eventually have to scale the Blackledge because they had come too far downstream to regain the valley and the passes that would let them make an easy descent. There was not enough time left them to try going all the way back; the demons would be everywhere by now. The Owl worried that they might already be searching along the river. He advised pressing ahead. The journey would be treacherous, but the demons would not be so quick to look for them here. A day, two at the most, and they should reach the mountains.

After a brief discussion, the remainder of the company agreed. None of them, with the exception of Wren and Garth, had been outside the city in almost ten years—and the Rover girl and her protector had passed through the country only once and knew little of how to survive its dangers. The Owl had lived out there for years. No one was prepared to second-guess him.

They began the trek through Eden's Murk. The Owl led, followed by Triss, Ellenroh, Eowen, Gavilan, Wren, Garth, and Dal. They proceeded in single file, strung out behind Aurin Striate as he worked to find a line of solid footing through the mire. He was successful most of the time, for there were still stretches where the swamp hadn't closed over completely. But there were times as well when they were forced to step down into the oily water and mud, easing along patches of tall grass and scrub, clutching with their hands to keep from losing their footing, feeling the muck suck eagerly in an effort to draw them in. They traveled slowly, cautiously through the gloom, warned by the Owl to stay close to the person ahead, peering worriedly into the haze whenever the water bubbled and the mud belched.

Eden's Murk, despite the pall of silence that hung over it, was a haven for any number of living things. Most were never seen and only barely heard. Winged creatures flew like shadows through the brume, silent in their passage, swift and furtive. Insects buzzed annoyingly, some iridescent and as large as a child's hand. Things that might have been rats or shrews skittered about the remaining trees, climbing catlike from view an instant after they were spied. There were other creatures out there as well, some of them massive. They splashed and growled in the stillness, hidden by the gloom, hunters that prowled the deeper waters. No one ever saw them, but it was never for lack of keeping watch.

The day wore on, a slow, agonizing crawl toward darkness. The company stopped once to eat, huddled together on a trunk that was half drowned by the swamp, backs to one another as their eyes swept the screen of vog. The air turned hot and cold by turns, as if Eden's Murk had been built of separate chambers and there were invisible walls all about. The swamp water, like the air, could be chilly or tepid, deep in some spots and shallow in others, a mix of colors and smells, none of which were pleasant, all of which pulled and dragged at the life above. Now and again the earth would shudder, a reminder that somewhere behind them Killeshan continued to threaten, gases and heat building within its core, lava spurting from its mouth to run burning down the mountainside. Wren pictured it as she slogged along with the others—the air choked with vog, the land a carpet of fire, everything enveloped by gathering layers of steam and ash. Already the Keel would be gone. What of the demons? she wondered. Would they have fled as well, or were they too mindless to fear even the lava? If they had fled, where would they have gone?

But she knew the answer to that last question. There was only one place for any of them to go.

They will be driven from their siege back across the Rowen, Garth signed grimly when she asked for his opinion. They walked together momentarily across a rare stretch of earth where the swamp was still held more than an arm's length at bay. *They will start back toward the cliffs, just as we have done. If we are too slow, they will be all about us before we can get clear.*

Perhaps they won't come this far downriver, she suggested hopefully, fingers flicking out the signs. *They may keep to the valley because it is easier.*

Garth didn't bother to respond. He didn't have to. She knew as well as he did that if the demons kept to the valley in their descent of the Blackledge, they would reach the lower parts of the island quicker than the company and be waiting on the beaches.

She thought often of Stresa, trying to remember when she had last seen the Splinterscat after the serpent's attack, trying to recall something that would give her even the faintest hope that he had escaped. But she could think of nothing. One moment he had been there, crouched amid the baggage, and the next he was gone along with everything else. She grieved silently for him, unable to help herself, more attached to him than she should have been, than she should have allowed herself to become. She clutched Faun tightly and wondered at herself, feeling oddly drawn away from who and what she had once been, a stranger to everything, no longer so self-assured by her training, so confident in her skills, so certain that she was a Rover first and always and that nothing else mattered.

More often than she cared to admit, her fingers stole beneath her tunic to find the Elfstones. Eden's Murk was immense and implacable, and it threatened to erode her courage and her strength. The Elfstones reassured her; the Elven magic was power. She hated herself for feeling so, for needing to rely on them. A single day out of Arborlon, and already she had begun to despair. And she was not alone. She could see the uneasiness in all of their eyes, even Garth's. Morrowindl did something to you that transcended reason, that buried rational thought in a mountain of fear and doubt. It was in the air, in the earth, in the life about them, a kind of madness that whispered insidious warnings and stole life with casual disregard. She again tried to picture the island as it had once been and again failed to do so. She could not see past what it was, what it had become.

What the Elves and their magic had made it.

And she thought once more of the secrets they were hiding—Ellenroh, the Owl, Gavilan, all of them. Stresa had known. Stresa would have told her. Now it would have to be someone else.

She touched Eowen on the shoulder at one point and asked in a whisper, "Are you able to see anything of what is to happen to us? Do you have use of the sight?"

But the pale, emerald-eyed woman only smiled sadly and replied, "No, Wren, the sight is clouded by the magic that runs through the core of the island. Arborlon gave me shelter to see. Here there is only madness. Perhaps if I am able to get beyond the cliffs to where the sun's light and the sea's smell reach . . ." She trailed off.

Then darkness descended in a slow setting of gray veils, one after another, that gradually screened away the light. They had been walking since midmorning and still there was no sign of Blackledge, no hint of the swamp's end. The Owl began to look for a place where they could spend the night, cautioning them to be especially careful now as shadows dappled the land and played tricks with their eyes. The day's silence gradually gave way to a rising tide of night sounds, a mix rough-edged and sharp, rising out of the darker patches to echo through the gloom. Bits and pieces of foliage began to glow with a silver phosphorescence, and flying insects glimmered and faded as they skipped across the mire.

Aurin Striate's lank form knifed steadily ahead, bent against the encroaching dark. Wren saw Ellenroh slip past Triss momentarily, leaning forward to say something to the Owl. The company was crossing a stretch of weeds grown waist high, and the fading light glimmered dully off the surface of the swamp to their left.

Abruptly the water geysered as something huge surfaced to snare unsuspecting prey, jaws closing with a snap as it sank again from sight. Everyone jumped, and for an instant all were distracted. Wren saw the Owl turn halfway back, warning with his hands. She saw something else, something half hidden in the gloom ahead. There was a flicker of movement.

A second later, she heard a familiar hissing sound.

Garth couldn't have heard it, of course, yet something warned him of the danger, and he launched himself atop Wren and Eowen both and threw them to the ground. Behind them, Dal dropped instinctively. Ahead, the Owl wrapped himself about Ellenroh Elessedil, shoving her back into Triss and Gavilan. There was a ripping, thrusting sound as a hail of needles sliced through the grasses and leaves. Wren heard a surprised grunt. Then they were all flat upon the earth, deep in the grasses, breathing heavily in the sudden stillness.

A Darter!

The name scraped like rough bark on bare skin as she screamed it in her mind. She remembered how close one had come to killing her on the way in. Garth's arm loosened about her waist, and she signed quickly to him as the hard, bearded face pushed up next to her own.

Ahead, she heard her grandmother sob.

Frantic now, forgetting everything else, she scrambled forward through the tall grass, the others crawling hurriedly after her. She passed Gavilan, who was still trying to figure out what was going on, and caught up with Triss as the Captain of the Home Guard reached the queen.

Ellenroh was half lying, half bent over the Owl, cradling him in the crook of one arm as she wiped his sweating face. The Owl's scarecrow frame looked as if all the sticks had been removed and nothing remained but the clothing that draped them. His eyes were open and staring, and his mouth worked desperately to swallow.

Dozens of the Darter's poisonous needles stood out from his body. He had taken the full brunt of the plant's attack.

"Aurin," the queen whispered, and his eyes swung urgently to find her. "It's all right. We're all here."

Her own eyes lifted to meet Wren's, and they stared at each other in helpless disbelief.

"Owl." Wren spoke softly, her hand reaching out to touch his face.

Aurin Striate's breath quickened sharply. "I can't . . . feel a thing," he gasped.

Then his breathing stopped altogether, and he was dead.

WREN DIDN'T SLEEP at all that night. She wasn't sure any of them did, but she kept apart from the others so she had no real way of knowing. She sat alone with Faun curled in her lap at the base of a shaggy cedar, its trunk overgrown with moss and vines, and stared out into the swamp. They were less than a hundred yards from where the attack had occurred, huddled down against the vog and the night, encircled by the sounds of things they could not see, too devastated by what had happened to worry about going farther until morning.

She kept seeing the Owl's face as he lay dying.

It was just a fluke, she knew, just bad luck. It was nothing they could have foreseen and there was nothing they could have done to prevent it. She had come across only one other Darter until now, one other on the whole of Morrowindl she had traveled through. What were the chances that she should find another here? What were the odds that of all of them it should end up striking down Aurin Striate?

The improbability of it haunted her.

Would things have turned out differently if Stresa had been there watching out for them?

There was no solid ground in which to bury the Owl, nothing but marshland where the beasts that lived in Eden's Murk would dig him up for food, so they found a patch of quicksand and sank him to where he could never be touched.

They ate dinner then, what they could manage to eat, talking quietly about nothing, not even able to contemplate yet what losing the Owl meant. They ate, drank more than a little ale, and dispersed into the dark. The Elven Hunters set a watch, Triss until midnight, Dal until dawn, and the silence settled down.

Just a fluke, she repeated dismally.

She had so many fond memories of the Owl, even though she had known him only a short time, and she clung to them as a shield against her grief. The Owl had been kind to her. He had been honest, too—as honest as he could be without betraying the queen's trust. What he could share of himself, he did. He had told her that very morning that he had been able to survive outside of Arborlon's walls all these years because he had accepted the inevitability of his death and by doing so had made himself strong against his fear of it. It was a necessary way to be, he had told her. If you are always frightened for yourself you can't act, and then life loses its purpose. You just have to tell yourself that, when you get right down to it, you don't matter all that much.

But the Owl had mattered more than most. Alone with her thoughts, the others either asleep or pretending to be, she allowed herself to acknowledge exactly how much he had mattered. She remembered how Ellenroh had cried in her arms when Aurin Striate was gone, like a little girl again, unashamed of her grief, mourning someone who had been much more than a faithful retainer of the throne, more than a lifetime companion, and more than just a friend. She had not realized the depth of feeling that her grandmother bore for the Owl, and it made her cry in turn. Gavilan, for once, was at a complete loss for words, taking Ellenroh's hands and holding them without speaking, impulsively hugging Wren when she most needed it, doing nothing more than just being there. Garth and the Elven Hunters were stone faced, but their eyes reflected what lay behind their masks. They would all miss Aurin Striate.

How much they would miss him would become evident at first light, and its measure extended far beyond any emotional loss. For the Owl was the only one among them who knew anything about surviving the dangers of Morrowindl outside the walls of Arborlon. Without him, they had no one to serve as guide. They would have to rely on their own instincts and training if they were to save themselves and all those confined within the Loden. That meant finding a way to get free of Eden's Murk, descending the Blackledge, passing through the In Ju, and reaching the beaches in time to meet up with Tiger Ty. They would have to do all that without any of them knowing the way they should travel or the dangers they should watch out for.

The more Wren thought about it, the more impossible it seemed. Except for Garth and herself, none of the others had any real experience in wilderness survival—and this was strange country for the Rovers as well, a land they had passed through only once and then with help, a land filled with pitfalls and hazards they had never encountered before. How much help would any of them be to the others? What chance did they have without the Owl?

Her brooding left her hollow and bitter. So much depended on whether they lived or died, and now it was all threatened because of a fluke.

Garth slept closest to her, a dark shadow against the earth, as still as death in slumber. He puzzled her these days—had done so ever since they had arrived on Morrowindl. It wasn't something she could easily define, but it was there nevertheless. Garth, always enigmatic, had become increasingly remote, gradually withdrawing in his relationship with her—almost as if he felt that she didn't need him any more, that his tenure as teacher and hers as student were finished. It wasn't in any specific thing he had done or way he had behaved; it was more a general attitude, evinced in a pulling back of himself in little, unobtrusive ways. He was still there for her in all the ways that counted, protective as always, watching out and counseling. Yet at the same time he was moving away, giving her a space and a solitude she had never experienced before and found somewhat disconcerting. She was strong enough to be on her own, she knew; she had been so for several years now. It was simply that she hadn't thought that where Garth was concerned she would ever find a need to say good-bye.

Perhaps the loss of the Owl called attention to it more dramatically than would have otherwise been the case. She didn't know. It was hard to think clearly just now, and yet she knew she must. Emotions would only distract and confuse, and in the end they might even kill. Until they were clear of Morrowindl and safely back in the Westland, there could be little time wasted on longings and needs, on what-ifs and what-might-have-beens, or on what once was and could never be again.

She felt her throat tighten and the tears spring to her eyes. Even with Faun sleeping in her lap, Garth a whisper away, her grandmother found again, and her identity known, she felt impossibly alone.

Sometime after midnight, when Triss had given over the watch to Dal, Gavilan came to sit with her. He didn't speak, just wrapped the blanket he had carried over around her and positioned himself at her side. She felt the warmth of his body through the damp and the chill of the swamp night, and it gave her comfort. After a time, she leaned against him, needing to be touched. He took her in his arms then, cradled her to his chest, and held her until morning.

AT FIRST LIGHT, they resumed their trek through Eden's Murk. Garth led now, the most experienced survivalist among them. It was Wren who suggested that he lead and Ellenroh who quickly approved. No one was Garth's equal as a Tracker, and it would take a Tracker's skill to get them free of the swamp.

But even Garth could not unravel the mystery of Eden's Murk. Vog hung over everything, shutting out the sky, wrapping everything close about so that nothing was visible beyond a distance of fifty feet. The light was gray and weak, diffused by the mist, reflected by the dampness, and scattered so that it seemed to come from everywhere. There was nothing from which to take direction, not even the lichen and moss that grew in the swamp, which seemed clustered like fugitives against the coming of night, as confused and lost as those of the company who sought their aid. Garth set a course and stayed with it, but Wren could tell that the signs he needed were not to be found. They traveled without knowing what direction they were taking, without being able to chart their progress. Garth kept his thoughts to himself, but Wren could read the truth in his eyes.

Travel was steady, but slow, in part because the swamp was all but impassable and in part because Ellenroh Elessedil was ill. The queen had caught a fever during the night, and it had spread through her with such rapidity that she had gone from headaches and dizziness to chills and coughing in a matter of hours. By midday, when the company stopped for a quick meal, her strength was failing badly. She could still walk, but not without help. Triss and Dal shared the task of supporting her, arms wrapped securely about her waist to hold her up as they traveled. Eowen and Wren both checked her for injuries, thinking that perhaps she had been scratched by the spikes of the Darter and poisoned. But they found nothing. There was no ready explanation for the queen's sickness, and while they administered to her as best they could, neither had a clue as to what remedy might help.

"I feel foolish," she confided to Wren at one point, her wan features bathed in a sheen of sweat. They sat together on a log, eating a little of the cheese and bread that was their meal, wrapped in their great cloaks. "I was fine when I went to sleep, then woke sometime during the night feeling . . . odd." She laughed dryly. "I do not know any other way to describe it. I just didn't feel right."

"You will be better again after another night's sleep," Wren assured her. "We are all worn down."

But Ellenroh was beyond simple weariness, and her condition worsened as the day wore on. By nightfall, she had fallen so often that the Elven Hunters were simply carrying her. The company had spent the afternoon wallowing about in a chilly bottomland, a pocket of cold that had strayed somehow into the broad stretch of the swamp's volcanic heat and become trapped there, sending down roots into the mire, turning water and air to ice. Ellenroh, already on the verge of exhaustion, was weakened further. What little strength remained to her seemed to seep quickly away. When they stopped finally for the night, she was unconscious.

Wren watched Eowen bathe her crumpled face as Gavilan and the Elven Hunters set camp. Garth was at her elbow, his dark face impassive but his eyes clouded with doubt. When she met his gaze squarely, he gave a barely perceptible shake of his head. His fingers gestured. *I cannot read the signs. I cannot even find them.*

The admission was a bitter one. Garth was a proud man and he did not accept defeat easily. She looked into his eyes and touched him briefly in response. *You will find a way,* she signed.

They ate again, mostly because it was necessary, huddled together on a small patch of damp earth that was dryer than anything about it. Ellenroh slept, wrapped in two blankets, shaking with cold and fever, mumbling from time to time, and tossing within her dreams. Wren marveled at her grandmother's strength of will. Not once while she had struggled with her illness had she relaxed her hold on the Ruhk Staff. She clutched it to her still, as if she might with her own body protect the city and people the Loden's magic enclosed. Gavilan had offered more than once to relieve her of the task of carrying the staff, but she had steadfastly refused to give it up. It was a burden she had resolved to shoulder, and she would not be persuaded to lay it down. Wren thought of what it must have cost her grandmother to become so strong—the loss of her parents, her husband, her daughter, her friends—almost everyone close to her. Her whole life had been turned about with the coming of the demons and the walling away of the city of Arborlon. All that she remembered as a child of Morrowindl was gone. Nothing remained of the promise she must have once felt for the future save the possibility that the Elves and their city might, through her resolve and trust, be reborn into a better world.

A world of Federation oppression and Shadowen fear, a world in which, like Morrowindl, use of magic had somehow gone awry.

Wren's smile was slow, bitter, and ironic.

She was struck suddenly by the similarities between the two, the island and the mainland, Morrowindl and the Four Lands— different, yet afflicted with the same sort of madness. Both worlds were plagued with creatures that fed on destruction; both were beset with a sickness that turned the earth and the things that lived upon it foul. What was Morrowindl if not the Four Lands in an advanced state of decay? She wondered suddenly if the two were somehow connected, if the demons and the Shadowen might have some common origin. She wondered again at the secrets that the Elves were keeping from her of what had happened on Morrowindl years ago.

And again she asked herself, *What am I doing here? Why did Allanon send me to bring the Elves back into the Four Lands? What is it that they can do that will make a difference, and how will any of us ever discover what that something is?*

She finished eating and sat for a time with her grandmother, studying the other's face in the fading light, trying to find in the ravaged features some new trace of her mother, of the vision she had claimed from that now long-ago, distant dream when her mother had pleaded, *Remember me. Remember me.* Such a fragile thing, her memory, and it was all that she had of either parent, all that remained of her childhood. As she sat there with her grandmother's head cradled in her lap, she contemplated asking Garth to tell her something more of what had been, though she no longer had any real expectation that there was anything else to be told, knowing only that she was empty and alone and in need of something to cling to. But Garth stood watch, too far away to summon without disturbing the others and too distanced from her to be of any real comfort, and she turned instead to the familiar touch of the Elfstones within their leather pouch, running the tips of her fingers over their hard, smooth surfaces, rolling the Stones idly beneath the fabric of her tunic. They were her mother's legacy to her and her grandmother's trust, and despite her misgivings as to their purpose in her life she could not give them up. Not here, not now, not until she was free of the nightmare into which she had so willingly journeyed.

I chose this, she whispered to herself, the words bitter and harsh. *I came because I wanted to.*

To learn the truth, to discover who and what she was, to bring past and future together once and for all.

And what do I know of any of that? What do I understand?

Eowen came to sit next to her, and she realized how tired

she had grown. She gave her grandmother over to the red-haired seer and crept silently away to her own bed. Wrapped in her blankets, she lay staring out into the impenetrable night, the swamp a maze that would swallow them all and care nothing for what it had done, the world a blanket of indifference and deceit, of dangers as numerous as the shadows gathered about, and of sudden death and the taunting ghosts of what might have been. She found herself thinking of the years she had trained with Garth, of what he had taught her, of what she had learned. She would need all of it if she were to survive, she knew. She would need everything she could summon of strength, experience, training and resolve, and she would need more than a little luck.

And one thing more.

Her fingers brushed against the Elfstones once more and fell away as if burned. Their power was hers to summon and command whenever she chose. Twice now she had called upon them to save her. Both times she had done so either out of ignorance or desperation. But if she used them again, she sensed, if she employed them a third time now that she knew the magic was there and understood what wielding it meant, she risked giving up everything she was and becoming something else entirely. Nothing would ever be the same for her again, she cautioned herself. Nothing.

Yet, as she considered the failure of strength, experience, training, and resolve to come to her aid, as she lamented the apparent absence of any luck, it seemed that the power of the Stones was all that was left to her, the only resource that remained.

She turned her head into the blankets and fell asleep in a spider's web of doubt.

17

REN DREAMED, and her dreams were of Ohmsfords come and gone, a kaleidoscopic, fragmented rush of images that exploded out of memory. They careened into her like an avalanche and swept her away, tossed and tumbled in a slide that would not end. A spectator with no voice, she watched the history of her ancestors take shape in bits and flashes of time, saw events unfold that she had never seen but only heard described, the legends of the past carried forward in the words of the stories Par and Coll Ohmsford told.

Then she was awake, sitting bolt upright, startled from her sleep with a suddenness that was frightening. Faun, curled at her throat, skittered hurriedly away. She stared into blackness, listening to the sound of her heartbeat in her throat, to the rush of her breathing. All around her, the others of the little company slept, save whoever among them kept guard, a dim, faceless shape at the edge of their camp.

What was it? she thought wildly. *What was it that I saw?*

For something in her dreams had brought her awake, something so unnerving, so unexpected, that sleep was no longer possible.

What?

The memory, when it came, was shocking and abrupt. Her hand flew at once to the small leather bag tucked within her tunic.

The Elfstones!

In her dreams of Ohmsford ancestors, she had caught a singular glimpse of Shea and Flick, one brief image out of many, one story out of all those told about the search for the Sword of Shannara. In that image, the brothers were lost with Menion Leah in the lowlands of Clete at the start of their journey toward Culhaven. No amount of skill or woodlore seemed able to help them, and they might have died there if Shea, in desperation, had not discovered that he possessed the ability to invoke the power of the Elfstones given him by the Druid Allanon—the same Elfstones she carried now. In that image, dredged up by her dreams out of a storehouse of tales only barely remembered, she uncovered a truth she had forgotten—that the magic could do more than protect, it could also seek. It could show the holder a way out of the darkest maze; it could help the lost be found again.

She bit her lip hard against the sharp intake of breath that caught in her throat. She had known once, of course—all of them had, all of the Ohmsford children. Par had sung the story to her when she was little. But it had been so long ago.

The Elfstones.

She sat frozen within the covering of her blankets, stunned by her revelation. She had possessed the power all along to get them free of Eden's Murk. The Elfstones, if she chose to invoke the magic, would show the way clear. Had she truly forgotten? she wondered in disbelief. Or had she simply blocked the truth away, determined that she would not be made to rely on the magic, that she would not become subverted by its power?

And what would she do now?

For a moment she did nothing, so paralyzed with the fears and doubts that using the Elfstones raised that she could only sit there, clutching her blankets to her like a shield, voicing within her mind the choices with which she had suddenly been presented in an effort to make sense of them.

Then abruptly she was on her feet, the blankets and the fears and doubts cast aside as she made her way on cat's feet to where her grandmother lay sleeping. Ellenroh Elessedil's breathing was shallow and quick, and her hands and face were cold. Her hair curled damply about her face, and her skin was tight against her bones. She lay supine within blankets that swaddled her like a burial shroud.

She's dying, Wren realized in dismay.

The choices fell away instantly, and she knew what she must do. She crept to where Garth slept, hesitated, then moved on past Triss to where Gavilan lay.

She touched his shoulder lightly and his eyes flickered open. "Wake up," she whispered to him, trying to keep her voice from shaking. *Tell him first,* she was thinking, remembering his kindness of the previous night. *He will support you.* "Gavilan, wake up. We're getting out of here. Now."

"Wren, wait, what are you . . . ?" he began futilely for she was already hastening to rouse the others, anxious that there be no delays, so worried and distracted that she missed the fear that sprang demonlike into his eyes. "Wren!" he shouted, scrambling up, and everyone came awake instantly.

She stiffened, watching the others rise up guardedly—Triss and Eowen, Dal come back from keeping watch at the campsite's edge, and Garth, hulking against the shadows. The queen did not stir.

"What do you think you are doing?" Gavilan demanded heatedly. She felt his words like a slap. There was anger and accusation in them. "What do you mean we're getting out? Who gave you the right to decide what we do?"

The company closed about the two as they came face to face. Gavilan was flushed and his eyes were bright with suspicion, but Wren stood her ground, her look so determined that the other thought better of whatever it was he was about to say next.

"Look at her, Gavilan," Wren pleaded, seizing his arm, turning him towards Ellenroh. Why couldn't he understand? Why was he making this so difficult? "If we stay here any longer, we will lose her. We haven't a choice anymore. If we did, I would be the first to take advantage of it, I promise you."

There was a startled silence. Eowen turned to the queen, kneeling anxiously beside her. "Wren is right," she whispered. "The queen is very sick."

Wren kept her eyes fixed on Gavilan, trying to read his face, to make him understand. "We have to get her out of here."

Triss pushed forward hurriedly. "Do you know a way?" he asked, his lean features lined with worry.

"I do," Wren answered. She glanced quickly at the Captain of the Home Guard, then back again at Gavilan. "I don't have time to argue about this. I don't have time to explain. You have to trust me. You have to."

Gavilan remained stubbornly unconvinced. "You ask too much. What if you're wrong? If we move her and she dies . . ."

But Triss was already gathering up their gear, motioning Dal to help. "The choice has been made for us," he declared quietly. "The queen has no chance if we don't carry her from this swamp. Do what you can, Wren."

They collected what remained of their supplies and equipment, and built a hasty litter from blankets and poles on which they placed the queen. When they were finished, they turned expectantly to Wren. She faced them as if she were condemned, thinking that she had no choice in this matter, that she must forget her fears and doubts, her resolutions, the promises she had made herself regarding use of the magic and the Elfstones, and do what she could to save her grandmother's life.

She reached down into her tunic and pulled free the leather bag. A quick loosening of the drawstrings, and the Elfstones tumbled into her hand with a harsh, blue glitter.

Feeling small and vulnerable, she walked to the edge of the campsite and stood staring out for a moment into the shadows and mist. Faun tried to scramble up her leg, but she reached down gently and shooed the Tree Squeak away. Vog swirled everywhere, a vile stench of sulfur and ash clinging to its skirts. A mix of haze and steam rose off the swamp's fetid waters. She was at the edge of her life, she sensed, brought there by circumstance and fate, and whatever happened next, she would never be the same. She longed for what once had been, for what might have been, for an escape she could not hope to find.

Frightened that she might change her mind if she considered the matter longer, she held forth the Elfstones and willed them to life.

Nothing happened.

Oh, Shades!

She tried again, concentrating, letting herself form the words carefully in her mind, thinking each one in order, picturing the power that lay within stirring, rising up. She had the Elven blood, she thought desperately. She had summoned the power before . . .

And then abruptly the blue fire flared, exploding out of the Stones as if a stopper had been pulled. It coalesced about her hand, brilliant and stunning, brightening the swamp as if daylight had at last broken through into the mire. The members of the company reeled away, crouching guardedly, shielding their eyes. Wren stood erect, feeling the power of the Stones flow through her, searching, studying, and deciding if it belonged. A pleasant, seductive warmth enveloped her. Then the light shot away to her right, scything through the mist and haze and the dying trees and scrub and vines, shooting across the empty waters hundreds of yards, farther than the eye should have been able to see, to fix upon a rock wall that lifted away into the night.

Blackledge!

As quickly as it had come, the light was gone again, the power of the Elfstones dying, returned from whence it had come. Wren closed her fingers about the Stones, drained and exhilarated both at once, swept clean somehow by the magic, invigorated but left weak. Shaking in spite of her resolve, she slipped the talismans back into their pouch. The others straightened uncertainly, eyes shifting to find her own.

"There," she said quietly, pointing in the direction that the light had taken.

For an instant, no one spoke. Wren's mind was awash with what she had done, the magic's rush still fresh within her body, warring now with the guilt she felt for betraying her vow. But she had not had a choice, she reminded herself quickly; she had only done what was needed. She could not let her grandmother die. It was this one time only; it need not happen again. This once, because it was her grandmother's life and her grandmother was all she had left . . .

The words dissipated with Eowen's soft voice. "Hurry, Wren," she urged, "while there is still time."

They set off at once, Wren leading until Garth caught up to her and she motioned him ahead, content to let someone else take charge. Faun returned from the darkness, and she scooped the little creature up and placed it on her shoulder. Dal and Triss bore the litter with the queen, and she dropped back to walk beside it. She reached down and took her grandmother's hand in her own, held it for a moment, then squeezed it gently. There was no response. She laid the hand carefully back in place and walked ahead again. Eowen passed her, the white face looking lost and frightened in the shadows, the red hair flaring against the night. Eowen knew how sick Ellenroh was; had she foreseen what would happen to the queen in her visions? Wren shook her head, refusing to consider the possibility. She walked alone for a time until Gavilan slipped up beside her.

"I'm sorry, Wren," he said softly, the words coming with difficulty. "I should have known you would not act without reason. I should have had more trust in your judgment." He waited for her response, and when it did not come, said, "It is this swamp that clouds my thinking. I can't seem to focus as I should . . ." He trailed off.

She sighed soundlessly. "It's all right. No one can think clearly in this place." She was anxious to make excuses for him. "This island seems to breed madness. I caught a fever on the way in and for a time I was incoherent. Perhaps a touch of that fever has captured you as well."

He nodded distractedly, as if he hadn't heard. "At least you see the truth now. Magic has made Morrowindl and its demons, and magic is what will save us from them. Your Elfstones and the Ruhk Staff. You wait. You will understand soon enough."

And he dropped back again, his departure so abrupt that Wren was once again unable to ask the questions that his comments called to mind—questions of how the demons had been made, what it was the magic had done, and how things had come to such a state. She half turned to follow him, then decided to let him go. She was too tired for questions now, too worn to hear the answers even if he would give them—which he probably would not. Biting back her frustration, she forced herself to continue on.

It took them all night to get free of Eden's Murk. Twice more Wren was forced to call upon the power of the Elfstones. Torn each time by conflicting urges both to shun its flow and welcome it, she felt the magic boil through her like an elixir. The blue light seared the blackness and cut away the haze, showing them the path to Blackledge, and by dawn they had climbed free of the mire and stood at last upon solid ground once more. Before them, Blackledge lifted away into the haze, a towering mass of craggy stone jutting skyward out of the jungle. They chose a clearing at the base of the rocks and set the litter with Ellenroh carefully at its center. Eowen bathed the queen's face and hands and gave her water to drink.

Ellenroh stirred and her eyes flickered open. She studied the faces about her, glanced down to the Ruhk Staff still clutched between her fingers, and said, "Help me to sit up."

Eowen propped her forward gently and gave her the cup. Ellenroh drank it slowly, pausing frequently to breathe. Her chest rattled, and her face was flushed with fever.

"Wren," she said softly, "you have used the Elfstones."

Wren knelt beside her, wondering, and the others crowded close as well. "How did you know?"

Ellenroh Elessedil smiled. "It is in your eyes. The magic always leaves its mark. I should know."

"I would have used them sooner, Grandmother, but I forgot what it was that they could do. I'm sorry."

"Child, there is no need to apologize." The blue eyes were kind and warm. "I have loved you so much, Wren—even before you came to me, ever since I knew from Eowen that you had been born."

"You need to sleep, Ellenroh," the seer whispered.

The queen closed her eyes momentarily and shook her head."No, Eowen. I need to speak with you. All of you."

Her eyes opened, worn and distant. "I am dying," she whispered. "No, say nothing. Hear me out." She fixed them with her gaze. "I am sorry, Wren, that I cannot be with you longer. I wish that I could. We have had too short a time together. Eowen, this is hardest for you. You have been my friend all of my life, and I would stay to keep you well if I could. I know what my dying means. Gavilan, Triss, Dal—you did for me what you could. But my time is here. The fever is stronger than I am, and while I have tried to break free of it, I find I cannot. Aurin Striate waits for me, and I go to join him."

Wren was shaking her head deliberately, angrily. "No, Grandmother, don't say this, don't make it so!"

The soft hand found her own and gripped it. "We cannot hide from the truth, Wren. You, of all people, should know this. I am weakened to the bone. The fever has cut me apart inside, and there is almost nothing left holding me together. Even magic would not save me now, I'm afraid—and none of us possesses magic that would help in any case. Be strong, Wren. Remember what we share of flesh and blood. Remember how much alike we are—how much like Alleyne."

"Grandmother!" Wren was crying.

"A medicine," Gavilan whispered urgently. "There must be some medicine we can give you. Tell us!"

"Nothing." The queen's eyes seemed to drift from face to face and away again, seeking something that wasn't there. She coughed and stiffened momentarily. "Am I still your queen?" she asked.

They murmured yes, all of them, an uncertain reply. "Then I have one last command to give you. If you love me, if you care for the future of the Elven people, you will not question it. Say that you will obey."

They did, but furtive looks passed from one to the other, questioning what they were about to hear.

"Wren." Ellenroh waited until her granddaughter had moved to where she could see her clearly. "This is yours now. Take it."

She held out the Ruhk Staff and the Loden. Wren stared at her in disbelief, unable to move. "Take it!" the queen said, and this time Wren did as she was bidden. "Now, listen to me. I entrust the magic to your care, child. Take the Staff and its Stone from Morrowindl and carry them back into the Westland. Restore the Elves and their city. Give our people back their life. Do what you must to keep your promise to the Druid's shade, but remember as well your promise to me. See that the Elves are made whole. Give them a chance to begin again."

Wren could not speak, stunned by what was happening, struggling to accept what she was hearing. She felt the weight of the Ruhk Staff settle in her hands, the smoothness of its haft, cool and polished. *No*, she thought. *No, I don't want this!*

"Gavilan. Triss. Dal." The queen whispered their names, her voice breaking. "See that she is protected. Help her to succeed in what she has been given to do. Eowen, use your sight to ward her against the demons. Garth . . ."

She was about to speak to the big man, but trailed off suddenly, as if she had come upon something she could not face. Wren glanced back at her friend in confusion, but the dark face was chiseled in stone.

"Grandmother, I should not be the one to carry this." Wren started to object, but the other's hand gripped her sharply in reproof.

"You are the one, Wren. You have always been the one. Alleyne was my daughter and would have been queen after me, but circumstances forced us apart and took her from me. She left you to act in her place. Never forget who you are, child. You are an Elessedil. It was what you were born and what you were raised, whether you accept it or not. When I am dead, you shall be Queen of the Elves."

Wren was horrified. *This can't be happening,* she kept telling herself, over and over. *I am not what you think! I am a Rover girl and nothing more! This isn't right!*

But Ellenroh was speaking again, drawing her attention back once more. "Give yourself time, Wren. It will all come about as it should. For now, you need only concern yourself with keeping the Staff and its Stone safe. You need only find your way clear of this island before the end. The rest will take care of itself."

"No, Grandmother," Wren cried out urgently. "I will keep the Staff for you until you are well again. Just until then and not one moment more. You will not die. Grandmother, you can't!"

The queen took a long, slow breath. "Let me rest now, please. Lay me back, Eowen."

The seer did as she was asked, her green eyes frightened and lonely as they followed the queen's face down. For a moment they all remained motionless, staring silently at Ellenroh. Then Triss and Dal moved away to settle their gear and set watch, whispering as they went. Gavilan walked off muttering to himself, and Garth slipped from view as well. Wren was left staring at the Ruhk Staff, gripped now in her own hands.

"I don't think that I should . . ." she started to say and couldn't finish. Her eyes lifted to find Eowen's, but the red-haired seer turned away. Alone now with her grandmother, she reached out to touch the other's hand, feeling the heat of the fever burning through her. Her grandmother slept, unresponsive. *How could she be dying? How could such a thing could be so? It was impossible!* She felt the tears come again, thinking of how long it had taken to find her grandmother, the last of her family, how much she had gone through and how little time she had been given.

Don't die, she prayed silently. *Please.*

She felt a scratching against her legs and looked down to discover Faun, wide-eyed and skittish, peering up. She released Ellenroh's hand long enough to lift the little creature into her arms, ruffle its fur, and let it snuggle into her shoulder. The Ruhk Staff lay balanced on her lap like a line drawn in the gray light between herself and the sickened queen.

"Not me," she said softly to her grandmother. "It shouldn't be me."

She rose then, carrying both the Tree Squeak and the Staff up with her, and turned to find Garth. The big Rover was resting against a section of the cliff wall a dozen paces off. He straightened as she came up to him. The hard look she gave him made him blink.

"Tell me the truth now," she whispered, signing curtly. "What is there between you and my grandmother?"

His gaze was impassive. *Nothing.*

"But the way she looked at you, Garth—she wanted to say something and was afraid!"

You were a child given into my care by her daughter. She wanted to be certain I did not forget. That was what she thought to tell me. But she saw that it was not necessary.

Wren faced him unmoving a moment longer. Perhaps, she thought darkly. But there are secrets here . . .

Trust no one, the Addershag had warned.

But she couldn't do that. She couldn't be like that.

She broke off the confrontation and moved away, still

stunned at the whirlwind of events that had surrounded her, at the way in which she was being rushed along without having any control over what was happening. She glanced again at her grandmother, feeling torn at the prospect of losing her and at the same time angry at the responsibilities she had been asked to assume. Wren Ohmsford, Queen of the Elves? It was laughable. She didn't care who she was or what her family background might be, her whole life was defined by how she perceived herself, and she perceived herself as a Rover. She couldn't just wish all that away, forget all the years she had spent growing up, accept what had happened in these last few weeks as if it were a mandate she could not refuse. How could her grandmother say that she had been raised as an Elessedil? Why would the Elves want her as their queen in any case? She wasn't really one of them, her birthright notwithstanding.

Almost without thinking about it, she stalked over to where Gavilan sat back against a moss-grown stump and squatted down beside him.

"What am I to do about this?" she demanded almost angrily, thrusting the Ruhk Staff in his face.

He shrugged, his eyes distant and empty. "What you were asked to do, I expect."

"But this isn't mine! It doesn't belong to me! It shouldn't have been given to me in the first place!"

His voice was bitter. "I happen to agree. But what you and I want doesn't count for much, does it?"

"That isn't true. Ellenroh would never have done this if she weren't so sick. When she's better . . ." She stopped as he looked pointedly away. "When she's better," she continued, snapping off each word like a broken stick, "she will realize this is all a mistake."

His gaze was flat. "She's not going to get better."

"Don't say that, Gavilan. Don't."

"Would you rather I lied?"

Wren stared at him, unable to speak.

Gavilan's face was hard. "All right, then. I realize that you didn't plan for any of this to happen, that the Elves aren't your people, that none of this really has anything to do with you, and that all you wanted to do was to find Ellenroh and deliver your message. You don't want to be Queen of the Elves? Fair enough. You don't have to. Give the Staff to me."

There was a long, empty silence as they stared at each other.

"The Elessedil blood flows through my body as well," he pointed out heatedly. "These are my people, and Arborlon is my city. I can do what is needed. I have a better grasp of things than you. And I am not afraid to use the magic."

Suddenly Wren understood what was happening. Gavilan had expected to be given the Ruhk Staff; he had expected Ellenroh to name him as her successor. If Wren had not appeared, it probably would have happened that way. In fact, Wren's coming to Arborlon had changed everything for Gavilan. She felt a momentary pang of dismay, but it gave way almost instantly to wariness. She remembered how Gavilan and Ellenroh had quarreled about the Loden. Gavilan favored use of the magic to change things back to how they had once been, to set things right again. Ellenroh believed it was time to give the magic up, to return to the Westland and live as the Elves had once lived. That conflict surely must have influenced Ellenroh's decision to give the Staff to Wren.

Gavilan seemed to sense her uncertainty. "Think about it, Wren. If the queen dies, her burden need not be yours. If you had not returned, it never would have been." He folded his arms defensively. "In any case, it is up to you. If you wish it, I will help. I told you that when we first met, and the offer still stands. Whatever I can do."

She didn't know what to say. "Thank you, Gavilan," she managed.

She moved away from him then, feeling decidedly uneasy about what he had suggested. As much as she wanted to be free of the responsibility of the Staff, she was not at all sure she should give it over to him. The magic was a trust; it should not be relinquished too quickly, not when the consequences of its use were so enormous. Ellenroh could have given the Staff to Gavilan, but had chosen not to. Wren was not prepared to question the queen's judgment without thinking the matter through.

But she cared for Gavilan; she relied on his friendship and support. That complicated things. She understood his disappointment, and she knew that he was right when he said that the Elves were his people and Arborlon his city and that she was an outsider. She believed that Gavilan wanted what was best as much as she did.

A harsh, desperate determination took root inside her. *None of this matters, because Grandmother will recover, because she must recover, she will not die, she will not!* The words were a litany in her mind, repeating over and over. Her breathing was ragged and angry, and her hands were shaking.

She shook her head and fought back her tears.

Finally she sat down again next to her grandmother. Numb with grief, she stared down at the ravaged face. *Please, get well. You must get well.*

Weariness stole over her like a thief and left her drained.

THEY REMAINED CAMPED at the cliff wall all that day, letting Ellenroh sleep, hoping that her strength would return. While Wren and Eowen took turns caring for the queen, the men kept watch. Time slipped away, and Wren watched it escape with a quickness that was frightening. They had been gone from Arborlon for three days now, but it seemed like weeks. All about them, the world of Morrowindl was gray and hazy, a bleak landscape of shadows and half-light. Beneath, the earth rumbled with Killeshan's discontent. How much time remained to them? How much before the volcano exploded and the island broke apart? How much before the demons found them? How much before Tiger Ty and Spirit decided that there was no point in searching any longer, that they were irretrievably lost?

She bathed Ellenroh's face and whispered and sang to her, trying to dispel the fever, searching for some small sign that her grandmother was mending and the sickness would pass. She stayed clear of the others, save for Eowen, and even when she was close to the seer she spoke little. Her mind was restless, however, and filled with misgivings to which she could not give voice. The Ruhk Staff was a constant reminder of how much was at stake. Thoughts of the Elves plagued her; she could see their faces, hear their voices, and imagine what they must be thinking, more trapped than she was, more powerless. It terrified her to be so inextricably tied to them. She could not shake the feeling that she was all they had, that they must rely on her alone and no one else in the company mattered. Their lives were her charge, and while she might wish it otherwise, the fact of it could not be easily changed.

Night fell, and Ellenroh's condition grew worse.

Wren sat alone at one point and cried without being able to stop, hollow with losses that suddenly seemed to press about her at every turn. Once she would have told herself that none of it mattered—that the absence of parents and family, of a history, of a life beyond the one she lived was of no consequence. Coming to Morrowindl and finding Arborlon and the Elves had changed that forever. What had once seemed of so little importance had inexplicably become everything. Even if she survived, she would never be the same. The realization of what had been done to her left her stunned. She had never felt more alone.

She slept then for a time, too exhausted to stay awake longer, her emotions gone distant and numb, and woke again with Garth's hand on her shoulder. She rose instantly, frightened by what he might have come to tell her, but he quickly shook his head. Saying nothing, he simply pointed.

From no more than six feet away, a bulky, spiked form stood staring at her with eyes that gleamed like a cat's. Faun was dancing about in front of it, chittering wildly.

Wren stared. "Stresa?" she whispered in disbelief. She scrambled up hurriedly, throwing her blanket aside, her voice shaking. "Stresa, is that really you?"

"Come back from the dead, rwwlll Wren of the Elves," the other growled softly.

Wren would have thrown her arms about the Splinterscat if she could have managed to find a way, but settled instead for a quick gasp of relief and laughter. "You're alive! I can't believe it!" She clapped her hands and hugged herself. "Oh, I am so glad to see you! I was certain you were gone! What happened to you? How did you escape?"

The Splinterscat moved forward several paces and seated himself, ignoring Faun, who continued to dart about excitedly. "The—ssppht—serpent barely missed me when it destroyed the raft. I was dragged beneath the surface and towed by the current all the way back—hsstttt—across the Rowen. Phhhffft. It took me several hours to find another crossing. By then, you had gone into Eden's Murk."

Faun skittered too close, and the spines rose threateningly. "Foolish Squeak. Hsssttt!"

"How did you find us?" Wren pressed. Garth was seated next to her now, and she signed her words as she spoke.

"Ha! Ssspptt! Not easily, I can tell you. I tracked you, of course—hssssstt—but you have wandered in every direction since you entered. Lost your way, I gather. I wonder that you managed to find the cliffs at all."

She took a deep breath. "I used the magic."

The Splinterscat hissed softly.

"I had to. The queen is very sick."

"Sssttt. And so the Ruhk Staff is yours now?"

She shook her head hurriedly. "Just until Ellenroh is better. Just until then."

Stresa said nothing, yellow eyes agleam.

"I'm glad that you're back," she repeated.

He yawned disinterestedly. "Phhfft. Enough talk for tonight. Time to get some rrwwoll rest."

He made a leisurely turn and ambled off to find a place to sleep, looking for all the world as if nothing unusual had happened, as if tonight were just like any other night. Wren stared after him for a moment, then exchanged a long look with Garth. The big Rover shook his head and moved away.

Wren pulled the blanket back around her shoulders and cradled Faun in her arms. After a moment, she realized that she was smiling.

18

LLENROH ELESSEDIL DIED at dawn. Wren was with her when she woke for the last time. The darkness was just beginning to lighten, a pale violet tinge within the mist, and the queen's eyes opened. She stared up at Wren, her gaze calm and steady, seeing something beyond her granddaughter's anxious face. Wren took her hand at once, holding it with fierce determination, and for just an instant there appeared the faintest of smiles. Then she breathed once, closed her eyes, and was gone.

Wren found it odd when she could not cry. It seemed as if she had no tears left, as if they had been used up in being afraid that the impossible might happen, and now that it had she had nothing left to give. Drained of emotion, she was yet left feeling curiously unprotected in her sense of loss, and because she had no one she wanted to turn to and nowhere else to flee she took refuge within the armor of responsibility her grandmother had given her for the fate of the Elves.

It was well that she did. It appeared no one else knew what to do. Eowen was inconsolable, a crumpled, frail figure as she huddled next to the woman who had been her closest friend. Red hair fallen down about her face and shoulders, body shaking, she could not manage even to speak. Triss and Dal stood by helplessly, stunned. Even Gavilan could not seem to summon the strength to take charge as he might have before, his handsome face stricken as he stared down at the queen's body. Too much had happened to destroy their confidence in themselves, to shatter any belief that they could carry out their charge to save the Elven people. Aurin Striate and the queen were both gone—the two they could least afford to lose. Trapped within the bottomland of Eden's Murk on the wrong side of Blackledge, they were consumed with a growing premonition of disaster that was in danger of becoming self-fulfilling.

But Wren found within herself that morning a strength she had not believed she possessed. Something of who and what she had once been, of the Rover girl she had been raised, of the Elessedil and Shannara blood to which she had been born, caught fire within her and willed that she should not despair.

She rose from the queen and stood facing them, the Ruhk Staff gripped in both hands, placed in front of her like a standard, a reminder of what bound them.

"She's gone," Wren said quietly, drawing their eyes, meeting them with her own. "We must leave her now. We must go on because that is what we have sworn we would do and that is what she would want. We have been asked to do something that grows increasingly difficult, something we all wish we had not been asked to do, but there is no point in questioning our commitment now. We are pledged to it. I don't presume to think I can be the woman my grandmother was, but I shall try my best. This Staff belongs in another world, and we are going to do everything we can to carry it there."

She stepped away from the queen. "I only knew my grandmother a short time, but I loved her the way I would have loved my mother had I been given the chance to know her. She was all I had of family. She was the best she could be for all of us. She deserves to live on through us. I do not intend to fail her. Will you help me?"

"Lady, you need not ask that," Triss answered at once. "She has given the Ruhk Staff to you, and while you live the Home Guard are sworn to protect and obey you."

Wren nodded. "Thank you, Triss. And you, Gavilan?"

The blue eyes lowered. "You command, Wren."

She glanced at Eowen, who simply nodded, still lost within her grief.

"Carry the queen back into the Eden's Murk," Wren directed Triss and Dal. "Find a sinkhole and give her back to the island so that she can rest." The words fought their way clear, harsh and biting. "Take her."

They bore the Queen of the Elves into the swamp, found a stretch of mire a hundred feet in, and eased her down. She disappeared swiftly, gone forever.

In silence, they retraced their steps. Eowen was crying softly, leaning on Wren's arm for support. The men were voiceless wraiths turned silver and gray by the shadows and mist.

When they reached the base of Blackledge, Wren faced them once again. "This is what I think. We have lost a third of our number and have barely gotten clear of Killeshan's slopes. Time slips away. If we don't move quickly, we won't get off the island, any of us. Garth and I know something of wilderness survival, but we are almost as lost as the rest of you here on Morrowindl. There is only one of us remaining who stands a chance of finding the way."

She turned to look at Stresa. The Splinterscat blinked.

"You brought us safely in," she said quietly. "Can you take us out again?"

Stresa stared at her for a long moment, his gaze curious. "Hrrwlll, Wren of the Elves, bearer of the Ruhk Staff, I will take a chance with you, though I have no particular reason to help the Elves. But you have promised me passage to the larger world, and I hold you to your promise. Yes, I will guide you."

"Do you know the way, Scat," Gavilan asked warily, "or do you simply toy with us?"

Wren gave him a sharp glance, but Stresa simply said, "Stttsst. Come along and find out, why don't you?" Then he turned to Wren. "This is not country through which I have traveled often. Here the Blackledge is impassable. Hssstt. We will need to—rrwwlll—travel south for a distance to find a pass through which to climb. Come."

They gathered what remained of their gear, shouldered it determinedly, and set out. They walked through the morning gloom, into the heat and the vog, following the line of the cliffs along the boundary of Eden's Murk. At noon they stopped to rest and eat, a gathering of hard-faced, silent men and women, their furtive, uneasy eyes scanning the mire ceaselessly. The earth was silent today, the volcano momentarily at rest. But from within the swamp there was the sound of things at hunt, distant cries and howls, the splashing of water, the grunting of bodies locked in combat. The sounds followed after them as they trudged on, an ominous warning that a net was being gathered in about them.

By midafternoon, they had found the pass that Stresa favored, a steep, winding trail that disappeared into the rocks like a serpent's tongue into its maw. They began their ascent quickly, anxious to put distance between themselves and the sounds trailing after, hopeful that the summit could be reached before nightfall.

It was not. Darkness caught them somewhere in midclimb, and Stresa settled them quickly on a narrow ledge partially in the shelter of an overhang, a perch that would have looked out over a broad expanse of Eden's Murk had it not been for the vog, which covered everything in a seemingly endless shroud of dingy gray.

Dinner was consumed quickly and without interest, a watch was set, and the remainder of the company prepared to settle in for the night. The combination of darkness and mist was so complete that nothing was visible beyond a few feet, giving the unpleasant impression that the entire island had somehow fallen away beneath them, leaving them suspended in air. Sounds rose out of the haze, guttural and menacing, a cacophony that was both disembodied and directionless. They listened to it in silence, feeling it track them, feeling it tighten about.

Wren tried to think of other things, wrapping her blanket close, chilled in spite of the heat given off by the swamp. But her thoughts were disjointed, scattered by a growing sense of detachment from everything that was real. She had been stripped of the certainty of who and what she was and left with only a vague impression of what she might be—and that a thing beyond her understanding and control. Her life had been wrenched from its certain track and settled on an empty plain, there to be blown where it would like a leaf in the wind. She had been given trusts by the shade of Allanon and by her grandmother, and she knew not enough of either to understand how they were to be carried out. She recalled why it was that she had accepted Cogline's challenge to go to the Hadeshorn in the first place, all those weeks ago. By going, she had believed, she might learn something of herself; she might discover the truth. How strange that belief seemed now. Who she was and what she was supposed to do seemed to change as rapidly as day into night. The truth was an elusive bit of cloth that would not be contained, that refused to be revealed. It fluttered away at each approach she made, ragged and worn, a shimmer of color and light. Still, she was determined that she would follow the threads left hanging in its wake, thin remnants of brightness that would one day lead to the tapestry from which they had come unraveled.

Find the Elves and bring them back into the world of Men.

She would try.

Save my people and give them a new chance at life.

Again, she would try.

And in trying, perhaps she would find a way to survive.

She dozed for a time, her back against the cliff wall, legs drawn up to her chest and arms wrapped guardedly about the polished length of the Ruhk Staff. Faun was asleep at her feet in the blanket's folds. Stresa was a featureless ball curled up within the shadows of a rocky niche. She was aware of movement about her as the watch changed; she even considered asking to take a turn, but let the thought pass. She had slept little in two nights and needed to regain her strength. There was time enough to take the watch another night. She rested her cheek against her knees and lost herself in the darkness behind her eyes.

Later that night, she was never sure when, she was roused by the rough scrape of a boot on rock as someone approached. She lifted her head slightly, peering out from the shelter of the blanket. The night was black and thick with vog, the haze creeping down the mountainside and settling onto the ledge like a snake at hunt. A figure appeared out of the gloom, crouched low, movements quick and furtive.

Wren's hand slowly reached for the handle of her knife.

"Wren," the figure said quietly, calling her name.

It was Eowen. Wren lifted her head in recognition and watched the other creep forward and settle down before her. Eowen was wrapped in her hooded cloak, her red hair wild and tossed, her face flushed, and her eyes wide and staring as if she had just witnessed something terrifying. Her mouth tightened as she started to speak, and then she began to cry. Wren reached out to her and pulled her close, surprised at the other's vulnerability, a softening of strength that until the queen's death had never once been in evidence.

Eowen stiffened, brushed at her eyes, and breathed deeply of the night air in an effort to compose herself. "I cannot seem to stop," she whispered. "Every time I think of her, every time I remember, I start to grieve anew."

"She loved you very much," Wren told her, trying to lend some comfort, remembering her own love as she did so.

The seer nodded, lowered her eyes momentarily, and then looked up again. "I have come to tell you the truth about the Elves, Wren."

Wren stayed perfectly still, saying nothing, waiting. She felt a cold, fathomless pit open within.

Eowen glanced back at the misty night, at the nothingness that surrounded them, and sighed. "I had a vision once, long ago now, in which I saw myself with Ellenroh. She was alive and vibrant, all aglow against a pale background that looked like dusk in winter. I was her shadow, attached to her, bound to her. Whatever she did, I did as well—moved as she did, spoke when she spoke, felt her happiness and her pain. We were joined as one. But then she began to fade, to disappear, her color to wash, her lines to blur. She disappeared—yet I remained, a shadow still, alone now, in search of a body to which I might attach myself. Then you appeared—I didn't know you then, but I knew who you were, Alleyne's daughter, Ellenroh's grandchild. You faced me, and I approached. As I did, the air about me went dark and forbidding. A mist fell across my eyes, and I could see only red, a brilliant scarlet haze. I was cold to the bone, and there was no life left within me."

She shook her head slowly. "The vision ended then, but I took its meaning. The queen would die, and when she did I would die as well. You would be there to witness it—perhaps to partake in it."

"Eowen." Wren breathed the seer's name softly, appalled.

The seer turned back quickly and the green eyes clouded. "I am not frightened, Wren. A seer's visions are both gift and curse, but always the rule of her life. I have learned neither to fear nor deny what I am shown, only to accept. I accept now that my time in this world is almost gone, and I would not die without telling you the truth that you are so desperate to know."

She hugged the cloak to her shoulders. "The queen could not do so, you know. She could not bring herself to speak. She wanted to. Perhaps in time she would have. But it was the horror of her life that the magic of the Elves had done so much harm and caused so much hurt. I was loyal to Ellenroh in life, but I am released now by her death—in this at least. You must know, Wren. You must know and judge as you will, for you are indeed your mother's daughter and meant to be Queen of the Elves. The Elessedil blood marks you plainly, and while you question still that such a thing could be so, be certain that it is. I have seen it in my visions. You are the hope of all of the Elves, now and in the future. You have come to save them, if they are fated to be saved. Seeing that you accept the trust of the Ruhk Staff and the Loden, knowing that the Elfstones will protect you, I find that all that remains left undone is the telling of that which has been hidden from you—the secret of the rebirth of the Elven magic and of the poisoning of Morrowindl."

Wren shook her head quickly. "Eowen, I have not yet decided about the trust . . ." she began.

"Decisions are made for us for the most part, Wren Elessedil." Eowen cut her short. "I understand that better than you. I understood it better than the queen, I think. She was a good person, Wren. She did the best she could, and you must not blame her in any way for what I will tell you. You must reflect on what I say; if you do so, you will see that Ellenroh was trapped from the beginning and all of the decisions it might seem she made of her own will were in fact made for her. If she kept the truth secret from you, it was because she loved you too well. She could not bear to think of losing you. You were all she had left."

The pale face reflected like a ghost's in the haze, the voice gone back again to a whisper.

"Yes, Eowen," Wren replied softly. "And she was all I had."

The seer's slender hands reached out to take her own, the skin as cold as ice. Wren shivered in spite of herself. "Then heed what I say, daughter of Alleyne, Elf-kind found. Heed carefully."

Emerald eyes glittered like frosted leaves at sunrise. "When the Elves first came to Morrowindl, the island was innocent and unspoiled. It was a paradise beyond anything they could have imagined, all clean and new and safe. The Elves remembered what they had left behind—a world already beginning to spoil, sickening where the Shadowen had crawled to birth and feed, buckling under the weight of Federation oppression and the advance of armies that knew only to obey and never to question. It was an old story, Wren, and the Elves had endured it for countless generations. They wanted no more of it; they wanted it to be gone.

"So they began to scheme of how they might keep their newfound world and themselves protected. The Federation might one day choose to extend itself even beyond the boundaries of the Four Lands. The Shadowen surely would. Only magic could protect them, they felt, and the magic they relied upon now came not out of Druid lore or new world teachings but out of the rediscovered power of their beginnings. Such magic was vast and wild, still in its infancy for this generation, and they forgot the lessons of the Druids, of the Warlock Lord and his Skull Bearers, and of all those who had fallen victim before. They would not succumb, they must have told themselves. They would be smarter, more careful, and more deft in their use."

She took another deep breath, and her hands released Wren's to brush back the tangle of her hair. "Some among them had . . . experience in making things with the magic. Living creatures, Wren—new species that could serve their needs. They had found a way to extract the essence of nature's creatures and with use of the magic could nurture it so that as it grew it became a variation of the thing on which it had been modeled. They could make dogs from dogs and cats from cats, only bigger, stronger, quicker, smarter. But that was only the beginning. They quickly progressed to combining life forms, creating animals that evidenced the most desirable traits of both. That was how the Splinterscats came to be—and dozens of other species.

They were the first experiments of the magic's new use, beasts that could think and speak as well as humans, beasts that could forage and hunt and stand guard against any enemy while the Elves remained safe.

"It was all right in the beginning, it seemed. The creatures flourished and served as they were intended to do, and all was well. But as time passed, some among the wielders began to advance new ideas for use of the magic. They had been successful once, the argument went. Why not again? If animals could be formed of the magic, why not something even more advanced? Why not duplicate themselves? Why not build an army of men that would fight in their place in the event of an attack while they remained safe behind the walls of Arborlon?"

Eowen shook her head slowly, delicate features twisting at some inner horror. "They made the demons then—or the things that would become the demons. They took parts of themselves, flesh and blood to begin with, but then memories and emotions and all the invisible pieces of their spirits, and they gave them life. These new Elves—for they were Elves, then—were made to be soldiers and hunters and guardians of the realm, and they knew nothing else and had no need or desire but to serve. They seemed ideal. Those who made them sent them forth to establish watch on the coasts of the island. They were self-sufficient; there was no need to feel concern for them."

Her voice dropped to a whisper. "For a time, they were almost forgotten, I am told—as if they were of no further consequence."

Again she reached for Wren's hands, clasping them tight. "Then the changes began. Little by little, the new Elves started to alter, their appearance and personality to change. It happened away from the city and out of the sight and mind of the people, and so there was no one to stop it or to warn against it. Some of the first creatures created by the magic, like the Splinterscats, came to the Elves and told what was happening, but they were ignored. They were just animals after all, despite their abilities, and their cautions were dismissed.

"The new Elves, already changing to demons, began to stray from their posts, to disappear into the jungles, to hunt and kill everything they came across. The Splinterscats and the others were the first victims. The Elves of Arborlon were next. Efforts were made to put an end to these monsters, but the efforts were scattered and misdirected, and the Elves still did not accept that the trouble lay not with just a few but with all of their creations. By the time they realized how badly they had misjudged the magic's effect, the situation was out of control.

"By then, Ellenroh was Queen. Her father had infused the Keel with the magic of the Loden to provide a shield behind which the Elves could hide, and in truth they seemed safe enough. But Ellenroh wasn't so sure. Determined to put an end to the demons, she took her Elven Hunters into the jungles to search them out. But the magic had worked too well in its specific intent, and the demons were too strong. Time and again, they threw the Elves back. The war went on for years, a terrible, endless struggle for supremacy of the island that ravaged Morrowindl and made living on her soil a nightmare beyond reason."

The hands tightened, hard and unyielding. "Finally, all other choices stripped from Ellenroh by the magic's intractability and the demons' savagery, she called the last of the Elves into the city. That was ten years ago. It marked the end of any contact with the outside world."

"But why couldn't the same magic that made these creatures be used to eliminate them?" Wren demanded.

"Oh, Wren, it was far too late for that." Eowen rocked as if comforting a child. "The magic was gone!" Her eyes had a distant, ravaged look. "All magic has a source. It is no different with Elven magic. Most of it comes from the earth, a weaving together of the life that resides there. The island was the source of the magic used to create the demons and the others before them—its earth, air, and water, the elements of its life. But magic is precious and not without its limits. Time replenishes what is used, but slowly. What the Elves did not realize was that the demons, as they changed, began to have need of the magic themselves. Created from it, they now discovered they required it in order to survive. They began to systematically siphon it from the earth and the things that lived upon it, killing whatever they fed upon. They devoured it faster than it could regenerate. The island began to change, to wither, to sicken and die. It was as if it could no longer protect itself from the creatures that ravaged it, demon and Elf alike. By the time the Elves recognized the truth, not enough magic remained to make a difference. The demons had grown too numerous to be destroyed. Everything beyond the city was abandoned to them. Morrowindl survived, if barely, but it had been subverted, changed so that it was either wasteland or carnivorous jungle, so that almost everything that lived upon it killed as swiftly and surely as the demons. Nature was no longer in balance. Killeshan came awake and boiled within its cauldron. And finally the island's magic began to dry up altogether, and that compelled the demons to lay siege to Arborlon. The scent of the Keel's magic was irresistible. It drew them as a magnet would iron, and they became determined to feed on it."

Wren paled. "And now they will come for us as well, won't they? We have the Keel's magic, all of the magic of Arborlon and the Elves, stored within the Loden, and they will seek it out."

"Yes, Wren. They must." Eowen's voice was a hiss. "But that is not the worst of what I have to tell you. There is more. Listen to me. It is bad enough that the Elves made the monsters that would destroy them, that they subverted Morrowindl beyond any possible salvation, that perhaps they have destroyed themselves as a people. Ellenroh could scarcely bear to think of it, of the part she played in stealing away the island's magic, or of her own failure to set things right again. But what devastated her was knowing why the Elves had come to Morrowindl in the first place. Yes, it was to escape the Federation and the Shadowen and all that they represented, to isolate themselves from the madness, to begin again in a new world. But, Wren, it was the Elves who ruined the old!"

Wren stared, disbelieving. "The Elves? How could that be? What are you saying, Eowen?"

The hands released her own and clasped together with white-knuckle determination, as if nothing less could persuade the red-haired seer to continue. "After the demons had claimed virtually all of Morrowindl, after it was clear that the island was lost and the Elven people had been made prisoners of their own folly, the queen had ferreted out and brought before her those who still sought to play with the power, foolish men and women who could not seem to learn from their mistakes, who persisted in thinking the magic could be mastered. Among them were those who had created the demons. She had them thrown from the walls of the city. She did so not because of what they had done but because of what they were attempting to do. They were attempting to use the magic in another way, a way that had been employed almost three hundred years earlier in the days following the death of Allanon and the disappearance of the Druids from the Four Lands."

She took a deep breath. "Not all of those who sought to reclaim the old ways went with us to Morrowindl. Not all of those who were Elves came out of the Four Lands. A handful of the magic-wielders remained behind, disowned by their people, cast out by the Elessedil rulers." Her voice lowered until it was almost inaudible. "That handful, Wren, created monsters of another sort."

There was a long, terrible silence as the seer and the Rover girl faced each other in the gloom. The cold in Wren's stomach began to snake into her limbs. "Shades!" she whispered in horror, realizing the truth now, a truth that had been hidden all this time from those summoned to the Hadeshorn by the shade of Allanon. "You're saying that the Elves made the Shadowen!"

"No, Wren." Eowen's voice choked as she struggled to finish. "The Elves didn't *make* the Shadowen. The Elves *are* the Shadowen."

Wren's breath caught in her throat, a knot that threatened to strangle her. She remembered the Shadowen at the Wing Hove, the one that had stalked her for so long, the one that in the end would have killed her if not for the Elfstones. She tried to picture it as an Elf and failed.

"Elves, Wren." Eowen's husky voice drew her attention back again. "My people. Ellenroh's. Your own. Just a few, you understand, but Elves still. There are others now, I expect, but in the beginning it was only Elves. They sought to be something better, I think, something more. But it all went wrong, and they became . . . what they are. Even then, they refused to change, to seek help. Ellenroh knew. All of the Elves knew, once upon a time at least. It was why they left, why they abandoned their homeland and fled. They were terrified of what their brethren

had done. They were appalled that the magic had been so misused. For it was an inaccurate and changeable magic at best, and
what they created was not always what they desired."

She smiled bitterly. "Do you see now why the queen could
not reveal to you the truth of things? Do you understand the
burden she carried? She was an Elessedil, and her forefathers
had allowed this to happen! She had aided in the misuse of the
magic herself, albeit because it was all she could do if she wished
to save her people. She couldn't tell you. I can barely stand doing
it myself! I wonder even now if I have made a mistake . . ."

"Eowen!" Wren seized the other's hands and would not let
go. "You were right to tell me. Grandmother should have done
so in the beginning. It is a terrible, awful thing, but . . ."

She trailed off helplessly, and her eyes locked on the seer's.
Trust no one, the Addershag had warned. Now she understood
why. The secrets of three hundred years lay scattered at her
feet, and only death's presence had given them away.

Eowen started up, freeing her hands. "I have given you
enough of truth this night," she whispered. "I wish it could have
been otherwise."

"No, Eowen . . ."

"Be kind, Wren Elessedil. Forgive the queen. And me. And
the Elves, if you can. Remember the importance of the trust
you have been given. Carry the Loden back into the Four Lands.
Let the Elves begin anew. Let them help set matters right again."

She turned, ignoring Wren's hushed plea to stay, and disappeared from view.

WREN SAT AWAKE after that until dawn, watching the mist swirl
against the void, staring out into the impenetrable night. She
listened to the movements of those on watch, to the breathing
of those who slept, to the empty whisper of her thoughts as
they wrestled with the truth that Eowen had left her.

The Shadowen are Elves.

The words repeated themselves, a whispered warning. She
was the only one who knew, the only one who could warn the
others. But she had to get off Morrowindl first. She had to
survive.

The night seemed to close about her. She had wanted the truth. Now she had it. It was a bitter, wrenching triumph, and the cost of attaining it had yet to be fully measured.

Oh, Grandmother!

Her hands gripped the Ruhk Staff, and frustration, anger, and sadness rushed through her. She had found her birthright, discovered her identity, learned the history of her life, and now she wished that it would all disappear forever. It was vile and tainted and marked with betrayal and madness at every turn. She hated it.

And then, when the darkness of her mood had reached a point where it appeared complete, where it seemed that nothing worse could happen, a thought that was blacker still whispered to her.

The Shadowen are Elves—and you carry the entire Elven nation back into the Four Lands.

Why?

The question hung like an accusation in the silence of her mind.

CHAPTER

19

WREN WAS STILL STRUGGLING with the ambiguity of what her grandmother had given her to do when the rest of the company awoke at sunrise.

On the one hand, thousands of lives depended on her carrying the Loden and the Ruhk Staff safely from the island of Morrowindl back into the Westland. The whole of the Elven nation, all save the Wing Riders who resided on the coastal islands far away and had not migrated with the Land Elves to Morrowindl, had been gathered up by the magic and enclosed, there to remain until Wren—or, she supposed, another of the company, should she die as Ellenroh had—set them free. If she failed to do so, the Elves would perish, the oldest Race of all, the last of the faerie people, an entire history from the time of the world's creation gone.

On the other hand, perhaps it was best.

She shivered every time she repeated Eowen's words: *The Elves are the Shadowen.* The Elves, with their magic, and with their insistence on recovering their past, had turned themselves into monsters. They had created the demons. They had devastated Morrowindl and initiated the destruction of the Four Lands. Practically every danger that threatened could be traced to them. It might be better, given that truth, if they ceased to exist altogether.

She did not think she was overstating her concerns. Once the Elves were restored to the Westland, there was nothing to prevent them from beginning anew with the magic, from trying to recall it yet again so that it could be used in some newly terrible and destructive way. There was nothing that said that Ellenroh had disposed of all those who sought to play with its power, that some one or two had not survived. It would be easy enough for those few to begin to experiment once again, to create new forms of monsters, new horrors that Wren did not care to envision. Hadn't the Elves already proved that they were capable of anything?

Like the Druids, she thought sadly, victims of a misguided need to know, of an injudicious self-confidence, of a foolish belief that they could master something which by its very nature was dependably unreliable.

How had they let it all come to this, these people with so many years of experience in using the magic, these faerie folk brought into the new world out of the devastation of the old by lessons they could not have failed to learn? Surely they must have had some small inkling of the dangers they would encounter when they began to make nature over in their own ill-conceived image. Surely they must have realized something was wrong. Yet time's passage had rendered the Elves as human as the other Races, changed them from faerie creatures to mortals, and altered their perceptions and their knowledge. Why shouldn't they be as prone to make mistakes as anyone else—as anyone else had, in fact, from Druids to Men?

The Elves. She was one of them, of course, and worse, an Elessedil. However she might wish it otherwise, she was consumed with guilt for what their misjudgments had wrought and with remorse for what their folly had cost. A land, a nation, countless lives, a world's sanity and peace—they had set in motion the events that would destroy it all. Her people. She might argue that she was a Rover girl, that she shared nothing with the Elves beyond her bloodline and appearance, but the argument seemed hollow and feckless. Responsibility did not begin and end with personal needs—Garth had taught her that much. She was a part of everything about her, and not only survival but the measure of her life was directly related to whether she accepted that truth. She could not back away from the unpleasantnesses of the world; she could not forget its pain. Once upon a time, the Elves had been foremost among Healers, their given purpose to keep the land whole and instill in others the wisdom of doing so. What had happened to that commitment? How had the Elves become so misdirected?

She ate without tasting her food and she spoke little, consumed by her thoughts. Eowen sat across from her, eyes lowered. Garth and the other men moved past them unseeing, focused on the trek before them. Stresa was already gone, scouting ahead to make certain of his path. Faun was a ball of fur in her lap.

What am I to do? she asked herself in despair. *What choice am I to make?*

The climb up the Blackledge resumed, and still she could not settle on an answer. The day was dark and hazy like all the ones before, the sun screened away by the vog, the air thick with heat and ash and the faint stench of sulfur. Swamp sounds rose behind them out of Eden's Murk, a jumbled collection of screams and cries, fragmented and distant for the most part, scattered in the mist. Below, things hunted and foraged and struggled to stay alive for another day. Above, there was only silence, as if nothing more than clouds awaited. The trail was steep and winding, and it cut back upon itself frequently, a labyrinthine maze of ledges, drops, and defiles. Sporadic showers swept across them, quick and furious, the rain dampening the earth and rock to slickness and then fading back into the heat.

Time passed, and Wren's thoughts drifted. She found herself missing things she had never even considered before. She was young still, barely a woman, and she was struck by the possibility that she might never have a husband or children and that she would always be alone. She found herself envisioning faces and voices and small scenes out of an imagined life where these things were present, and without reason and to no particular purpose she mourned their loss. It was the discovery of who and what she was that triggered these feelings, she decided finally. It was the trust she carried, the responsibilities she bore that induced this sense of solitude, of aloneness. There was nothing for her beyond fleeing Morrowindl, beyond determining the fate of the Elven people, beyond coming to terms with the horror of what she had discovered. Nothing of her life seemed simple anymore, and the ordinary prospects of things like a husband and children were as remote as the home she had left behind.

She made herself consider the possibility then, a tentative conjecture brought on by a need to establish some sense of purpose for all that had come about, that what she might really have been given to do—by Allanon's shade, by Ellenroh, and by choice and chance alike—was to be for her people both mother and wife, to accept them as her family, to shepherd them, to guide and protect them, and to oversee their lives for the duration of her own. Her mind was light and her sense of things turned liquid, for she had barely slept at all now in three days and her physical and emotional strength had been exhausted. She was not herself, she might argue, and yet in truth she had perhaps found herself. There was purpose in everything, and there must be a purpose in this as well. She had been returned to her people, given responsibility over whether they lived or died, and made their queen. She had discovered the magic of the Elfstones and assumed control of their power. She had been told what no one else knew—the truth of the origin of the Shadowen. Why? She gave a mental shrug. Why not, if not to make some difference? Not so much where the Shadowen were concerned, although there could be no complete separation of problems and solutions, as Allanon had indicated in making his charges to the children of Shannara. Not so much in the future of the Races, for that was too broad an undertaking for one person and must inevitably be decided by the efforts of many and the vagaries of fortune. But for the Elves, for their future as a people, for the righting of so many wrongs and the correcting of so many mistakes—in this she might find the purpose of her life.

It was a sobering thought, and she mulled it through as the ascent of Blackledge wore on, lost within herself as she considered what an undertaking of such magnitude would require. She was strong enough, she felt; there was little she could not accomplish if she chose. She had resolve and a sense of right and wrong that had served her well. She was conscious of the fact that she owed a debt—to her mother, who had sacrificed everything so that her child would have a chance to grow up safely; to her grandmother, who had entrusted her with the future of a city and its people; to those who had already given their lives to help preserve her own; and to those who were prepared to do so, who trusted and believed in her.

But even that was not enough by itself to persuade her. There must be something more, she knew—something that transcended expectations and conscience, something more fundamental still. It was the existence of need. She already knew, deep within herself, that genocide was abhorrent and that she must find some other solution to the dilemma of the future of the Elves and their magic. But if they lived, if she was successful in restoring them to the Westland, what would become of them then if she was to walk away? Who would lead them in the fight that lay ahead? Who would guide and counsel them? Could she leave the matter to chance, or even to the dictates of the High Council? The need of the Elven people was great, and she did not think she could ignore it even if it meant changing her own life entirely.

Even so, she remained uncertain. She was torn by the conflict within herself, a war between choices that refused to be characterized as simply right or wrong. She knew as well that none of the choices might be hers to make, for while leadership had been bestowed upon her by Ellenroh, ultimately it was the Elves who would accept or reject it. And why should they choose to follow her? A Rover, an outsider, a girl barely grown— she had much to answer for.

Her reasonings fell apart about her like scraps of paper tumbled by the wind, a collapse of distant plans in the face of present needs. She looked about her at the rock and scrub, at the screen of Vog, and at the dark, bent forms of those who traveled with her. Staying alive was all she could afford to worry about for now.

The trek continued until it was nearing midday, and then Stresa brought them to an uncertain halt. Wren pushed forward from behind Garth to discover what was happening. The Splinterscat stood at the mouth of a cavern that burrowed ahead into the rock. To the right, the trail they followed continued sharply up the slope of the cliff face and disappeared into a tangle of vegetation.

"See, Wren of the Elves," the Splinterscat said softly, bright eyes fixing on her. "We have a choice now. Phhfft! The trail winds ahead to the summit, but it is slow and difficult from here—ssspppptt—not clear at all. The tunnel opens into a series of lava tubes formed by the pphhhtt fire of the volcano years ago. I have traveled them. They, too, lead to the summit."

Wren knelt. "Which is your choice?"

"Rwwll. There are dangers both ways."

"There are dangers everywhere." She dismissed his demurral. About her, the haze swirled and twisted against the island's thick growth, as if seeking its own way. "We rely on you to lead us, Stresa," she reminded him. "Choose."

The Splinterscat hissed his discontent. "The tunnels, then. Phhfftt!" The bulky body swung about and back again. The spikes lifted and fell. "We need light."

While Triss went off in search of suitable torch wood, the remainder of the company rummaged through backpacks and pockets for rags and tinder. Gavilan had the latter, Eowen the former. They placed them carefully inside the tunnel entrance and sat down to eat while waiting for Triss to return.

"Did you sleep?" Eowen asked softly, seating herself beside Wren. She kept her gaze carefully averted.

"No," Wren answered truthfully. "I couldn't."

"Nor I. It was as difficult to speak the words as it was to hear them."

"I know that."

The red hair shimmered damply as the pale face lifted into view. "I have had a vision—the first since leaving Arborlon."

Wren turned to meet the seer's gaze and was frightened by what she saw there. "Tell me."

Eowen shook her head, a barely perceptible movement. "Only because it is necessary to warn you," she whispered. She leaned in so that only Wren could hear. "In my vision, you stood alone atop a rise. It was clear that you were on Morrowindl. You held the Ruhk Staff and the Elfstones, but you could not use them. The others, those here, myself included, were black shadows cast upon the earth. Something approached you, huge and dangerous, yet you were not afraid—it was as if you welcomed it. Perhaps you did not realize that it threatened. There was a glint of bright silver, and you hastened to embrace it."

She paused, and her breath seemed to catch in her throat. "You must not do that, Wren. When it happens, remember."

Wren nodded, feeling numb and empty inside. "I will remember."

"I'm sorry," Eowen whispered. She hesitated a moment, like a hunted creature brought to bay with nowhere left to flee, then rose and swiftly moved away. *Poor Eowen,* Wren thought. She looked after the seer a moment, thinking. Then she beckoned to Garth. The big man came at once, eyes questioning, reading already her concern. She shifted so that only he could see her.

Eowen has had a vision of her own death, she signed, not bothering to speak the words this time. Garth showed nothing. *Watch out for her, will you? Try to keep her safe?*

Garth's fingers gestured. *I don't like what I see in her eyes.*

Wren sighed, then nodded. *Neither do I. Just do the best you can.*

Triss returned a few moments later bearing two hunks of dry wood that he had managed to salvage from somewhere on the rain-soaked slopes. He glanced over his shoulder as he approached. "There is movement below," he advised them, passing one of the pieces to Dal. "Something is climbing toward us."

For the first time since they had escaped the swamp, they experienced a sense of urgency. Until now, it had almost been possible to forget the things that hunted them. Wren thought instantly of the Loden's magic, wondering if the demons could indeed scent it, if the smell of the Keel's recovered magic was strong enough to draw them even when it was not in use.

They bound the strips of cloth in place about the wood and used the tinder to set it afire. When the brands were burning, they started ahead into the tunnels. Stresa led, a night creature comfortable in darkness, his burly body trundling smoothly ahead into the gloom. Triss followed close behind with one torch, while Dal trailed the company with the other. In between walked Wren, Gavilan, Eowen, and Garth. The air in the lava tube was cool and stale, and water dripped off the ceiling. In places, a narrow stream meandered along the gnarled floor. There were no projections, no obstructions; the passage of the red-hot lava years earlier had burned everything away. Stresa had explained to her while they waited for Triss how the pressure of heat and gases at the volcano's core forced vents in the earth, carving tunnels through the underground rock to reach the surface, the lava burning its way free. The lava burned so hot that the passageways formed were smooth and even. These tubes would run for miles, curling like giant worm burrows, eventually creating an opening through Morrowindl's skin that in turn would release the pressure and allow the lava to flow unobstructed to the sea. When the volcano cooled, the lava subsided and the tubes it had formed remained behind. The one they followed now was part of a series that cut through miles of Blackledge from crown to base.

"If I don't get us lost, we'll be atop the rrwwllll ridge by nightfall," the Splinterscat had promised.

Wren had wanted to ask him where he had learned about the tubes, but then decided the Splinterscat's knowledge had probably come from the Elves and it would only make him angry to talk about it. In any event, he seemed to know where he was going, nose thrust forward, pushing out at the edge of the torchlight as if seeking to drag them along in his wake, never hesitating once, even when he reached divergent passageways and was forced to choose. They twisted and wound ahead through the cool rock, climbing steadily, hauling themselves and their packs through the gloom, and brushing at the drops of water that fell on their faces and hands with cold, stinging splats. Their booted feet echoed hollowly in the deep stillness, and their breathing was an uneven hiss. They listened carefully for the sounds of pursuit, but heard nothing.

At one point they were forced to descend a particularly steep drop to a cross vent where the lava had cut through to a hollow core within the mountain and left a yawning hole that fell away into blackness. Farther on, there was a cavern where the lava had gathered and pooled for a time, forming a series of passageways that crisscrossed like snakes. In each instance, Stresa knew what to do, which tunnel to follow, and where the passage lay that would take them to safety.

The hours slipped away, and the trek wore on. Wren let Faun ride on her shoulder. The Tree Squeak's bright eyes darted left and right, and its voice was a low murmur in her ear. She quit thinking for a time and concentrated instead on putting one foot in front of the other, on studying the hypnotically swaying shadows they cast in the torchlight, on these and a dozen other mundane, purposeless musings that served to give her weary mind and emotions a much needed rest.

It was nightfall when they finally emerged from the tunnels, exiting the smokey blackness to stand amid a copse of thin-limbed ash and scrub backed up against the cliff face. Before them, a ledge spread away into the mist; behind, the mountain sloped upward to a broken, empty ridgeline. Overhead, the sky was murky and clouded, and a light rain was falling.

They moved away from the tunnels into a stretch of acacia near the rim of Blackledge, and there settled in for the night. They spread their gear and ate a hurried meal, then wrapped themselves in their cloaks and blankets and prepared for sleep. It was cold atop the mountain, and the wind blew at them in sharp gusts. Far distant, Wren could hear Killeshan's rumble and see the red glow of its fire shimmering through the haze. The earth had begun to tremble again, a slow, ominous vibration that loosened rock and earth and sent them tumbling, that caused the trees to sway and leaves to whisper like startled children.

Wren sat back against a half-fallen acacia whose exposed roots maintained a tenuous grip on the mountain rock. The Ruhk Staff rested on her lap, momentarily forgotten. Faun burrowed into her shoulder for a time as the tremors continued, then disappeared down inside her blanket to hide. She watched the small, solid figure of Dal slip past to take the first watch. Her eyes were heavy as she stared out at the dark, but she found she was not yet ready to sleep. She needed to think awhile first.

She had been sitting there for only a few moments when Gavilan appeared. He came out of the darkness rather suddenly, and she started in spite of herself.

"Sorry," he apologized hurriedly. "Can I sit with you awhile?"

She nodded wordlessly, and he settled himself next to her, his own blanket wrapped loosely about his shoulders, his hair tangled and damp. His handsome face was etched with fatigue, but a hint of the familiar smile appeared.

"How are you feeling?"

"I'm all right," she answered.

"You look very tired."

She smiled.

"Would that we had known," he murmured.

She glanced over. "Known what?"

"Everything. Anything! Something that would have prepared us better for what we're going through." His voice sounded odd to her, almost frenetic. "It is almost like being cast adrift in an ocean without a map and being told to navigate to safety and at the same time to refrain from using the little bit of drinking water we are fortunate enough to carry with us."

"What do you mean?"

He turned. "Think about it, Wren. We have in our possession both the Loden and the Elfstones—magic enough to accomplish almost anything. Yet we seem afraid to invoke that magic, almost as if we were restrained from doing so. But we aren't, are we? I mean, what is to prevent it? Look at how much better things became when you used the Elfstones to find a way out of Eden's Murk. We should be using that magic every step of the way! If we did, we might be to the beach by now."

"It doesn't work that way, Gavilan. It doesn't do just anything . . ."

But he wasn't listening. "Even worse is the way we ignore the magic contained in the Loden. Yes, it is needed to preserve the Elves and Arborlon for the journey back. But all of it? I don't believe it for a moment!" He let his hand come to rest momentarily on the Ruhk Staff. His words were suddenly fervent. "Why not use the magic against these things that hunt us? Why not just burn a path right through them? Or better still, why not make something that will go out there and destroy them!"

Wren stared at him, unable to believe what she was hearing. "Gavilan," she said quietly. "I know about the demons. Eowen told me."

He shrugged. "It was time, I suppose. Ellenroh was the only reason no one told you sooner."

"However that may be," she continued, her voice lowering, taking on a firmness, "how can you possibly suggest using the magic to make anything else?"

His face hardened. "Why? Because something went wrong

when it was used before? Because those who used it hadn't the ability or strength or sense of what was needed to use it properly?"

She shook her head, voiceless.

"Wren! The magic has to be used! It has to be! That is why it is there in the first place! If we don't make use of it, someone else will, and then what? This isn't a game we play. You know as much. There are things out there so dangerous that . . ."

"Things the Elves made!" she said angrily.

"Yes! A mistake, I agree! But others would have made them if we had not!"

"You can't know that!"

"It doesn't matter. The fact remains we made them for a good cause! We have learned a lot! The making is in the soul of the wielder of the power! It simply requires strength of purpose and channeling of need! This time we can do it right!"

He broke off, waiting for her response. They faced each other in silence. Then Wren took a deep breath and reached down to remove his hand from the Staff. "I don't think you had better say anything more."

His smile was bitter, ironic. "Once you were angry because I hadn't said enough."

"Gavilan," she whispered.

"Do you think this will all go away if we don't talk about it, that everything will somehow just work out?"

She shook her head slowly, sadly.

He bent to her, his hands closing firmly on her own. She didn't try to pull away, both fascinated and repelled by what she saw in his eyes. She felt something like grief well up inside. "Listen to me, Wren," he said, shaking his head at something she couldn't see. "There is a special bond between us. I felt it the moment I first saw you, the night you came to Arborlon, still wondering what it was that you had been sent to do. I knew. I knew it even then, but it was too early to speak of it. You are Alleyne's daughter and you have the Elessedil blood. You have courage and strength. You have done more already than anyone had a right to expect from you.

"But, Wren, none of this is your problem. The Elves are not

your people or Arborlon your city. I know that. I know how foreign it must all feel. And Ellenroh never understood that you couldn't ask people to accept responsibility for things when the responsibility was never theirs to begin with. She never understood that once she sent you away, she could never have you back the same. That was how she lost Alleyne! Now, look. She has given you the Ruhk Staff and the Loden, the Elves and Arborlon, the whole of the future of a nation, and told you to be queen. But you don't really want any part of it, do you?"

"I didn't," she admitted. "Once."

He missed her hesitation. "Then give it up! Be finished with it! Let me take the Staff and the Stone and use them as they should be used—to fight against the monsters that track us, to destroy the ones that have turned Morrowindl into this nightmare!"

"Which set of monsters?" she asked softly.

"What?"

"Which set? The demons or the Elves? Which do you mean?"

He stared at her, uncomprehending, and she felt her heart break apart inside. His eyes were clear and angry, his face intense. He seemed so convinced. "The Elves," she whispered, "are the ones who destroyed Morrowindl."

"No," he answered instantly, without hesitation.

"They made the demons, Gavilan."

He shook his head vehemently. "Old men made them in another time. A mistake like that wouldn't happen again. I wouldn't let it. The magic can be better used, Wren. You know that to be true. Haven't the Ohmsfords always found a way? Haven't the Druids? Let me try! I can stand against these things; I can do what is needed! You don't want the Staff; you said so yourself! Give it to me!"

She shook her head. "I can't."

Gavilan stiffened, and his hands drew away. "Why not, Wren? Tell me why not."

She couldn't tell him, of course. She couldn't find the words, and even if she had been able to find the words, she wouldn't have been able to speak them.

"I have given my promise," she said instead, wishing he would let the matter die, that he would give up his demand, that he would see how wrong it was for him to ask.

"Your promise?" he snapped. "To whom?"

"To the queen," she insisted stubbornly.

"To the queen? Shades, Wren, what's the worth of that? The queen is dead!"

She hit him then, struck him hard across the face, a blow that rocked his head back. He remained turned away for a moment and then straightened. "You can hit me again if it will make you feel any better."

"It makes me feel terrible," she whispered, curling up inside, turning to ice. "But that was a wrong thing to say, Gavilan."

He regarded her bitterly for a moment, and she found herself wishing that she could have him back as he was when they were still in Arborlon, when he was charming and kind, the friend she needed, when he had kissed her outside the High Council, when he had cared for her.

The handsome face tightened with determination. "You have to let me use the Loden's magic, Wren."

She shook her head firmly. "No."

He thrust forward aggressively, almost as if to attack her. "If you don't, we won't survive. We can't. You haven't the—"

"Don't, Gavilan!" she interjected, her hand flying to cover his mouth. "Don't say it! Don't say anything more!"

The sudden gesture froze them both momentarily, and the wind that blew past them in a sudden gust caused Wren to shiver. Slowly she took her hand away. "Go to sleep," she urged, fighting to keep her voice from breaking. "You're tired."

He rocked back slightly, a small motion only, one that moved him just inches away from her—yet she could feel the severing of ties between them as surely as if they were ropes cut with a knife.

"I'll go," he said quietly, the anger in his voice undiminished. He rose and looked down at her. "I was your friend. I would be still if you would let me."

"I know," she said.

He stayed where he was momentarily, as if undecided about what to do next, whether to stay or go, whether to speak or keep silent. He looked back through the darkness into the haze. "I won't die here," he whispered.

Then he wheeled and stalked away. Wren sat where she was, looking after him until he could no longer be seen. Tears came to her eyes, but she brushed them quickly away. Gavilan had hurt her, and she hated it. He made her question everything she had decided, made her wonder if she had any idea at all what she was doing. He made her feel stupid and selfish and naive. She wished that she had never gone to speak with the shade of Allanon, never come to Morrowindl, never discovered the Elves and their city and the horror of their existence—that none of it had ever happened.

She wished she had never met her grandmother.

No! she admonished herself sharply. *Don't ever wish that!*

But deep down inside, she did.

CHAPTER

20

DAYBREAK ARRIVED, a stealthy apparition cloaked iron-gray against the shadow of departing night as it crept uncertainly out of yesterday in search of tomorrow. The company rose to greet it, weary-eyed and disheartened, the weight of time's passage and shortening odds a mantel of chains that threatened to drag them down. Pulling cloaks and packs and weapons across their shoulders, they set out once more, wrapped in the silence of their separate thoughts, grim-faced against a rising wall of fear and doubt.

If I could sleep but one night, Wren was thinking as she tried to blink away her exhaustion. *Just one.*

There had been little rest for her last night, restless again as she lay awake in the stillness, beset by demons of all shapes and kinds, demons that bore the faces of those who had been or were closest, friends and family, the tricksters of her life. They whispered words to her, they teased and taunted, they warned of secrets she could not know, they gave her trails to follow and burdens to carry, and then they faded from her side like the morning mist.

Her hands clasped the Ruhk Staff and she leaned upon it for support as she climbed. *Trust no one,* the Addershag hissed again from out of memory.

The climb was short, for they had emerged from the lava tubes close to the summit at the end of yesterday's trek, with the ridgeline already in view. They reached it quickly this day, scrambling up the final stretch of broken trail to stand atop the wall, pausing to look back into the mists that cloaked the country they had passed through—almost as if they expected to find something waiting there. But there was nothing to see, the whole of it shrouded in clouds and fog, a world and a life vanished into the past. They could see it still in their minds, picture it as if it were drawn on the air before them. They could remember what it had cost them to come through it, what it had taken from them, and how little it had given back. They stared a moment longer, then quickly turned away.

They walked then through narrow stretches of rocks separated by trees that stretched from the edge of Blackledge like fingers until everything abruptly ended at a ragged tangle of ravines and ridges that split and folded back on themselves, huge wrinkles in the land's skin. A lava flow had passed this way some years back, come down out of Killeshan's maw to sweep the crest of Blackledge clean. Everything had been burned away save a scattering of silvered tree trunks standing bare and skeletal, some fallen away at strange angles, some propped against one another in hapless despair. Scrub grew out of the lava in gnarled clumps, and patches of moss darkened the shady side of roughened splits.

Stresa brought them to the edge of this forbidding world, lumbering to a halt atop a small rise, spines lifting guardedly. The company stared out bleakly at what lay ahead, listening for and hearing nothing, looking at and seeing nothing, feeling death's presence at every turn. The devastation spread away before them, a vast and empty landscape wrapped in gray silence.

On Wren's shoulder, Faun sat up stiffly and leaned forward, ears pricked. She could feel the Tree Squeak shiver.

"What is this place?" Gavilan asked.

A heavy rumble distracted them momentarily, causing them to glance north to where Killeshan's bulk loomed darkly, seemingly as close to them now as it had been on their leaving Arborlon. The rumble receded and died.

Stresa swung slowly about. "This is the Harrow," he said. "Hssttt! This is where the Drakuls live."

A form of demon—or Shadowen—Wren recalled. Stresa had mentioned them before. Dangerous, he had intimated.

"Drakuls," Gavilan repeated, weary recognition in his voice.

Killeshan rumbled again, more insistent than before, an un-necessary reminder of its presence, of the anger it bore them for having stolen the magic away, for having disrupted the balance of things. Morrowindl shuddered in response.

"Tell me about the Drakuls," Wren instructed the Splinterscat quietly.

Stresa's dark eyes fixed on her. "Demons, like the others. Phhfftt! They sleep in daylight, come out at night to feed. They drain the life out of the living things they catch—the blood, the fluids of the body. They make—hssstt—some into creatures like themselves." The blunt nose twitched. "They hunt as wraiths, but take form to feed. As wraiths, they cannot be harmed." He spit distastefully.

"We will go around," Triss announced at once.

Stresa spit again, as if the taste wouldn't go away. "Around! Phaaww! There is no 'around'! North, the Harrow runs back toward Killeshan, miles and miles—back toward the valley and the demons that hunt us. Rwwlll. South, the Harrow stretches to the cliffs. The Drakuls hunt its edges, too. In any case, we would never—hrraaggh—get around it before nightfall and we must if we are to live. Crossing in daylight is our only chance."

"While the Drakuls sleep?" Wren prompted.

"Yes, Wren of the Elves," the Splinterscat growled softly. "While they sleep. And even so—hsssttt—it will not be entirely safe. The Drakuls are present even then—as voices out of air, as faces on the mist, as feelings and hunches and fears and doubts. Phhffttt. They will try to distract and lure, try to keep us within the Harrow until nightfall."

Wren stared off into the blasted countryside, into the haze that hung from the skies to the earth. *Trapped again*, she thought. *The whole island is a snare.*

"There is no other passage open to us?"

Stresa did not answer—did not need to.

"And on the other side of the Harrow?"

"The In Ju. And the beaches beyond."

Triss had moved up beside her. His lean face was intense. "Aurin Striate used to speak of the Drakuls," he advised softly.

His gaze fixed on her. "He said there was no defense against them."

"But they sleep now," she replied, just as softly.

The gray eyes shifted away. "Do they?"

A new rumble shook the island, deep and forbidding, rising like a giant coming awake angry, thunderous as the tremors built upon themselves. Cracks appeared in the ground about them and rock and silt fell away into the void. Steam and ash belched out of the Killeshan, showering skyward in towering geysers, arcing away into the gloom. Fire trailed ominously from the volcano's lip, a trickle only, just visible in the haze.

Garth caught Wren's attention, a simple shifting of his shoulders. His fingers moved. *Be quick, Wren. The island begins to shake itself apart.*

She glanced at them in turn—Garth, as enigmatic and impassive as ever; steady Triss, her protector now, given over to his new charge; Dal, restless as he stared out into the haze—she had never even heard him speak; Eowen, a white shadow against the gray, looking as if she might disappear into it; and Gavilan, uneasy, unpredictable, haunted, lost to her.

"How long will it take us to cross?" she asked Stresa. Faun scrambled down off her shoulder and moved away, picking at the earth.

"Half a day, a little more," the Splinterscat advised.

"A lifetime if you are wrong, Scat," Gavilan intoned darkly.

"Then we will have to hurry," Wren declared, and called Faun back to her shoulder. She brought the Ruhk Staff before her, a reminder. "We have no choice. Let's be off. Stay close to each other. Keep watch."

They struck out across the flats, winding down into the maze of depressions, through the tangle of tree husks, cautious eyes scanning the blasted land about them. Stresa took them along as quickly as he could, but travel was slow, the terrain broken and uneven, filled with twists and turns that prevented either rapid or straight passage. The Harrow swallowed them after only moments, gathering about them almost magically until there was nothing else to be seen in any direction. Mist swirled and spun in the wind currents, steam rose out of cracks in the earth that burrowed all the way to Killeshan's core, and vog drifted down from where it spewed out of the volcano. Nothing moved in the land; it was still and empty all about. Shadows played, black lines cast earthward by the skeletal trees, iron bars against the light. All the while the earth beneath rumbled ominously, and there was a sense of something dangerous awakening.

The voices began in the first hour. They lifted out of nothingness, whispers on the air that might have come from anywhere. They called compellingly, and for each of the company the words were different. Each would look at the others, thinking that all must have heard, that the voices were unmistakable. They asked, anxious, intense: *Did you hear that? Did you hear?* But none had, of course—only the speaker, called specifically, purposefully, drawn on by some mirror of self, by a reflection of sense and feeling.

The images came next, faces out of the air, figures that quickly formed and just as quickly faded in the shifting haze, visions of things peculiar to whomever they addressed—personifications of longings, needs, and hopes. For Wren, they took the form of her parents. For Triss and Eowen, it was the queen. For the others, something else. The images worked the fringes of their consciousness, struggling to break through the barriers they had erected to keep them at bay, working to turn them from their chosen path and lead them away.

It went on relentlessly. The voices were never loud, the images never clear, and the whole of the experience not unpleasant, not threatening, not even real—a false memory of what had never been. Stresa, familiar with the danger, started them talking to each other to ward off the attack—for there was no mistaking what it was. The Drakuls stalked them even in sleep, some part of what they were rising up to follow after, seeking to delay or detain, to turn aside or lead astray, to keep them within the Harrow until nightfall.

Time slowed, as cautious and measured as the haze through which they walked, as bleak as the landscape that stretched ahead. The depressions deepened, and in places the lifeless trees formed a barrier that could not be crossed, but had to be got around. Wren called to the others as they trudged ahead, pushing past the voices, casting through the faces, working to keep them all together, to keep them moving. Noon approached, and the day darkened. Clouds massed overhead, heavy with rain. It began to drizzle, then to pour. The wind quickened, and the rain blew into them in sheets. It would sweep across in a curtain, fade away to scattered drops, and start the cycle over again. It lasted for a time and was gone. The earth's heat returned, and the mist began to thicken. It closed about them, and soon nothing was visible beyond a dozen feet. They stayed close then, so close they were tripping over each other, bumping together as if made sightless, feeling their way through the gloom.

"Stresa! How much farther?" Wren shouted through the cacophony of voices that whirled about her ears.

"Spptptt! Close, now," the reply came. "Just ahead."

They passed down into a particularly deep ravine, a jagged knife cut across the surface of the lava rock, all shadows and shifting haze. Wren knew it was dangerous, almost called them back, but saw, too, that it sliced directly across their pathway out, that it was the only way they could go. She descended into the gloom, the Ruhk Staff gripped before her like a shield. Faun chittered wildly on her shoulder, another sound to blend with the others, the unseen voices that buzzed and raged and filled her subconscious with a growing need to scream. She saw Triss a step ahead, with Stresa a faint dark spot beyond. She heard footsteps behind, someone following, the others . . .

And then the hands had her, abrupt, startling, as hard as iron. They reached up from nowhere, materializing from out of the mist, closed about her legs and ankles, and yanked her from the pathway. She yelled in fury and struck downward with the butt of the Ruhk Staff. White fire burst from the earth, flaring out in all directions, the magic of the talisman responding. It shocked her, stunned her that the magic should come so easily. There were shouts from the others, cries of warning. Wren wheeled about wildly, and the hands that had fastened on her fell away. Something moved in the mist—things, dozens of them, faceless, formless, yet there. The Drakuls, she realized, awake somehow when they should not have been. Perhaps it was dark enough here in this cut, black enough to pass for night. She cried out to the others, summoned them to her, and led them toward the ravine's far slope. The figures swirled all about, grasping, touching, nonsubstantive, yet somehow real. She saw faces drained of life, pale images of her own, eyes empty and unseeing, teeth that looked like the fangs of animals, sunken cheeks and temples, and bodies wasted away to nothing. She fought through them, for they seemed centered on her, drawn to her as if she were the one who mattered most to them. It was the magic, she realized. Like all the Shadowen, it was the magic that drew them first.

Drakul wraiths materialized in front of her and Garth bounded past, short sword hacking. The images dissipated and reformed, unharmed. Wren wheeled about as she reached the floor of the ravine. *One, two* . . . She counted frantically. All six were there. Stresa was already scrambling ahead, and she turned to follow him. They went up the slope in a tangle, clawing their way over the rain-slick lava rock, past the scrub and fallen trees. The images followed, the voices, the phantoms come from sleep, undead monsters trailing after. Wren fought them off with anger and repulsion, with the fury of her movement, conscious of Faun clinging to her neck as if become a part of her, of the heat of the Ruhk Staff in her hands as its magic sought to break free again. Magic that could do anything, she lamented, that could create anything—even monsters like these. She recoiled inwardly at the prospect, at the horror of a truth she wished had never been, a truth she feared would rise up to haunt her if she were to keep the promise she had made to her grandmother to save the Elves.

Over the top of the ravine the members of the little company stumbled and began to run. The gloom was thick and shifted like layers of gauze before them, but they did not slow, racing ahead heedlessly, calling words of encouragement to each other, fighting back against their pursuers. The Drakuls hissed and spit like cats, the venom of their thoughts a fire that burned inside. Yet it was only voices and images now and no longer real, for the Drakuls could not leave the darkness of their shelter to venture into the Harrow while it was yet daylight. Slowly their presence faded, drawing away like the receding waters of some vast ocean, gone back with the tide. The company began to slow, their breathing heavy in the sudden stillness, their boots scraping as they came to a ragged halt.

Wren looked back into the haze. There was nothing there but the mist and the faint shadow of the scrub land and tree bones beyond, empty and stark. Faun poked her head up tentatively. Stresa lumbered over to join them, panting, tongue licking out. The Splinterscat spit. "Hsssttt! Stupid wraiths!"

Wren nodded. In her hands, the heat of the Ruhk Staff dissipated and was gone. She felt her own body cool in response. A small measure of relief welled up within.

Then abruptly Garth crowded forward, startled by something she had missed, intense and anxious as he searched the mist. Wren followed his gaze, frightened without yet knowing why. She saw the others glance at one another uneasily.

Her heart jumped. *What was wrong?*

She saw it then. There were only five of them. Eowen was missing.

At first she thought such a thing impossible, that she must be mistaken. She had counted all six when they had climbed from the ravine. Eowen had been among them; she had recognized her face . . .

She stopped herself. Eowen. She saw the red-haired seer in her mind, trailing after—too pale, too ephemeral. Almost as if she wasn't really there—which, of course, she hadn't been. Wren experienced a sinking feeling in the pit of her stomach, an aching that threatened to break free and consume her. What she had seen had been another image, one more clever and calculated than the others, an image designed to make them all believe they were together when in fact they were not.

The Drakuls had Eowen.

Garth signed hurriedly. *I was watching out for her as I promised I would. She was right behind us when we climbed from the ravine. How could I lose her?*

"You didn't," Wren replied instantly. She felt an odd calm settle over her, a resignation of sorts, an acceptance of the inevitability of chance and fate. "It's all right, Garth," she whispered.

She felt the ground open beneath her, a hole into which she

must surely fall. She waited for the feeling to pass, for stability to take hold. She knew what she had to do. Whatever else happened, she could not abandon Eowen. To save her, she would have to go back into the Harrow, back among the Drakuls. She could send the others, of course; they would go if she asked. But she would never do that—would never even consider it. Tracker skills, Rover experience, Elven Hunter training—all would be useless against the Drakuls. Only one thing would make any difference.

She took a few uncertain steps and stopped. Reason screamed at her to reconsider. She was aware of the others coming forward one by one to stand with her, their eyes following her own as she peered out into the Harrow's gloom.

"No!" Stresa warned. "Phffft! It's already growing dark!"

She ignored him, turning instead to Gavilan. Wordlessly she took his measure, then held forth the Ruhk Staff. "It is time for you to be a friend to me again, Gavilan," she told him quietly. "Take the Staff. Hold it for me until my return. Keep it safe."

Gavilan stared at her in disbelief, then cautiously reached for the talisman. His hands closed over it, tightened about it, and drew it away. She did not allow her eyes to linger on his, frightened of what she would find there. He was all that remained of her family; she had to trust him.

Triss and Dal had dropped their packs and were cinching their weapons belts. Garth already had his short sword out.

"No," she told them. "I am going back alone."

They started to protest, the words quick and urgent, but she cut them off instantly. "No!" she repeated. She faced them. "I am the only one who stands a chance of finding Eowen and bringing her out again. Me." She reached within her tunic and pulled forth the pouch with the Elfstones. "Magic to find her and to protect me—nothing less will do. If you come with me, I shall have to worry about protecting you as well. These things can't be hurt by your weapons, and this one time at least you cannot help me."

She put a hand on Triss's arm, gentle but firm. "You are pledged to watch over me, I know. But I am ordering you to watch over the Loden instead—to stay with Gavilan, you and

Dal, to see to it that whatever else happens, the Elves are kept safe."

The hard, gray eyes narrowed. "I beg you not to do this, Lady. The Home Guard serve the queen first."

"And the queen, if that is what in truth I am, believes you will serve best by staying here. I order it, Triss."

Garth was signing angrily. *Do what you wish with them. But I have no purpose in remaining. I come with you.*

She shook her head, and her fingers moved as she spoke. "No, Garth. If I am lost, they will need you to see them safely to the beaches and to Tiger Ty. They will need your experience. I love you, Garth, but you can do nothing to help me here. You must stay."

The big man looked at her as if she had struck him.

"This is the time we always knew would come," she told him, quiet and insistent, "the time for which you have worked so hard to train me. It is too late now for any further lessons. I have to rely on what I know."

She took Faun from her shoulder and placed her on the ground beside Stresa. "Stay, little one," she commanded, and stepped away.

"Rrrwwlll! Wren, of the Elves, take me!" Stresa snapped, spines bristling. "I can track for you—better than any of these others!"

She shook her head once more. "The Elfstones can track better still. Garth will see you safely to the Westland, Stresa, if I should fail to return. He knows of my promise to you."

She removed her pack, dropped her weapons—all but the long knife at her waist. The four men, the Splinterscat, and the Tree Squeak watched in silence. Carefully she shook the Elfstones from their pouch, dropping them into her open hand. Her fingers closed.

Then, before she could think better of it, she turned and stalked into the mist.

SHE WALKED STRAIGHT AHEAD for a time, simply concentrating on putting one foot in front of the other, distance between herself and those who would keep her safe. She crossed the bare lava rock, a solitary hunter, feeling herself turn cold within, numb from the intensity of her determination. Eowen spoke to her out of memory, telling her of the vision she had seen so long ago, the vision of her own death. *No,* Wren swore silently. *Not now, now while I still breathe.*

The Drakuls began to whisper to her, urging her on, calling her to them. Within, fury battled back against fear. *I will come to you, all right—but not as you would have me!*

She passed through a line of silvered trunks, wood stakes barren and stark, a gate into the netherworld of the dead. She saw faces appear, gaunt and empty, skulls within the mist. She brought up the Elfstones, held them forth, and summoned their power. It came at once, obedient to her will, blazing to life with blue fire and streaking out into the haze. It took her left along a flat where nothing grew, where no trace of what had been survived. Ahead, far in the distance, she could see a gathering of white forms, bodies shifting, turning as if to greet her. Voices reached out, cries and whispers, a summons to death.

The blue fire faded, and she walked blindly on.

Wren, she heard Eowen call.

She shut her sense of urgency away, forcing herself to move cautiously, watching everything around her, the movement of shadows and mist, the hint of life coming awake. Stresa had been right. It was growing dark now, the afternoon lengthening toward evening, the light beginning to fail. She knew she would not reach Eowen before nightfall. It was what the Drakuls intended; it was what they had planned all along. Eowen's magic drew them like her own—but it was hers that they wanted, that was most powerful, that would feed them best. Eowen was bait for the trap that was meant to snare her.

She shut her eyes momentarily against the inevitability of it. She should have known all along.

The voices grew louder, more insistent, and she saw figures begin to take form at the edges of her vision, faint and ethereal in the mist. A ravine opened before her—the one in which she had lost Eowen? she wondered. She didn't know and didn't care. She went down into it without slowing, following the magic's lead, feeling the iron of it fill her now with its heat, fired in the

forge of her soul. She didn't know how much time had passed—
an hour, more? She had lost all track of time, all sense of everything but what she had come to do. Queen of the Elves,
keeper of the Rikh Staff and Loden, bearer of Druid magic, and
heir to the blood of Elessedils and Ohmsfords alike—she was all
these and she was none, made instead of something more, something undefinable.

Nothing, she told herself, could stand against her.

The darkness closed about as she reached the bottom of the
ravine, the faint light above lost in mist and shadows. The Drakuls appeared boldly now, skeletal forms come slowly into view,
gaunt and stripped of all life but that which their Shadowen
existence gave them. They were hesitant still, afraid of the magic
and at the same time eager for it. They looked upon her with
hungry eyes, anxious to taste her, to make her their own. She
felt the Elfstones burn against her palm in warning, but still she
did not summon their magic. She walked ahead boldly, the living among the dead.

Wren, she heard Eowen call again.

A wall of pale bodies blocked her way. They were human
of a sort, shaped as such, but twisted, pale imitations of what
they had been in life. They turned to meet her, no longer ap-
paritions that shimmered and threatened to dissolve at a breath
of wind, but things taking on the substance of life.

"Eowen!" she cried out.

One by one the Drakuls stood away, and there was Eowen.
She lay cradled in their arms, as white-skinned as they save for
her fire-red hair and emerald eyes. The eyes glittered as they
sought Wren's own, alive with horror. Eowen's mouth was open
as if she were trying to breathe—or scream.

The mouths of the Drakuls were fastened to her body, feeding.

For an instant Wren could not move, stricken by the sight,
trapped in a web of indecision.

Then Eowen's head jerked up, and her lips parted in a snarl
to reveal gleaming fangs.

Wren howled in dismay, and the Drakuls came for her. She
brought the Elfstones up with the quickness of thought, called
forth their power in rage and terror, and turned the fire of the

magic on everything in sight. It swept through her attackers like a scythe, incinerating them. Those who had taken solid form, those feeding and Eowen with them, were obliterated. The others, wraiths still, vanished. Flames engulfed everything. Wren scattered fire in every direction, feeling the magic course through her, hot and raw. She howled, exultant as the fire burned the ravine from end to end. She gave herself over to its heat—anything to block away the image of Eowen. She embraced it as she would a lover. Time and place disappeared in the rush of sensations.

She began to lose control.

Then, a bare instant before she would have disappeared into the power completely, she realized what was happening, remembered who she was, and made a last, desperate attempt to recover herself. Frantically she clamped her fingers about the Stones. The fire continued to leak through. Her hand tightened, and her body convulsed. She doubled over with the effort, falling to her knees. Finally, the magic swept back within her, raked her one final time with the promise of its invincibility, and was gone.

She crouched in the mist, fighting to regain mastery of herself, seeing once more with her mind's eye a picture of the Drakuls and Eowen as they disappeared into flames, consumed by the Elfstone magic.

Power! Such power! How she longed to have it back!

Shame swept through her, followed by despair.

She lifted her eyes wearily, already knowing what she would find, fully cognizant now of what she had done. Before her, the ravine stretched away, empty. Smoke and ash hung on the air. Her throat tightened as she tried to breathe. She had not had a choice, she knew—but the knowledge didn't help. Eowen had been one of them, brought to her death as Wren watched, her own prophecy fulfilled. Though Wren had tried, she could not change the outcome of the seer's vision. Eowen had told her once that her life had been built around her visions and she had come to accept them—even the one that foretold her death.

Wren felt tears fill her eyes and run down her cheeks.

Oh, Eowen!

CHAPTER

21

A T SOUTHWATCH TIME DRIFTED away like a cloud across the summer blue, and Coll Ohmsford could only watch helplessly as it passed him by. His imprisonment continued unchanged, his life an uneasy compendium of boredom and tension. His thoughts were unfettered, but led him nowhere. He dreamed of the past, of the life he had enjoyed in the Vale, and of the world that lay without the black walls of his confinement, but his dreams had turned tattered and faded. No one came for him. He began to accept that no one would.

He spent his days in the exercise yard, sparring with Ulfkingroh, the gnarled, scarred, taciturn fellow into whose care Rimmer Dall had given him. Ulfkingroh was as tough as nails and he worked Coll until the Valeman thought he would drop. With padded cudgels, heavy staffs, blunted swords, and bare hands, they exercised and trained as if fighters preparing for battle, sometimes all day, frequently until they were sweating so hard that the dust they raised in the yard ran from their bodies in black stripes. Ulfkingroh was a Shadowen, of course—but he didn't seem like one. He seemed like any normal man, albeit harder and more sullen. At times, Coll almost liked him. He spoke little, content to let his expertise with weapons do his talking for him. He was a skilled and experienced fighter, and it became a point of pride with him that he pass what he knew on to the Valeman. Coll, for his part, made the best of his situation, taking advantage of the one diversion he was allowed, learning what he could of what the other was willing to teach, playing at battle as if it meant something, and keeping fit for the time when it really would.

Because sooner or later, he promised himself over and over again, he would have his chance to escape.

He thought of it constantly. He thought of little else. If no one knew he was there, if no one would come to save him, then clearly it was up to him to save himself. Coll was resourceful in the manner of all Valemen; he was confident he would find a way. He was patient as well, and his patience was perhaps the more important attribute. He was watched whenever he was out of his cell, whenever he went down the dark halls of the monolith to the exercise yard and whenever he went back up again. He was allowed to spend as much time sparring with Ulfkingroh as he wished and allowed as well to visit with the rugged fellow to the extent that he was able to engage the other in conversation, but always he was watched. He could not afford to make a mistake.

Still, he never doubted that he would find a way.

He saw Rimmer Dall only twice after the First Seeker visited him in his cell. Each time it was from a distance, an unexpected glimpse that lasted only a moment before the other was gone. Each time the cold eyes were all he could remember afterward. Coll looked for him everywhere at first until he realized it was becoming something of an obsession and that he had to stop it. But he never stopped thinking of what the big man had told him, of how Par was a Shadowen, too, of how the magic would consume him if he did not accept the truth of his identity, and of how in his madness he was a danger to his brother. Coll did not believe what Rimmer Dall had told him—yet he could not bring himself to disbelieve either. The truth, he decided, lay somewhere in between, in that gray area amid the speculations and lies. But the truth was hard to decipher, and he would never learn it there. Rimmer Dall had his own reasons for what he was doing and he was not about to reveal them to Coll. Whatever they were, whatever the reality of the Shadowen and their magic, Coll was convinced that he had to reach his brother.

So he trained in the exercise yard by day, lay awake sorting out chances and possibilities by night, and all the while fought back against the insidious possibility that nothing would come of any of it.

Then one day, several weeks after he had been released from his cell, while sparring once again with Ulfkingroh in the exercise yard, he caught sight of Rimmer Dall passing down a walkway between two alcoves. At first it looked as if part of him had been cut away. Then he realized that the First Seeker was carrying something draped over one arm—something that at first seemed like nothing because it was so black it had the appearance of a piece of a new moon's night. Coll stopped in his tracks, then backed away, staring. Ulfkingroh glared in irritation, then glanced back over his shoulder to see what had caught the Valeman's eye.

"Huh!" he grunted when he saw what Coll was looking at. "There's nothing there that concerns you. Put up your hands."

"What is it he carries?" Coll pressed.

Ulfkingroh braced his staff against the ground and leaned on it with exaggerated patience. "A cloak, Valeman. It's called a Mirrorshroud. See how black it is? See how it steals away the light, just like a spill of black ink? Shadowen magic, little fellow." The rough face tightened about a half smile. "Know what it does?" Coll shook his head. "You don't? Good! Because you're not supposed to! Now put up your hands!"

They went back to sparring, and Coll, who was no little fellow and every bit as big and strong as Ulfkingroh, gained a measure of revenge by striking the other so hard he was knocked from his feet and left stunned for several minutes after.

That night Coll lay awake thinking about the Mirrorshroud and wondering what it was for. It was the first tangible piece of Shadowen magic he had ever seen. There were other magics, of course, but they were hidden from him. The biggest and most important was something kept deep in the bowels of the tower that hummed and throbbed and sometimes almost sounded as if it were screaming, something huge and very frightening. He envisioned it as a dragon that the Shadowen had managed to chain, but he knew he was being too simplistic. Whatever it was, it was far more impressive and terrible than that. There were other things as well, concealed behind the doors through which he was never allowed, secreted in the catacombs into which he could never pass. He could sense their presence, the brush of it against his skin, the whisper of it in his mind. Magic, all of it, Shadowen conjurings and talismans, things dark and evil.

Or not, if you believed Rimmer Dall. But he did not believe the First Seeker, of course. He never had believed him.

Still, he could not help wondering.

Two days later, while he was taking a break in the yard, the sweat still glistening on his body like oil, the First Seeker appeared out of the shadows of a door and came right up to him. Over one arm he carried the Mirrorshroud like a fold of stolen night. Ulfkingroh started to his feet, but Rimmer Dall dismissed him with a wave of his gloved hand and beckoned Coll to follow. They walked from the light back into the cooler shadows, out of the midday sun, away from its glare. Coll squinted and blinked as his eyes adjusted. The other man's face was all angles and planes in the faint gray light, the skin dead and cold, but the sharp eyes certain.

"You train hard, Coll Ohmsford," he said in that familiar whispery voice. "Ulfkingroh loses ground on you every day."

Coll nodded without speaking, waiting to hear what the other had really come to tell him.

"This cloak," Rimmer Dall said, as if in answer. "It is time that you understood what it is for."

Coll could not hide his surprise. "Why?"

The other glanced away as if thinking through his answer. The gloved hand lifted and fell again, a black scythe. "I told you that your brother was in danger, that you in turn were in danger, all because of the magic and what it might do. I had thought to use you to bring your brother to me. I let it be known you were here. But your brother remains in Tyrsis, unwilling to come for you."

He paused, looking for Coll's response. Coll kept his face an expressionless mask.

"The magic he hides within himself," the First Seeker whispered, "the magic that lies beneath the wishsong, begins to consume him. He may not even realize it yet. He may not understand. You've sensed that magic in him, haven't you? You know it is there?"

He shrugged. "I had thought to reason with him when I found him. I think now that he may refuse to listen to me. I had hoped that having you at Southwatch would make a difference. It apparently has not."

Coll took a deep breath. "You are a fool if you think Par will come here. A bigger fool if you think you can use me to trap him."

Rimmer Dall shook his head. "You still don't believe me, do you? I want to protect you, not use you. I want to save your brother while there is still time to do so. He is a Shadowen, Coll. He is like me, and his magic is a gift that can either save or destroy him."

A gift. Par had used that word so often, Coll thought bleakly. "Let me go to him then. Release me."

The big man smiled, a twisting at the corners of his mouth. "I intend to. But not until I have confronted your brother one more time. I think the Mirrorshroud will let me do so. This is a Shadowen magic, Valeman—a very powerful one. It took me a long time to weave it. Whoever wears the cloak appears to those he encounters as someone they know and trust. It masks the truth of who they are. It hides their identity. I will wear it when I go in search of your brother." He paused. "You could help me in this. You could tell me where I might find him, where you think he might be. I know he is in Tyrsis. I don't know where. Will you help me?"

Coll was incredulous. How could Rimmer Dall even think of asking such a thing? But the big man seemed so sure of himself, as if he were right after all, as if he knew the truth far better than Coll.

Coll shook his head. "I don't know where to find Par. He could be anywhere."

For a long moment Rimmer Dall did not respond, but simply stood looking at the Valeman, measuring him carefully, the hard eyes fixed on him as if the lie could be read on his face.

"I will ask again another time," he said finally. The heavy boots scraped on the stone of the walkway. "Return to your sparring. I will find him on my own, one way or the other. When I do, I will release you."

He turned and walked away. Coll stared after him, looking

not at the man now but at the cloak he carried, thinking, *If I could just get my hands on that cloak for five seconds . . .*

HE WAS STILL THINKING ABOUT IT when he woke the next day. A cloak that when worn could hide the identity of the wearer from those he encountered, making him appear to be someone they trusted—here at last was a way out of Southwatch. Rimmer Dall might envision the Mirrorshroud as a subterfuge that would allow him to trap Par, but Coll had a far better use for the magic. If he could find a way to get possession of the cloak long enough to put it on . . . His excitement at the prospect would not allow him to finish the thought. How could he manage it? he wondered, his mind racing as he dressed and paced the length of his cell, waiting for his breakfast.

It occurred to him then, for just a moment, that it was extraordinarily careless of Rimmer Dall to show him such a magic when the Shadowen had been so careful to keep all their other magics hidden. But then the First Seeker had been anxious for his help in locating Par, hadn't he, and the cloak was useless unless they found Par, wasn't it? Probably Dall had hoped to persuade Coll simply by letting him know he possessed such magic.

Then the first suspicion was abruptly crowded aside by a second. What if the cloak was a trick? How did he know that the Mirrorshroud could do what was claimed? What proof did he have? He started sharply as the metal food tray slid through the slot at the bottom of his door. He stared at it helplessly a moment, wondering. But why would the First Seeker lie? What did he stand to gain?

The questions besieged and finally overwhelmed him, and he brushed them aside long enough to eat his breakfast. When he was finished, he went down to the exercise yard to train with Ulfkingroh. He needed to talk with Rimmer Dall again, to find out more about the cloak and to discover the truth of its magic. But he could not afford to seem too interested; he could not let the First Seeker surmise his true motive. That meant he had to wait for Rimmer Dall to come to him.

But the First Seeker did not appear that day or the next, and it was not until three days later as sunset approached that he materialized from the shadows as Coll was trudging wearily back to his cell and fell in beside him.

"Have you given further thought to helping me find your brother?" he asked perfunctorily, his face lowered within the cowl of his black cloak.

"Some," Coll allowed.

"Time passes swiftly, Valeman."

Coll shrugged casually. "I have trouble believing anything you tell me. A prisoner is not often persuaded to confide in his jailor."

"No?" Coll could almost feel the other's dark smile. "I would have thought it was just the opposite."

They walked in silence for a few paces, Coll's face burning with anger. He wanted to strike out at the other, having him this close, alone in these dark halls, just the two of them. He fought down the temptation, knowing how foolish it would be to give in to it.

"I think Par would see through the magic of the Mirror-shroud," he said finally.

Dall glanced over. "How?"

Coll took a deep breath. "His own magic would warn him."

"So you think I would fail to get close enough even to speak with him?" The whispery voice was hoarse and low.

"I wonder," Coll replied.

Dall stopped and turned to face him. "How would it be if I tested the magic on you? Then you could make your own judgment."

Coll frowned, hiding the elation that surged abruptly within. "I don't know. It might not make any difference whether it works with me."

The gloved hand lifted, a lean blackness stealing the light from the air. "Why not let me try? What harm can it do?"

They went down the hallway and up a dozen flights of stairs until they were only several floors below the cell where Coll was kept imprisoned. At a door marked with a wolf's head and red lettering that Coll could not decipher, Rimmer Dall produced a key, inserted it in a heavy lock, and pushed the door back. Inside was a single window through which a narrow band of sunlight shone on a tall wooden cabinet. Rimmer Dall walked to the cabinet, opened its double doors, and took out the Mirrorshroud.

"Look away from me for a moment," he ordered.

Coll turned his head, waiting.

"Coll," a voice came.

He turned back. There was his father, Jaralan, tall and stooped, thick shouldered, wearing his favorite leather apron, the one he used for his woodworking. Coll blinked in disbelief, telling himself that it wasn't his father, that it was Rimmer Dall, and still it was his father he saw.

Then his father reached up to remove the apron, which instantly became the Mirrorshroud, and Rimmer Dall stood before him once more.

"Who did you see?" the First Seeker asked softly.

Coll could not bring himself to answer. He shook his head. "I still think Par will recognize you."

Rimmer Dall studied him a moment, the big, rawboned face flat and empty, the strange eyes as hard as stone. "I want you to think about something," he said finally. "Do you remember those pitiful creatures in the Pit at Tyrsis, the ones driven mad by Federation imprisonment, their magic consuming them? That is what will happen to your brother. It may not happen today or tomorrow or next week or even next month, but it will happen eventually. Once it does, there will be no help for him."

Coll fought to keep the fear from his eyes.

"I want you to think about this as well. All Shadowen have the power to invade and consume. They can inhabit the bodies of other creatures and become them for as long as it is needed." He paused. "I could become you, Coll Ohmsford. I could slip beneath your skin as easily as a knife blade and make you my own." The harsh whisper was a hiss against the silence. "But I don't choose to do that because I don't want to hurt you. I spoke the truth when I told you I wanted to help your brother. You will have to decide for yourself whether or not to believe me, but think about what I have just told you as you do."

He turned, shoved the Mirrorshroud back into its locker, and closed the door. Whether he was angry or frustrated or something else was difficult to tell, but his walk was purposeful as he led Coll from the room and pulled the door closed behind them. Coll listened automatically for the click of the lock and did not hear it. Rimmer Dall was already moving away, so Coll went after him without slowing. The First Seeker took him to a stairway and pointed up.

"Your quarters lie that way. Think carefully, Valeman," he warned. "You play with two lives while you delay."

Coll turned wordlessly and started up the stairs. When he glanced back over his shoulder a dozen steps later, Rimmer Dall was gone.

IT WAS STILL LIGHT, if barely, when he went out once again, passing along the hallway to the stairs, then winding his way downward through the shadows toward the exercise yard. He had left his tunic there; he had forgotten it earlier. He didn't require it, of course, but it provided the excuse he needed to discover whether the door to the room that held the Mirrorshroud had been left unlocked.

His breathing was rapid and harsh-sounding in the silence of his descent. It was a reckless thing he was attempting to do, but his desperation was growing. If he did not get free soon, something bad was going to happen to Par. His conviction of this was based mostly on supposition and fear, but it was no less real for being so. He knew he wasn't thinking as clearly as he should; if he had been, he would never have even considered taking this risk. But if the lock had not released back into place, if the room was still open and the Mirrorshroud still in its locker, waiting . . .

Footsteps sounded from somewhere below, and he froze against the stair wall. The steps grew momentarily louder and then disappeared. Coll wiped his hands on his pants and tried to think. Which floor was it? Four, he had counted, hadn't he? He worked his way ahead again, then stepped onto the fourth landing down and with his body pressed against the stone, peered around the corner.

The hallway before him stood empty.

He took a deep breath to steady himself and stepped from hiding. Down the hall he crept, swift and silent, casting anxious glances ahead and behind as he went. The Shadowen were always watching him. Always. But there were none now, it seemed, none that he could see. He kept going. He checked each door as he passed it. A wolf's head with red lettering below—where was it?

If he was caught . . .

Then the door he was searching for was before him, the wolf's eyes glaring into his own. He stepped up to it quickly, put his ear close and listened. Silence. Carefully he reached out and turned the handle.

It gave easily. The door opened before him and he was through.

The room was empty save for the wooden cabinet, a tall, shrouded coffin propped against the far wall. He could hardly believe his good fortune. Swiftly he went to the cabinet, opened it, and reached inside. His hands closed about the Mirrorshroud. Cautiously he took it out, lifting it toward the graying light. The fabric was soft and thick, the cloak as light as dust. Its blackness was disconcerting, an inkiness that looked as if it could swallow you whole. He held the cloak before him momentarily, studying it, weighing a final time the advisability of what he was about to do.

Then quickly he swung it over his shoulders and let it settle into place. He could barely feel it, a presence no greater than the shadow he cast in the failing daylight. He tied its cords about his neck and lifted the hood into place. He waited expectantly. Nothing seemed different. Everything was the same. He wished suddenly for a mirror in which to study himself, but there was none.

After closing the locker behind him, he crossed the room and stepped out into the hallway.

He hadn't taken a dozen steps when a Shadowen appeared from out of the stairwell.

Coll felt his heart sink. He had no weapons, no means of protection, and no time or place in which to hide. He kept walking toward his discoverer, unable to think what else to do.

The Shadowen went by him without slowing. A brief nod, a barely perceptible lifting of the dark face, and the other was past, moving away as if nothing had happened.

Coll felt a rush of elation coupled with relief. The Shadowen hadn't recognized him! He could scarcely believe it. But there was no time to revel in his good fortune. If he was ever to escape Southwatch and Rimmer Dall, it must be now.

Down he went through the corridors and stairwells of the monolith, skirting well-lit places in favor of darker ones, knowing only one way to go but determined to be noticed as little as possible, cloak or no cloak. His hands clutched the dark folds protectively, and his eyes searched the shadows as the daylight faded to dusk. He reached the exercise yard unchallenged. Weapons and armor stood stacked in racks and hung on pegs, metal edges and fastenings glinting dully. Ulfkingroh was nowhere to be seen. Coll helped himself to a brace of long knives, which he stuffed beneath his cloak. He circled the open area for the doors that led to the outer courts. A pair of Shadowen appeared and went past in the manner of the one before, oblivious. Coll felt his muscles tighten with tension, but his confidence in the Mirrorshroud was growing.

Momentarily he considered going down into the bowels of Southwatch to discover what the Shadowen were hiding there. But the risk was too great, he decided. Better to get clear as quickly as possible. Whatever else, he must be free.

He hastened along the corridors that led to the outer courts, another of twilight's shadows. He reached the courts without challenge, passed through, and almost before he realized it stood before an outer door. He glanced around hurriedly. No one was in sight.

He released the lock, pushed the door open, and stepped out.

He stood within an alcove that sheltered him from the coming night. Beyond, the Rainbow Lake spread away in a glimmer of silver, the surrounding forests a dark, irregular mass that buzzed and hummed with life, the smell of leaves, earth, and grasses wafting sweetly on the summer air.

Coll Ohmsford took a deep breath and smiled. He was free.

He would have preferred to wait until it was completely dark, but he couldn't chance the delay. It wouldn't be long before he was missed. Crouching low against the sawgrass, he sprinted from the shadows of the wall into the trees.

From the window of a darkened room thirty feet up, Rimmer Dall watched him go.

THERE WAS NEVER ANY QUESTION in Coll Ohmsford's mind as to where he would go. He worked his way through the trees that separated Southwatch from the Mermidon, chose a quiet narrows a mile or so upstream, swam the river, and began his trek toward Tyrsis and his brother. He did not know how he would find Par once he reached the city; he would worry about that later. His most immediate concern was that the Shadowen were already searching for him. They seemed to materialize within moments of his escape, black shadows that slipped through the night like wraiths at haunt, silent and spectral. But if they saw him, and he was certain they must have, the Mirrorshroud disguised him from them. They passed without slowing, without interest, disappearing as anonymously as they had come.

But so many of them!

Oddly enough, the cloak seemed to give him a heightened sense of who and where they were. He could feel their presence before he saw them, know from which direction they approached, and discern in advance how many there were. He did not try to hide from them; after all, if the cloak's magic failed, they would search him out in any case. Instead, he tried to appear as an ordinary traveler, keeping to the open grasslands, to the roads when he found them, walking easily, casually, trying not to look furtive.

Somehow it all worked. Though the Shadowen were all about, obviously hunting him, they could not seem to tell who he was.

He slept for a few hours before dawn and resumed his journey at daybreak. He thought on more than one occasion to remove the cloak, but the presence of so many of the black things kept him from doing so. Better to be safe, he told himself. After all, as long as he wore the cloak, he would not be found out.

He passed other travelers on the road as he went. None seemed interested in what they saw of him. A few offered greetings. Most simply passed him by.

He wondered how he appeared to them. He must not have seemed someone they recognized or they would have said something. He must have seemed an ordinary traveler. It made him wonder why Rimmer Dall had looked like his father in the cloak. It made him wonder why the magic acted differently toward him.

The first day passed swiftly, and he camped in a small copse of ash still within view of the Runne. The sun collapsed behind the Westland forests in a splash of red-gold, and the warm night air was scented by grassland wildflowers. He built a fire and ate wild fruit and vegetables. He had a craving for meat, but no real way to catch any. The stars came out, and the night sounds died.

Again the Shadowen appeared, hunting him. Sometimes they came close—and again he was reluctant to remove the cloak. He did so long enough to wash, careful to keep concealed within the trees, and then quickly put it back on again. He was finding it more comfortable to wear now, less constricting and less unfamiliar. He was actually growing to like the sense of invisibility it gave him.

He went on again at first light, striding out across the grasslands, fixing on the dark edges of the Dragon's Teeth where they broke the blue skyline north. Just this side of those mountains lay Tyrsis and Par. The heat of this new day seemed more intense, and he found the light uncomfortable. Perhaps he would begin traveling at night, he decided. The darkness seemed somehow less threatening. He took shelter at midday in a cluster of rocks, crouching back within their shadows, hidden. His mind wandered, scattering to things that were forgotten almost as soon as they were remembered. He hunched down, his cowled head lowered between his knees, and he slept.

Nightfall took him from his shelter. He hunted down a rabbit, spying it out in the dark and chasing it to its den as if he were a cat. He dug down to it with his hands, wrung its neck, carried it back to his rock-walled shelter, and ate it before it was finished cooking over the little fire. He sat staring at the bones afterward, wondering what creature it had been.

Stars and moon brightened in the darkening sky. Somewhere distant, an owl hooted. Coll Ohmsford no longer searched for the Shadowen that hunted him. Somehow, they no longer mattered.

When the night had settled comfortably in about him, he rose, kicked out the fire, and crept from his place of concealment like an animal. Far distant still, but growing closer, was the city. He could smell it in the wind.

There was a rage inside him that he could not explain. There was a hunger. Somehow, though he could not yet determine how, it was tied to Par.

Swiftly he passed north toward the mountains. In the moonlight his eyes glinted blood-red.

22

NIGHTFALL.

Wren Ohmsford walked back across the Harrow through the deepening gloom, empty of feeling. Shadows layered the lava rock, cast by the bones of the ravaged trees and the shifting mists. Daylight had faded to a tinge of brightness west, a candle's slender glow against the dark. The Harrow stretched silent and lifeless all about, a mirror of herself. The magic of the Elfstones had scoured her clean. The death of Eowen had hardened her to iron.

Who am I? she asked herself.

She chose her path without really thinking about it, moving in the direction from which she had come because that was the only way she knew to go. She stared straight ahead without seeing; she listened without hearing.

Who am I?

All of her life she had known the answer to that question. The fact of it had been her one certainty. She was a Rover girl, free of the constraints of personal history, of the ties and obligations of family, and of the need to live up to anyone's expectations but her own. She had Garth to teach her what she needed to know and she could do with herself as she pleased. The future stretched away intriguingly, a blank slate on which her life could be written with any words she chose.

Now that certainty was gone, disappeared as surely as her youthful misconceptions of who and what she would be. She would never be as she had been or had thought she would be.

Never. She had lost it all. And what had she gained? She almost laughed. She had become a chameleon. Just look at her; she could be anyone. She couldn't even be sure of her name. She was an Ohmsford and an Elessedil both. Choose either—it would fit. She was an Elf and a human. She was the child of several families, one who birthed her, two more who raised her.

Who am I?

She was a creature of the magic, heir to the Elfstones, keeper of the Ruhk Staff and the Loden. She bore them all, trusts she had been given to hold, responsibilities she had been empowered to manage. The magic was hers, and she hated the very thought of it. She had never asked for it, certainly never wanted it, and now could not seem to get rid of it. The magic was a shadow within, a dark reflection of herself that rose on command to do her bidding, a trickster that made her feel as nothing else could and at the same time stole away her reason and sanity and threatened to take her over completely. The magic even killed for her—enemies to be sure, but friends as well. *Eowen. Hadn't the magic killed Eowen?* She bit down against her despair. It destroyed—which was all right because that was what she expected it to do, but at the same time was all wrong because it was indiscriminate and even when it chose properly it emptied her a little further of things like compassion, tenderness, remorse, and love, the soft that balanced the hard. It burned away the complexity of her vision and left her stripped of choices.

As she was now, she realized.

A wind had come up, slow and erratic at first, now quick and rough as it gusted across the flats, causing the spines of the trees to shiver and the ravines to hum and moan. It blew across her shoulders, pushing her sideways in the manner of a thoughtless stranger in a crowd. She lowered her head against it, another distraction to be suffered, another obstacle to be overcome. The light west had disappeared, and she was cloaked in darkness. It wasn't so far to go, she told herself wearily. The others were just ahead at the Harrow's edge, waiting.

Just ahead.

She laughed. What did it matter whether they were there or not? What did any of it matter? Her life would do with her as it chose, just as it had been doing ever since she had come in search of herself. No, she corrected, longer ago than that. Forever, perhaps. She laughed again. Come in search of herself, her family, the Elves, the truth—such foolishness! She could hear the mocking sounds of her own voice as the thoughts chased after one another.

A voice that echoed in the wind.

What matter? it whispered.

What difference?

Her thoughts returned unbidden to Eowen, kind and gentle, doomed in spite of her seer's gifts, fated to be swallowed up by them. What good had it done Eowen to know her future? What good would it do any of them? What good, in fact, even to try to determine it? Useless, she raged, because in the end it would do with you what it chose in any case. It would make you what it wished, take you where it willed, and leave you in its own good time.

All about her, the wind voice howled. *Let go!*

She heard it, nodded in recognition, and began to cry. The words caressed her like a mother's hands, and she welcomed their touch. Everything seemed to be fading away. She was walking—where? She didn't stop, didn't pause to wonder, but simply kept moving because movement helped, taking her away from the hurt, the anguish. She had something to do—what? She shook her head, unable to determine, and brushed at her tears with the back of her hand.

The hand that held the Elfstones.

She looked down at it wonderingly, surprised to discover the Stones were still there. The magic pulsed within her fist, within the fingers tightly wrapped about, its blue glow seeping through the cracks, spilling out into the dark. Why was it doing that? She stared blankly, vaguely aware that something was wrong. Why did it burn so?

Let go, the wind voice whispered.

I want to! she howled in the silence of her mind.

She slowed, looking up from the pathway her feet had been following, from the emptiness of the ground. The Harrow had taken on a different cast, one of brightness and warmth. There were faces all about, strangely alive against the haze, filled with understanding of her need. The faces were familiar, of friends and family, of all those who had loved and supported her, living and dead, come out of her imagination into life. She was surprised when they appeared, but pleased as well. She spoke to them, a word or two, tentative, curious. They glanced her way and whispered in reply.

Let go.

Let go.

The words repeated insistently in her mind, a glimmer of hope. She slowed and finally stopped, no longer knowing where she was and no longer caring. She was so tired. Her life was a shambles. She could not even pretend that she had any control over it. It rode her as a rider would a horse, but without pause or rest, without destination, endlessly into night.

Let go.

She blinked, then smiled. Understanding flooded through her. Of course. So simple, really. Let go of the magic. Let go, and the weariness and confusion and sense of loss would pass. Let go, and she would have a chance to start over again, to regain possession of her life, to return to who and what she had been. Why hadn't she seen it before?

Something tugged at her in warning, some part of her deep within that had become buried in the sound of the wind's voice. Curious, she tried to uncover it, but feathery touches on her skin distracted her. There was a burning against the skin of her palm from the Elfstones, but she ignored it. The touches were more intriguing, more inviting. She lifted her face to find their source. The faces were all about her now, milling at the edge of the darkness and the mist, taking on form. She knew them, didn't she? Why couldn't she remember?

Let go.

She cocked the hand that grasped the Elfstones in response, barely conscious of the act, and a sliver of blue light escaped the cracks of her fingers, lancing into the dark. Instantly the faces were gone. She blinked in confusion. What was she doing? Why had she stopped walking? She glanced about in alarm, seeing the darkness and the mist of the Harrow, realizing she was lost somewhere within, that she had strayed. The Drakuls were there, watching. She could feel their presence. She swallowed against her fear. What had she been thinking?

She started moving again, trying to sort out what had happened. She was dimly aware that for a time she had lost track of everything, that she must have wandered aimlessly. She remembered bits and pieces of her thoughts, like the fragments of dreams on waking. She had been about to do something, she thought worriedly. But what?

The minutes passed. Far ahead, lost in the howl of the wind, she heard the call of her name. It was there, hanging momentarily in a lull, then gone. She moved toward it, wondering if she was still going in the right direction. If she was unable to determine so soon, she would have to use the Elfstones. The thought was anathema. She never wanted to use them again. All she could see in her mind's eye was their fire exploding into the monster that had once been Eowen and turning her to ash.

Again she began to cry and again quickly stopped herself. There was no use in it, no point. Leafless trees and fire-washed lava rock spread away from her, an endless, changeless expanse. The Harrow seemed to go on forever. She was lost, she decided, become turned about somehow. She stopped and glanced around wearily. Exhaustion flooded through her, and in anguish and despair she closed her eyes.

The wind whispered. *Let go.*

Yes, she replied silently, *I want to.*

The spell of the words folded about her like a warm cloak, wrapped her and held her close. She resisted but a moment, then gave herself over to it. When she opened her eyes, the faces were back again, surrounding her in a circle of faint light and feathery touches. She saw that she was at the edge of a ravine—a familiar place, it seemed. Once again, everything began to fade. She forgot that she was trying to escape the Harrow, that the faces about her were something other than what they appeared to be. The haze of the mist crept into her mind and settled there, thick and murky. Her ice-bound thoughts melted and ran like liquid through her body; she could feel their cold. She was so tired, so weary of everything.

Let go.

The hand that clutched the Elfstones lowered, and the faces clustered about her began to take on shape and size. Lips brushed her throat.

Let go.

She let her eyes close again. Her fingers loosened. It would all be so easy. Let the Elfstones fall, and she would escape the magic's chain forever.

"Lady Wren!"

The shout was an anguished howl, and for a moment's time it didn't register. Then her eyes snapped open, and her body tensed. The strange sleep that had almost claimed her hovered close, a whisper of insistent need. Through its fog, beyond its pall, she saw two figures crouched at the edge of the light. They held swords in their hands, the metal glinting faintly.

"Phfftt! Don't move, Wren of the Elves!" she heard another cry out in warning. Stresa.

"Stay where you are, Lady Wren," the first cautioned frantically. Triss.

The Captain of the Home Guard inched forward, his weapon held before him. She saw his face now, lean and hard, filled with determination. Behind him was Garth, a larger form, darker, inscrutable. Leading them both, spines bristling, was the Splinterscat.

A cold place opened in the pit of her stomach. What were they doing here? What had happened to bring them? She felt a surge of fear strike her, a sense that something was about to happen and she had not even been aware of it.

She forced back the lassitude, the calm, and the whisper of the wind and made herself see again. The cold turned to ice. The light surrounding her emanated from the things that clustered close. Drakuls, all about. They were so close she could feel their breath—or seem to. She could see their dead eyes, their gaunt, nearly featureless faces, and their ivory fangs. There were dozens of them, pressed about her, parted only at the point where Triss and Garth and Stresa sought to approach, a window into the dark of the Harrow. Their hands and fingers clutched her, held her fast, bound her in ropes of hunger. They had lured her to them, lulled her almost to slumber as they must have done Eowen. Turned from phantoms to things of substance, they were about to feed.

For an instant Wren hung suspended between being and nonbeing, between life and death. She could feel the draw of two choices, very different, each compelling. One would have her break free of the soothing, deadly bonds that held her, would have her rise up in revulsion and fury and fight for her life because that was what her instincts told her she must do. The other would have her do as the wind voice had whispered and simply let go because that was the only way she would ever be free of the magic. Time froze. She weighed the possibilities as if detached from them, a judging that seemed to bring into focus the whole of her existence, past, present, and future. She could see her rescuers creep nearer, their gestures unmistakable. She could feel the Drakuls draw a fraction of an inch closer. Neither seemed to matter. Each was a distant, slow-moving reality that could change in the blink of an eye.

Then fangs brushed her throat—a whisper of hunger and need.

Drakuls.

Shadowen.

Elves.

An evolution of horror—and only she knew.

If I do not escape Morrowindl and return to the Four Lands, who else will ever know?

"Lady Wren!" Triss called softly to her, his voice pleading, desperate, angry and lost.

She stepped back from the precipice and took a long, deep breath. She could feel the strength of her body return, a rising up out of lethargy. But she would still be too slow. She flexed gently, almost imperceptibly, seeking to discover if she could move, testing the limits of her freedom. There were none; the hands that secured her held her so fast that she might as soon have been chained to the earth.

One chance, then. One hope. Her mind focused, hard and insistent, reaching deep within. Her fingers slipped open.

Now.

Blue fire exploded into the night, racing up her body to sheathe her in flames. The fangs jerked back, the hands fell away, the Drakuls shrieked in fury, and she was free. She stood within a cylinder of fire, the magic's heat racing over her, wrapping her about as she waited for the pain to begin, anticipated what it would feel like to be burned to ash. *Better that than to become one of them*, the thought flashed through her mind, the corner of her life's need turned and become a certainty she would not question again. *Just let it be quick!*

The fire pillared over her, rising up against the black, searing the curtain of the vog. The Drakuls flung themselves into the flames, desperately trying to reach her, moths bereft of reason. They died in sudden bursts of light, incinerated as quick as thought. Wren watched them come at her, reach for her, become entangled in the fire and disappear. Her eyes snapped open seeking the Elfstones. She found them in the cup of her open hand, white with magic, as brilliant as small suns.

Yet she did not burn. The fire raged about her, swallowed her attackers, and left her untouched.

Oh, yes!

Now the exhilaration began, the sense of power that the magic always gave her. She felt invincible, indestructible. The fire could not hurt her, would not—and she must have known as much. She flung her hands out, carrying the fire away from her in a sweep, into the maelstrom of Drakuls that circled about her. They were engulfed and consumed, shrieking in despair. *For you, Eowen!* She watched them perish and felt nothing beyond the joy that use of the magic gave her, the Drakuls reduced to things of no consequence, as insignificant to her as dust. She embraced the magic's power and let it carry her beyond reason, beyond thought.

Use it, she told herself. *Nothing else matters.*

For an instant, she was lost completely. Forgotten were Triss and Garth, the need to escape Morrowindl and return to the Four Lands, the truths she had learned and planned to tell, the history of who and what she was, and the lives that had been given into her trust, everything. Forgotten was any purpose beyond the wielding of the Elfstones.

Then some small, ragged corner of her conscience reclaimed her once again, a whisper of sanity that reached past the mix of fear and exhaustion and despair that threatened to turn determination to madness. She saw Triss and Garth and Stresa as they fought the Drakuls turning now on them, back to back as the circle closed. She heard their cries to her and heard the voice within herself that echoed in reply. She sensed the island of self on which she had retreated beginning to sink into the fire.

Down came the hand with the Elfstones, the pillar of flames dying to a flare of light that curled about her hand, brought under control once more. She saw the darkness and the mist again, the ragged slopes of the ravine, the lava rock, jagged and black. She smelled the night, the ash and fire and heat. She wheeled toward the Drakuls and hissed at them as a snake might. They backed away in fear. She moved toward her friends, and the attackers that ringed them fell away. She carried death in her hand, certain annihilation for things who understood all too well what annihilation meant. They shimmered about her, losing substance. She stalked into their midst, unafraid, swinging the light of her magic this way and that, threatening, menacing, alive with deadly promise. The Drakuls did not challenge; in an instant they faded and were gone.

She came then to where Garth and Triss stood crouched, weapons in hand, uncertainty in their eyes. She stopped before Stresa, who stared up at her as if she were a thing beyond comprehension. She closed her fingers tight about the Elfstones, and the fire winked out.

"Help me walk from the ravine," she whispered, so weary she was in danger of collapse, knowing she could not, realizing that the Drakuls still watched.

Triss had his arm about her instantly. "Lady, we thought you lost," he said as he turned her gently about.

"I was," she answered, her smile tight.

Slowly, a step at a time, eyes sweeping the island night, they began to climb.

IT TOOK THEM UNTIL MIDNIGHT to get clear of the Harrow. The Drakuls had drawn Wren deep into their lair, far from the pathway she had thought to follow, turning her about so completely after discovering Eowen that she had ended up wandering across the flats in the wrong direction. Stresa had managed to track her, but it hadn't been easy. They had come in search of her at nightfall, despite her command that they were not to do so, worried by then because she had been gone so long, determined to make certain that she was safe, even at the risk of their own lives. They knew they had no effective protection against the Drakuls, but that no longer mattered. Both Garth and Triss were decided. Dal was left to keep watch over Gavilan and the Ruhk Staff. Stresa had come because no one else could find Wren's trail in the dark. They might not have found her even then if the Drakuls hadn't been so preoccupied with their quarry. Even a handful of the wraiths would have been enough to disrupt the rescue effort. But Wren, bearer of the Elfstone magic, was a lure for the Drakuls, and all had joined in the hunt, anxious to share in the feeding, Shadowen to the end. Stresa had been able to track her unhindered. They had found her, it seemed, just in time.

Wren told them in turn of Eowen's fate, of how the Drakuls had subverted her, of how she had been made one of them. She described the seer's death, unwilling to gloss past it, needing to hear the words, to give voice to her grief. It felt as if she were speaking from some hollow place within, wrapped in a haze of emptiness and exhaustion. She was so tired. Yet she would not slow; she would not rest. She disdained all help once clear of the ravine. She walked because she would not let herself be carried, because that would be another demonstration of weakness and she had shown weakness enough for one night. She was dismayed by what had happened to her, appalled at how easily she had been misled by the wind voice, how close she had come to dying, and how willing she had been to allow it to happen—Wren Elessedil, called Queen of the Elves, bearer of the trust of a people, heir of so much magic. She could still remember how inviting the wind voice had made it seem for her to give up her life. She had been so ready, welcoming the peace she had supposed she would find. All of her life she had been strong in the face of death, never giving way to the possibility of it finding her, always certain that she would fight for her last breath. What had happened in the Harrow had shaken her confidence more than she cared to admit. She had failed to resist as she had always told herself she would. She had let exhaustion and despair work through her so thoroughly that she was as hollowed out as wormwood and as quick to crumble. She saw the way the magic pulled her, first one way, then the other, the Drakul's, her own. Just as Eowen had been a prisoner of her visions, so Wren was now becoming a prisoner of the Elven magic. She hated herself for it. She despised what she had become.

I am nothing of what I believed, she thought in despair. *I am a lie.*

She talked to keep from thinking of it, speaking of what she had seen as she wandered the Harrow, of how the wind voice of the Drakuls had lulled her, of how Eowen—so vulnerable to visions and images—must have become ensnared. She rambled at times, the sound of her voice helping to distract her from dark thoughts, keeping her awake, keeping her moving. She thought of the dead on this nightmare journey, of Ellenroh and Eowen in particular. She was consumed by their loss, ravaged by feelings of helplessness at having been unable to save them and by guilt at being inadequate for the task they had left her. She clutched the Elfstones tightly in her hand, unable to persuade herself to put them away, frightened that the Drakuls would come again. They did not. Not even the wind voice whispered in the darkness now, gone back into the earth, leaving her alone. She gazed out into the black and felt it a mirror of the void within. She was heartsick for what she had become and what she feared she yet might be. The world was a place she no longer understood. She could not even decide which was the greater evil—the monsters or the monster makers. Shadowen or Elves—which should bear the blame? Where was the balance to life that should come from lessons learned and experience gained? Where was the sense that the madness would pass, that a purpose would be revealed for everything that was happening? She had no answers. The magic had caught them all up in a whirlwind, and it would drop them where it chose.

This night, it picked a darker hole than she would have imagined could exist. They came off the Harrow bone weary and numb, relieved to be clear, anxious to be gone. They would rest until dawn, then continue on. The greater part of Blackledge was behind them now, left in the shadow of Killeshan's vog. Ahead, between themselves and the beaches, there was only the In Ju. They would pass through the jungle quickly, two days if they hurried, and reach the shores of the Blue Divide in two more. Quick, now, they urged themselves silently. Quick, and get free.

They reached the spot where their companions had been left, a clearing within a cluster of lava rocks in the shadow of a fringe of barren vines and famished scrub. Faun raced through the darkness, come out of hiding from some distance off, chittering wildly, springing to Wren's shoulder and hunkering there as if no other haven existed. Wren's hands came up reassuringly. The Tree Squeak was shivering with fear.

They found Dal then, sprawled at the clearing's far edge, a lifeless tangle of arms and legs, his skull split wide. Triss bent close and turned the Elven Hunter over.

He looked up, stunned. Dal's weapons were still sheathed.

Wren glanced away in despair, a dark certainty already taking hold. She didn't have to look further to know that Gavilan Elessedil and the Ruhk Staff were gone.

CHAPTER
23

PAR OHMSFORD CROUCHED in the shadow of the building wall, as dark as the night about him within the covering of his cloak, listening to the sounds of Tyrsis as she stirred restlessly beneath her blanket of summer heat, waiting for morning. The air was still and filled with the city's smells, sweet, sticky, and cloying. Par breathed it in reluctantly, wearily, peering out from his shelter into the pools of light cast by the street lamps, watchful for things that didn't belong, that crept and hunted, that searched relentlessly.

The Federation.

The Shadowen.

They were both out there, stalkers that never seemed to sleep and that refused to quit. For almost a week now Damson and he had been running from them, ever since they had fled the Mole's underground hideout and made their way back through the sewers of the city to the streets. A week. He could barely sort through the debris of its passing, his memory in fragments, a jumble of buildings and rooms, of closets and crawl-ways, and of one concealment after another. They had not been able to rest anywhere for more than a few hours, always discovered somehow just when they had thought themselves safe, forced to run again, to flee the dark things that sought to claim them.

How was it, Par wondered for what must have been the thousandth time, that they were always found so quickly?

At first he had attributed it to luck. But luck would only

take you so far, and the regularity of their discovery had soon ruled out any possibility that it was luck alone. Then he had thought that it might be his magic, traced somehow by Rimmer Dall—for it was the Seekers that came most often, sometimes in Federation guise, but more often revealed as the monsters they were, dark shadows cloaked and hooded. But he hadn't used his magic since they had escaped the sewers, and if he hadn't used it, how could it be traced?

"They have infiltrated the Movement," Damson had declared, tight-lipped and wan before leaving him only hours earlier to search anew for a hiding place about which their pursuers did not know. "Or they have caught one of us and extracted all of our secrets. There is no other explanation."

But even she had been forced to admit that no one other than Padishar Creel knew all the hiding places she used. No one else could have betrayed them.

Which led, in turn, to the disquieting possibility that despite their hopes to the contrary, the fall of the Jut had yielded the Federation the catch it had been so anxious to make.

Par let his head fall back to rest against the rough, heated stone, his eyes closing momentarily in despair. Coll dead. Padishar and Morgan missing. Wren and Walker Boh. Steff and Teel. The company. Even the Mole—there had been no word of him since they had fled his subterranean chambers. There was no sign of him, nothing to reveal what had happened. It was maddening. Everyone he had started out with weeks ago— his brother, his cousin, his uncle, and his friends—had disappeared. It sometimes seemed as if everyone he came in contact with was doomed to fall off the face of the earth, to be swallowed by some netherworld blackness and never resurface again.

Even Damson . . .

No. His eyes snapped open again, anger reflected in the glimmer from the lamps. *Not Damson. He would not lose her. It would not happen again.*

But how much longer could they keep running like this? How long before their enemies finally ran them to earth?

There was sudden movement at the corner of the wall ahead where it turned the building to follow the street west toward the bluff, and Damson appeared. She scurried through the shadows in a crouch and came up next to him, breathless and flushed.

"Two other safe holes are discovered," she said. "I could smell the stench of the things that watch for us even before I saw them." Her long red hair was tangled and damp against her face and neck, tied back by a cloth band about her forehead. Her smile, when it came, was unexpected. "But I found one they missed."

Her hand reached out to brush his cheek. "You look so tired, Par. Tonight you will sleep well. This place—I remembered it, actually. A cellar beneath an old gristmill that was once something else, I forget what. It hasn't been used in more than a year—not by anyone. Once, Padishar and I . . ." She stopped, the memory retrieved at the verge of its telling and drawn back again—too painful, her eyes said, to relate. "They will not know of this one. Come with me, Valeman. We'll try again."

They hurried off into the night, twin shadows that appeared and faded again as quick as the blink of an eye. Par felt the weight of the Sword of Shannara against his back, flat and hard, its presence a reminder of the travesty his quest had become and of the confusions that plagued him. Was this, in fact, the ancient talisman he had been sent to find, or some trick of Rimmer Dall's meant to bring him to his destruction? If it was the Sword, why had he not been able to make it work when face to face with the First Seeker? If it was a fake, what had become of the real Sword?

But the questions, as always, yielded no answers, only further questions, and as always, he quickly abandoned them. Survival was all that counted for the moment, evasion of the black things and, more important, escape from the city. For their flight had been that of rats in a maze, trapped behind walls from which they could not break free. All efforts at getting clear of Tyrsis to regain the open country beyond had been thwarted. The gates were carefully watched, all the exits guarded, and Damson lacked sufficient skill, in the absence of the Mole, to navigate the tunnels beneath the city that provided the only other means of escape. So there was nothing left for them but to continue to run and hide, to scurry from one hole to the next, and to wait for an opportunity to arise or a means to present itself that would at last set them free.

They turned down a side street dappled with shards of light cast through the slats of shutters closed against windows high on a back wall, hearing laughter and the clink of drinking glasses from the alehouse within. Garbage littered the street, damp and stinking. Tyrsis wore her cheapest perfume in this quarter, and the smell of her body was rank and shameless where the poor and the homeless had been crowded away by the occupiers. Once a proud lady, she was used up and cast off now, a chattel to be treated as the Federation wished, a spoil of a war that had been over before it had begun.

Damson paused, searched carefully the empty swath of a lighted crossing, listened momentarily for sounds that didn't belong, then took him swiftly across. They passed down a second side street, this one as silent and musty as an unopened closet, then through an alcove and into an alley that connected to another street. Par was thinking of the Sword of Shannara again, wondering how he could discover if it was real and what test he could put it to that would determine the truth.

"Here," Damson whispered, turning him abruptly through the broken opening of an ancient board wall.

They stood in a barnlike room thick with gloom, the rafters overhead barely visible in the faint light of other buildings where it seeped through cracks in the split, dry boards of the walls. Machines hunkered down like animals crouched to spring, and rows of bins yawned empty and black. Damson steered him across the room, their boots crunching on stone and straw in the deep silence. Close to the back wall she stopped, reached down, seized an iron ring embedded in the floor, and pulled free a trapdoor. A glimmer of light showed stairs leading down into blackness.

"You first," she ordered, motioning. "Just inside, then stop."

He did as he was told, listened to the sound of her footsteps as she followed, then of the trapdoor as it closed behind them. They stood listening for a moment, then she pushed carefully past and fumbled quietly in the dark. A spark struck, a flame appeared, and the pitch of a torch caught and began to burn.

Light filled the chamber in which they stood, weak and hazy, revealing a low cellar filled with old iron-banded casks and disintegrating crates. She gestured for him to follow, and they moved ahead through the debris. The cellar stretched on for a time, then ended at a passageway. Damson bent low against the black, thrust the torch ahead of her, and entered. The passage took them down a series of intersecting corridors to a room that had once been a sleeping chamber. A worn bed was positioned against one wall, a table and chairs against another. A second passage led out the other side and back into blackness. Where the torchlight ended, Par could just make out the beginning of a set of ancient stairs.

"We should be safe here for tonight, maybe longer," she advised, turning now so that the light caught her features, the bright gleam of her green eyes, the softness of her smile. "It's not much, is it?"

"If it's safe, it's everything," he replied, smiling back. "Where do the stairs lead?"

"Back to the street. But the door is locked from the outside. We would have to break it down if we needed to escape that way, if we were unable to use the cellar entry. Still, that's at least a measure of protection against being trapped. And no one will think to look where the lock is old and rusted and still in place."

He nodded, took the torch from her hand, looked about momentarily, then carried it to a ruined lamp bracket and jammed it in place. "Home it is," he declared, unslinging the Sword of Shannara and leaning it against the bed. His eyes lingered momentarily on the crest graven in its hilt, the upraised hand with its burning torch. Then he turned away. "Anything to eat in the cupboard?"

She laughed. "Hardly." Impulsively she went to him, put her arms about his waist, held him momentarily, then kissed his cheek. "Par Ohmsford." She spoke his name softly.

He hugged her, stroked her hair, felt the warmth of her seep through him. "I know," he whispered.

"It will be all right for you and me."

He nodded without speaking, determined that it would be, that it must.

"I have some fresh cheese and bread in my pack," she said, pulling away. "And some ale. Good enough for refugees like us."

They ate in silence, listening to the muffled tick of cooling iron nails embedded in the building's walls, tightening as the night grew deeper. Once or twice there were voices, so distant the words were indistinguishable, carried from the street through the padlocked door and down the ancient stairs. When they had finished, they carefully packed away what was left, extinguished the torch, wrapped themselves in their blankets, lay close together on the narrow bed, and quickly fell asleep.

Daybreak brought a glimmer of light creeping through cracks and crevices, cool and hazy, and the sounds of the city grew loud and distinct as people began to venture forth on a new day's business. Par woke refreshed for the first time in a week, wishing he had water in which to wash, but grateful simply to be shed momentarily of his weariness. Damson was bright-eyed and lovely to look upon, tousled and at the same time perfectly ordered, and Par felt as if the worst might at last be behind them.

"The first order of business is to find a way out of the city," Damson declared between bites of her breakfast, seated across from him at the little table. Her forehead was lined with determination. "We can't go on like this."

"I wish we could find out something about the Mole."

She nodded, her eyes shifting away. "I've looked for him when I've been out." She shook her head. "The Mole is resourceful. He has stayed alive a long time."

Not with the Shadowen hunting for him, Par almost said, then thought better of it. Damson would be thinking the same thing anyway. "What do I do today?"

She looked back at him. "Same as always. You stay put. They still don't know about me. They only know about you."

"You hope."

She sighed. "I hope. Anyway, I have to find a way for us to get past the walls, out of Tyrsis to where we can discover what's happened to Padishar and the others."

He folded his arms across his chest and leaned back. "I feel useless just sitting around here."

"Sometimes waiting is what works best, Par."

"And I don't like letting you go out alone."

She smiled. "And I don't like leaving you here by yourself. But that's the way it has to be for now. We have to be smart about this."

She pulled on her street cloak, her magician's garb, for she still appeared regularly in the marketplace to do tricks for the children, keeping up the appearance that everything was the same as always. A pale shaft of light penetrated the gloom of the passageways that had brought them, and with a wave back to him she disappeared into it and was gone.

He spent the remainder of the morning being restless, prowling the narrow confines of his shelter. Once, he climbed to the top of the stairs leading back to the street where he tested the lock that fastened the heavy wooden door and found it secure. He wandered back through the tunnels that branched from the gristmill cellar and discovered that each dead-ended at a storage hold or bin, all long empty and abandoned. When noon came, he took his lunch from the remains of yesterday's foodstuffs, still cached in Damson's backpack, then stretched out on the bed to nap and fell into a deep sleep.

When he finally woke, the light had gone silver, and the day was fading rapidly into dusk. He lay blinking sleepily for a moment, then realized that Damson had not returned. She had been gone almost ten hours. He rose quickly, worried now, thinking that she should have been back long ago. It was possible that she had come in and gone out again, but not likely. She would have woken him. He would have woken himself. He frowned darkly, uneasily, twisted his body from side to side to ease the kinks, and wondered what to do.

Hungry, in spite of his concern, he decided to eat something, and finished off the last of the cheese and bread. There was a little ale in the stoppered skin, but it tasted stale and warm.

Where was Damson?

Par Ohmsford had known the risks from the beginning, the dangers that Damson Rhee faced every time she left him and went out into the city. If the Mole was captured, they would make him talk. If the safe holes were compromised, she might be, too. If Padishar was taken, there were no secrets left. He knew the risks; he had told himself he had accepted them. But faced for the first time since escaping from the sewers that the worst had happened, he found he was not prepared after all. He found that he was terrified.

Damson. If anything had happened to her . . .

A scuffing sound caught his attention, and he left the thought unfinished. He started, then wheeled about, searching for the source of the noise. It was behind him, at the top of the stairs, at the door leading to the street.

Someone was playing with the lock.

At first he thought it must be Damson, forced for some reason to try to enter through the back. But Damson did not have a key. And the sound he was hearing was of a key scraping in the lock. The fumbling continued, ending in a sharp *snick* as the lock released.

Par reached down for the Sword of Shannara and strapped it quickly across his back. Whoever was up there, it was not Damson. He snatched up the backpack, thinking to hide any trace of his being there. But his bootprints were everywhere, the bed was mussed, and small crumbs of food littered the table. Besides, there was no time. The intruder had lifted the lock from its hasp and was opening the door.

Daylight flooded through the opening, an oblique shaft of wan gray. Par backed hastily from the room into the tunnels. He left the torch. He no longer needed it to find his way. The morning's explorations had left him with a clear vision of which way to go, even in the near dark. Boots thudded softly on the wooden steps, too heavy and rough to be Damson's.

He went down the tunnel in a noiseless crouch. Whoever had entered would know he had been there, but would not know how long ago. They would wait for him to return, thinking to catch him unprepared. Or Damson. But he could wait for Damson somewhere close to the entrance to the old mill and warn her before she entered. Damson would never come through the back entrance with the lock sprung. His thoughts raced through his mind in rapid succession, propelling him on through the darkness, silent and swift. All he had to do was escape detection, to get back through the cellar and out the door to the street.

He could no longer hear footsteps. Good. The intruder had

stopped to view the room, was wondering who had been there, how many of them there had been, and why they had come. More time for Par to get away, a better chance for him to escape.

But when he reached the cellar, he moved too quickly toward the stairs leading up and stumbled into an empty wooden crate, tripped, and fell. The rotting wood cracked and splintered beneath him, the sound reverberating sharply through the silence.

As he pulled himself back to his feet, furious, breathless, he could hear the sound of footsteps coming toward him.

He broke for the stairs, no longer bothering to hide his flight. The footsteps gave chase. Not Shadowen, he thought—they would be silent in their coming. Federation, then. But only one. Why just one?

He gained the stairs and scrambled up. The trapdoor was a faint silhouette above. He wondered suddenly if others might be waiting above, if he was being driven into a trap. Should he stand his ground and face the one rather than allow himself to be herded toward the others? But it was all speculation, and besides there wasn't time left to decide. He was already at the trapdoor.

He shoved upward against it. The trapdoor did not move.

Shafts of fading daylight found their way through gaps in the heavy wooden boards and danced off his sweat-streaked face, momentarily blinding him. Lowering his head, he shoved upward a second time. The door was solidly in place. He squinted past the light, trying to see what had happened.

Something large and bulky was sitting atop the front edge of the trapdoor.

In desperation, he threw himself against the barrier, but it refused to budge. He backed down the steps, casting a quick glance over his shoulder. His heart was beating so loudly in his ears he could barely manage to hear the muffled voice that called his name.

"Par? Par Ohmsford?"

A man, someone he knew it seemed, but he wasn't sure. The voice was familiar and strange all at once. The speaker was still back in the tunnels, lost in the darkness. The gristmill cellar stretched low and tight to the dark opening, dust motes dancing on the air in the gloom, a haze that turned everything to shadow. Par looked at the trapdoor once more, then back again at the cellar.

He was trapped.

The line of his mouth tightened. Sweat was running down his body in the wake of his exertion and fear, and his skin was crawling.

Who was back there?

Who was it who would know his name?

He thought again of Damson, wondering where she was, what had become of her, whether she was safe. If she had been taken, then he was the only one left she could depend upon. He could not let himself be captured because then there would be no one to help her. Or him. Damson. He saw her flaming red hair, the quirk of her mouth as she smiled at him, and the brightness of her green eyes. He could hear her voice, her laughter. He could feel her touching him. He remembered how she had worked to save his life, to keep him from the madness that had claimed him when Coll had died.

The feelings he experienced in that instant were overwhelming, so intense he almost cried them out.

Anger and determination replaced his fear. He reached back and started to draw free the Sword of Shannara, then let it slip back into its sheath. The Sword was meant for other things. He would use his magic, use it even though it frightened him now, an old friend who had turned unexpectedly strange and unfamiliar. The magic was unreliable, quixotic, and dangerous.

And of questionable use, he realized suddenly, if what he faced was human.

His thoughts scattered, leaving him bereft of hope. He reached back a second time and pulled free the Sword. It was his only weapon after all.

A shadow appeared at the mouth of the tunnel, breath hissing softly in the sudden silence, a cloaked form, dark and featureless in the failing light. A man, it looked, taller than Par and broader as well.

The man stepped clear of the dark and straightened. He

started forward and then abruptly stopped, seeing Par crouched on the cellar stairs, weapon in hand. The long knife in his own hand glinted dully. For an instant they faced each other without moving, each trying to identify the other.

Then the intruder's hands reached up slowly and slid back the hood of his dusty black cloak.

CHAPTER

24

RISS STRAIGHTENED, his movements leaden and stiff. They stared wordlessly at one another, the Captain of the Home Guard, Wren, and Garth, faceless in Morrowindl's vog-shrouded night. They stood like statues about the crumpled form of Dal, as if sentinels set at watch, frozen in time. They were all that remained of the company of nine who had set out from beneath Killeshan's shadow to bear Arborlon and the Elves from their volcanic grave to life anew within the forests of the Westland. Three, Wren emphasized through her anguish, for Gavilan was lost to them as surely as her own innocence.

How could she have been so stupid?

Triss shifted abruptly, breaking his bonds. He walked away, bent down to examine the earth, stood again, and shook his head. "What could have done this? There must be tracks . . ." He trailed off.

Wren and Garth exchanged glances. Triss still didn't understand. "It was Gavilan," she said softly.

"Gavilan?" The Captain of the Home Guard turned. He stared at her blankly.

"Gavilan Elessedil," she repeated, speaking his full name, hoping that the saying of it would make what had happened real for her. Against her shoulder, Faun still shivered. "He's killed Dal and taken the Ruhk Staff."

Triss did not move. "No," he said at once. "Lady Wren, that could not happen. You are wrong. Gavilan is an Elf, and no Elf would harm another. Besides, he is a prince of the Elessedil blood! He is sworn to serve his people!"

Wren shook her head in despair. She should have seen it coming. She should have read it in his eyes, his voice, his changing behavior. It was there, and she had simply refused to recognize it. "Stresa," she called.

The Splinterscat lumbered up from out of the dark, spines prickling belligerently. "Hssssttt! I warned you about him!"

"Thank you for reminding me. Just tell me what the signs say. Your eyes are sharpest, your nose better able to measure. Read them for me, please."

Her words were gentle and filled with pain. The Splinterscat saw and edged quietly away. They watched as he began to skirt the clearing, sniffing, scanning, pausing frequently, then continuing on.

"He could not have done this," Triss murmured anew, the words hard-edged with disbelief. Wren did not reply. She looked away at nothing. The Harrow was a gray screen behind them, the In Ju a black hole ahead. Killeshan was a distant rumble. Morrowindl hunched over them like an animal with a bone.

Then Stresa was back. "Nothing—phhhfft—has passed through the place we stand in the last few hours except us. Sssttt. Our tracks come out from the Harrow, go in, then come out again—over there. Just us—no monsters, no intruders, nothing." He paused. "There." He swiveled in the opposite direction. "A newer set of tracks depart, west, toward the In Ju. His scent. I'm sorry, Wren Elessedil."

She nodded, her own last vestige of hope shredded. She looked pointedly at Triss.

"Why?" he asked, a worn and defeated whisper.

Because he was terrified, she thought. Because he was a creature of order and comfort, of walls and safe havens, and this was all too much for him, too overwhelming. Because he thought them all dead and was afraid that he would die too if he didn't run. Or because he was greedy and desperate and wanted the power of the Ruhk Staff and its magic for himself.

"I don't know," she said wearily.

"But Dal . . . ?"

"What difference does it make?" she interrupted, more angry than she should have been, regretting her harshness immediately. She took a deep breath. "What matters is that he has taken the Ruhk Staff and the Loden, and we have to get them back. We have to find him. Quickly."

She turned. "Stresa?"

"No," the Splinterscat said at once. "Hssstt. It is too dangerous to track at night. Stay here until daybreak."

She shook her head deliberately. "We don't have that much time."

"Rrrwwll Wren Elessedil. We had best find it then, if we want to stay alive!" Stresa's rough voice deepened to a growl. "Only a fool would venture down off the Blackledge and into the In Ju at night."

Wren felt her anger building. She did not care to be challenged just now. She could not permit it. "I have the Elfstones, Stresa!" she snapped. "The Elven magic will protect us!"

"The Elven magic you—hssstt—are so anxious not to use?" Stresa's words were a taunt. "Phhffft. I know you cared for him, but . . ."

"Stresa!" she screamed.

". . . the magic will not protect against what you cannot see," the other finished, calm, unruffled. "Ssstttpp! We must wait until morning."

The silence was immense. Inside, Wren could hear herself shriek. She looked up as Garth stepped in front of her. *The Splinterscat is right. Remember your training, Wren. Remember who you are.*

What she could remember at the moment was the look she had seen in Gavilan Elessedil's eyes when she had given him the Ruhk Staff. She met Garth's gaze squarely. What she saw in his eyes stayed her anger. Reluctantly she nodded. "We'll wait until morning."

She kept watch then while the others slept, her own exhaustion forgotten, buried in her anger and despair over Gavilan. She could not sleep while feeling so unsettled, her mind racing and her emotions in disarray. She sat alone with her back against a stand of rocks while the men curled up in sleep a dozen feet away and Stresa hunkered down at the clearing's edge, perhaps asleep, perhaps not. She stared into blackness, stroking Faun absently, thinking thoughts darker than the night.

Gavilan. He had been so charming, so comfortable when she had met him. She had liked him—perhaps more than liked him. She had harbored expectations for them that even now she could not bring herself to admit. He had promised to be a friend to her, to look after her, to give her what answers he could to the questions she asked, and to be there when she needed him. He had promised so much. Perhaps he could have kept those promises if they had not been forced to leave the protection of the Keel. For she had not been mistaken in assessing Gavilan's weakness; he was not strong enough for what lay beyond the safety of Arborlon's walls. The changes in him had been apparent almost immediately. His charm had faded into worry, then edginess, and finally fear. He had lost the only world he had ever known and been left naked and unprotected in a waking nightmare. Gavilan had been as brave as he could manage, but everything he had known and relied upon had been stripped away. When the queen had died and the Staff had been entrusted to Wren, it had just been too much. He had counted himself the queen's logical successor, and with the power of the Elven magic he still believed he could accomplish anything. He was committed to it; he had made it his cause. He was convinced that he could save the Elves, that he was destined to do so, that the magic would give him the means.

Let me have the Staff, she could still hear him plead.

And she had foolishly given it to him.

Tears came to her eyes. He probably panicked, she thought. He probably decided that she was dead, that they were all dead, and that he was alone. He tried to leave, and Dal stopped him, telling him, no, wait, underestimating the depth of his fear, his madness. He would have heard the sounds of the Drakuls, the whispers, and the lures. They would have affected him. He killed Dal then because . . .

No! She was crying, unable to stop. She let herself, furious that she should try to make excuses for him. But it hurt so to admit the truth, harsh and unavoidable—that he had been weak, that he had been greedy, that he had rationalized instead of reasoned, and that he had killed a man who was there to protect him. Stupid! Such madness! But the stupidity and the madness were everywhere, all about them, a mire as vast and impenetrable as Eden's Murk. Morrowindl fostered it, succored it within each of them, and for each there was a threshold of endurance that once crossed signaled an end to sanity. Gavilan had crossed that threshold, unable to help himself perhaps, and now he was gone, faded into mist. Even if they found him, what would be left?

She bit at her wrist, making herself feel pain. They must find him, of course—even though he no longer mattered. They must regain possession of the Ruhk Staff and the Loden or everything they had gone through to get clear of Morrowindl and all of the lives that had been given up—her grandmother's, the Owl's, Eowen's, and those of the Elven Hunters—would have been for nothing. The thought burned through her. She could not tolerate it. She would not permit them to fail. She had promised her grandmother. She had promised herself. It was the reason she had come—to bring the Elves back into the Westland and to help find a way to put an end to the Shadowen. Allanon's charge—hers now as well, she admitted in black fury. Find yourself, and she had. Discover the truth, and she had. Too much of both, but she had. Her life was revealed now, past, present, and future, and however she felt about it she would not let it be taken away without her consent.

I don't care what it takes, she vowed. *I don't care!*

She was sleeping when Triss touched her shoulder and brought her awake again. "Lady Wren," he whispered gently. "Go lie down. Rest now."

She blinked, accepting the blanket he slipped about her. "In a minute," she replied. "Sit with me first."

He did so, a silent companion, his lean brown face strangely untroubled, his eyes distant. She remembered how he had looked when she had told him of Gavilan's treachery. *Treachery, wasn't that what it was?* That look was gone now, washed away by sleep or by acceptance. He had found a way to come to terms with it. Triss, the last of those who had come out of Arborlon's old life—how alone he must feel.

He looked over at her, and it seemed as if he could read her thoughts. "I have been Captain of the Home Guard for almost eight years," he ventured after a moment. "A long time, Lady Wren. I loved your grandmother, the queen. I would have done anything for her." He shook his head. "I have spent my whole life in service to the Elessedils and the Elven throne. I knew Gavilan as a child; we were children together. I grew to manhood with him. We played. My family and his still wait within the Loden, friends, . . ." He drew a deep breath, groping for words, understanding. "I knew him. He would not have killed Dal unless . . . Could it be that something happened to change him? Could one of the demons have done something to him?"

She had not considered that possibility. It could have happened. There had been opportunity enough. Or why not something else, a poison, for instance, or a sickening like that which had killed Ellenroh? But she knew in her heart that it was none of those, that it was simply a wearing away of his spirit, a breaking apart of his resolve.

"It could have been a demon," she lied anyway.

The strong face lifted. "He was a good man," he said quietly. "He cared about people; he helped them. He loved the queen. She would have named him king one day, perhaps."

"If not for me."

He turned away, embarrassed. "I should not have said that. You are queen." He looked back again. "Your grandmother would not have given the Staff to you if she had not believed it best. She would have given it to Gavilan instead. Perhaps she saw something in him that the rest of us missed. Yours is the strength the Elven people need."

She faced him. "I didn't want any part of this, Triss. None of it."

He nodded, smiled faintly. "No. Why would you?"

"I just wanted to find out who I was."

She saw a flicker of despair in his dark eyes. "I don't pretend to understand what brought you to us," he told her. "I only know that you are here and you are Queen of the Elves." He kept his eyes fixed on her. "Don't abandon us," he said quietly, urgently. "Don't leave us. We need you."

She was amazed at the strength of his plea. She placed her hand on his arm reassuringly. "Don't worry, Triss. I promise I won't run away. Ever."

She left him then, went over to where Garth slept and curled up next to her big friend, needing both his warmth and bulk for comfort this night, wanting to retreat into the past, to recover the protection and safety it had once offered, to recapture what was irretrievably lost. She settled instead for what was there and finally slept.

At dawn she was awake, more rested than she had a right to expect. The light was faint and gray through the haze, and the world about them was still and empty feeling, smelling of rot. Killeshan's rumble was distant and faint, yet steady now for the first time since they had begun their journey, a slow building of tremors that promised bigger things to come. Time was running out, Wren knew—quicker now, swifter with the passing of each hour. The volcano's fire was beginning to build at the core of the island toward a final conflagration, and when it exploded everything would be swept away.

They set out immediately, Stresa leading, Garth a step behind, Wren following with Faun, and Triss trailing. Wren was calmer now, less distraught. Gavilan, she reasoned, had nowhere to go. He might run for the beaches in search of Tiger Ty and Spirit, but how likely was he to find his way through the In Ju? He was not a Tracker and had no experience in wilderness survival. He was already half mad with fear and despair. How far could he get? He would likely travel in circles, and they would find him quickly.

Yet in the back of her mind lurked the specter of his somehow managing to get clear of the jungle, finding his way down to the beach, convincing Tiger Ty that everyone else was dead, and having himself and the Ruhk Staff carried safely away while the rest of the company was left behind. The possibility infuriated her, the more so when she considered the possibility that Gavilan didn't really think her dead at all and had simply decided to strike out on his own, convinced of the rightness of his cause and the inevitability of his rule.

Unable to ponder the matter further, she brushed it roughly aside.

Blackledge began to drop away from the Harrow almost immediately, but it was not as steep here as where Garth and she had climbed up. The cliff face was craggy and thick with vegetation, and it was not difficult for them to find a pathway down. They descended quickly, Stresa keeping Gavilan's scent firmly before them as they went. Broken limbs and crushed leaves marked clearly the Elven Prince's passing; Wren could have followed the trail alone, so obvious was it. Time and again they discovered places where the fleeing man had fallen, apparently heedless of his safety, anxious only to escape. He must be frantic, Wren thought sadly. He must be terrified.

They reached the edge of the In Ju at midday and paused to eat. Stresa was gruffly confident. They were only a few hours behind Gavilan, he advised. The Elven Prince was staggering badly now, clearly exhausted. Unless something happened to change things, they would catch him before nightfall.

Stresa's prediction was prophetic—but not in the way they had hoped. Shortly after they resumed tracking Gavilan's futile efforts to circumvent the In Ju, it began to rain. The air had grown hotter with the descent off the mountain, a swelter that built slowly and did not recede. When the rain commenced, it was a dampness that layered the air, a thick moisture that hung like wet silk draped against their skin, beading on their leather clothing. After a time, the dampness turned to mist, then drizzle, and finally a torrent that washed over them with ferocious determination. They were blinded by it and forced to take shelter beneath a giant banyan. It swept through quickly and took Gavilan's scent with it. Stresa searched carefully in the aftermath, but all trace was gone.

Garth studied the damp green tangle of the jungle. He beckoned Wren. *The marks of his passing are still evident. I can track him.*

She let Garth assume the lead with Stresa a half step behind, the former searching for signs of their quarry's passing, the latter keeping watch for Darters and other dangers. *Their quarry,* Wren thought, repeating the words. Gavilan had been reduced to that. She felt pity for him in spite of herself, thinking he should have stayed within the city, reasoning she should have done more to keep him safe, still wishing for what could never be.

They progressed more slowly now. Gavilan had given up his efforts to bypass the In Ju and plunged directly in. What signs they found—broken twigs and small branches, vegetation disturbed, an occasional print—suggested he had abandoned any attempt at stealth and was simply trying to reach the beaches by the shortest possible route. Speed over caution was a poor choice, Wren thought to herself. They tracked him steadily, without difficulty, and at each turn Wren expected to find him, the chase concluded and the inevitable confirmed. But somehow he kept going, evading the pitfalls that were scattered everywhere, the bogs and sinkholes, the Darters, the things that lay in wait for the unwary, and the traps and the monsters made of the Elven magic he so foolishly thought to wield. How he managed to stay alive, Wren could only wonder. He should have been dead a dozen times over. A step either way, and he would have been. She found herself wishing it would happen, that he would make that one mistake and that the madness would cease. She hated what they were doing, hunting him like an animal, chasing after him as if he were prey. She wanted it to stop.

At the same time, she dreaded what it would take to make that happen.

When they began to catch sight of the Wisteron's webbing, she despaired. *Not like that,* she found herself pleading with whatever fate controlled such things. *Give him a quick end.* Trip lines were strung all about, draped from the trees, looped along the vines, and attached in deadly nets. Stresa retook the lead from Garth in order to guide them past the snares, pausing often to listen, to sniff the air, and to judge the safety of the land ahead. The jungle thickened into a maze of green fronds and dark trunks that crisscrossed one another in jigsaw fashion. Shadows moved slowly and ponderously about them, but the sounds they made were anxious and hungry. The afternoon shortened toward evening, and it grew dark. Far distant, screened by the mountain they had descended, Killeshan rumbled. Tremors shook the island, and the jungle's green haze shivered with the echo. Explosions began to sound, muffled still, but growing stronger. Whole trees trembled with the reverberations, and steam geysered out of swamp pools, hissing with relief. As the light darkened, Wren could see through the ever-present haze of vog and mist the sky above Killeshan turn red.

It has begun, she thought as Garth's worried eyes met her own.

She wondered how much time was left to them. Even if they regained the Staff, it was still another two days to the beach. Would Tiger Ty be there waiting? How often had he promised he would come? Once a week, wasn't it? What if a whole week must pass before he was scheduled to return? Would he see the volcano's glare and sense the danger to them?

Or had he given up his vigil long ago, convinced that she had failed, that she had died like all the others and that there was no point in searching further?

She shook her head in stern admonishment. No, not Tiger Ty. She judged him a better man than that. He would not give up, she told herself. Not until there was no hope left.

"Phhffttt! We have to stop soon," Stresa warned. "Hssstt. Find shelter before it grows any darker, before the Wisteron hunts!"

"A little farther," Wren suggested hopefully.

They went on, but Gavilan Elessedil was not to be found. His ragged trail stretched before them, worming ahead into the In Ju, a line of bent and broken stalks and leaves disappearing into the shadows.

Finally, they quit. Stresa found shelter for them in the hollow stump of a banyan toppled by age and erosion, a massive trunk with entries through its base and a narrow cleft farther up. They blocked off the larger and set themselves to keep watch at the smaller. Nothing of any size could reach them. It was dark and close within their wood coffin and as dry as winter earth. Night descended, and they listened to the jungle's hunters come awake, to the sounds of coughing roars, of sluggish passage, and of prey as it was caught and killed. They huddled back to back with Stresa hunched down before them, spikes extended back toward the faint light. They took turns standing guard, dozing because they were too tired to stay awake but too anxious to sleep. Faun lay cradled in Wren's arms, as still as death. She stroked the little creature affectionately, wondering at how it could have survived in such a world. She thought of how much she hated Morrowindl. It was a thief that had stolen everything from her—the lives of her grandmother and her friends, the innocence she had harbored of the Elves and their history, the love and affection she had discovered for Gavilan, and the strength of will she had thought she would never lose. It was the loss of the latter that bothered her most, her confidence in who and what she was and in the certainty that she could determine her own fate. So much was gone, and Morrowindl, this once paradise made into a Shadowen nightmare, had taken it all. She tried to picture life beyond the island and failed. She could not think past escape, for escape was still uncertain, still a fate that hung in the balance. She remembered how once she had thought that traveling to find Allanon and speak with his shade might be the beginning of a great adventure. The memory was ashes in her mouth.

She slept for a time, dreamed of dark and terrible things, and came awake sweating and hot. At watch, she found her thoughts straying once again to Gavilan, to small memories of him—the way he had touched her, the feel of his mouth kissing hers, and the wonder he had invoked in her through nothing more than a chance remark or a passing glance. She smiled as she remembered. There was so much of him she had liked; she hurt for the loss of him. She wished she could bring him back to her and return him to the person he had been. She even wished she could find a way to make the magic do what nature could not—to change the past. It was foolish, senseless thinking, and it teased her mercilessly. Gavilan was lost to her. He had fallen prey to Morrowindl's madness. He had killed Dal and stolen the Ruhk Staff. He had turned himself into something unspeakable. Gavilan Elessedil, the man she had been so attracted to and cared so much for, was no more.

At daybreak they rose and set out anew. They did not have to bother with breakfast because there was nothing left to eat. Their supplies were exhausted, those that hadn't been lost or abandoned. There was a little water, but not more than enough for another day. While they traveled the In Ju, they would find nothing to sustain them. One more reason to get clear quickly.

Their search that day was over almost before it began. In

less than an hour, Gavilan's trail abruptly ended. They crested a ravine, slowed on Stresa's warning hiss, and stopped. Below, amid the wreckage of small plants and grasses trampled almost flat in what must have been a frantic struggle, lay the shreds of one of the Wisteron's webs.

Stresa eased down into the ravine, sniffed cautiously about, and climbed out again. The dark, bright eyes fixed on Wren. "Hsssttt. It has him, Wren Elessedil."

She closed her eyes against the horrific vision the Splinterscat's words evoked. "How long ago?"

"Ssspptt. Not long. Maybe six hours. Just after midnight, I would guess. The net snared the Elf Prince and held him until the Wisteron came. Rwwlll. The beast carried him away."

"Where, Stresa?"

The other pricked his ears. "Its lair, I expect. It has one deep within a hollow at the In Ju's center."

She felt a new weariness steal through her. Of course, a lair—there would have to be. "Any sign of the Ruhk Staff?"

The Splinterscat shook his head. "Gone."

So unless Gavilan had abandoned it—something he would never do—it was still with him. She shuddered in spite of her resolve. She was remembering her brief encounter with the Wisteron on her way in. She was remembering how just its passing had made her feel.

Poor, foolish Gavilan. There was no hope for him now.

She looked at the others, one by one. "We have to get the Ruhk Staff back. We can't leave without it."

"No, Lady Wren, we can't," Triss echoed, hard-eyed.

Garth stood, his great hands limp at his sides.

Stresa shook out his quills and his sharp-nosed face lifted to her own. "Rrwwll Wren of the Elves, I expected nothing less of you. Hssttt. But you will have to—ssppppttt—use the Elf Magic if we are to survive. You will have to, against the Wisteron."

"I know," she whispered, and felt the last vestige of her old life drop away.

"Chhttt. Not that it will make any difference. Phhfftt. The Wisteron is—"

"Stresa," she interrupted gently. "You needn't come."

The silence of the moment hung against the screen of the jungle. The Splinterscat sighed and nodded. "Phhfft. We have come this far together, haven't we? No more talk. I will take you in."

CHAPTER

25

N THE LONG, deep silence of Paranor's endless night, in the limbo of her gray, changeless twilight, Walker Boh sat staring into space. His hand was closed into a fist on the table before him, his fingers locked like iron bands about the Black Elfstone. There was nothing more to do— no other options to consider, no further choices to uncover. He had thought everything through to the extent that it was possible to do so, and all that remained was to test the right and wrong of it.

"Perhaps you should take a little more time," Cogline suggested gently.

The old man sat across from him, a frail, skeletal ghost nearly transparent where caught against the light. Increasingly so, Walker thought in despair. White, wispy hair scattered like dust motes from the wrinkled face and head, robes hung like laundry set to dry on a line, and eyes flickered in dull glimmerings from out of dark sockets. Cogline was fading away, disappearing into the past, returning with Paranor to the place from which it had been summoned. For Paranor would not remain within the world of men unless there was a Druid to tend it, and Walker Boh, chosen by time and fate to fill those dark robes, had yet to don them.

His eyes drifted over to Rumor. The moor cat slouched against the far wall of the study room in which they were settled, black body as faint and ethereal as the old man's. He looked down at himself, fading as well, though not as quickly. In any event, he had a choice; he could leave if he chose, when he chose. Not so Cogline or Rumor, who were bound to the Keep for all eternity if Walker did not find a way to bring it back into the world of Men.

Strangely enough, he thought he had found that way. But his discovery terrified him so that he was not certain he could act on it.

Cogline shifted, a rattle of dry bones. "Another reading of the books couldn't hurt," he pressed.

Walker's smile was ironic. "Another reading and there won't be anything left of you at all. Or Rumor or the Keep or possibly even me. Paranor is disappearing, old man. We can't pretend otherwise. Besides, there is nothing left to read, nothing to discover that I don't already know."

"And you're still certain that you're right, Walker?"

Certain? Walker was certain of nothing beyond the fact that he was most definitely not certain. The Black Elfstone was a deadly puzzle. Guess wrong about its workings and you would end up like the Stone King, enveloped by your own magic, destroyed by what you trusted most. Uhl Belk had thought he had mastered the Stone's magic, and it had cost him everything.

"I am guessing," he replied. "Nothing more."

He allowed his hand to open, and the Elfstone to come into the light. It lay there in the cup of his palm, smooth-faced, sharp-edged, opaque and impenetrable, power unto itself, power beyond anything he had ever encountered. He remembered how it had felt to use the Stone when he had brought back the Keep, thinking it would end then, that the retrieval out of limbo where Allanon had sent it was all that was required. He remembered the surge of power as it joined him to the Keep, the entwining of flesh and blood with stone and mortar, the reworking of his body so that he was as much ghost as man, changing him so that he could enter Paranor, so that he could discover the rest of what he must do.

A metamorphosis of being.

Within, he had encountered Cogline and Rumor and heard the tale of how they had survived the attack of the Shadowen by being caught up in the protective shield of the Druid Histories' magic and spirited into Paranor. Though Walker had brought Paranor out of the limbo place into which Allanon had dispatched it, it would not be fully returned until he had found a way to complete his transformation, to become the Druid it was decreed he must be. Until then, Paranor was a prison that only he could leave—a prison rapidly drawing back into the space from which it had come.

"I am guessing," he repeated, almost to himself.

He had read and reread the Druid Histories in an effort to discover what it was that he must do and found nothing. Nowhere did the Histories relate how one became a Druid. Despairing, he had thought the cause lost to him when he had remembered the Grimpond's visions, two of which had come to pass, the third of which, he realized, would happen here.

He faced the old man. "I stand within a castle fortress empty of life and gray with disuse. I am stalked by a death I cannot escape. It hunts me relentlessly. I know I must run from it, yet cannot. I let it approach, and it reaches for me. A cold settles within, and I can feel my life ending. Behind me stands a dark shadow holding me fast, preventing my escape. The shadow is Allanon."

The words were a familiar litany by now. Cogline nodded patiently. "Your vision, you said. The third of three."

"Two came to pass already, but neither as I anticipated. The Grimpond loves to play games. But this time I shall use that gamesplaying to my advantage. I know the details of the vision; I know that it will happen here within the Keep. I need only decipher its meaning, to separate the truth from the lie."

"But if you have guessed wrong . . ."

Walker Boh shook his head defiantly. "I have not."

They were treading familiar ground. Walker had already told the old man everything, testing it out on someone who would be quick to spot the flaws he had missed, putting it into words to see how it would sound.

The Black Elfstone was the key to everything.

He repeated from memory that brief, solitary passage inscribed in the Druid Histories:

Once removed, Paranor shall remain lost to the world
of men for the whole of time, sealed away and invisible

within its casting. One magic alone has the power to return it—that singular Elfstone that is colored Black and was conceived by the faerie people of the old world in the manner and form of all Elfstones, combining nevertheless in one stone alone the necessary properties of heart, mind, and body. Whosoever shall have cause and right shall wield it to its proper end.

He had assumed until now that the Black Elfstone was meant to restore Paranor to its present state of half-being and to gain him entry therein. But the language of the inscription didn't qualify the extent of the Elfstone's use. One magic alone, it said, had the power to restore Paranor. One magic. The Black Elfstone. There wasn't any another magic mentioned, not anywhere. There wasn't another word about returning Paranor to the world of men in all the pages of all the Druid Histories.

Suppose, then, that the Black Elfstone was all that was required, but that it must be used not just once, but twice or even three times before the restoration process was complete.

But used to do what?

The answer seemed obvious. The magic that Allanon had released into the Keep three hundred years ago was a sort of watchdog set loose to do two things—to destroy the Keep's enemies and to dispatch Paranor into limbo and keep it there until it was properly summoned out again. The magic was a living thing. You could feel it in the walls of the castle; you could hear it stir in its bowels. It watched and listened. It breathed. It was there, waiting. If the Keep was to be restored to the Four Lands, the magic Allanon had loosed must be locked away again. It was reasonable to assume that only another form of magic could accomplish this. And the only magic at hand, the only magic even mentioned in the Druid Histories where Paranor was concerned, was the Black Elfstone.

So far, so good. Druid magic to negate Druid magic. It made sense; it was the Black Elfstone's stated power, the negation of other magics. One magic, the inscription read. And Walker must wield it, of course. He had done so once, proved that he could. *Whosoever shall have cause and right.* Himself. Use the Black Elfstone against the watchdog magic and secure it. Use the Black Elfstone and bring Paranor all the way back.

But there was still something missing. There was no explanation of how the Black Elfstone would work. It was infinitely more complicated than simply calling up the magic and letting it run loose. The Black Elfstone negated other magics by drawing them into itself—and into its holder. Walker Boh had already been changed when he had used the Elfstone to bring Paranor back and gain entry, turned from a whole man into something incorporeal. What further damage might he do to himself if he used the Elfstone on the watchdog? What further transformation might take place?

And then, abruptly, he realized two things.

First, that he was still not a Druid and would not become one until he had established his right to do so—that his right would not come from study, or learning, or wisdom gleaned from a reading of the Druid Histories, that it was not foreordained, not predetermined by the bestowal of Allanon's blood trust to Brin Ohmsford three hundred years earlier, but that it would come at the moment he found a way to subdue the watchdog that guarded the Keep and brought Paranor fully back into the world of Men, because that was the test that Allanon had set him.

Second, that the third vision the Grimpond had shown him, the one that would take place within Paranor, the one where he was confronted by a death he could not escape, held fast by the ghost of Allanon, was a glimpse of that moment.

His arguments were persuasive. The Druids would not commit to writing a process as inviolate as this one when there was a better way. Only Walker Boh could use the Black Elfstone. Only he had the right. Somehow, in some way, that use would trigger the required transformation. When it was necessary to know, Walker would discover what was needed. So much of the Druid magic relied on acceptance—use of the Elfstones, of the Sword of Shannara, even of the wishsong. It was only reasonable that it would be the same here.

And the Grimpond's vision only cemented his thinking. There would have to be a confrontation of the sort depicted. A literal reading of the vision suggested that such a confrontation would result in Walker's death, that Allanon by sending him here had bound him so that he must die, and that whatever he might try to do to escape would be futile. But that was too simplistic. And it made no sense. Why would Allanon send him all this way to certain death? There had to be another interpretation, another meaning. The one he favored was the one that ended one life and began another, that established him once and for all as a Druid.

Cogline was not so sure. Walker had guessed wrong on both of the Grimpond's previous visions. Why was he so convinced that he was not guessing wrong here as well? The visions were never what they seemed, devious and twisted bits of half-truth concealed amid lies. He was taking a terrible gamble. The first vision had cost him his arm, the second Quickening. Was the third to cost him nothing? It seemed more reasonable to believe that the vision was open to a number of interpretations, any one of which could come to pass in the right set of circumstances, including Walker's death. Moreover, it bothered Cogline that Walker had no clear idea of how use of the Black Elfstone was to effect his transformation, how it was to subdue the Druid watchdog, how Paranor itself was to be brought fully alive—or how any of this was to work. It could not possibly be as easy as Walker made it sound. Nothing involving use of the Elven magic ever was. There would be pain involved, enormous effort, and the very real possibility of failure.

So they had argued, back and forth, for longer than Walker cared to admit, until now, hours later, they were too tired to do anything but exchange a final round of perfunctory admonishments. Walker's mind was made up, and they both knew it. He was going to test his theory, to seek out and confront the thing that Allanon had let loose within Paranor and use the magic of the Black Elfstone to resecure it. He was going to discover the truth about the Black Elfstone and put an end to the last of the Grimpond's hateful visions.

If he could make himself rise from this table, take up the talisman, and go forth.

Though he had sought to keep it hidden from Cogline with hard looks and confident words, his terror bound him. So much uncertainty, so many guesses. He forced his fingers to close again over the Black Elfstone, to grip so hard he could feel pain.

"I will go with you," Cogline offered. "And Rumor."

"No."

"We might be able to help in some way."

"No," Walker repeated. He looked up, shaking his head slowly. "Not that I wouldn't like you to. But this isn't something you can help me with, either of you. It isn't something anyone can help me with."

He could feel an ache where his missing arm should be, as if it were somehow there and he simply couldn't see it. He shifted uneasily, trying to relieve muscles that had tightened and cramped while he had stayed seated with the old man, arguing. The movement gave him impetus, and he forced himself to rise. Cogline stood with him. They faced each other in the half-light, in the fading transparency of the Keep.

"Walker." The old man spoke his name quietly. "The Druids have made us both their creatures. We have been twisted and turned in every direction, made to do things we did not wish to do and become involved in matters we would rather have left alone. I would not presume to argue with you now the merits of their manipulation. We are both beyond the point where it matters."

He leaned forward. "But I would tell you, would ask you to remember, that they choose their paladins wisely." His smile was worn and sad. "Luck to you."

Walker came around the table, wrapped his good arm about the old man, and hugged him tight. He held him momentarily, then released him and stepped away.

"Thank you," he whispered.

There was nothing more to be said. He took a deep breath, walked over to scratch Rumor between his cocked ears, gazed into the luminous eyes, then turned and disappeared out the door.

WITH SLOW, cautious steps, moving through the vast, empty hallways as if the walls might hear him coming, as if his intentions could be divined, he proceeded toward the center of the Keep. Shadows hung about him in colorless folds, a sleep-shroud that cloaked his thoughts. He buried himself in the sanctuary of his mind, drawing his determination and strength of will about him in protective layers, summoning from deep within the resolve that would give him a chance at life.

For the truth of things was that he had no real idea what would happen when he confronted the Druid watchdog and called upon the Black Elfstone's magic to subdue it. Cogline was right; there would be pain and the process would be more complex and difficult than he wanted to admit. There would be a struggle, and he might not emerge the victor. He wished he had some better idea of what it was he faced. But there was no point in wishing for what could never be, for what had never been. The Druid ways had been secretive forever.

He turned down the main hallway, heading now to the doors that opened into the Keep—and to the well in which the watchdog slumbered. Or perhaps simply laired, for it seemed to the Dark Uncle that the magic was awake and watching, following him with its eyes as he moved through the castle, trailing along in a ripple of changing light, an invisible presence. Allanon's shade was there as well, a tightening at his back, a cramping of the muscles in his shoulders where the great hands gripped. He was held fast already, he thought to himself. He was propelled to this confrontation as much as if he were deadwood carried on the crest of a river in flood, and he could not turn aside from it.

Speak to me, Allanon, he pleaded silently. *Tell me what to do.*

But no answer came.

The doors of empty rooms and the dark tunnels of other halls and corridors came and went. He felt again the ache of his missing arm and wished that he were whole again, if only for the moment of this confrontation. He gripped the Black Elfstone tightly in his good hand, feeling its smooth facets and sharp edges press reassuringly against his flesh. He could summon the power within, but he could not predict what it would do. *Destroy you,* the thought came unbidden. He breathed slowly, deeply, to calm himself. He tried to remember the passage on the Stone's usage from the Druid History, but his memory suddenly failed him. He tried to remember what he had read in all the pages of all those books and could not. Everything was melting away within, lost in the rush of fear and doubt that surged through him, anxious and threatening. Don't give way to it, he admonished himself. Remember who you are, what has been promised you, what you have told yourself will happen.

The words were dead leaves caught in a strong wind.

Ahead, a broad alcove opened into the stone of the walls, arched and shadowed so deeply that it was as black as night. There, a set of tall iron doors stood closed.

The entry to the well of the Druid's Keep.

Walker Boh came up to the doors and stopped. All around him he could hear a whispering of voices, taunting, teasing in the manner of the Grimpond, telling him to go back, urging him to go on, a maddening whirl of conflicting exhortations. Memories stirred from somewhere within—but they were not his own. He could feel their movement along his spine, a reaching out of fingers that coiled and tightened. Before him, he could see a trace of wicked green light probe at the cracks and crevices of the door frame. Beyond, he could sense movement.

In that instant, he almost bolted. Had he been able to do so, he would have thrown down the Black Elfstone and run for his life, the whole of his resolve and purpose abandoned. His fear was manifest; it was so palpable that it seemed he could reach out and touch it. It did not wear the face he had expected. His fear was not of the confrontation, of the vision's promise, or even of dying. It was of something beyond that, something so intangible he was unable to define it and at the same time was certain it was there.

But Allanon's shade held him fast, just as in the vision, a contrivance of fate and time and manipulation of centuries gone combining to assure that Walker Boh fulfilled the purpose the Druids had set for him.

He reached forward with his closed fist, seeing his hand as if it belonged to another person, watching as it pushed against the iron doors.

Soundlessly they swung open.

Walker stepped through, his body numb and his head light and filled with small, terror-filled cries of warning. *Don't*, they whispered. *Don't.*

He stopped, breathless. He stood on a narrow stone landing within the well of the Keep. Stairs coiled upward along the wall of the tower like a spike-backed serpent. Weak gray light filtered through slits cut in the stone, piercing the shadows. There was nothing below where he stood but emptiness—a vast, yawning abyss out of which rose the hollow echo of the iron doors as they thudded closed behind him. He listened to his heart pound in his ears. He listened to the silence beyond.

Then something stirred in the abyss. Breath released from a giant's lungs, quick and angry. Greenish light flared, dimmed again, turned to mist, and began to swirl sluggishly.

Walker Boh felt the vastness of the Keep settle down about him, a monstrous weight he could not escape. Tons of stone ringed him, and the blackness it sealed away was a death shroud. The mist rose, a dark and ancient magic, the Druid watchdog roused and come forth to investigate. It came for him in a sweeping, lifting motion, curling along the stone, eating away at the dark, a morass that would swallow him without a trace.

Still he would have run but for the certainty that it was too late, that he had begun something that must be finished, that time and events had caught up with him at last, and now here, alone, he would have to resolve the puzzle of his Druid-shaped life. He made himself move forward to the landing's edge, frail flesh a drop of water against the ocean of the power below. It hissed at him as if it saw, a whisper of recognition. It seemed to gather itself, a tightening of movement.

Walker brought up the hand with the Black Elfstone.

Wait.

The voice rose out of the mist. Walker froze. The voice belonged to the Grimpond.

Do you know me?

The Grimpond? How could it be the Grimpond? Walker blinked rapidly. The mist had begun to take form at its center, a pillar of swirling green that bore upward into the light, that lifted through the shadows, steady, certain, until it was even with him, hanging in air and silence.

Look.

It became a human figure all cloaked and hooded and face-less. It grew arms and hands that stretched to embrace Walker. Fingers curled and flexed.

Who am I?

A face appeared, shadows and light shifting within the mist. Walker felt as if his soul had been torn away.

The face he saw was his own.

WITHIN THE DARK SECLUSION of the vault that housed the Druid Histories, Cogline lurched to his feet. Something was happening. Something. He could feel it in the air, a vibration that stirred the shadows. The wrinkled face tightened in con-centration; the aged eyes stared into space. The silence was unbroken, vast and changeless, time suspended, and yet . . .

Across the room from him, Rumor's head snapped up and the moor cat gave a deep, low, angry growl. He moved into a crouch, turning first this way, then that, as if seeking an enemy that had made itself invisible. He, too, sensed something. Cog-line's eyes flickered right and left. On the table before him, the pages of the open book began to tremble.

It begins, the old man thought.

He gathered his robes close in an unconscious motion, thinking of all that had brought him to this place and time, of all that had gone before. After so many years, what price? he wondered. But the price would be paid not by him, but by Walker Boh.

I must do what I can, he decided.

He focused deep within, one of those few skills he retained from his once-Druid past. He retreated down inside until he was free enough to leave. He could travel short distances so, see within small worlds. He sped through the castle corridors, still within his mind, seeing and hearing everything. He swept through the darkness, through the gray half-light, to the tower of the Keep.

There he found Walker Boh face to face with immortality and death, frozen by indecision. He realized what was hap-pening.

His voice was surprisingly calm.

Walker. Use the Stone.

WALKER BOH HEARD the old man's voice, a whisper in his mind, and he felt his body respond. His arm straightened, and he tensed.

The thing before him laughed. *Do you still not know me?*

He did—and didn't. It was many things at once, some of which he recognized, some of which he didn't. The voice, though—there could be no mistake. It was the Grimpond's, taunting, teasing, calling his name.

You have found your third vision, haven't you, Dark Uncle?

Walker was appalled. How could this be happening? How could the Grimpond be both this thing he had come to subdue and the avatar imprisoned in Darklin Reach? How could it be in two places at once? It didn't make sense! The Druids hadn't created the Grimpond. Their magics were diverse and opposed. Yet the voice, the movement, and the feel of the thing . . .

The shadow before him was growing larger, approaching.

I am your death, Walker Boh. Are you prepared to embrace me?

And abruptly the vision was back in Walker's mind, as clear as the moment it had first appeared to him—the shade of Allanon behind him, holding him fast, the dark shadow before him, the promise of his death, and the castle of the Druids all about.

Why don't you flee? Flee from me!

It was all he could do to keep from screaming. He groped away from it, beseeching help from any quarter. Cogline's voice was gone, buried in black fear. Resolve and purpose were scattered in pieces about him. Walker Boh was disintegrating while still alive.

Yet some small part of him did not give way, held fast by memory of what had brought him, by the promise he had made himself that he would not die willingly or in ignorance. Cogline's face was still there, the eyes frantic, the lips moving, trying to speak. Walker reached down inside for the one thing that had sustained him over the years, for that core of anger that burned at the thought of what the Druids had done to him. He fanned it until it blazed. He cupped it to his face and let it sear him.

He breathed it in until the fear was forced to give way, until there was only rage.

Then an odd thing happened. The voice of the thing before him changed. The voice became his own, frantic, desperate.

Flee, Walker Boh!

The voice was no longer coming from the mist; it was coming from himself! He was calling his own name, urging himself to flee!

What was happening?

And suddenly he understood. He wasn't listening to the thing before him; he was listening to himself. It was his own voice he had been hearing all along, a trick of his subconscious—a trick, he realized in fury, of the Grimpond. The wraith had implanted in Walker's mind, along with that third vision, a suggestion of his death, a voice to convince him of it, and a certainty that it was the Grimpond itself who came forth in another form to deliver it. Revenge on the descendants of Brin Ohmsford—it was what the Grimpond had been after from the first. If Walker listened to that voice, faltered in his resolve, and turned away from the purpose that had brought him . . .

No!

His fingers opened and the Black Elfstone flared to life.

The nonlight streaked forth, spreading like ink across the shadowed well of the Keep to embrace the mist. *No more games!* Walker's shout was a euphoric, silent cry within his mind. The Grimpond—so insidious, so devious—had almost undone him. *Never again. Never . . .*

Then everything began to happen at once.

Nonlight and mist meshed and joined. Back through the tunnel of the magic's dark flooded the mist, a greenish, pulsing fury. Walker had only an instant to catch his breath, to question what had gone wrong, and to wonder if perhaps he had failed to outsmart the Grimpond after all—and then the Druid magic was on him. It exploded within, and he screamed in helpless dismay. The pain was indescribable, a fiery incandescence. It felt as if another being had entered him, carried within by the magic, drawn out of the concealment of the mist. A physical presence, it burrowed into bone and muscle and flesh and blood until it was all that Walker could bear. It expanded and raged until he thought he would be torn apart. Then the sense of it changed, igniting a different kind of pain. Memories flooded through him, vast and seemingly endless. With the memories came the feelings that accompanied them, emotions charged with horror and fear and doubt and regret and a dozen other sensations that rolled through Walker Boh in an unstoppable torrent. He staggered back, trying to resist, to fling them away. His hand fought to close over the Black Elfstone in an effort to shut this attack off, but his body would no longer obey him. He was gripped by the magics—those of both Elfstone and mist—and they held him fast.

Like Allanon and the specter of death in the third version! *Shades! Had the Grimpond been right after all?*

He was seeing other places and times, viewing the faces of men and women and children he did not know, witnessing events transpire and fade, and above all feeling a wrenching series of emotions emanate from the being inside. Walker's sense of where he was disappeared. He was transported into the mind of his invader. A man? Yes, a man, he realized, a man who had lived countless lifetimes, centuries, far longer than any normal human, someone so different . . .

The images abruptly changed. He saw a gathering of black robes, dark figures concealed behind castle walls, closeted in chambers where the light barely reached, hunched over ancient books of learning, writing, reading, studying, discussing . . .

Druids!

And then he realized the truth—a jarring, shocking recognition that cut through the madness with a razor's edge.

The being that the mist had carried within him was Allanon—his memories, his experiences, his feelings, and his thoughts, everything but the flesh and blood he had lost in death.

How had Allanon managed this? Walker asked himself in disbelief, fighting to breathe against the rush of memories, against the suffocating blanket of the other's thoughts. But he already knew the answer to that. A Druid's magic allowed almost anything. The seeds had been planted three hundred years ago. Why, then? And that answer, too, came swiftly, a red flare of certainty. This was how the Druid lore was to be passed on to him. All that Allanon had known and felt was stored within the mist, his knowledge kept safe for three hundred years, waiting for his successor.

But there was more, Walker sensed. This was how he was to be tested as well. This was how it was to be determined if he should become a Druid.

His speculation ended as the images continued to rush through him, recognizable now for what they were, the whole of the Druid experience, all that Allanon had gleaned from his predecessors, from his studies, from the living of his own life. Like footprints in soft earth, they embedded in Walker's mind, their touch fiery and harsh, each a coal laid against his skin. The words and impressions and feelings descended in an avalanche. It was too much, too fast. *I don't want this!* he screamed in terror, but still the feeding continued, relentless, purposeful— Allanon's self transferring into Walker. He fought back against it, groping through the maze of images for something solid. But the black light of the Elfstone was a funnel that refused to be stoppered, drawing in the greenish mist, absorbing it, and chan- neling it into his body. Voices spoke words, faces turned to look, scenes changed, and time rushed away—a composite of all the years Allanon had been alive, struggling to protect the Races, to assure that the Druid lore wasn't lost, that the hopes and aspirations the First Council had envisioned centuries ago were carried forth and preserved. Walker Boh became privy to it all, learned what it had meant to Allanon and those whose lives he had touched, and experienced for himself the impact of life through almost ten centuries.

Then abruptly the images ceased, the voices, the faces, the scenes out of time—everything that had assailed him. They vanished in a rush, and he was standing alone again within the Keep, a solitary figure slumped against the stone-block wall.

Still alive.

He lifted away unsteadily, looking down at himself, making certain he was whole. Within, there was a rawness, like skin reddened from too much sun, the implant of all that Druid knowledge, of all that Allanon had intended to bequeath. His spirit felt leavened and his mind filled. Yet his command over the knowledge was disjointed, as if it could not be brought to bear, not called upon. Something was wrong. Walker could not seem to focus.

Before him, the Black Elfstone pulsed, the nonlight a bridge that arced into the shadows, still joined with what remained of the mist—a roiling, churning mass of wicked green light that hissed and sparked and gathered itself like a cat about to spring.

Walker straightened, weak and unsteady, frightened anew, sensing that something more was about to happen and that the worst was still to come. His mind raced. What could he do to prepare himself? There wasn't time enough left . . .

The mist launched itself into the nonlight. It came at Walker and enveloped him in the blink of an eye. He could see its anger, hear its rage, and feel its fury. It exploded through the new skin of his knowledge, a geyser of pain. Walker shrieked and doubled over. His body convulsed, changing within the covering of his robes. He could feel the wrenching of his bones. He closed his eyes and went rigid. The mist was within, curling, settling, feeding.

He experienced a rush of horror.

All of his life, Walker Boh had struggled to escape what the Druids had foreordained for him, resolved to chart his own course. In the end, he had failed. Thus he had gone in search of the Black Elfstone and then Paranor with the knowledge that if he should find them it would require that he become the next Druid, accepting his destiny yet promising himself that he would be his own person whatever was ordained. Now, in an instant's time, as he was wracked by the fury of what had hidden within the mist, all that remained of his hopes for some small measure of self-determination was stripped away, and Walker Boh was left instead with the darkest part of Allanon's soul. It was the Druid's cruelest self, a composite of all those times he had been forced by reason and circumstance to do what he abhorred, all those situations when he had been required to expend lives and faith and hope and trust, and all those years of hardening and tempering of spirit and heart until both were as carefully forged and as indestructible as the hardest metal. It was a rendering of the limits of Allanon's being, the limits to which he had been forced to journey. It revealed the weight of responsibility that came with power. It delineated the understanding that experience bestowed. It was harsh and ragged and terrible, an accumulation of ten normal lifetimes, and it inundated Walker like floodwaters over the wall of a dam.

Down into blackness the Dark Uncle spiraled, hearing himself cry out, hearing as well the Grimpond's laughter—imagined or real, he could not tell. His thoughts scattered before the flaying of his spirit, of his hopes, and of his beliefs. There was nothing he could do; the force of the magic was too powerful. He gave way before it, a monstrous strength. He waited to die.

Yet somehow he clung to life. He found that the torrent of dark revelation, while testing his endurance in ways he had not believed possible, had failed nevertheless to destroy him. He could not think—there was too much pain for that. He did not try to see, lost within a bottomless pit. Hearing availed him nothing, for the echo of his cry reverberated all about him. He seemed to float within himself, fighting to breathe, to survive. It was the testing he had anticipated—the Druid rite of passage. It battered him senseless, filled him with hurt, and left him broken within. Everything washed away, his beliefs and understandings, all that had sustained him for so long. Could he survive that loss? What would he be if he did?

Through waves of anguish he swam, buried within himself and the force of the dark magic, borne to the edge of his endurance, an inch from drowning. He sensed that his life could be lost in the tick of a moment's passing and realized that the measure of who and what he was and could be was being taken. He couldn't stop it. He wasn't sure he even cared. He drifted, helpless.

Helpless.

To be ever again who he had thought he would. To fulfill any of the promises he had made to himself. To have any control over his life. To determine if he would live or die.

Helpless.

Walker Boh.

Barely aware of what he was doing, separated from conscious reasoning, driven instead by emotions too primal to identify, the

Dark Uncle thrashed clear of his lethargy and exploded through the waves of pain, through nonlight and dark magic, through time and space, a bright speck of fiery rage.

Within, he felt the balance shift, the weight between life and death tip.

And when he broke at last the surface of the black ocean that had threatened to drown him, the only sound he heard, as it burst from his lungs, was an endless scream.

CHAPTER

26

T WAS LATE MORNING. The last three members of the company of nine worked their way cautiously through the tangle of the In Ju, following after the bulky, spiked form of Stresa, the Splinterscat, as he tunneled steadily deeper into the gloom.

Wren breathed the fetid, damp air and listened to the silence.

Distant, far removed from where they labored, Killeshan's rumble was a backdrop of sound that rolled across earth and sky, deep and ominous. Tremors snaked through Morrowindl, warning of the eruption that continued to build. But in the jungle, everything was still. A sheen of wetness coated the In Ju from the ground up, soaking trees and scrub, vines and grasses, a blanket that muffled sound and hid movement. The jungle was a vault of stunning green, of walls that formed countless chambers leading one into the other, of corridors that twisted and wound about in a maze that threatened to suffocate. Branches intertwined overhead to form a ceiling that shut out the light, canopied over a patchwork floor of swamp and quicksand and mud. Insects buzzed invisibly and things cried out from the mist. But nothing moved. Nothing seemed alive.

The Wisteron's webbing was everywhere by now, a vast networking that layered the trees like strips of gauze. Dead things hung in the webbing, the husks of creatures drained of life, the remains of the monster's feedings. They were small for the most part; the Wisteron took the larger offerings to its lair.

Which lay somewhere not far ahead.

Wren watched the shadows about her, made more anxious by the lack of any movement than by the silence. She walked in a dead place, a wasteland in which living things did not belong, a netherworld she traversed at her peril. She kept thinking she would catch sight of a flash of color, a rippling of water, or a shimmer of leaves and grasses. But the In Ju might have been sheathed in ice, it was so frozen. They were deep within the Wisteron's country now, and nothing ventured here.

Nothing save themselves.

She held the Elfstones clutched tightly in her hand, free now of their leather bag, ready for the use to which she knew they must be put. She harbored no illusions as to what would be required of her. She bore no false hope that use of the Elfstones might be avoided, that her Rover skills might be sufficient to save them. She did not debate whether it was wise to employ the magic when she knew how its power affected her. Her choices were all behind her. The Wisteron was a monster that only the Elfstones could overcome. She would use the magic because it was the only weapon they had that would make any difference in the battle that lay ahead. If she allowed herself to hesitate, if she fell prey yet again to indecision, they were all dead.

She swallowed against the dryness in her throat. Odd that she should be so dry there and so damp everywhere else. Even the palms of her hands were sweating. How far she had come since her days with Garth when she had roamed the Tirfing in what seemed now to have been another life, free of worry and responsibility, answerable only to herself and the dictates of time.

She wondered if she would ever see the Westland again.

Ahead, the gloom tightened into pockets of deep shadow that had the look of burrows. Mist coiled out and wound through the tree limbs and vines like snakes. Webbing cloaked the high branches and filled the gaps between—thick, semitransparent strands that shimmered with the damp. Stresa slowed and looked back at them. He didn't speak. He didn't have to. Wren was aware of Garth and Triss at either shoulder, silent, expectant. She nodded to Stresa and motioned for him to go on.

She thought suddenly of her grandmother, wondering what Ellenroh would be feeling if she were there, imagining how she would react. She could see the other's face, the fierce blue eyes in contrast to the ready smile, the imposing sense of calm that swept aside all doubt and fear. Ellenroh Elessedil, Queen of the Elves. Her grandmother had always seemed so much in control of everything. But even that hadn't been enough to save her. What then, Wren wondered darkly, could she rely upon? The magic, of course—but the magic was only as strong as the wielder, and Wren would have much preferred her grandmother's indomitable strength just now to her own. She lacked Ellenroh's self-assurance; she lacked her certainty. Even determined as she was to recover the Ruhk Staff and the Loden, to carry the Elven people safely back into the Westland, and to fulfill the terms of the trust that had been given her, she saw herself as flesh and blood and not as iron. She could fail. She could die. Terror lurked at the fringes of such thoughts, and it would not be banished.

Triss bumped up against her from behind, causing her to jump. He whispered a hasty apology and dropped back again. Wren listened to the pounding of her blood, a throbbing in her ears and chest, a measure of the brief space between her life and death.

She had always been so sure of herself . . .

Something skittered away on the ground ahead, a flash of dark movement against the green. Stresa's spines lifted, but he did not slow. The forest opened through a sea of swamp grass into a stand of old-growth acacia that leaned heavily one into the other, the ground beneath eroded and mired. The company followed the Splinterscat left along a narrow rise. The movement came again, quick, sudden, more than one thing this time. Wren tried to follow it. Some sort of insect, she decided, long and narrow, many legged.

Stresa found a patch of ground slightly broader than his body and turned to face them.

"Phhhfft. Did you see?" he whispered roughly. They nodded. "Scavengers! Orps, they are called. Hsssst! They eat anything. Hah, everything! They live off the leavings of the Wisteron. You'll see a lot more of them before we're finished. Don't be frightened when you do."

"How much farther?" Wren whispered back, bending close.

The Splinterscat cocked its head. "Just ahead," he growled. "Can't you smell the dead things?"

"What's back there?"

"Ssssttt! How would I know that, Wren of the Elves? I'm still alive!"

She ignored his glare. "We'll take a look. If we can talk, we will. If not, we will withdraw and decide what to do."

She looked at Garth and Triss in turn to be certain they understood, then straightened. Faun clung to her like a second skin. She was going to have to put the Tree Squeak down before she went much farther.

They burrowed ahead through the grasses and into the collapsing trees. Orps appeared from everywhere now, scattering at their approach. They looked like giant silverfish, quick and soundless as they disappeared into earth and wood. Wren tried to ignore them, but it was difficult. The surface water of the swamp bubbled and spit about them, the first sound they had heard in some time. Killeshan's reach was lengthening. They passed out of the grasses and through the trees, the gloom settling down about them in layers. It went still again, the air empty and dead. Wren breathed slowly, deeply. Her hand tightened about the Elfstones.

Then they were through the stand of acacia and moving across a mud flat to a cluster of huge fir whose limbs wrapped about one another in close embrace. Strands of webbing hung everywhere, and as they neared the far side of the flats Wren caught sight of bones scattered along the fringe of the trees. Orps darted right and left, skimming the surface of the flats, disappearing into the foliage ahead.

Stresa had slowed their pace to a crawl.

They gained the edge of the flats, eased down through an opening in the trees on hands and knees, and froze.

Beyond the trees lay a deep ravine, an island of rock suspended within the swamp. The fir trees lifted from its bedding in a jumble of dark trunks that looked as if they had been lashed together with hundreds of webs. Dead things hung in the webs, and bones littered the ravine floor. Orps crawled over everything, a shimmering carpet of movement. The light was gray and diffuse above the ravine, filtered down to faint shadows by the vog and mist. The smell of death hung over everything, captured within the rocks and trees and haze. It was quiet within the Wisteron's lair. Except for the scurrying Orps, nothing moved.

Wren felt Garth's hand grip her shoulder. She glanced over and saw him point.

Gavilan Elessedil hung spread-eagle in a hammock of webbing across from them, his blue eyes lifeless and staring, his mouth open in a silent scream. He had been gutted, his torso split from chest to stomach. Within the empty cavity, his ribs gleamed dully. All of his body fluids had been drained. What remained was little more than a husk, a grotesque, frightening parody of a man.

Wren had seen much of death in her short life, but she was unprepared for this. *Don't look!* she admonished herself frantically. *Don't remember him like this!* But she did look and knew as she did that she would never forget.

Garth touched her a second time, pointing down into the ravine. She peered without seeing at first, then caught sight of the Ruhk Staff. It lay directly beneath what remained of Gavilan, resting on the carpet of old bones. Orps crawled over it mindlessly. The Loden was still fixed to its tip.

Wren nodded in response, already wondering how they could reach the talisman. Her gaze shifted abruptly, searching once more.

Where was the Wisteron?

Then she saw it, high in the branches of the trees at one end of the ravine, suspended in a net of its own webbing, motionless in the haze. It was curled into a huge ball, its legs tucked under it, and it had the curious appearance of a dirty cloud. It was covered with spiked hair, and it blended with the haze. It seemed to be sleeping.

Wren fought down the rush of fear that seeing it triggered. She glanced hurriedly at the others. They were all looking. The

Wisteron shifted suddenly, a straightening out of its surprisingly lean body, a stretching of several limbs. There was a flash of claws and a hideous insectlike face with an odd, sucking maw. Then it curled up again and went still.

In Wren's hand, the Elfstones had begun to burn.

She took a last despairing look at Gavilan, then motioned to the others and backed out of the trees. Wordlessly they retraced their steps across the flats until they had gained the cover of the acacia, where they knelt in a tight circle.

Wren searched their eyes. "How can we get to the Staff?" she asked quietly. The image of Gavilan was fixed in her mind, and she could barely think past it.

Garth's hands lifted to sign. *One of us will have to go down into the ravine.*

"But the Wisteron will hear. Those bones will sound like eggshells when they're stepped on." She put Faun down next to her. The dark eyes stared upward intently into her own.

"Could we lower someone down?" Triss asked.

"Phhhfft! Not without making some sound or movement," Stresa snapped. "The Wisteron isn't—ssstttt—asleep. It only pretends. It will know!"

"We could wait until it does sleep, then," Triss pursued. "Or wait until it hunts, until it leaves to check its nets."

"I don't know that we have enough time for that . . ." Wren began.

"Hssstt! It doesn't matter if there is enough time or not!" Stresa interjected heatedly. "If it goes to hunt or to check its nets, it will catch our scent! It will know we are here!"

"Calm down," Wren soothed. She watched the spiky creature back off a step, its cat face furrowed.

"There has to be a way," Triss whispered. "All we need is a minute or two to get down there and out again. Perhaps a diversion would work."

"Perhaps," Wren agreed, trying unsuccessfully to think of one.

Faun was chittering softly at Stresa, who replied irritably. "Yes, Squeak, the Staff! What do you think? Phfftt! Now be quiet so I can think!"

Use the Elfstones, Garth signed abruptly.

Wren took a deep breath. "As a diversion?" They were where she had known they must come all along. "All right. But I don't want us to separate. We'll never find each other again."

Garth shook his head. *Not as a diversion. As a weapon.*

She stared.

Kill it before it can kill us. One quick strike.

Triss saw the uncertainty in her eyes. "What is Garth suggesting?" he demanded.

One quick strike. Garth was right, of course. They weren't going to get the Ruhk Staff back without a fight; it was ridiculous to suppose otherwise. Why not take advantage of the element of surprise? Strike at the Wisteron before it could strike at them. Kill it or at least disable it before it had a chance to hurt them.

Wren took a deep breath. She could do it if she had to, of course. She had already made up her mind to that. The problem was that she was not at all certain the magic of the Elfstones was sufficient to overcome something as large and predatory as the Wisteron. And the magic depended directly on her. If she lacked sufficient strength, if the Wisteron proved too strong, she would have doomed them all.

On the other hand, what choice did she have? There was no better way to reach the Staff.

She reached down absently to stroke Faun and couldn't find her. "Faun?" Her eyes broke from Garth's, her mind still preoccupied with the problem at hand. Orps darted away as she shifted. Water pooled in the depressions left by her boots.

Through the cover of the trees in which they knelt, across the mud flats, she caught sight of the Tree Squeak entering the ravine.

Faun!

Stresa spotted her as well. The Splinterscat whirled, spines jutting forth. "Foolish ssstttt Squeak! It heard you, Wren of the Elves! It asked what you wished. I paid no attention—phfftt—but . . ."

"The Staff?" Wren lurched to her feet, horror clouding her eyes. "You mean she's gone for the Staff?"

She was moving instantly then, racing from the trees onto

the flats, running as silently as she could. She had forgotten that Faun could communicate with them. It had been a long time since the Tree Squeak had even tried. Her chest tightened. She knew how devoted the little creature was to her. It would do anything for her.

It was about to prove that now.

Faun! No!

Her breath came in quick gasps. She wanted to cry out, to call the Tree Squeak back. But she couldn't; a cry would wake the Wisteron. She reached the far edge of the flats, Orps racing away in every direction, dark flashes against the damp. She could hear Garth and Triss following, their breathing harsh. Stresa had gotten ahead of her somehow, the Splinterscat once again quicker than she expected; he was already burrowing through the trees. She followed, crawling hurriedly after, her breath catching in her throat as she broke free.

Faun was halfway down the side of the ravine, slipping smoothly, soundlessly across the rocks. Strands of webbing lay across Faun's path, but she avoided them easily. Above, the Wisteron hung motionless in its net, curled tight. The remains of Gavilan hung there as well, but Wren refused to look on those. She focused instead on Faun, on the Tree Squeak's agonizing, heartstopping descent. She was aware of Stresa a dozen feet away, flattened at the edge of the rocks. Garth and Triss had joined her, one to either side, pressed close. Triss gripped her protectively, trying to draw her back. She yanked her arm free angrily. The hand that gripped the Elfstones came up.

Faun reached the floor of the ravine and started across. Like a feather, the Squeak danced across the carpet of dry bones, carefully choosing the path, mincing like a cat. She was soundless, as inconsequential as the Orps that scattered at its coming. Above, the Wisteron continued to doze, unseeing. The vog's gray haze passed between them in thick curtains, hiding the Tree Squeak in its folds. *Shades, why didn't I keep hold of her?* Wren's blood pounded in her ears, measuring the passing of the seconds. Faun disappeared into the vog. Then the Squeak was visible again, all the way across now, crouched above the Staff.

It's too heavy, Wren thought in dismay. *She won't be able to lift it.*

But somehow Faun managed, easing it away from the layers

of human deadwood, the sticks of once-life. Faun cradled it in her tiny hands, the Staff three times as long as she was, and began to walk a tightrope back, using the Staff as a pole. Wren came to her knees, breathless.

Triss nudged Wren urgently, pointing. The Wisteron had shifted in its hammock, legs stretching. It was coming awake. Wren started to rise, but Garth hurriedly pulled her back. The Wisteron curled up again, legs retracting. Faun continued toward them, tiny face intense, sinewy body taut. She reached the near side of the ravine again and paused.

Wren went cold. *Faun doesn't know how to climb out!*

Then abruptly Killeshan coughed and belched fire, miles distant, so far removed that the sound was scarcely a murmur in the silence. But the eruption triggered shock waves deep beneath the earth, ripples that spread outward from the mountain furnace like the rings that emanate from the splash of a stone. Those tremors traveled all the way to the In Ju and to the Wisteron's island lair, and swiftly a chain reaction began. The shock waves gathered force, turned quickly to heat, and the heat exploded from the mud flats directly behind Wren in a fountain of steam.

Instantly the Wisteron was awake, legs braced in its webbing, head swiveling on a thick, boneless stalk as its black mirrored eyes searched. Faun, caught unprepared for the tremors and explosion, bolted up the side of the ravine, lost her grip, and immediately fell back again. Bones clattered as the Ruhk Staff tumbled down. The hiss of the Wisteron matched that of the geyser. It spun down its webbing with blinding speed, half spider, half monkey, and all monster.

But Garth was faster. He went over the side of the ravine with the swiftness of a shadow cast by a passing cloud at night. Down the rocky outcropping he bounded, as nimble as light, dropping the last dozen feet without slowing. He landed in a crash of broken bones, stretched for the Ruhk Staff, and snatched it up. Faun was already scrambling for the safety of his broad back. Garth whirled to start up again, and the Wisteron's shadow closed over him as the creature spun down its webbing to smash him flat.

Wren came to her feet, her hand opened and her arm thrust

forth, and she summoned the Elfstone power. As quick as thought it responded, streaking forth in a blinding rope of fire. It caught the Wisteron still descending, hammered into it like a massive fist, and sent it spinning away. Wren felt all of her strength leave her as the blow struck. In her urgency to save Garth, she held nothing back. The exhilaration swept through her in an instant and was gone. She gasped in shock, started to collapse, and Triss caught her about the waist. Stresa yelled at them to run.

Garth heaved up out of the ravine, his face sweat-streaked and grim, the Ruhk Staff in one hand, Faun in the other. The Tree Squeak flew to Wren, shivering. On hands and knees they crawled frantically back through the trees, rose, and began to run across the mud flats.

Wren shot a frantic glance over one shoulder.

Where was the Wisteron?

It appeared an instant later. It did not come through the trees as she had expected, but over them. It cleared the topmost limbs, surged into view in a cloud of gray, and dropped on them like a stone. Triss flung himself at Wren and knocked her from its path or she would have been crushed. Stresa turned into a ball of needles and was knocked flying. The Wisteron hissed, one clawed foot bristling with the Splinterscat's spines, and landed in a crouch. Garth dropped the Staff and turned to face it, broadsword drawn. Using both hands, the big Rover slashed at the Wisteron's face, missing as the beast drew back. It spit at Garth, a steaming spray that burned through the air like fire. "Poison!" Stresa screamed from what sounded like the bottom of a well, and Garth went down, flat against the mud.

The moment he dropped, the Wisteron charged.

Wren scrambled up again, arms extending. The Elfstones flared, and the magic responded. Fire exploded into the Wisteron from behind, sending it tumbling away in a cloud of smoke and steam. Howling in triumph, she went after it, a red haze across her vision, the power of the magic surging through her once again. She could not think; she could only react. Gathering the magic within herself, she attacked. The fire struck the Wisteron over and over, pounding it, burning it. The monster hissed and screeched, twisted away, and fought to stand upright. Out of the corner of her eye, Wren saw Garth stagger back to his feet. One hand snatched up the fallen Ruhk Staff, the other the broadsword. The big man was caked with mud. Wren saw him, then forgot him, the magic a veil that enveloped and swept away. The magic was an elixir that filled her with wonder and excitement and white heat. She was invincible; she was supreme!

But then abruptly her strength deserted her once again, drained in an instant's time, and the fire died in her hand. She closed her fingers protectively and dropped to one knee. Garth and Triss were both there at once, dragging her away, hauling her as if she were a child, racing back across the flats. Faun came out of nowhere to scramble up her leg and burrow in her shoulder. Stresa was still screaming in warning, the words unintelligible, the voice rising from somewhere back in the old growth.

Then the Wisteron shot out of the haze, burned and smoking, its sinewy body stretched out like a wolf's in flight. It slammed into them and everyone went sprawling. Wren lurched to her hands and knees in the monster's shadow, half dazed, still weak, mud in her eyes and mouth. In desperation, her protectors fought to save her. Garth stood astride her, broadsword swinging in a deadly arc. Bits and pieces of the Wisteron flew as it pressed the big Rover back. Triss appeared, hacking wildly, cutting one of the monster's legs out from under it with a bone-jarring blow. Shouts and cries filled the fetid air.

But the Wisteron was the largest and strongest of all Morrowindl's demons, of any Shadowen birthed in the lapse of the Elven magic's use, and it was the equal of them all. It whipped its tail against Triss and knocked him thirty feet to land in a crumpled heap. When Garth missed in a quick cut at its head, the beast sliced through clothing and flesh with one black-clawed limb and ripped the broadsword away. Garth had his short sword out in an instant, but a second blow sent him reeling back, tumbling over Wren to land helplessly on his back.

They would have been lost then if not for Faun. Terrified for Wren, who lay exposed now in the Wisteron's path, the Tree Squeak launched itself directly into the monster's face, a shrieking ball of fur, tiny hands tearing and ripping. The Wisteron was caught by surprise, flinched instinctively, and drew back. It reached for the Tree Squeak, anxious to crush this insignificant threat, but Faun was too quick, already scrambling along the monster's ridged back. The Wisteron twisted about in an effort to catch it, incensed.

Get up! Wren told herself, fighting to stand. The Elfstones were white heat in her tightened hand.

Then Garth was back, ragged and bloodied, broadsword flashing against the light. One massive stroke knocked the Wisteron back on two legs. A second almost severed one arm. The Wisteron hissed and writhed, curling back on itself. Faun leapt free and dashed away. Garth swung the broadsword in a deadly arc, blade sweeping, cutting, rending the air.

Wren staggered to her feet, the white heat of the Elfstones transferring from her hand to her chest, then deep into her heart.

Before her lay the Ruhk Staff, fallen from Garth's hand.

Abruptly the Wisteron spun and about and spit a stream of liquid poison at Garth. This time the big man wasn't quick enough, and it struck him in the chest, burning like acid. He dropped to the mud in agony, rolling to cleanse himself.

The Wisteron was on him instantly. One clawed limb pinned him to the earth and began to press.

With both hands cupped about the Elfstones, Wren called forth the fire one final time. It exploded out of her with such force that it rocked her backward like the blow of a fist. The Wisteron was struck full on, picked up like deadwood and spun helplessly away. Fire enveloped it, a raging inferno. Wren pressed forward, the white heat of the magic reflecting in her eyes. Still the Wisteron struggled to break free, fighting to reach the girl. Between them, Garth raised himself to his hands and knees, blood everywhere, the broken blade of the broadsword gripped in one hand. For Wren, everything slowed to a crawl, a dream that was happening only in her mind. Triss was a vague shape stumbling back out of the mist, Stresa a voice without a body, Faun a memory, and the world a shifting, endless haze. Garth's dark eyes looked up at her from his ragged, broken form. At her feet lay the Ruhk Staff and the Loden, the last hope of the Elven people, their vessel of safekeeping, their chance at life. She shrugged it all away and buried herself in the power of the Elfstones, in the magic of her blood, shaping it, directing it, and knowing in some dark, secretive place that her own chance at life had come down to this.

Before her, the Wisteron surged back to its feet.

Help me! she cried out in the silence of her mind.

Then she directed the fire against the mud on which the Wisteron stood, melting it to soup, to a mire as liquid and yielding as quicksand. The Wisteron lurched forward and sank to its knees. The mud bubbled and spit like Killeshan's flow, sucking at the thing that floundered within it. The Wisteron hissed and spit and struggled to break free. But its weight was significant and drew it down; its legs could find no footing. The Elfstone fire burned about it, coring the mud deeper and deeper, pooling it in a bottomless pit. The Wisteron thrashed frantically, steadily sinking. It shrieked, a sound that froze the air to silence.

Then the mud closed over it, the roiling surface glazing orange and yellow with fire, and it was gone.

CHAPTER

27

REN'S FINGERS CLOSED over the Elfstones, mechanical appendages that seemed to belong to someone else. The fire flared once in response and died. She stood frozen in place for a moment, unable to find the strength to make herself move—light-headed, floating, a half step out of time. The magic spit and hissed within her, making small dashes along her arms and legs that caused her to gasp and shiver. She had trouble breathing; her chest was constricted, and her throat was dry and raw.

Before her, the flames that seared the surface of the mud flats diminished to small blue tongues and died into steam. Garth was still braced on hands and knees, head lowered and chest heaving. All about, the In Ju was cavernous and still.

Then Faun darted out of nowhere, scrambled up her arm, and nuzzled into her neck and shoulder, squeaking softly. She closed her eyes against the warm fur, remembering how the little creature had saved her, thinking it was a miracle that any of them were still alive.

She moved finally, forcing herself to take one step and then another, driven by her fear for Garth and by the sight of all that blood. She forced aside the last traces of exhilaration that were the magic's leavings, groped past her craving to savor the power anew, slipped the Elfstones into her pocket, and knelt hurriedly beside her friend. Garth lifted his head to look at her. His face was muddied almost beyond recognition, but the dark eyes were bright and certain.

"Garth," she whispered.

He was ripped open from shoulder to ribs on his left side, and his chest was burned black by the poison. Caked mud had helped to slow the flow of blood, but the wounds needed cleaning or they would become infected.

She eased Faun down gently, then put her arms around Garth and tried to help him to his feet. She could barely move him.

"Wait," a voice called out. "I'll help."

It was Triss, stumbling out of the mist, looking only marginally better off than Garth. He was streaked with mud and swamp water. His left arm hung limp; he carried his short sword in his right. One side of his face was a sheet of blood.

But the Captain of the Home Guard seemed unaware of his injuries. He draped Garth's arm about his shoulders and with a heave brought the big man to his feet. With Wren supporting from the other side, they recrossed the mud flats toward the old-growth acacia.

Stresa lumbered into view, quills sticking out in every direction. "This way! Phhffft! In here! In the shade!"

They bore Garth to a patch of dry earth that lay in the cradle of a cluster of tree roots and laid him down again. Wren worked quickly to cut away his tunic. She had only a little fresh water left, but used almost all of it to clean his wounds. The rest she gave to Triss for his face. She used sewing thread and a needle to stitch the gash closed and bound the big man with strips of cloth torn from the last of her extra clothing. Garth watched her work, silent, unmoving, as if trying to memorize her face. She signed to him once or twice, but he merely nodded and did not sign back. She did not like what she saw.

Then she worked on Triss. The face wound was superficial, merely a deep abrasion. But his left arm was broken. She set it, cut splints of wood and bound them with his belt. He winced once or twice as she worked, but did not cry out. He thanked her when she was done, solemn, embarrassed. She smiled at him.

Only then did she remember the Ruhk Staff, still lying somewhere out in the mud. Hurriedly she went back for it, leaving the cover of the old growth, crossing the flats once again. Orps scurried away at her approach, flashing bits of silver light. The air was empty and still, but the sound of Killeshan's rumble echoed ominously from beyond the wall of the mist, and the earth shivered in response. She found the Ruhk Staff where it had fallen and picked it up. The Loden sparkled like a cluster of small stars. So much given up on its behalf, she thought, on behalf of the Elven people, trapped inside. She experienced a dark moment of regret, a sudden urge to toss it aside, to sink it as deep within the mud as the Wisteron. The Elves, who had done so much damage with their magic, who had created the Shadowen with their ambition and who had abandoned the Four Lands to a savagery for which they were responsible, might be better gone. But she had made her decision on the Elves. Besides, she knew it was not the fault of these Elves, not of this generation, and it was wrong to hold an entire people accountable for the acts of a few in any case. Allanon must have counted on her thinking like that. He must have foreseen that she would discover the truth and decide for herself the wisdom of his charge. *Find the Elves and return them to the Four Lands.* She had wondered why many times. She thought now she was beginning to see. Who better than the Elves to right the wrong that had been done? Who better to lead the fight against the Shadowen?

She trudged back across the flats, numbness setting in, the last traces of the magic's euphoria fading away. She was tired and sad and oddly lost. But she knew she could not give in to these feelings. She had the Ruhk Staff back again, and the journey to the beaches and the search for Tiger Ty lay ahead. And there were still the demons.

Stresa was waiting at the edge of the trees. The rough voice was a whisper of warning. "Hsstt. He is badly hurt, Wren of the Elves. Your big friend. Be warned. The poison is a bad thing. Phffttt. He may not be able to come with us."

She brushed past the Splinterscat, irritated, abrupt. "He'll manage," she snapped.

With help from Triss, she got Garth to his feet once more and they started out. It was past midday, the light faint and hazy through the screen of vog, the heat a blanket of sweltering damp. Stresa led, working his way doggedly through the jungle's maze, choosing a path that gave those following a chance to maneuver with Garth. The In Ju seemed empty, as if the death of the

Wisteron had killed everything that lived within it. But the silence was mostly a response to the earth tremors, Wren thought. The creatures of Morrowindl sensed that all was not well, and for the moment at least they had suspended their normal activities and gone into hiding, waiting to discover what would happen.

She watched Garth's face as they walked, saw the intensity of his eyes, the mask of pain that stretched his skin tight across his bones. He did not look at her, his gaze fixed purposefully on the path ahead. He was keeping upright through sheer determination.

It was twilight by the time they cleared the In Ju and passed into the forested hill country beyond. They found a clearing with a spring, and she cleaned her giant friend's wounds anew. There was nothing to eat; all of their provisions had been consumed or lost, and they were uncertain which of the island's roots and tree fruit was safe. They had to make do with spring water. Triss found enough dry wood to make a fire, but it began to rain almost immediately, and within seconds everything was soaked. They huddled back within the shelter of a broad-limbed koa, shoulder to shoulder against the encroaching dark. After a time, Stresa moved out to where he could keep watch, muttering something about being the only one left who was fit for the job. Wren didn't argue the point; she was half-inclined to agree. The light faded steadily from silver to gray to black. The forest was transformed, suddenly alive with movement as the need for food brought its creatures forth to hunt, but nothing that went abroad made any attempt to approach their refuge. Mist seeped through the trees and grasses in lazy tendrils. Water dripped softly from the leaves. Faun squirmed in Wren's arms, burrowing deep into her shoulder.

At midnight, Killeshan erupted. Fire belched out in a shower of sparks and flaming debris, and ash and smoke spewed forth. The sound it made was terrifying, a booming that shattered the night stillness and brought everyone awake with a start. The initial explosion turned quickly to a series of rumbles that built one upon the other until the entire island was shaking. Even from as far away as they were, the eruption was visible, a deep red glow against the black that lifted skyward and seemed to hang there. Close at hand, the earth split in small rents and steam rose in geysers, hissing and burning. In the shadows beyond, the island's creatures raced wildly about, fleeing without direction or purpose, frightened by the intensity of the tremors, by the sound and the glare. The company huddled back against the koa, fighting the urge to join them. But flight in such blackness was dangerous, Wren knew, and Stresa was quick to remind her that they must stay put until daylight.

The eruptions continued all night long, one after the other, a series of thundering coughs and fiery convulsions that threatened to rend Morrowindl from end to end. Fires burned high on Killeshan's slopes as lava flows began their descent to the sea. Cliffs slid away in a roar of broken stone, avalanches that tore free whole mountainsides. Giant trees snapped at their centers and tumbled to the earth.

Wren closed her eyes and tried unsuccessfully to sleep.

Toward dawn, Stresa rose to scout the area leading out and Triss took the Splinterscat's place at watch. Wren was left alone with Garth. The big man slept fitfully, his face bathed in sweat, his body wracked with convulsions. He was running a fever, and the heat of his body was palpable. As she watched him twist and turn against his discomfort, she found herself thinking of all they had been through together. She had worried about him before, but never as much as now. In part, her concern was magnified by her sense of helplessness. Morrowindl remained a foreign world to her, and her knowledge of it was too little. She could not help thinking that there must be something more that she could do for her big friend if she only knew what. She was reminded of Ellenroh, stricken by a fever similar to Garth's, a fever that none of them had understood. She had lost her grandmother; she did not intend to lose her best friend. She reassured herself over and over that Garth was strong, that he possessed great endurance. He could survive anything; he always had.

It was growing light, and she had just closed her eyes against her fatigue and depression when the big man surprised her by touching her gently on the arm. When she lifted her head to look at him, he began to sign.

I want you to do something for me.

She nodded, and her fingers repeated her words. "What?"

It will be difficult for you, but it is necessary.

She tried to see his eyes and couldn't. He was turned too far into the shadows.

I want you to forgive me.

"Forgive you for what?"

I have lied to you about something. I have lied repeatedly. Ever since I have known you.

She shook her head, confused, anxious, weary to the bone. "Lied about what?"

His gaze never faltered. *About your parents. About your mother and father. I knew them. I knew who they were and where they came from. I knew everything.*

She stared, not quite ready to believe what she was hearing.

Listen to me, Wren. Your mother understood the impact of Eowen's prophecy far better than the queen. The prophecy said that you must be taken from Morrowindl if you were to live, but it also said that you would one day return to save the Elves. Your mother correctly judged that whatever salvation you could provide your people would be tied in some way to a confrontation with the evil they had created. I did not know this at the time; I have surmised it since. What I did know was that your mother was determined that you be raised to be strong enough to withstand any danger, any foe, any trial that was required of you. That was why she gave you to me

Wren was stunned. "To you? Directly to you?"

Garth shifted, pushing himself into a sitting position, giving his hands more freedom. He grunted with the effort. Wren could see blood soaking through the bandages of his wounds.

She came with her husband to the Rovers, sent by the Wing Riders. She came to us because she was told that we were the strongest of the free peoples, that we trained our children from birth to survive because survival is the hardest part of every Rover's life. We have always been an outcast people and as such have found it necessary to be stronger than any other. So your mother and your father came to us, to my family, a tribe of several hundred living on the plains below the Myrian, and asked if there were someone among us who could be trusted in the schooling of their daughter. They wished her to be trained in the Rover way, to begin learning as soon as she was old enough how to survive in a world where everyone and everything was a potential enemy. I was recommended. We talked, your parents and I, and I agreed to be your teacher.

He coughed, a deep, racking sound that tore from the depths of his chest. His head lowered momentarily as he gasped for breath.

"Garth," she whispered, frightened now. "Tell me about this later, after you have rested."

He shook his head. *No. I want this finished. I have carried it with me for too long.*

"But you can hardly breathe, you can barely . . ."

I am stronger than you think. His hand closed over her own momentarily and released. *Are you afraid I might be dying?*

She swallowed against her tears. "Yes."

Does that frighten you so? After all I have taught you?

"Yes."

The dark eyes blinked, and he gave her a strange look. *Then I will not die until you are ready for me to do so.*

She nodded wordlessly, not understanding what he meant, wary of the look, anxious only that he live, whatever bargain it required.

His breath exhaled in a thick rattle. *Good. Your mother, then. She was everything you have been told—strong, kind, determined, devoted to you. But she had decided that she must return to her people. She had made up her mind before she left Morrowindl, I think. Your father acquiesced. I don't know the reason for their decision; I only know that your mother was bound in countless ways to her own mother and to her people, and your father was desperately in love with her. In any case, it was agreed that you should be sent to live with the Ohmsfords in Shady Vale until you were five—the beginning age for training a Rover child—and then given back to me. You were to be told that your mother was a Rover and your father an Ohmsford and that your ancestors were Elves. You were to be told nothing else.*

Wren shook her head in disbelief. "Why, Garth? Why keep it all a secret from me?"

Because your mother understood how dangerous it was to try to influence the workings of a prophecy. She could have tried to keep you safe, to prevent you from returning to Morrowindl. She could have stayed with you and told you what was foreordained. But what harm might she have caused by interfering so? She knew enough of prophecies to recognize the threat. It was better, she believed, that you grow to womanhood without knowing the specifics of what Eowen had foretold, that you find your destiny on your own, however it was meant to be. It was given to me to prepare you.

"So you knew everything? All of it? You knew about the Elfstones?"

No. Not about the Elfstones. Like you, I thought them painted rocks. I was told to make certain that you knew where they came from, that they were your heritage from your parents. I was to see to it that you never lost them. Your mother was convinced, I suppose, that like your destiny, the power of the Elfstones would reveal itself when it was time.

"But you knew the rest, all the time I was growing up? And after, when I went to the Hadeshorn, when I was sent in search of the Elves?"

I knew.

"And didn't tell me?" There was a hint of anger in her voice now, the first. The impact of what he was telling her was beginning to set in. "Never a word, even when I asked?"

I could not.

"What do you mean, you could not?" She was incensed. "Why?"

Because I promised your mother. She swore me to secrecy. You were to know nothing of your true heritage, nothing of the Elessedils, Arborlon, or Morrowindl, nothing of the prophecy. You were to discover it on your own or not, as fate decreed. I was not to aid you in any way. I was to go with you when it came time if I chose. I was to protect you as best I could. But I was to tell you nothing.

"Ever?"

The big man's breath rattled in his chest, and his fingers hesitated. *I swore an oath. I swore that I would tell you nothing until the prophecy came to pass, if it ever did—nothing until you had come back into Arborlon, until you had discovered the truth for yourself, until you had done whatever it was you were fated to do to help your people. I promised.*

She sank back on her heels, despair washing through her. *Trust no one*, the Addershag had warned. *No one.* She had believed she realized the impact of those words. She had thought she understood.

But this . . .

"Oh, Garth," she whispered in dismay. "I trusted you!"

You lost nothing by doing so, Wren.

"Didn't I?"

They faced each other, silent, motionless. Everything that had happened to Wren since Cogline had first come to her those many weeks past seemed to gather and settle on her shoulders like an enormous weight. So many harrowing escapes, so many deaths, so much lost—she felt it all, the whole of it, come together in a single moment, in this truth terrible and unexpected.

Had you known before coming, it might have changed everything. Your mother understood that. Your father as well. Perhaps I would have told you if I could, but my promise bound me. The big frame shifted, and the sharply etched bones of the other's face lifted into the light. *Tell me, if you can, that I should have done otherwise. Tell me, Wren, that I should have broken my promise.*

Her mouth was a tight, bitter line. "You should have."

He held her gaze, dark eyes flat and expressionless.

"No," she admitted finally, tears in her eyes. "You shouldn't have." She looked away, empty and lost. "But that doesn't help. Everyone has lied to me. Everyone. Even you. The Addershag was right, Garth, and that's what hurts. There were too many lies, too many secrets, and I wasn't part of any of them."

She cried silently, head lowered. "Someone should have trusted me. My whole life has been changed, and I have had nothing to say about it. Look what's been done!"

One big hand brushed her own. *Think, Wren. The choices have all been yours. No one has made them for you; no one has shown you the way. Had you known the truth of things, had you understood the expectations held for you, would it have been the same? Could you say the choices were yours in that case?*

She looked back, hesitant.

Would it have been better to know you were Ellenroh Elessedil's granddaughter, that the Elfstones you thought painted rocks were real, that when you grew to womanhood you would one day be expected to travel to Morrowindl and, because of a prophecy given before you were born, save the Elves? How free would you have been to act then? How much would you have grown? What would you have become?

She took a deep breath. "I don't know. But perhaps I should have been given the chance to find out."

The light was stronger now as dawn broke somewhere beyond the pall of the mist and trees. Faun lifted her head from out of Wren's lap where she had lain motionless. Triss had come back from the edge of the dark; he stood watching them in silence. The night sounds had died away, and the frantic movement had ceased. In the distance, the sounds of Killeshan's eruption continued unabated, steady and ominous. The earth shook faintly, and the fire of the lava rose skyward into gray smoke and ash.

Garth stirred, his hands moving. *Wren,* he signed. *I did what I was asked, what I promised. I did the best I could. I wish it had not been necessary to deceive you. I wish I had been able to give you the chance you ask for.*

She looked at him for a long time, and finally nodded. "I know."

The strong, dark face was rigid with concentration. *Don't be angry with your mother and father. They did what they thought they had to do, what they believed was right.*

She nodded again. She did not trust herself to speak.

You must find a way to forgive us all.

She swallowed hard. "I wish . . . I wish I didn't hurt so much."

Wren, look at me.

She did so, reluctantly, warily.

We are not finished yet. There is one thing more.

She felt a chill settle in the pit of her stomach, an ache of something sensed but not yet fully realized. She saw Stresa appear out of the trees to one side, lumbering heavily, winded and damp. He slowed as he approached them, aware that something was happening, a confrontation perhaps, a revelation, a thing inviolate.

"Stresa," Wren greeted quickly, anxious to avoid hearing any more from Garth.

The Splinterscat swung his blunt cat face from one human to the other. "We can go now," he said. "In fact, we should. The mountain is coming down. Sooner or later it will reach here."

"We must hurry," she agreed, rising. She snatched up the Ruhk Staff, then looked down anxiously at her injured friend. "Garth?"

We need to speak alone first.

Her throat tightened anew. "Why?"

Ask the others to go ahead a short distance and wait for us. Tell them we won't be long.

She hesitated, then looked at Stresa and Triss. "I need a moment with Garth. Wait for us up ahead. Please."

They stared back at her without speaking, then nodded reluctantly, Triss first, lean face expressionless, and Stresa with sharp-eyed suspicion.

"Take Faun," she asked as an afterthought, disengaging the Tree Squeak from its perch on her shoulder and setting it gently on the ground.

Stresa hissed at the little creature and sent it racing off into the trees. He looked back at her with sad, knowing eyes. "Call, rwwwlll Wren of the Elves, if you need us."

When they had gone, the sound of their footsteps fading, she faced Garth once more, the Staff gripped tightly in both hands. "What is it?"

The big man beckoned. *Don't be frightened. Here. Sit next to me. Listen a moment and don't interrupt.*

She did as he asked, kneeling close enough that her leg was pressed up against his body. She could feel the heat of his fever. Mist and pale light obscured him in a shading of gray, and the world about was fuzzy and thick with heat.

She lay the Ruhk Staff down beside her, and Garth's big hands began to sign.

Something is happening to me. Inside. The Wisteron's poison, I think. It creeps through me like a living thing, fire that sears and deadens. I can feel it working about, changing me. It is a bad feeling.

"I'll wash the wounds again, rebind them."

No, Wren. What is happening now is beyond that, beyond anything you can do. The poison is in my system, all through me.

Her breath was hurried, angry. "If you are too weak, we will carry you."

I was weak at first, but the weakness is passing now. I am growing stronger again. But the strength is not my own.

She stared at him, not really understanding, but frightened all the same. She shook her head. "What are you saying?"

He looked at her with fierce determination, his dark eyes

hard, his face all angles and planes, chiseled in stone. *The Wisteron was a Shadowen. Like the Draculs. Remember Eowen?*

She shuddered, jerked back and tried to rise. He grabbed her and held her in place, keeping their eyes locked. *Look at me.*

She tried and couldn't. She saw him and at the same time didn't, aware of the lines that framed him but unable to see the colors and shadings between, as if doing so would reveal the truth she feared. "Let me go!"

Then everything broke within her, and she began to cry. She did so soundlessly, and only the heaving of her shoulders gave her away. She closed her eyes against the rage of feelings within, the horror of the world about her, the terrible price it seemed to require over and over again. She saw Garth even there, etched within her mind—the dark confidence and strength radiating from his face, the smile he reserved exclusively for her, the wisdom, the friendship, and the love.

"I can't lose you," she whispered, no longer bothering to sign, the words a murmur. "I can't!"

His hands released her, and her eyes opened. *Look at me.*

She took a deep breath and did so.

Look into my eyes.

She did. She looked down into the soul of her oldest and most trusted friend. A wicked red glimmer looked back.

It already begins, he signed.

She shook her head in furious denial.

I can't let it happen, Wren. But I can't do it alone. Not and be sure. You have to help me let go.

"No."

One hand slipped down to his belt and pulled free the long knife, its razor-sharp blade glinting in the half-light. She shuddered and drew back, but he grabbed her wrist and forced the handle of the knife into her palm.

His hands signed, quick, steady. *There is no more time left to us. What we've had has been good. I do not regret a moment of it. I am proud of you, Wren. You are my strength, my wisdom, my skill, my experience, my life, everything I am, the best of me. And still your own person, distinct in every way. You are what you were meant to be—a Rover girl become*

Queen of the Elves. I can't give you anything more. It is a good time to say good-bye.

Wren couldn't breathe. She couldn't see clearly. "You can't ask this of me! You can't!"

I have to. There is no one else. No one I could depend upon to do it right.

"No!" She dropped the knife as if it had burned her skin. "I would rather," she choked, crying, "be dead myself!"

He reached down for the knife and carefully placed it back in her hand. She shook her head over and over, saying no, no. He touched her, drawing her eyes once more to his own. He was shivering now, just cold perhaps, but maybe something more. The red glow was more pronounced, stronger.

I am slipping away, Wren. I am being stolen from myself. You have to hurry. Do it quickly. Don't let me become . . . He couldn't finish, his great, strong hands shaking now as well. *You can do it. We have practiced often enough. I can't trust myself. I might . . .*

Wren's muscles were so tight she could barely move. She glanced over her shoulder, thinking to call Stresa back, or Triss, desperate for anyone. But there was no one who could help her, she knew. There was nothing anyone could do.

She turned quickly back. "There must be an antidote that will counteract the poison, mustn't there?" Her words were frantic. "I'll ask Stresa! He'll know! I'll get him back!"

The big hands cut her short. *Stresa already knows the truth. You saw it in his eyes. There isn't anything he can do. There never was. Let it go. Help me. Take the knife and use it.*

No!

You have to.

No!

One hand swept up suddenly as if to strike her, and instinctively she reacted with a block to counter, the hand with the knife lifting, freezing, inches above his chest. Their eyes locked. For an instant, everything washed away within Wren but the terrible recognition of what was needed. The truth stunned her. She caught her breath and held it.

Quick, Wren . . . She did not move. He took her hand and gently lowered it until the knife blade was resting against his tunic, against his chest. *Do it.*

Her head shook slowly, steadily from side to side, a barely perceptible movement.

Wren. Help me.

She looked down at him, deep into his eyes, and into the red glare that was consuming him, that rose out of the horror growing within. She remembered standing next to him as a child when she had first come to live with the Rovers, barely as tall as his knee. She remembered herself at ten, whip-thin, leather-tough, racing to catch him in the forest. She remembered their games, constant, unending, all directed toward her training.

She felt his breath on her face. She felt the closeness of him and thought of the comfort it had given her as a child.

"Garth," she whispered in despair, and felt the great hands come up to tighten over her own.

Then she thrust the long knife home.

CHAPTER

28

HE FLED THEN. She ran from the clearing into the trees, numb with grief, half blind with tears, the Ruhk Staff clutched before her in both hands like a shield. She raced through the shadows and half-light of the island's early morning, oblivious to Killeshan's distant rumble, to Morrowindl's shudder in response, lost to everything but the need to escape the time and place of Garth's death, even knowing she could never escape its memory. She tore past brush and limbs with heedless disregard, through tall grasses and brambles, along ridges of earth encrusted with lava rock, and over deadwood and scattered debris. She sensed none of it. It was not her body that fled; it was her mind.

Garth!

She called out to him endlessly, chasing after her memories of him, as if by catching one she might bring him back to life. She saw him race away, spectral, phantasmagoric. Parts of him appeared and faded in the air before her, blurred and distant images from times gone by. She saw herself give chase as she had so many times when they had played at being Tracker and prey, when they had practiced the lessons of staying alive. She saw herself that last day in the Tirfing before Cogline had appeared and everything had changed forever, skirting the shores of the Myrian, searching for signs. She watched him drop from the trees, huge, silent, and quick. She felt him grapple for her, felt herself slip away, felt her long knife rise and descend. She heard herself laugh. *You're dead, Garth.*

And now he really was.

Somehow—it was never entirely clear—she stumbled upon the others of the little company, the few who remained alive, Triss, the last of the Elves, the last besides herself, and Stresa and Faun. She careened into them, spun away angrily as if they were hindrances, and kept going. They came after her, of course, running to catch up, calling out urgently, asking what was wrong, what had happened, where was Garth?

Gone, she said, head shaking. Not coming.

But it was okay. It was all right.

He was safe now.

Still running, she heard Triss demand again, *What is wrong?* And Stresa reply, *Hssssttt, can't you see?* Words, whispered furtively, passed between them, but she didn't catch their meaning, didn't care to. Faun leapt from the pathway to her arm, clinging possessively, but she shook the Tree Squeak off roughly. She didn't want to be touched. She could barely stand to be inside her own skin.

She broke free of the trees.

"Lady Wren!" she heard Triss cry out to her.

Then she was scrambling up a lava slide, clawing and digging at the sharp rock, feeling it cut into her hands and knees. Her breath rasped heavily from her throat, and she was coughing, choking on words that wouldn't come. The Ruhk Staff fell from her hands, and she abandoned it. She cast everything away, the whole of who and what she was, sickened by the thought of it, wanting only to flee, to escape, to run until there was nowhere left to go.

When she collapsed finally, exhausted, stretched flat on the slide, sobbing uncontrollably, it was Triss who reached her first, who cradled her as if she were a child, who soothed her with words and small touches and gave her a measure of the comfort she needed. He helped her to her feet, turned her about, and took her back down to the forest below. Carrying the Ruhk Staff in one arm and supporting her with the other, he guided her through the morning hours like a shepherd a stray lamb, asking nothing of her but that she place one foot before the other and that she continue to walk with him. Stresa took the lead, his bulky form becoming the point of reference on which she focused, the steadily changing object toward which she moved, first one foot, then the other, over and over again. Faun returned for another try at scrambling up her leg and onto her arm, and this time she welcomed the intrusion, pressing the Tree Squeak close, nuzzling back against the little creature's warmth and softness.

They traveled all day like this, companions on a journey that required no words. The few times they paused to rest, Wren accepted the water Triss gave her to drink and the fruit he pressed into her palm and did not bother to ask where it came from or if it was safe to eat. The daylight dimmed as clouds massed from horizon to horizon, as the vog thickened beneath. Killeshan stormed behind them, the eruptions unchecked now, fire and ash and smoke spewing skyward in long geysers, the smell of sulfur thick in the air, the island shaking and rocking. When darkness finally descended, the crest of the mountain was bathed in a blood-red corona that flared anew with each eruption and sent trailers of fire all down the distant slopes where the lava ran to the sea. Boulders grated and crunched as the molten rock carried them away, and trees burned with a sharp, crackling despair. The wind died to nothing, a haze settled over everything, and the island became a fire-rimmed cage in which the inhabitants bumped up against one another in frightened, angry confusion.

Stresa settled them that night in a cleft of rock that sheltered on three sides amid a grove of wiry ironwood stripped all but bare of foliage. They huddled in the dark with their backs to the wall and watched the holocaust beyond grow brighter. They were still a day from the beaches, a day from any rendezvous with Tiger Ty, and the destruction of the island was imminent. Wren came back to herself enough to realize the danger they were in. Sipping at the cup of water Triss gave her, listening to the sound of his voice as he continued to speak quietly, reassuringly, she remembered what it was that she was supposed to do and that it was Tiger Ty alone who could help her to do it.

"Triss," she said finally, unexpectedly, seeing him for the first time, speaking his name in acknowledgment, making him smile in relief.

Shortly after, the demons appeared, Morrowindl's shad-

owen, the first of those that had escaped Killeshan's fiery
flow, fled down out of the hills toward the beaches, lost and
confused and ready to kill anything they came upon. They
stumbled out of the fiery gloom, a ragged collection of misshapen horrors, and attacked unthinkingly, responding to instinct and to their own peculiar madness. Stresa heard them
coming, sharp ears picking out the sound of their approach, and
warned the others seconds before the attack. Sword drawn, Triss
met the rush, withstood it, and very nearly turned it aside, almost a match for the things even with only one useful arm. But
the demons were crazed past fear or reason, driven from their
high country by something beyond understanding. These humans were a lesser threat. They rallied and attacked anew, determined to exact some measure of revenge from the source at
hand.

But now Wren was facing them, consumed by her own madness, cold and reasoned, and she sent the magic of the Elfstones
scything into them like razors. Too late, they realized the danger. The magic caught them up and they vanished in bursts of
fire and sudden screams. In seconds nothing remained but smoke
and ash.

Others came all during the night, small bunches of them,
launching out of the darkness in frenzied rushes that carried
them to quick and certain deaths. Wren destroyed them without
feeling, without regret, and then burned the forest about until
it was as fiery as the slopes above where the lava rivers steamed.
As morning approached, the whole of their shelter for fifty yards
out was barren and smoking, a charnel house of bodies blackened beyond recognition, a graveyard in which only they survived. There was no sleep, no rest, and little respite against the
assaults. Dawn found them hollow-eyed and staring, gaunt and
ragged figures against the coming light. Triss was wounded in
half a dozen new places, his clothing in rags, all of his weapons
lost or broken but his short sword. Wren's face was gray with
ash, and her hands shook with the infusion of the Elfstones'
power. Stresa's quills fanned out in every direction, and it did
not seem as if they would ever settle back in place. Faun
crouched next to Wren like a coiled spring.

As the light crept out of the east, silver sunrise through the

haze of fire and smoke, Wren told them finally what had become of Garth, needing at last to tell, anxious to rid herself of
the solitary burden she bore, the bitter knowledge that was hers
alone. She told them quietly, softly, in the silence that followed
the last of the attacks. She cried again, thinking that perhaps
she would never stop. But the tears were cleansing this time, as
if finally washing away some of the hurt. They listened to her
wordlessly, the Captain of the Home Guard, the Splinterscat,
and the Tree Squeak, gathered close so that nothing would be
missed, even Faun, who might or might not have understood
her words, nestled against her shoulder. The words flowed from
her easily, the dam of her despair and shame giving way, and a
kind of peace settled deep within her.

"Rwwlll Wren, it was what was needed," Stresa told her solemnly when she had finished.

"You knew, didn't you?" she asked in reply.

"Hssstt. Yes. I understood what the poison would do. But I
could not tell you, Wren of the Elves, because you would not
have wanted to believe. It had to come from him."

And the Splinterscat was right, of course, although it no
longer really mattered. They talked a bit longer while the light
seeped slowly past the gloom, brightening the world about them,
their world of black ruin in which smoke still curled skyward
in wispy spirals and the earth still trembled with the fury of
Killeshan's discontent.

"He gave his life for you, Lady Wren," Triss offered solemnly. "He stood over you when the Wisteron would have
claimed you and fought to keep you safe. None of us would
have fared as well. We tried, but only Garth had the strength.
Keep that as your memory of him."

But she could still feel herself pushing against the handle of
the long knife as it slipped into his heart, still feel his hands
closing over hers, almost as if to absolve her of responsibility.
She would always feel them there, she thought. She would always see what had been in his eyes.

They started out again soon after, crossing the charred bat-
tleground of the night gone past to the fresh green landscape of
the day that lay ahead, passing toward the last of the country
that separated them from the beach. The tremors underfoot

were constant still, and the fires of the lava rivers were burning closer, streaming down the mountainside above. Things fled about them in all directions, and even the demons did not pause to attack. Everything raced to escape the burning heat, driven by Killeshan's fury toward the shores of the Blue Divide. Morrowindl was turning slowly into a cauldron of fire, eating away at itself from the center out. Cracks were beginning to appear everywhere, vast fissures that opened into blackness, that hissed and spit with steam and heat. The world that had flourished in the wake of the Elven magic's use was disappearing, and within days only the rocks and the ashes of the dead would remain. A new world was evolving about the little company as it fled, and when it was complete nothing of the old would be left upon it.

They passed down into the meadows of tall grasses that bounded the final stretches of old growth bordering the shoreline. The grasses had already begun to curl and die, smoked and steamed by heat and gases, the life seared out of them. Scrub brush broke apart beneath their boots, dried and lifeless. Fires burned in hot spots all about, and to their right, across a deep ravine, a thin ribbon of red fire worked its way relentlessly through a patchwork of wildflowers toward a stand of acacia that waited in helpless, frozen anticipation. Clouds of black soot roiled down out of the heights of the In Ju, where the jungle burned slowly to the waterline, the swamp beneath already beginning to boil. Rock and ash showered down from somewhere beyond their vision like hail out of clouds, thrown by the volcano's continuing explosions. The wind shifted and it grew harder to see. It was midday, and the sky was as raw and gray and hazy as autumn twilight.

Wren's head felt light and substanceless, a part of the air she breathed. Her bones were loose within her body, and the fire of the Elfstones' magic still flared and sparked like embers cooling. She searched the land about her and could not seem to focus. Everything drifted in the manner of clouds.

"Stresa, how much farther?" she asked.

"A ways," the Splinterscat growled without turning. "Phhfftt. Keep walking, Wren of the Elves."

She did, knowing that her strength was failing and wondering absently if it was from so much use of the magic or from exhaustion. She felt Triss move close, one arm coming about her shoulders.

"Lean on me," he whispered, and took her weight against his own.

The meadows passed away with the sweep of the sun west, and they reached the old growth. Already it was aflame to the south, the topmost branches burning, smoke billowing. They pushed through rapidly, skidding and slipping on moss and leaves and loose rock. The trees were silent and empty, the pillars of a hall roofed in low-hanging clouds and mist. Growls and snarls rose up out of the haze, distant, but all about.

The trek wore on. Once something huge moved in the shadows off to one side, and Stresa wheeled to face it, spines lifting. But nothing appeared, and after a moment they moved on. The sound of water crashing against rocks sounded ahead, the rise and fall of the ocean. Wren found herself smiling, clasping the Ruhk Staff tight against her breast. There was still a chance for them, she thought wearily. There was still hope that they might escape.

Then finally, as daylight faded behind them and sunset brightened into silver and red ahead, they broke clear of the trees and found themselves staring out from a high bluff over the vast expanse of the Blue Divide. Smoke and ash clouded the air close at hand, but beyond its screen the horizon was ablaze with color.

The company staggered forward and stopped. The bluff fell away sharply to a shoreline jagged with rocks. There were no beaches anywhere and so sign of Tiger Ty.

Wren leaned heavily on the Staff, searching the sky. It stretched away, a vast and empty expanse.

"Tiger Ty!" she whispered in despair.

Triss released her and moved away, searching the bluff. "Down there," he signaled after a moment, pointing north. "There's a beach, if we can get to it."

But Stresa was already shaking his grizzled head. "Ssssstt! We'll have to go back through the woods, back into the smoke and the things it hides. Not a smart idea with darkness coming. Phffftt!"

Wren watched helplessly as the sun settled down against the ocean's edge and began to disappear. In minutes it would be dark. They had come so far, she thought, and whispered, "No," so that only she could hear.

She laid down the Staff and slipped free the Elfstones. Holding them forth, she sent the white magic streaking across the sky from end to end, a flare of brightness against the gray twilight. The light shimmered like fire and disappeared. They all stood looking after it, watching the dark approach, watching the sun paint the sky with color as it sank from view.

Behind them, the hunters began to gather, the demons come down from the heights, the black things either tracking them or drawn by the magic. Their shadows pushed against the edges of the twilight, growling, snarling, edging steadily closer. Wren and her companions were trapped on the bluff, caught against the drop into the ocean. Wren felt the rattle of her bones, of her breath, of her failing strength. It was too much to expect that Tiger Ty would be there for them after all this time, too much to hope for. Yet she refused to let go of the only hope left to them. Once more she would use the magic, if need be. Once more, for good measure. Because there wasn't enough left in any case to keep them alive another night. There was not enough strength left in her to use it, not enough left in any of them to matter.

Triss stepped out to confront the shadows in the trees, lean and hard, broken arm hanging stiff, sword arm bent and ready. "Keep behind me," he ordered.

The seconds slipped quickly away. The colors in the western sky faded into gray. Twilight deepened to a pale shade of ash.

"There!" Stresa warned.

Something launched itself out of the dark, a massive form, hammering into Triss, throwing him down. Another rushed in behind it, and Stresa showered it with quills. Wren swung the Elfstones up and sent the magic streaking forth, burning the things closest. They screamed and hastily withdrew. Triss lay unconscious on the earth.

Wren sagged to her knees, exhausted.

"Sssttt stand up!" Stresa growled desperately.

A handful of misshapen forms detached themselves anew and began to inch forward.

"Stand up!"

Then a shriek split the near silence, a sound like the tearing out of a human life, and a huge shadow swept the bluff. Claws raked the edges of the trees and sent the attackers scattering into the dark. Wren stared upward in disbelief, speechless. *Had she seen . . . ?* The shadow swung away, black wings knifelike against the sky, and another shriek emitted from its throat.

"Spirit!" Wren screamed in recognition.

Back swung the Roc and plummeted to the bluff edge where it settled with a mad beating of wings. A small, wiry form leapt down, yelling and shouting wildly.

"Ho, this way, quick now! They won't stay frightened long!"

Tiger Ty!

And when Wren pulled Triss to his feet and staggered forward to meet the little man, she found the Tiger Ty she remembered from all those weeks ago, wrinkled and smiling within his brown skin, a scarecrow of bones and leather, rough hands ready and bright eyes quick. He looked at her, at her companions, at the Ruhk Staff she carried, and he laughed.

"Wren Elessedil," he greeted. "You are as good as your word, girl! Come back out of death to find me, come back to spit in my face, to prove you could do it after all! Shades, you must be tough as nails!"

She was too happy to see him to disagree.

HE HURRIED THEM atop Spirit then—but only after a sharp glance at Stresa and a pointed warning to the Splinterscat that he had best keep his quills to himself. Muttering something about Wren's choice of traveling companions, he wrapped the Splinterscat in a leather coverlet and boosted him up. Although Stresa remained still and compliant, his eyes darted anxiously. Wren bound Faun to her back, mounted Spirit, and pulled a semiconscious Triss up in front of her where she could hold him in place. Her hands full, she jammed the Ruhk Staff beneath her legs in the harness. They worked swiftly, Tiger Ty and she, chased by the snarls and growls that rose from the darkness of the trees, driven by their fear of the things hidden there. Twice black forms darted from the shadows as if to attack, but each time Spirit's angry shriek sent them scrambling away again.

It seemed to take them forever, but finally they were settled. With a quick last check of the harness straps, Tiger Ty sprang atop the Roc.

"Up, now, old bird!" he yelled urgently.

With a final cry, Spirit spread his great wings and lifted away. A handful of demons broke cover, racing to catch them in a last desperate effort, flinging themselves across the bluff. Several caught hold of the Roc's feathers, dragging the great bird down. But Spirit shook himself, twisted and raked wildly with his claws, and the attackers fell away into the dark. As the Roc swept out over the Blue Divide and began to rise, Wren glanced back a final time. Morrowindl was a furnace glowing against the night, all mist and steam and ash, Killeshan's mouth spitting out streams of molted rock, rivers of fire running to the sea.

She closed her eyes and did not look back again.

She was never sure how long they flew that night. It might have been hours; it might have been only minutes. She clung to Triss and the restraining straps as she fought to stay awake, exhausted to the point of senselessness. Faun's arms were wrapped about her neck, warm and furry, and she could feel the Tree Squeak's worried breath against her neck. Somewhere behind, Stresa rode in silence. She heard Tiger Ty call back to her once or twice, but his words were lost in the wind, and she did not bother to try to answer. A vision of Morrowindl in those last minutes floated spectrally before her eyes, harsh and un-yielding, a nightmare that would never recede into sleep.

When they landed, whatever time had passed, it was still night, but the sky was clear and bright about her. Spirit settled down on a small atoll green with vegetation. The sweet smell of flowers wafted on the air. Wren breathed the scents gratefully as she slid down the Roc's broad back, reaching up in numb response for Triss and then Stresa. Imagine, she thought diz-zily—a moon and stars, a night bright with their light, no mist or haze, no fire.

"This way, over here, girl," Tiger Ty advised gently, taking her arm.

He led her to a patch of soft grass where she lay down and instantly fell asleep.

The sun was red against the horizon when she woke again, a scarlet sphere rising from the ocean's crimson-colored waters into skies black with thunderheads. The storm and its fire seemed settled in a single patch of earth and sky. She raised herself on her elbow and peered at the strange phenomenon, wondering how it could be.

Then Tiger Ty, keeping watch at her side, whispered, "Go back to sleep, Miss Wren. It's still night. That's Morrowindl out there, all afire, burning up from the inside out. Killeshan's let go with everything. Won't be anything left soon, I'd guess."

She did go back to sleep, and when she woke again it was midday, the sun sitting high in a cloudless blue expanse over-head, the air warm and fragrant, and the birdsong a bright tril-ling against the rush of the ocean on the rocks. Faun chittered from somewhere close by. She rose to look, and found the Tree Squeak sitting on a rock and pulling at a vine so it could nibble its leaves. Triss still slept, and Stresa was nowhere to be seen. Spirit sat out at the edge of cliff, his fierce eyes gazing out at the empty waters.

Tiger Ty appeared from behind the bird and ambled over. He handed her a sack with fruit and bread and motioned her away from the sleeping Triss. She rose, and they walked to sit in the shade of a palm.

"Rested now?" he asked, and she nodded. "Eat some of this. You must be starved. You look as if you haven't eaten in days."

She ate gratefully, then accepted the ale jug he offered and drank until she thought she would burst. Faun turned to watch, eyes bright and curious.

"You seem to have gathered up some new friends," Tiger Ty declared as she finished. "I know the Elf and the Splinterscat by name, but what's this one called?"

"Her name is Faun. She's a Tree Squeak." Wren's eyes locked on his. "Thanks for not leaving us, Tiger Ty. I was counting on you."

"Ha!" he snorted. "As if I would miss the chance of finding out how things had worked out! But I admit I had my doubts, girl. I thought your foolishness might have outstripped your fire. Looks like it almost did."

She nodded. "Almost."

"I came back looking for you every day after the volcano blew. Saw it erupt twenty miles out. I said to myself, she's got something to do with that, you mark me! And you did, too, didn't you?" He grinned, face crinkling like old leather. "Anyway, we circled about once a day, Spirit and me, searching for you. Had just finished last night's swing when we saw your light. Might have left, otherwise. How did you do that, anyway?" He pursed his lips, then shrugged. "No, hold off, don't tell me. That's the Land Elf magic at work or I miss my guess. It's better I don't know."

He paused. "In any case, I'm very glad you're safe."

She smiled in acknowledgment, and they sat silently for a moment, looking at the ground. Fishing birds swooped and dove across the open waters like white arrows, wings cocked back, and long necks extended. Faun came down from her perch to crawl up Wren's arm and burrow into her shoulder.

"I guess your big friend didn't make it," Tiger Ty said finally.

Garth. The pain of the memory brought tears to her eyes. She shook her head. "No. He didn't."

"I'm sorry. I think maybe you'll feel his loss a long time, won't you?" The shrewd eyes slid away. "Some kinds of pain don't heal easily."

She didn't speak. She was thinking of her grandmother and Eowen, of the owl and Gavilan Elessedil, of Cort and Dal, all lost in the struggle to escape Morrowindl, all a part of the pain she carried with her. She stared out over the water into the distance, searching the skyline. She found what she was searching for finally, a dark smudge against the horizon where Morrowindl burned slowly to ash and rock.

"And what of the Elves?" Tiger Ty asked. "You found them, I guess, judging from the fact that one of them came with you."

She looked back at him again, surprised by the question, forgetting momentarily that he had not been with her. "Yes, I found them."

"And Arborlon?"

"Arborlon as well, Tiger Ty."

He stared at her a moment, then shook his head. "They wouldn't listen, would they? They wouldn't leave." He announced it matter-of-factly, undisguised bitterness in his voice. "Now they're all gone, lost. The whole of them. Foolish people."

Foolish, indeed, she thought. But not lost. Not yet. She tried to tell Tiger Ty about the Loden, tried to find the words, but couldn't. It was too hard to speak of any of it just now. She was still too close to the nightmare she had left behind, still floundering through the harsh emotions that even the barest thought of it invoked. Whenever she brought the memories out again, she felt as if her skin was being flayed from her body. She felt as if fire was searing her, burning down to her bones. The Elves, victims of their own misguided belief in the power of the magic—how much of that belief had been bequeathed to her? She shuddered at the thought. There were truths to be weighed and measured, motives to be examined, and lives to be set aright. Not the least of those belonged to her.

"Tiger Ty," she said quietly. "The Elves are here, with me. I carry them . . ." She hesitated as he stared at her expectantly. "I carry them in my heart." Confusion lined his brow. Her eyes lowered, searching her empty hands. "The problem is deciding whether they belong."

He shook his head and frowned. "You're not making sense. Not to me."

She smiled. "Only to myself. Be patient with me awhile, would you? No more questions. But when we get to where we're going, we'll find out together whether the lessons of Morrowindl have taught the Elves anything."

Triss awoke then, stirring sluggishly from his sleep, and they rose to tend him. As they worked, Wren's thoughts took flight. Like a practiced juggler she found herself balancing the demands of the present against the needs of the past, the lives of the Elves against the dangers of their magics, the beliefs she had lost against the truths she had found. Silent in her deliberation, her concentration complete, she moved among her companions as if she were there with them when in fact she was back on Morrowindl, watching the horror of its magic-induced evolution, discovering the dark secrets of its makers, reconstructing the bits and pieces of the frantic, terrifying days of her struggle to fulfill the charges that had been given her. Time froze, and while it stood statuelike before her, carved out of a chilling, silent introspection, she was able to cast away the last of the tattered robes that had been her old life, that innocence of being that had preceded Cogline and Allanon and her journey to her past, and to don at last the mantle of who and what she now realized she had always been meant to be.

Good-bye Wren that was.

Faun squirmed against her shoulder, begging for attention. She spared what little she could.

An hour later, Splinterscat, Tree Squeak, Captain of the Elven Home Guard, Wing Rider, and the girl who had become the Queen of the Elves were winging their way eastward atop Spirit toward the Four Lands.

29

I T TOOK THE REMAINDER of the day to reach the mainland. The sun was a faint melting of silver on the western horizon when the coastline finally grew visible, a jagged black wall against the coming night. Darkness had fallen, and the moon and stars appeared by the time they descended onto the bluff that fronted the abandoned Wing Hove. Their bodies were cramped and tired, and their eyes were heavy. The summer smells of leaves and earth wafted out of the forest behind them as they settled down to sleep.

"Phfffttt! I could grow to like this land of yours, Wren of the Elves," Stresa said to her just before she fell asleep.

They flew out again at dawn, north along the coastline. Tiger Ty rode close against Spirit's sleek head, eyes forward, not speaking to anyone. He had given Wren a long, hard look when she had told him where she wanted to go and he had not glanced her way since. They rode the air currents west across the Irrybis and Rock Spur and into the Sarandanon. The land gleamed beneath them, green forests, black earth, azure lakes, silver rivers, and rainbow-colored fields of wildflowers. The world below appeared flawless and sculpted; from this high up, the sickness that the Shadowen had visited on it was not apparent. The hours slipped by, slow and lazy and filled with memories for the Roc's riders. There was an ache in the heart on such perfect days, a longing that they could last forever stitched against the knowledge that tomorrow would be different, that in life few promises were given.

They landed at noon in a meadow on the south edge of the Sarandanon and ate fruit and cheese and goat's milk provided by Tiger Ty. Birds flitted in the trees, and small animals disappeared along branches and into burrows. Faun watched everything as if she were seeing it for the first time. Stresa sniffed the air, cat's face wrinkling and twitching. Triss was well enough to sit and stand alone now, though bandaged and splinted still, his strong face scarred and bruised. He smiled often at Wren, but his eyes remained sad and distant. Tiger Ty continued to keep to himself. Wren knew he was mulling over what she was about, wanting to ask but unwilling to do so. She found him a curious man.

They continued their journey when their meal was finished, sweeping down the valley toward the Rill Song. By midafternoon they were following the river's channel north in a slow, steady glide toward sunset.

It was approaching twilight when they reached the Carolan. The rock wall rose in stark relief from the eastern shore of the river to a vast, empty bluff that jutted outward from a protective wall of towering hardwood and sheltering cliffs that rose higher still. The bluff was rocky and bare, a rugged stretch of earth on which only isolated patches of scrub grass grew.

It was atop the Carolan that Arborlon had been built. It was from here more than a hundred years ago that the city had been taken away.

Tiger Ty directed Spirit downward, and the giant Roc dropped smoothly to the center of the bluff. The riders dismounted, one after the other, Wren and Tiger Ty working side by side in silence to unwrap Stresa and set him on the ground. They stood clustered together for a moment, staring across the empty plain at the forest dark east and the cliff drop west. The country beyond was hazy with shadows, and the skies were faintly tinged with purple and gold.

"Ssssttt! What is this place?" Stresa questioned uncomfortably, staring about at the ravaged bluff.

"Home," Wren answered distantly, lost somewhere deep within herself.

"Home! Sssppph!" The Splinterscat was aghast.

"What are we doing here, if you don't mind my asking?" Tiger Ty snapped, unable to contain himself any longer.

"What Allanon's shade asked of me," she said.

She reached up along Spirit's harness and pulled free the Ruhk Staff. The walnut haft was marred and dirtied and the once gleaming surface dulled and worn. Fastened in the clawed grips at one end, the Loden shone with dull, worn persistence in the fading light.

She put the Staff butt downward against the earth and gripped it before her with both hands. Her eyes fixed on the Stone, and her thoughts traveled back to Morrowindl again, to the long, endless days of mist and darkness, of demon Shadowen, of monsters and pitfalls, and of horror born of the Elven magic. The island world rose up out of memory and gathered her in, a frantic, doomed lover too dangerous for any to hold. The faces of the dead paraded before her—Ellenroh Elessedil, to whom the care of the Elves had been given and who in turn had given it to her; Eowen, who had seen too much of what was to be; Aurin Striate, who had been her friend; Gavilan Elessedil, who could have been; Cort and Dal, her protectors; and Garth, who had been, in the end, all of these. She greeted them silently, reverently, promising each that a measure of what had been given would be returned, that she would keep the trust that had been passed on to her, and that she would respect what it had cost to keep it safe.

She closed her eyes and sealed away the past, then opened them again to stare into the faces of those gathered about her. Her smile was, for an instant, her grandmother's. "Triss, Stresa, Tiger Ty, and you, little Faun—you are my best friends now, and if you can, I would like you to stay with me, to be with me, for as long as you are able. I will not hold you—not even you, Triss. I do not charge you in any way. I ask that you decide freely."

No one spoke. There was uncertainty in their eyes, a hint of confusion. Faun edged forward and pulled at her leg anxiously.

"No, little one," she said. She beckoned to the others. "Walk with me."

They moved across the Carolan—the girl, the Elf, the Wing Rider, his Roc, and the two creatures from Morrowindl—trailing their shadows in the dust behind them. Birdsong rose from the trees and cliff rocks as darkness fell, and the Rill Song churned steadily below.

When they reached the cliff edge, she turned, then stepped away several paces so that the others were behind her. She was facing back across the bluff toward the forest, back into the closing night. Above the trees, stars were coming out, bright pinpoints against the deepening black. Her hands tightened on the Ruhk Staff. She had anticipated this moment for days, and now that it was here she found herself neither anxious nor excited, but only weary. Once, she had wondered if she would be able to invoke the Loden's magic when it was time—what she would decide, how she would feel. She had wondered without cause, she thought. She felt no hesitation now. Perhaps she had always known. Or perhaps all the wondering had simply resolved itself somewhere along the way. It didn't matter, in any case. She was at peace with herself. She even knew how the magic worked, though her grandmother had never explained. Because it hadn't been necessary? Because it was instinctive? Wren wasn't sure. It was enough that the magic was hers to call upon and that she had determined at last to do so.

She breathed the warm air as if drawing in the fading light. She listened to the sound of her heart.

Then she jammed the Ruhk Staff into the earth, twisting it in her hands, grinding it into the soil. Earth magic, Eowen had told her. All of the Elven magic was earth magic, its power drawn from the elements within. What came from there must necessarily be returned.

Her eyes fixed on the gleaming facets of the Loden. The world around her went still and breathless.

Her hands loosened their grip on the Staff, her fingers light and feathery on the gnarled, polished wood, a lover's caress. She need only call for them, she knew. Just think it, nothing more. Just will it. Just open your mind to the fact of their existence, to their life within the confines of the Stone. Don't debate it, don't question it. Summon them. Bring them back. Ask for them.

Yes.

I do.

The Loden flared brightly, a fountain of white light against the darkness, springing forth like fire, then building with blinding intensity. Wren felt the Ruhk Staff tremble in her hands and begin to heat. She tightened her grip on it, her eyes squinting against the brightness, then lowering into shadow. The light rose and began to spread. There was shape and movement within. And suddenly there was wind, a wind that seemed to come from nowhere, whipping across the bluff, sweeping up the light and carrying it across the barren expanse to the trees and rocks and back again, spreading it from end to end. The wind roared, yet lacked strength and impact as it raced past, all sound and brightness as it swallowed the light.

Wren tried to glance back at her companions to make certain they were safe, that the magic had not harmed them, but she could not seem to turn her head. Her hands were clutched tight about the Ruhk Staff now, and she was joined to it, enmeshed in the workings of the magic, given over to that alone.

The light filled the bluff plain, building on itself, rising up until the trees and cliffs that bracketed it had disappeared entirely, until the skies had folded into it and everything was colored silver. There was a wrenching sound, a rending of earth and rock, and a settling of something heavy. Through the slits of her eyes she could see the shapes in the light growing large and taking form as buildings and trees, roadways and paths, and lawns and parks appeared. Arborlon was coming back into being. She watched it materialize as if seeing it from behind a window streaked with rain, hazy and indistinct. At its center, like a gleaming arch of silver and scarlet in the mist, was the Ellcrys. She felt her strength begin to fail, the power of the magic stealing it away for its own use, and she found herself fighting to stand upright. White light whirled and spun like clouds before a storm, gathering in force until it seemed it must explode everything about it in a roar of thunder.

Then it began to fade, dimming steadily, wanning back into darkness like water into sand.

It was finished then, Wren knew. She could see Arborlon within the haze, could even pick out the people standing in clusters at the edges of the brightness as they peered to see what lay without. She had done what her grandmother had asked of her, what Allanon had asked, and had accomplished all with which she had been charged by others—but not yet that with which she had charged herself. For it would never be enough simply to restore the Elves and their city to the Westland. It would never be enough to give them back to the Four Lands, a people returned out of self-imposed exile. Not after Morrowindl. Not when she knew the truth about the Shadowen. Not while she lived with the horror of the possibility that the magic might be misused again. The lives of the Elves had been given to her on others' terms; she would give them back again on her own.

She clamped her hands about the Ruhk Staff and sent what was left of its magic soaring out into the light, burning downward into the earth, all of it that remained, all that could ever be. She drained it in a final fury that sent a crackle of fire exploding through the shimmering air. It swept out like lightning, flash after flash. She did not let up. She expended it all, emptying the Staff and the Stone, burning the power away until the last of it flared a final time and was gone.

Darkness returned. A haze hung on the night air momentarily, then dissipated into motes of dust and began to settle. She followed its movement, seeing grass now beneath her feet where there hadn't been grass before, smelling the scents of trees and flowers, of burning pitch, of cooking foods, of wood and iron, and of life. She looked past the dark line of the Ruhk Staff to the city, to Arborlon returned, buildings lit by lamps, streets and tree lanes stretching its length and breadth like dark ribbons.

And the people, the Elves, stood before her, thousands of them, gathered at the city's edge, staring wide-eyed and wondering. Elven Hunters stood at the forefront, weapons drawn. She faced them, saw their eyes fix on her, on the Staff she held. She was aware of Tiger Ty's mutter of disbelief, of Triss coming up to stand next to her, and of Stresa and Faun. She could feel their heat against her back, small touches flicking against her skin.

Barsimmon Oridio and Eton Shart emerged from the crowd

and came slowly forward. When they were a dozen feet away, they stopped. Neither seemed able to speak.

Wren took her weight off the Ruhk Staff and straightened. For the first time she glanced up at the Loden. The gleaming facets had disappeared into darkness. The magic had gone back into the earth. The Loden had turned to common stone.

She brought the Ruhk Staff close to her face and saw that it was charred and brittle and dead. After taking it firmly in both hands, she brought it down across raised knee, snapped it in two, and cast the remains to the ground.

"The Elves are home," she said to the two who stood open-mouthed before her, "and we won't ever leave again."

Triss stepped past her, his body still splinted and bandaged, but his eyes filled with pride and determination. He walked to where he could be seen, standing close to the Commander of the Elven armies and the First Minister, and called out. "Home Guard!"

They appeared instantly dozens of them, gathering before their captain in row after row. There was a murmuring in the crowd, an anticipation.

Then Triss turned back to face Wren, dropped slowly to one knee, and placed his right hand over his heart in salute. Behind him, the lamps of the city flickered like fireflies in the dark. "Wren Elessedil, Queen of the Elves!" he announced. "The Home Guard stand ready to serve!"

His Elven Hunters followed his lead to a man, kneeling and repeating the words in a jumbled rush. Some among the crowd did the same, then more. Eton Shart went down, then after a moment's hesitation Barsimmon Oridio as well. Whether they did it out of recognition of the truth or simply in response to Triss, Wren never knew. She stood motionless as they knelt before her, the whole of the Elven nation, her charge from Ellenroh, her people found.

There were tears in her eyes as she stepped forward to greet them.

THE DRUID'S KEEP SHUDDERED one final time, a massive stone giant stirring in sleep, and went still.

Cogline waited, braced against the heavy reading table, eyes closed, head bowed, making sure his strength had returned. He stood once more within the vault that sealed away the Druid Histories, come back to himself after his search to find Walker Boh, after leaving his body in the old Druid way. He had found Walker and warned him but been unable to remain— too weak now, too old, a jumble of bones filled with stiffness and pain. It had taken all of his strength just to do as much as he had.

He waited, and the tremors did not return.

Finally he pushed himself upright, released his grip on the table, let his eyes open, and looked carefully around. The first thing he saw was himself—his hands and arms, then his body, all of him—made whole again. He caught his breath, rubbed his hands together experimentally, and touched himself to be certain that what he was seeing was real. The transparency was gone; he was flesh and blood once more. Rumor crowded up against him, big head shoving into his scarecrow body so hard it threatened to knock the old man down. The moor cat was himself again as well, no longer faint lines and shadows, no longer wraithlike.

And the room—it stone walls were hard and clear, its colors sharply detailed, and its lines and surfaces defined by substance and light.

Cogline took a long, slow breath. Walker had done it. He had brought Paranor back into the world of men.

He went out from the little room through the study beyond to the halls of the Keep. Rumor padded after. Sunlight filled the corridors, streaming through the high windows, motes of dust dancing in the glow. The old man caught a glimpse of white clouds against a blue sky. The smell of trees and grasses wafted on the summer air.

Back.

Alive.

He began to search for Walker, moving through the corridors of the Keep, his footsteps scraping softly on the stone. Ahead, he could hear the faint rush of something rising from within the castle's bowels, a low rumbling sound, a huffing like . . . And then he knew. It was the fire that fed the Keep from the earth's core, fire that had been cold and dead all this time, now alive again with Paranor's return.

He turned into the hall that ran to the well beneath the Keep.

In the shadows ahead, something moved.

Cogline slowed and stopped. Rumor dropped to a crouch and growled. A figure materialized out of the gloom, come from a place where the sunlight could not reach, all black and featureless. The figure approached, the light beginning to define it, a man hooded and cowled, tall and thin against the gloom, moving slowly but purposefully.

"Walker?" Cogline asked.

The other did not reply. When he was less than a dozen feet away, he stopped. Rumor's growl had died to heavy breathing. The man's arm reached up and drew back the hood.

"Tell me what you see," Walker Boh said.

Cogline stared. It was Walker, and yet it was not. His features were the same, but he was bigger somehow, and even with his white skin he seemed as black as wet ashes, the cast of him so dark it seemed any light that approached was being absorbed. His body, even beneath the robes, gave the impression of being armored. His left arm was still missing. His right hand held the Black Elfstone.

"Tell me," Walker asked him again.

Cogline stared into his eyes. They were flat and hard and depthless, and he felt as if they were looking right through him.

"I see Allanon," the old man answered softly.

A shudder passed through Walker Boh and was gone. "He is part of me now, Cogline. That was what he left to guard the Keep when he sent it from the Four Lands; that was what was waiting for me in the mist. They were all there, all of the Druids—Galaphile, Bremen, Allanon, all of them. That was how they passed on their knowledge, one to the next—a kind of joining of spirit with flesh. Bremen carried it all when he became the last of the Druids. He passed it on to Allanon, who passed in turn to me."

His eyes were bright; there were fires there that Cogline could not define. "To me!" Walker Boh cried out suddenly.

"Their teachings, their lore, their history, their madness—all that I have mistrusted and avoided for so long! He gave it all to me!"

He was trembling, and Cogline was suddenly afraid. This man he had known so well, his student, at times his friend, was someone else now, a man made over as surely as day changed to night.

Walker's hand tightened about the Black Elfstone as he lifted it before him. "It is done, old man, and it can't be undone. Allanon has his Druid and his Keep back in the world of men. He has his charge to me fulfilled. And he has placed his soul within me!" The hand lowered like a weight pressing down against the earth. "He thinks to make the Druids over through me. Brin Ohmsford's legacy. He gives me his power, his lore, his understanding, his history. He even gives me his face. You look at me, and you see him."

A distant look came into the dark eyes. "But I have my own strength, a strength I gained by surviving the rite of passage he set for me, the horror of seeing what becoming a Druid means. I have not been made over completely, even in this."

He stared hard at Cogline, then stepped forward and placed his arm about the thin shoulders. "You and I, Cogline," he whispered. "The past and the future, we are all that remain of the Druids. It will be interesting to see if we can make a difference."

He turned the old man slowly about, and together they began to walk back along the corridor. Rumor stared after them momentarily, sniffed at the floor where Walker Boh's feet had trod as if trying it identify his scent, then padded watchfully after.

HERE ENDS BOOK THREE of *The Heritage of Shannara*. Book Four, *The Talismans of Shannara*, will conclude the series as Walker, Wren, Par, Coll, and their friends engage in a final struggle against Rimmer Dall and the Shadowen.

About the Author

Terry Brooks was born in Illinois in 1944. He received his undergraduate degree from Hamilton College, where he majored in English Literature, and his graduate degree from the School of Law at Washington & Lee University.

A writer since high school, he published his first novel, *The Sword of Shannara*, in 1977. It became the first work of fiction ever to appear on the *New York Times* Trade Paperback Bestseller List, where it remained for over five months. *The Elfstones of Shannara* followed in 1982 and *The Wishsong of Shannara* in 1985. *Magic Kingdom for Sale—Sold!* began a bestselling new series for him in 1986. The Heritage of Shannara series, a four-book set, debuted with publication of *The Scions of Shannara* in 1990.

The author was a practicing attorney for many years, but now writes full-time. He lives with his wife, Judine, in the Pacific Northwest.